ECLIPSE

William Stevenson

ECLIPSE

DOUBLEDAY & COMPANY, INC.
GARDEN CITY, NEW YORK
1986

Library of Congress Cataloging in Publication Data

Stevenson, William, 1925–
  Eclipse.

  I. Title.
PR9199.3.S7876E2   1986   813'.54

ISBN: 0-385-23209-8
Library of Congress Catalog Card Number 85-7038
Copyright © 1986 by William Stevenson, Ltd.
All Rights Reserved
Printed in the United States of America
First Edition

"Hess, the Deputy Fuehrer," by A. P. Herbert reprinted by permission of Lady Herbert.

To Monika and Alexandra

ACKNOWLEDGMENTS

Material has been excerpted from:
War in a Stringbag, by Commander Charles Lamb, DSO, DSC, Bantam Books, Inc., New York; *The Fox in the Attic*, by Richard Hughes, Harper & Row, New York.

"Hess, the Deputy Fuehrer,"
by A. P. Herbert, 1941,
after Hess parachuted into
England:

He is insane.
He is the Dove of Peace.
He is Messiah.
He is Hitler's niece.
He is the one clean honest man they've got.
He is the worst assassin of the lot.
He has a mission to preserve mankind.
He's non-alcoholic. He was a "blind."
He has been dotty since the age of ten.
But all the time was top of Hitler's men.

Part I
Flashback

1

Scott Talbott watched his air bubbling up into the brilliant blue. He slow-rolled over white sands and relished the freedom from gravity and his release from the burdens above.

Today he was a diver. Soon, he must go back to being America's favorite newsman, star of the weekly television newsmagazine *Newsmag*. Its name opened the doors of the rich, the famous and powerful, for it was in many ways richer and more powerful. The program of scoops and hard-nosed interviews was also a court of last resort for the underdog. Known to everyone as just plain Talbott, the show's chief correspondent was acclaimed wherever the network sold his stories abroad. Even America's enemies, pirating the program for whatever it might reveal, watched Talbott with attentive respect.

He zoomed up between coral cliffs, enjoying the boom of the surf in the reef, the soft pulse of the regulator feeding him air. This was the closest he got now to the exuberance of piloting a fighter aircraft. He was back in a war long ago, only the fun remembered. He had chosen to forget everything else about that war.

The mirror between sun and sea splintered. A girl swam through the shards and beckoned.

She was back in the dive boat by the time he surfaced. "New York was calling," she said. "It's about Hess."

He backed off, treading water. "What did you tell them?"

"You were busy."

"Thanks, Mandy." He pulled down his mask, prepared to escape below again.

"Blasted impudence!" Mandy burst out, to hold him as much as anything. "They seem to think 'busy' means you're in my bed. My response was a trifle rude."

He bet it was. Dr. Mandy Melda Roberts was a black Jamaican who had struggled out of the slums on a series of scholarships. She had pride, and a command of language that must have burned their ears in New York.

"Then they told me," she added, "this producer of yours . . . Bronfmann? He's vanished or something in Germany."

She grabbed his air bottle and weights as Talbott heaved himself on board and lunged for the radiophone.

The call went through Mandy's house on the Jamaican shoreline. The connection was bad. Not bad enough, she reflected. She'd pulled strings to get a medical post back here after UN assignments in Africa and Asia. She'd earned some playtime. Talbott was an undemanding part of it. She cursed silently while that desirable male torso curled up under the radio mast astern. He *needed* to play. He'd told her the whole news business had become too complex, with its support teams and producers who turned reporters into marionettes. He was sick of being the everlasting spectator. Probably he'd exaggerated because he was tired. He wanted to quit, he said. Yet listen to him now!

"There's a flight out of Montego Bay this afternoon," she heard him say. "Schedule the General Massey interview before he vanishes too. And yes, I'll see Hess if he'll see me."

"Hess?" Mandy asked Talbott later. "Hess, as in the last Nazi?"

"Hitler's deputy." Talbott tossed clothes into his overnight bag. "He's been in jail for half a century, if you count the time he served while writing *Mein Kampf* with Hitler. They keep him locked up as if it's a way to confine evil."

"Who's 'they'?"

"That's what Bronfmann was trying to find out," said Talbott.

"Why did Deputy Fuehrer Hess fly to England in 1941?" Talbott asked the old man sitting in a wheelchair under the hot studio lights. *"Was* there a secret deal between London and Berlin?"

"Nobody knows," said General Quex Massey. His forehead glistened. He hated this confinement under the fierce lights, but it had been his decision to come to the network news center in Manhattan. He couldn't complain.

"If there was some kind of secret pact, how could it be kept secret so long?" Talbott persisted.

"Same way these wartime photographs of the Nazi death camps were concealed from me!" Quex indicated the glossies piled on the stage coffee table.

Talbott held one up for Camera 2. "This says, 'Auschwitz. Photographed by U.S. Air Force bombers 7th July 1944.' You should have been fully informed about Auschwitz by then?"

"Of course! For three years I knew."

"Because in that time you'd become history's most powerful spy master?"

"Adviser!" admonished Quex Massey. "Intelligence adviser to President Roosevelt."

"You had enormous resources?"

"There was nothing I couldn't get—for *aggressive* subversion, sabotage, assassination—in terms of money, equipment, talent. But I could *not* get things like why Hess flew to England. Others dealt with demands to bomb the death camps."

"Wouldn't our bombers have only killed the inmates?"

"Our bombers could have stopped the death traffic. Between the time we could have struck and the end of the war, millions were murdered in those camps. Yet we blasted open other Nazi prisons from the air, to release Resistance fighters, who mostly escaped unhurt. But, for that, we needed precise intelligence."

"These labels seem precise enough," said Talbott, displaying another photograph. "Here, printed right into this aerial shot, we read, 'German officers make selections . . . Condemned line up for gas chambers . . . Slave-labor quarters . . . Crematoria . . .' "

The general thumped his gold-topped cane on the studio floor. "The air force had specialists in that kind of intelligence. They told me the camps were beyond range."

"These photographs testify that our bombers recorded the death camps on film and flew on to hit military targets. What do you make of that?"

"There must have been a secret decision at the top not to bomb the camps."

"A dangerous assertion?"

"People get killed for making it."

"Still you persist in trying to prove it?"

"I must," said the general, tilting his musician's shapely head. "Personal honor demands it. But I'm not appealing for information to satisfy an old man's ego. Much bigger matters are at stake . . ." He waited a beat. "Others must have said to the German generals, 'If you attack Bolshevism in Russia, we promise not to attack you in the rear.' The German generals replied something like, 'Yes, but we'll have to keep Hitler busy. He's quite mad, you know. He's got this thing about Jews. If you give Hitler his Jews, then we'll get on with destroying the Russian menace.' I'm not saying this did happen, but as I gather new evidence, the probability increases."

"What kind of evidence?"

"Well, I can't go into details here."

"A f'rinstance?"

"For instance, the connection between Hess flying to meet British leaders and Hitler's invasion of Russia soon after. It was a massive failure of *my* intelligence never to find the link."

"You say you want to make up for such failures. No other motive?"

"What other could I have?"

Talbott examined his clipboard, and a memo about expenses. To General Massey, it appeared to be a researcher's brief. Talbott looked up sharply. "Isn't it true, sir, you yourself sacrificed Jews for political reasons?"

Anger shadowed Massey's face. "I'm not aware of it!"

"Citadel!" Talbott jerked out the word. "Does the code name 'Citadel' mean anything to you?"

Quex's fine features turned to stone. Talbott fiddled with the clipboard. He wanted to give the old man some leeway. Quex must see, if he denied everything, another trap could open.

"We ran many missions," said Quex finally.

"Let me help." Talbott seemed to read from notes. " 'Zionists cannot be trusted. These volunteers are Jewish terrorists, however, and their use is recommended. Nobody is expected to return from Operation Citadel.' " Talbott raised his eyes. "General Massey, did you not draft this?"

"Absolutely not." Quex gripped the sides of his wheelchair. His voice was icy calm. "That is the kind of murderous lie you'd expect from those hiding the truth. They can't kill me with bullets, so they destroy me with words."

Quex had a granddaughter. She was a field producer with the network's London news bureau. Sally Ryan used her mother's family name, not wishing to be accused of trading on Quex's. She flew into New York at Talbott's urgent request. There was speculation he would offer her an enviable promotion to the newsmagazine. She sat through the packaging of a *Newsmag* segment. She knew Talbott by way of the goggle box only. There was a reverse side to TV images, and she watched for that. Boob-tube pussycats often turned out to be holy terrors off camera; champions of the underdog sometimes proved to be lumps of lard. Professionally, she respected Talbott's performance, but she knew that meeting the performer could resemble enjoying goose liver and then meeting the goose.

Talbott had only to voice the studio links. He hurtled away from the cameras the moment he was done, and skidded into a ninety-degree turn when he spotted her sitting quietly offstage. "Sally Ryan!" He took her arm. "Welcome aboard!"

"I'm still working for News," she said dryly.

"Now you'll work with me."

"I haven't decided that yet, have I?"

He had steered her to his office and now flung himself into a chair, making a pantomime of his astonishment that anyone could turn down such an enviable promotion. "You diddled around with this Hess piece for Arnold Bronfmann. Now Bronfmann's gone, why not replace him?"

The callous logic took her breath away. So did the word *diddle* to describe being briefly loaned to Bronfmann because of her West German contacts. She said, "Bronfmann hasn't checked in for several days, that's all." She sank into Talbott's one and only settee, a sagging off-white relic. "I've no intention of jumping into his shoes as if— as if he's dead!"

Talbott was secretly delighted by her reaction. She had Quex's integrity. She also had his finely cut features. As a blonde, she'd had offers to go before the cameras. It is a truism that television as well as gentlemen prefer blondes. She'd chosen instead the hard legwork of field research, moving up to the physical and creative challenge of producing. She regarded journalism as a public trust, not as show biz. He'd gleaned this from colleagues, and he was glad it seemed true.

He said, "Your grandfather warned you'd be difficult."

"He told you *what?*" She rose to the bait. "He'd no right . . . to reveal our relationship. Is that why I'm getting this offer?"

Talbott stood and moved guardedly to the door. "You know better than that. We go by work, not by family connections."

"With Grandpa on the network board, it *looks* bad." She stared up at him, thinking he was as untidy as his office. He had thrown aside his on-camera jacket and tie. What remained, unseen on screen, were worn corduroy pants, a shapeless short-sleeved yellow shirt and sneakers. His leathery face was plugged with a boxer's bent nose, a scar decorated the brow of one sharp blue eye. His brown hair was gray where it curled around his neck. He must be the despair of makeup, thought Sally, because he doesn't care how he looks, not really. Still, she felt obliged to dislike him. "What," she demanded belligerently, "do you want from me?"

Talbott relaxed. "Just, for the moment, wait here. There's something you'd better see."

Left alone, Sally made her appraisal. The office was confusing, the chaos contrived. Other correspondents, glimpsed through plate-glass windows along the *Newsmag* talent row, looked neat as pins. Their offices twinkled with awards and portraits, as if they were always on public display. Talbott's walls were spotted with notes about stories long done with; his desk was awash in outdated files; old transcripts were marked OBE, for overtaken-by-events. None of Talbott's rivals, snooping around here from their nearby offices, could possibly guess what scoops he might have up his sleeve. And all six of the newsmagazine's correspondents were notoriously competitive . . .

He shot back into the office. "I'm afraid to leave this lying around," he said, and dropped a package in her lap.

The wrapping was old-fashioned butcher's waxed paper. Words were stenciled there in a livid red scrawl, like marks on a prime cut of meat: BRONFMANN DIES UNLESS YOU COME TO GET HIM.

Inside was a tarnished metal badge with the swastika and eagle on one side. She turned it over and read, "Geheime Staatspolizei." She pushed it away. "Gestapo! Bloody, *bloody* neo-Nazis! They think because he's Jewish he'll quit and run."

"But this was sent to me."

"He knows his life's at stake."

"You're sure?"

"He told me about the first threats. He didn't want to make a big thing of it. He'd found some new angles on Hess and he was like a fox terrier. He wouldn't let go."

"Shouldn't you have warned us?"

"He was afraid you'd take him off the story. Anyway," Sally added defiantly, "I wasn't working for you. I was back in the London newsroom, which is probably where I should be now."

"You'll help your grandfather if you stay."

"Help him salvage his precious reputation?"

"Or save his immortal soul."

"Is that the old buzzard's line, then?" Sally bristled. "My God, he gets high-flown when he wants! He never could bear to be wrong. Now he's caught out in the biggest blooper in the history of secret warfare."

"So why would he publicize it now, in your opinion?" asked Talbott.

"To get things off his chest before he goes to his grave? Isn't that what he told you?"

"Perhaps."

"But Grandpa Massey's going to live forever! Did you know he'd turned eighty when he began the last of his scientific potboilers? A book about dolphin sonar! He'll write, talk, about anything under the sun, the vain old coot!"

Where vanity entered, Talbott did not learn. The door swung open and a bull-like man barged in, head drawn down into thick shoulders.

"Miss Ryan? We never met. I'm Sol Farkas."

The words were so abrupt, Talbott felt obliged to make some genial intervention. "A senior vice president, Sally. He's responsible for news and public affairs. Or thinks he is."

Sol Farkas brushed this aside. "Who," he demanded, confronting the girl, "is Jacob Slominsky?"

"I— I don't believe I know," she whispered.

Sol took a deep breath. He was in shirt-sleeves and jeans. His bald head accentuated his bushy red eyebrows. He had cauliflower ears and heavy, prizefighter fists. "Let me tell you, then," he said. "Slominsky's better known today as Jake Cooke. A terrorist, if you like."

"I don't like!" retorted Sally. "Jake Cooke, I've known a long time.

He's no terrorist! He was a Jewish underground fighter before Israel was born. *Terrorism?* British propaganda!"

"But he gave you those death-camp photographs?" persisted Sol.

"Of course! He'd got them from the CIA."

"Bronfmann was never told that. The poor bastard thought Cooke found them and turned them over to you," said Sol.

"Goddammit! If you'd read my background notes and not relied on Bronfmann"—Sally's anger evaporated—"Oh, my God! What's become of Bronfmann?"

Sol's expression softened. Her blond hair reminded him of Quex's silver candytuft. She possessed the same icy blue eyes, shading subtly to aqua-green with changing moods. Her fragility was that of a rose of the wind, frail to look at because of its delicate beauty, but full of the wildflower's secret tenacity. Sol sighed. "Bronfmann's become a police matter, Miss Ryan. Does that help your memory?"

The girl sat in obstinate silence.

"Bronfmann vanished without trace," Sol Farkas ground on. "His hotel room's empty. It's the West German police who talk about terrorists." His face turned red again. He banged a fist on Talbott's desk. "If the police have a reason, they haven't told me."

Talbott said in sudden alarm, "Sally, who knows where you're staying in New York?"

"The London bureau. And your office booked the hotel."

Sol cut in. "Take her to your apartment. I'll collect her things myself." He saw the color rise in her face. "Aw, come on!" he joked, "Talbott's harmless!"

"You don't understand—" Sally stopped. Of course they wouldn't understand. Some envious little ape in the London bureau had asked, pretending to joke: "Would you sleep with Talbott to get the job?" It was the macho reporter's way of handling a woman's promotion. "I daresay," he'd sneered, "it won't be through the normal channels."

Talbott misunderstood her hesitation. "You've probably got friends to see. Invite them over. I'll bunk somewhere nearby."

Sally cut him short. "That defeats the purpose."

"Of protecting you?"

"No," Sally shot back. "Of keeping an eye on me."

General Massey hung down in a large white bin, image and voice cut up into dangling strips of 16-millimeter film and sound track.

Sally gaped. *"Film?* Didn't anyone notice there's been a videotape revolution?"

"Middleton sticks to film," said Talbott. "He's the executive producer. The brains behind the show. It's his invention. It's his baby. He loves film. The network's afraid to touch any ingredient in a formula that keeps us top of the ratings."

FLASHBACK was the word on the door to the editing cubicle. On a workbench were pages of transcript from the Massey interview of three days before. Sally wondered what her grandfather had said while she was still in London. She was torn between curiosity and resistance to Talbott's assumption she wanted to go straight to work.

"All I want is a rough cut," Talbott said. "It hasn't been assigned any special slot, so we'll hold it for our occasional 'Flashback' segments." He still had things to do before leaving for the day and thought Sally might as well review the Massey interview. "It was shot just to get it on the record before someone gets the general with a gun." He'd apologized immediately afterwards for that unfeeling remark.

Now he stuck his head back around the door. "Take out the stuff about Hess."

"Grandpa talked about Hess?" She tried to hide her surprise.

"Yes. I'd like to keep that part separate for when we interview him."

"Interview Hess?" She was feeling a little giddy from the transatlantic Concorde crossing. She was also peeved with Talbott. He seemed afraid she might sneak off to rest after the journey, or to get her hair fixed, or something equally flighty.

So now she laughed. She leaned back and her mirth echoed down the corridor. Editors in other rooms paused in envy. Sally's laughter was one of her chief charms. She wasn't exercising it now with seductive intent. It was a spontaneous hoot. *"Hess?"* She recovered her breath. "Nobody, ever, interviews Hess!"

"Nonetheless," said Talbott, a bit put out, "we've asked before and we're asking again."

"Hess?" She swallowed. "He's not even allowed to see his wife. Nor his son. Except, once a month, for one hour, with only one of them, either or. He's forbidden to talk about anything except weather and . . . and *space!* An interview? Even his wretched notes are burned at the end of each day *without his knowing it!* When he dies, he'll be incinerated too." There was a new quality in her voice. "When he dies, he'll leave no trace."

Talbott forgot his annoyance with her. "What is it?" he asked. "Revenge? Punishment?"

"You decide. Every other big Nazi's been hanged or got a life sentence that was commuted long ago. Only the deputy fuehrer remains, a living dummy. The only living witness—"

"To a foolish and wicked conspiracy?"

"Ah, you *did* read my research!" said Sally in triumph.

"Of course." Talbott hid a sudden embarrassment. He waved vaguely at the editing machine. "Well, do what you can with the rough cut. Lock everything away, out-takes and all. Too much leaks from here as it is."

He hurried back to the office. Arnold Bronfmann, his youngest producer, had not been aware that the story he was scouting in Europe stemmed from off-the-record discussions with General Massey. Nor had

Sally been told, when the London bureau lent her to Bronfmann, about her grandfather's involvement. Whatever Bronfmann and Sally dug up, in preliminary inquiries, had been later synthesized in New York. Talbott now searched out Sally's "preinterviews." These were not filmed. They established what the interviewees knew and could say when confronted by the correspondent. He found her reports on a chief British army surgeon and on Dame Rebecca West.

The surgeon had written a book, *The Murder of Rudolf Hess*. About this, Rebecca West had commented, "The medical evidence forcibly suggests we put the name 'Hess' between inverted commas." She believed each of the great powers of World War II still had something to hide in the Hess case. Soviets and Americans had a common interest in burying Hess alive. The British were suspected of drugging him in wartime experiments that turned him into a cabbage. Some said he'd been replaced by a double. Others that he was a Soviet agent from the start, suffering solitary confinement to serve his cause with mystical fanaticism. Dame Rebecca West had called publicly for an investigation "into whether governments themselves have become parties to a foolish and wicked conspiracy."

Reading Sally's material, Talbott wondered why she'd lied about Slominsky. Or had she genuinely not connected the name with Jake Cooke? Her integrity shone through these pages. He'd first scanned them before a New York researcher amalgamated the material, and he'd paid scant attention to the initials SR. Sally Ryan. Now he could put a face to those anonymous initials. She seemed quick-witted, capable, organized. If Sol Farkas distrusted her, it was because Sol had great hopes for Bronfmann's professional future, and right now would suspect anyone who'd been close to Bronfmann when he vanished. But Talbott had made up his own mind about Sally. He'd need her if he was to move quickly on the story without Bronfmann. He made a separate pile of reports initialed AB. Arnold Bronfmann. Why on earth would anyone want to hurt Arnie Bronfmann? He was disarmingly young, he seemed small and inoffensive, and few would guess he could turn into a bulldog when he got his teeth into anything.

2

At this moment in West Germany, what Arnie Bronfmann was sinking his teeth into was his own tongue. His mouth filled with blood and the froth slid down his chin. He was bound and naked, knees drawn up, his head alone free to move.

"You like biting your tongue, then Sami happy to help," said the man standing behind him, putting more syllables into the sentence than it seemed to require. He loosened his grip on the American's jaw. Bronfmann took deep bubbling gasps before the air was cut off again by pressure on his skull and under his chin. Fresh waves of pain flared. He prayed for death.

He understood that nobody intended him to die. Whoever they were, his abductors wanted him merely to talk. Their crude lack of imagination in the use of torture offended him. He refused to answer their questions. Each refusal bore consequences which carried him to fresh levels of pain. Finally, left alone in his windowless cell, he had remembered something from his days as a police reporter: the Mafia's men in Sicily were terrified of being caught acting as police informers, or "grassing"; for Mafia vengeance outweighed the worst police brutality. Illiterate men under interrogation had been known to bite out their own tongues. The stump, "chew-pulp" in their jargon, was proof they could not have talked.

Until now, Bronfmann thought such self-mutilation impossible except among fanatics. He had never considered himself a fanatic before he'd stumbled across information that frightened him, not for his own sake, but for his people. He was a Jew. Not exactly mother's pride and joy when it came to religious observances. Not especially aware of his own Jewishness. But nonetheless a Jew in his reaction to discovering that there existed another Jew who was alive today and carrying upon his shoulders the fate, quite possibly, of all Jews. It seemed to Bronfmann this other Jew must have been selected by the Lord, the circumstances were so bizarre and even terrifying. Bronfmann had himself groaned, "Why me, O Lord!" not because he was that particular Jew bearing that particular load, but because the knowledge of the other man's existence dropped upon him an awesome responsibility.

"Just tell us what you know," his tormentors had said, giving the rack another turn. He'd only the vaguest notion of the passing hours: a day, a week, a month. At first his senses were keenly attuned and he could guess where they'd brought him. There was a ludicrous giant in the costume of a Russian cossack, and a deep-throated woman in a garish gown split at the back to display her bare buttocks. These two had been waiting when he was hustled from the car, down basement stairs, with the heavy rock beat of a nightclub band disturbing the warm autumnal air. He knew this quarter of Düsseldorf, where the rich played at being bohemians and picked up half-assed artists and called themselves only half jokingly patrons of the arts. There was a place where they ran live sex shows and advertised porn movies, and he had a pretty good idea this was where they'd brought him.

"My Uncle Feelie's followed your movements many weeks," said the woman in the split gown. "Your TV program is very thorough, but it doesn't like lawsuits. Uncle Feelie's very well informed, so we mustn't piss on him, must we, Herr Bronfmann?"

Uncle Feelie turned out to be the comic-opera cossack. He had called the woman Madame Obedience, or Madame O. When Bronfmann first set eyes on these two penny dreadfuls, the woman had simpered, dropped a curtsey and said, "Everything that goes in must come out, in and out. All we want from you, little Yid, is lubrication." And she bared one fat breast with a nipple painted to look like an eye surrounded by false eyelids. Bronfmann had thought he heard faint flutterings and remembered, in that curiously distracted and irrelevant way people have when caught in unthinkable crises, that Mae West's many eyelids had made the same butterfly clicks, or so people said. The cossack and the vamp seemed faintly comic until Sami appeared, naked to the waist, his dark skin covered in tattoos. Sami had inflicted deep pain on Bronfmann between unnatural acts by Madame O and Uncle Feelie. In the best of conditions, Bronfmann would have been difficult to titillate; he was seriously involved with a super-bright *Newsmag* researcher in New York. He hardly ever used foul language. He believed sex was a most precious and singular expression of love. In some perverse way, that was how the lubricious pair undid him. They flung him back and forth between gross acts and extreme pain. The obscene Madame O, clipped and pedantic, said, "The Cretan wives did this for their men, home from the long siege of Troy, as proof they really had missed them. Scholars later deleted all accounts of what they condemned as the ultimate in sexual perversion. Let me show you why it was really quite irresistible." Madame O stripped Bronfmann of his pride, proved him as fallible as any man, and fell back at intervals to let Uncle Feelie reinforce Bronfmann's vulnerability. Between acts, Sami turned the screws.

Bronfmann felt suffocated by a sense of human degradation. Once he fully grasped their purpose, he knew it was too late to warn Talbott. That was when he tried to bite off his tongue.

His head had fallen forward and he heard through renewed pain a fresh voice bark. A new hand jerked his head back by the hair. Two powerful fingers dug into his mouth and prevented his jaws from closing.

The newcomer peered into Bronfmann's face. "You'll keep your tongue *and* talk, Jewish bastard!" The man could hardly contain his fury against the other three. "Flaming idiots!" he called them. "Turds!" They had almost succeeded in depriving Bronfmann of speech. He struck Bronfmann across the face to punctuate his renewed questions. "Who flew with Hess? Was it a Jew? What's happened to the Jewish pig coward?"

These were the only questions that seemed to matter now. Bronfmann was almost provoked into snarling, "He's no coward, this Jew who brought Hess to England!" Bronfmann couldn't do it, because the Jew was still alive. The weight of that knowledge was immense, it filled the universe, it bore down upon Bronfmann, who could only pray again, "Why me, O Lord? Why *me?*"

Now a tiny seed of hope sprouted. Bronfmann decided that if the Lord had dumped this load upon his head, there had to be a reason. Maybe he was meant to survive. If he could last out, he would warn Talbott, who was at the center of this maelstrom to judge by the earlier questions. To save Talbott, though, he'd have to keep the facts straight in his head.

But what is fact? Well, on that Saturday night of May 10, 1941, Hess parachutes into England. The Nazis are winning. Every other country hit by Hitler's blitzkriegs has surrendered. There is no obvious reason for Hitler's deputy to fly into the camp of an enemy who is already beaten. The Americans are not rushing to the rescue. Any day now, Hitler is expected to invade England.

That Saturday, a lone German fighter-bomber heads for the northern coastline of Great Britain. The man hunched in the second crewman's position is Rudolf Hess . . . *That* is fact! A fact nobody else ever even considered before. The conventional wisdom is that Hess flew *alone*.

Bronfmann had dug out particulars and he could reconstruct the rest.

"How long to target?" Hess asks with the haughty self-assurance of the deputy fuehrer, popularly supposed to be Hitler's favorite.

The pilot makes his calculations. He's flown for nearly two hours across

Nazi Germany and then another two hours outside the range of British radar over the North Sea. That much is in the official records.

"Another thirty minutes," says the pilot, using the honorific appropriate to the man one step below dictator.

"We can abandon the masquerade now!" snaps the passenger.

"Certainly, comrade!"

The Messerschmidt crawls onto British radar eventually and is labeled "Raid 42," commencing shortly after ten that evening. Two RAF fighters rise unseen to intercept, but the German pilot is already hitting the deck. No British plane can catch up with the Me-110. This "Destroyer" version has two giant Daimler-Benz motors. No Destroyer is known to carry enough fuel for such a long flight. Yet it continues to fly clean across Scotland. Then it turns and climbs until the pilot says, "Ready?"

"Ready!"

The pilot slides back the canopy. The blast of ice-cold air drowns out everything else, but not before the two men exchange their last courtesies.

"Remember, forget me!" says the passenger.

"You remember to forget me!" yells back the pilot. Then he half-rolls the aircraft. The passenger, his intercom unplugged, his harness undone, his oxygen mask disconnected, drops into the void. The pilot rights the aircraft and fancies he sees his companion's parachute ghosting through the gloom below. He counts off the seconds and then puts his feet against the control column, pushing the machine into an outside loop that catapults him free. His leg strikes a tail fin. He prays no bones are broken. He will have to manage without medical aid, once down.

"Do you mean to tell me," demands Winston Churchill, "the deputy fuehrer is in our hands?"

"That is correct," says the Duke of Hamilton. "He came down near my house."

"He flew *alone?*"

"Without question, sir. His machine's splattered all over the estate."

Churchill has to take the Duke's word for it, for Hamilton is a fighter pilot himself who flew north to examine the man claiming to be Hess, and then flew down again to report to Churchill at his country retreat. Great air battles are raging over Britain, and this night has seen the heaviest bombing yet. The Duke is itching to get back into the air. Churchill is eager to leave the dinner table to watch a Marx Brothers movie. So all Churchill says is, "You're satisfied it's Hess?"

"I knew him before the war," replies the Duke. "He liked to talk about my flight over Everest."

Churchill sighs. "Well, Hess or no Hess," he declares, "I'm going to see the Marx Brothers."

Stalin questions Churchill about Hess at a Kremlin banquet in October 1944. The Soviet leader suspects there has been a secret deal between the West and Hitler to encourage the Nazi invasion of Russia.

Churchill writes later: "Remembering what a wise man [Stalin] is, I was surprised to find him silly on this point." He rebukes Stalin for thinking the British Secret Service is behind the Hess mission.

"There are lots of things happen here in Russia which our own Secret Service do not necessarily tell me about!" retorts Stalin.

Bronfmann, trussed like a chicken, jaws wired, waited for the punishment to resume. Yanked back from death, his mind would not now stop racing. Everyone said Hess had flown alone. It was in all the history books. Bronfmann did not kid himself: he was no great detective; therefore others must have found clues to the existence of A. N. Other, the faceless pilot who left no trace.

Had Churchill later suspected Stalin was right? "Something nasty in the Gothic line." Wasn't it Churchill who said that, years later? Or someone else who'd followed the trail and finished up, like Bronfmann, trapped in something Gothic and nasty?

3

It was dusk when Talbott let Sally into his apartment on East Sixty-first at Lexington. She crossed to the windows.

"When I lived near here," she said, "that thing up there reminded me of a lost soul scuttling back and forth, never sure what side it's on." She was pointing to a gondola that swayed up into a cat's-cradle of cables above the Queensboro Bridge.

"The Roosevelt Island Tramway," he said, amused. "Nothing more."

"I saw it as a pendulum between contradictions. Easily swayed. Like me."

"Nonsense!" He was puzzled now. "It looks at both sides but stays the course."

The first words exchanged in an intimate relationship tend to etch themselves upon the memory. Both parties, though still unconscious of what is in store, instinctively file them for future reference. Sally, as if to escape the inevitable, moved restlessly around the room. "You don't care that I worked with Jake Cooke at one time?"

"Should I?"

"You might see him as 'the other side.'"

She stopped again by the windows. The little red-and-silver tramway car had jerked out over the river. "Do *you* believe Grandpa Massey wrote the Citadel memo?" It was the passage in the transcripts of the interview that most disturbed her professional balance. "All those awful things about getting rid of Jewish terrorists by dropping them behind Nazi lines?"

"No."

"Jake does."

Talbott waited.

"I'm sorry," said Sally. "Small talk's beyond me, right this minute." She darted into the small kitchen. "But I can cook . . . My God, your cupboards *are* bare." She turned into all the women he'd ever known, peering into cabinets, judging the owners' competence.

"You want the larder filled, I'll do it," said Talbott, sensing something else. "Make yourself at home."

He returned with groceries bought indiscriminately from Fortnum & Mason and a Korean food mart. Sally smiled at the mixture of ritzy and brown-paper bags. "I'm never home enough to bother—" Talbott began defensively, and then the phone rang.

"Yes, she's here." Talbott stood at the kitchen phone, staring blankly at her. "She looks okay to me. Why? I see . . . Uh-huh. I'll call you back." He hung up. "Sally, your room at the hotel's been ransacked. That was Sol Farkas."

Sally's hand fluttered up to her face. The Westcliffe was a discreet apartment hotel, protective of the network's itinerants. "It's impossible to break in there. Was anything missing? But nobody else would know except me." She spoke rapidly, seeming to voice whatever question came into her head and then answering it. "What about the police? The hotel won't want a scandal."

"Nor do we," Talbott cut in. "We'll keep the police out of this. Sol said it didn't seem like robbery."

A faint shadow crossed Sally's face. She shrugged. "Then, it's all right, isn't it?" She turned back to the grocery bags, as though dismissing the matter.

Talbott watched her. Icy calm, like her grandfather, caught in a crisis. Or caught in a lie? He walked through the kitchen archway into the living area and stopped by his desk. "Found what you wanted?" he called out, staring down at a jammed drawer.

"As a matter of fact, yes." Her tone was defiant. She joined him and began jerking open the drawer. "You like your producers to do their homework, right? And you'd want to know more about your captor if you were in my shoes?"

"Captor?" Talbott watched her withdraw a frayed photograph showing himself in naval uniform beside a much younger General Massey.

"*Did* you work for my grandfather once?" Sally swung round on him.

"Ask him. If you can locate him."

"Of course I can." She put her hand on the desk phone.

"Go ahead, call the house. You won't find him home."

"Then, I'll go to where he is."

"If he sends for you. The general's disappeared underground. Again."

"Don't be ridiculous." The photograph slipped from her fingers.

Talbott retrieved it from the floor. "Don't fight this, Sally. He's being kept . . . safe."

She disliked the way he split the last sentence. "More captors?"

Talbott seemed not to hear. He was regarding the snapshot with an odd expression. Regret? Surprise? *"Eh?"* He looked up. "Come off it, Sally, I'm not holding you prisoner. If you'd stuck around your hotel, or your grandfather around his home—"

"Who would have hurt us? Say it! *Say* who went through my bags, and goes after old men."

"I don't know who."

"Or you don't trust me enough to say?" Her eyes returned to the redand-silver gondola swinging into view again. "You're probably right."

"Still loyal to Jake Cooke?" Talbott grinned suddenly. The smile was used to disconcert Talbott's victims on camera. There was a frankness in the smile that reassured the innocent. Sally felt her guard lowering.

"Don't let it worry you," Talbott continued cheerfully. "I've been through the same thing myself."

Sally nodded uncertainly and began to rummage through the shopping bags. She knew he was waiting for more disclosures. Well, she still wasn't ready. She said, "You buy grub the way you run your office, untidily. I can't imagine what kind of a meal you had in mind. This is all odds and ends. The veal's perfect, but it calls for trimmings." She began to write on a message pad. "Here's a list of what I want. *Comprenez?"*

Talbott understood, all right. What she really wanted was more time alone. He took her list, went to the elevators, couldn't wait, ran down the backstairs and headed straight for a pay phone on Lexington. Shoppers swelled the homing flocks of office workers. Thunder threatened, darkening the sky.

"Sol?" He clasped one ear to muffle the street noises. "What in God's name are we doing?"

"Maybe this embarrasses you," he heard Sol grumble. "But *I* have the dirty work. I searched her personal stuff. Nothing in it."

"Well, *of course* there's nothing in it."

Silence. It was obvious Sol was thinking the girl was pretty, plausible, and already winding Talbott around her finger. Talbott matched Sol's silence. Outside, large drops of rain bespattered the dusty windshield of a police cruiser. Young blacks hastily packed away their curbside bazaar of stolen goods. A gust of wind sent old shopping bags, newspapers, wrappings and ribbons into a gutter-crawling swirl. Summer was a distant memory and a new television season was in full stride.

"She might double-cross you, fella!" he heard Sol Farkas saying. With an effort, Talbott paid attention.

"Sol, we can't take the law into our own hands—"

"Save your finer feelings for when we get Bronfmann back!" The statement was unanswerable. "You've more finished stories than all the other correspondents combined. So don't plead you haven't time for this one. It could be the biggest."

"But that's not the motive, is it?" Talbott stared despairingly at the suddenly darkening street. Like an African safari, three black youths hopped and darted between cars, bundles of briefcases and plastic bags balanced on their heads. Again his mind had to be jerked back to what Sol was saying.

"Just now, at your apartment, you said you'd call me back . . . Did Sally hear you?"

Talbott shifted his gaze to the phone in his hand. "What? Yes, I guess— *She* must guess I went to phone you. O shit! Sol, why don't we tell her the truth?" There was no reply except the telephone's smug purr.

He began walking slowly back, feeling sick inside.

Sally had beaten a strategic retreat to the bathroom. There she could use the phone and cover the sound by flushing the toilet if Talbott returned suddenly. She gave the operator a Düsseldorf number. She did not use her network credit card. She reversed charges and asked for Jake Cooke, person to person. She wanted no record of the call that Talbott might see. She could have cried with relief when she heard the familiar, guttural accents. She spoke rapidly, and concluded: "They're not going to let me out of their sight, so God knows when I contact you again."

"Get Talbott here," was the only response.

"It's the busiest time for stories."

"Tell him this will be his greatest, ever."

"Darling Jake, you know *nothing* about this business!" Sally broke off, and then hissed, "He's back!" She had heard the front door. A rush of water drowned the *ping!* of the replaced phone and she felt grateful for ancient, noisy plumbing.

Talbott stood in the entryway, smiling ruefully. The bathroom phone was not as inconspicuous as Sally supposed. She'd certainly got Quex Massey's blood in her veins. According to Sol, the general wanted Sally driven out to his Long Island home the moment word was passed to Talbott. Meanwhile, it was all very awkward and distasteful. He'd have to keep the girl just a bit off balance. No cozy conversations. Television? He went into the study and leafed through the *TV Times.* There was Shakespeare on PBS. Sally would be the Shakespeare type. *The Tempest.* Channel 13. Not the best of omens. But better than swapping lies in the guise of life stories. What was it Prospero ends *The Tempest* with? ". . . pardon the deceiver . . ."

He dialed Sol Farkas again, using a phone on a separate line. No extension. No way Sally, lingering in the bathroom, could eavesdrop. He told Sol what had just happened, knowing the news chief had the telephone-company contacts to discover whom Sally had called. He heard the girl come up behind, and quickly switched the conversation. "And make sure we keep pressing on the Mother application."

Sol understood and played along. When Talbott finally turned to Sally, she said scornfully, "What a pair of schoolboys! Talking in code, yet."

"Mother," Talbott said stiffly, "is leader of the Soviet Union. The application for an interview's been in the works since he took power. The Kremlin's suddenly receptive. That merits some elementary secrecy in our competitive business, doesn't it?"

"But I knew all that."

"Oh?" Talbott got up to mask his surprise and fiddled with a window blind.

"Ever since Bronfmann went to the Soviets in London," said Sally.

What the hell was Bronfmann doing with the Russians? Masking his surprise, Talbott stared at the cinema across the street. The marquee lights flashed the name of some remake of a James Bond classic. If only the real world could be compressed into these neat little morality plays. If only one side were always good.

He faced Sally. "You'd better tell me what you know about Mother," he said.

4

Yuri Gorin, who had invented his own niche in history as Little Mother of all the Russias, sat in the gloom of a KGB briefing theater near Moscow listening to a report on Talbott's filmed interview with General Quex Massey. Mother's visit had not been anticipated. Soviet leaders were not expected to interfere openly in KGB affairs. High-minded reasons are given for the execution of those who have tried. Their fall from grace is blamed upon a dictatorial attitude and their cultivation of the cult of personality. It boils down in the end, though, to power. As the man who ran the armed forces, the presidium, the politburo *and* the security agencies, Yuri Gorin might be described with some justice as a dictator. Since party theology teaches the impossibility of one-man rule surviving within the great Soviet enlightenment, and since the party is infallible, nobody was calling Yuri Gorin a dictator.

His effective control of the KGB and its sister services was being quietly challenged by General Helmuth Henkell, chief of the East German HVA intelligence service, the Haupt Verwaltung Aufklärung. In private, Henkell not only called Mother a dictator but many other unflattering names. It was Henkell who now stood in front of the large screen showing a recent photograph of Quex Massey.

"Yes, he is old," Henkell agreed in response to a question. "His memory is still phenomenal, though, and he has a considerable reputation as the symbol of duty, honor and a narrow patriotic dedication to old imperial concepts. He feels compelled to investigate his own failures, and this presents us with our greatest opportunity yet. It doesn't matter if the Americans never publicly show the Quex Massey interview. My team will insert the appropriate segments and use the final results at the appropriate time."

Mother sucked through the gaps in his iron teeth. That faint whistle was a warning to Nikolai Kerensky, chief of his personal secretariat. Nick Kerensky, sitting beside Mother in the isolation of the theater's VIP back rows, had always known there must soon come a day of reckoning with satellite zealots like Henkell. The man was more Marxist than Marx, more wedded to terrorism as an instrument of policy than Lenin. Beneath Henkell's blather lurked a German nationalist who had polished the most effective covert-action forces within the Soviet bloc and saw them first and foremost as German; just as he saw Karl Marx as German and the first true Marxist revolution as German-inspired. Now Henkell strode up the center aisle to the epidiascope, his hair golden in the projector's stream of blinding light. How ironic! thought Kerensky. Henkell was the blond embodiment of Hitler's super race: tall, athletic, godlike.

"Vital to the project is this man Talbott." Henkell put up a *Newsmag* publicity photograph on the screen. "You heard the line of questioning in that interview. It followed exactly the pattern we desired . . ."

Yuri Gorin rose and shuffled heavily toward the rear exit. Not a Russian there could fail to sense his secret arrival and stealthy departure. None dared turn a head. Not even Henkell's insolence was up to making an acknowledgment of Mother's brief presence.

Nick Kerensky caught up with him outside.

"I want General Massey eclipsed," said Mother.

"Someone else might get to him first," Kerensky warned. At private moments like this, his real task permitted him to discard formality.

Mother removed his tinted glasses to give Kerensky the full benefit of a bright albino eye. "That would be better," he conceded. "So long as nothing connects the . . . ah, incident, with this country." He gazed up into the blue dome of that marvelous autumn sky as if sniffing the brisk air. Kerensky knew all the mannerisms. The shortsighted, crouching walk. The lifting of the long snout bracketed by black-ringed eyes; one so brown it was almost black, the other a milky blue. The baring of the iron teeth. Yuri Gorin wanted the people to see in him the strength and cunning of their symbolic Russian bear. He had taught them to call him Mother, to identify him with the Soviet motherland. An attack on Mother was an attack on Mother Russia.

They paced the boardwalk to the paved road. "Bring me everything," rumbled Mother, "on Operation Citadel. You got the name?"

"Naturally." Kerensky had also heard Henkell use the Hebrew name. The East German liked to show off his familiarity with Zionist plots, his distinguished service as former director of the KGB special department for Jewish affairs. Henkell claimed nobody better understood the Jewish problem than a German, especially a German like Henkell, born in the Soviet Union during the secret mutual-help alliance of Stalin and Hitler.

It was on the tip of Kerensky's tongue to say that Henkell had probably kept the Citadel file when promoted to his present East German post. Mother forestalled him.

"If the file still exists, you will find it in the Jewish special department at Minsk."

It sounded to Kerensky like the first hint of overdue confrontation with the pestilential Germans. Action was what he had missed since being requisitioned by the Kremlin. He felt a marvelous apprehension, a welcome void in the stomach heralding danger.

"Well?" demanded Mother. "What are we waiting for? Jack Frost?"

Kerensky collected himself. "The American. Talbott. Why not eclipse him, too?"

Mother reared back. "I said eclipse *one*, not massacre the lot."

Kerensky wondered what was wrong with a massacre. But Mother was breaking into a shambling trot as a burnished black ZIL stretched lazily at the end of the boardwalk. You had to think ahead to keep up with the old warrior. "Anticipate!" he was always urging Kerensky, who now stood back while faceless men encircled Mother. They were snatching him away from the leftover mysteries of World War II. The public saw it recycled daily through television. You could justify every excess on the basis of national security, thought Kerensky; and the Great Patriotic War was all about the betrayal of that security. Hitler's lies were reemployed. World Zionism was a conspiracy for global war from which the Jews would profit. Now, now! he warned himself. Mustn't get bitter! That bloody war's my bread and butter.

Mother vanished into the ZIL. Kerensky had intended to warn that an eclipse team in New York ran the danger of colliding with Henkell's own assassins. Probably it didn't matter who killed Quex Massey. What was odd, though, was Mother's response to eclipsing Talbott. Kerensky sensed Mother was disturbed, deep down, by that proposal. As if . . . as if Talbott were a visitor from the past. That's absurd! thought Kerensky. With Soviet leaders, there was never a past, only an official biography.

The secretary turned back to the briefing theater. He begrudged time spent here in Potma: a concentration of thirty-six prison camps served by private railroad out of Moscow. When Kerensky was fresh from hack duties at the Washington embassy, this place had reminded him of the Dallas Market Center in Texas. He knew better now. Here, the KGB sold guns instead of glitz. Kerensky took a deep, regretful breath and ducked back into the theater and the smell of moldy carpets.

"The project should be ready for our national Spy Day," Helmuth Henkell was telling his faintly hostile audience.

Spy Day! Kerensky froze. What bloody insolence! Spy Day was an East German indulgence. No other ally had such nerve! Erich Honecker, the DDR leader, inviting Moscow's rage, had declared it "the day this country's secret agents must be honored as heroic fighters on the invisible frontier." Now Henkell openly taunted senior KGB men with the same crap.

He thinks nobody can touch him, reflected Kerensky, remembering his last visit to East Berlin, when the German had waved airily in the direction of the old jail and said, "Don't threaten us, Kerensky. We've got the biggest spy in history right there. Anything happens to me, Hess will spill the beans."

Kerensky had been warning the locals of Moscow's displeasure should they insist on going ahead with some independent operation in the West. He was only the messenger, and to show there was nothing personal, he had slapped Henkell on the back and joked, "We can bump off Hess any time we choose."

But Henkell was not laughing. "You can't," he said softly. "Not in front of the other three powers. He's never been out of their sight in forty years. Murder Hess, you'd start another war. Terminate me, old son, and the documentation would pop out automatically in the one place you Russians can't reach!"

The two men had drawn back their lips, grinning at each other with bared fangs. No two mutually hostile men had ever discovered such a common bond, not since Stalin made his deals with Hitler in a time when both were vulnerable.

Secretary Kerensky now sat aghast. Here were the fruits of his compulsive partnership! And no way in sight to break it. Henkell could not, must not press on with a project originating outside the Kremlin. And yet it was so.

On stage, General Henkell conjured up charts while the jargon tripped off his tongue, glib but unassailable . . . in the best spirit of the indissoluble ties between our countries . . . Berlin offers you technical expertise and by far the greatest number of illegals in place in the West . . . Not of course boasting . . . matter of record that millions from East Germany now live in the West and share with it an ethnic identity . . . leadership is yours, comrades . . . building socialism at the heart of . . .

All the party claptrap could not conceal the truth: Henkell's project was too far along. It would be a betrayal of solidarity to oppose Henkell openly, unless you were Mother. Mother could do it, but then only with subtlety. Nobody else smoked out heretics with greater unobtrusive skill. That brutal resolve, hidden inside a kid glove of sophistication, had won Kerensky's undying devotion. Mother would send Henkell to the stake, as he'd done others. The proof of Mother's genius was his survival.

5

"Age," said General Quex Massey. "Everything improves with age."

"Me? Or the car?" asked the woman at the wheel of an ancient Packard with its hood folded back.

"This charabanc, sweetie. Friskier with each passing year. Chivalry alone forbids me saying the same about you."

The woman laughed. "Then, I'll say it. In old age, I'll still give anyone a run for their money."

The teasing drifted in drowsy harmony with the Packard's stately progress along a highway near the tip of Long Island. It was the morning after Sally Ryan's first encounter with Talbott. Her grandfather was in high good humor. Sally would have condemned it as theatrical. Indeed the conversation *did* seem to play to some unseen gallery. Quex wore a straw boater and striped blazer. The woman was equally flamboyant with a scarlet Thai silk scarf tied around auburn hair. Indian summer had settled across the eastern United States, and out over the Atlantic fell an appropriate sprinkle of rain from a great blue cloud flanked by amethyst and amber.

The woman abruptly dropped her pose. "We've hooked the blighters!" she hissed. "Hang on to your hat, lover-boy!"

Quex gave a muffled whoop and tipped his hat to a more rakish angle. The woman whipped the car round onto a dirt road, shoving her foot down hard on the pedal. The old tourer squirted a plume of du. into the path of a charcoal-gray Buick sedan stealing up behind.

Unable to contain himself, Quex yelped, "That's the stuff to give the troops!" The woman tapped the dashboard, shushing him.

She drove fast through the narrow, winding lane. Lashed to the Packard's trunk was a whitewalled spare wheel. It flashed like a rabbit tail between thickets of wormwood and ash, head-high thistles and dense hedgerows. The woman braked, accelerated, and teased the pursuing Buick before she suddenly threw the car into a skidding turn and plunged over a sand river, up onto the old Montauk road, where two more Buicks waited, purring, on the soft shoulders.

"Good thinking," whispered Quex.

The Buicks all looked the same. They came charging up, three in single file now, the lead car pulling abreast of the Packard and thumping it sideways. A running board was ripped away before the woman got the Packard clear. She took the blow calmly. Seconds later she said, "Oh, blast!" and then smothered the next word. "Cops!"

She slowed down, gears grinding. The entire pack of Buicks braked hastily too. The oncoming police cruiser sailed past. Quex gravely returned an amiable salute from the police driver. They all watched in their rearview mirrors, the woman and Quex and their pursuers, until the police had safely disappeared around the receding bend. Then the Packard leapt forward again. It was not part of anyone's plan to drag the police into this deadly game.

"Fishhook coming up!" warned the old man, pointing ahead.

The woman saw the gap she was seeking. It led down to a ridge, another lane, then a path into the deserted old Montauk horse-show grounds. She wrenched the car into another tight turn, the wooden carriage creaking like a schooner in a sudden squall. The maneuver surprised the hunters, who overshot the nearly invisible, unmarked turnoff. By the time they had reversed and hurtled up a second ridge, overlooking the horse-show grounds, all they could see among the empty green huts below was the Packard's bunny-tail hippity-hopping to disaster.

The Buicks drew up in a row along the ridge. The drop to the vacant parking lot was dangerously steep. There was a bang from behind the huts. Smoke drifted across the cracked tarmac.

One of the Buicks nosed cautiously down the ridge until the driver dared go no farther. There was no need. He could see the two bundles sprawled like scarecrows between two distant sand dunes. An engine was rammed into the ladies' washrooms. A mudguard hung from a tree. A woman's auburn wig, followed by the straw boater, went whirling on the wind off the sea.

If the driver had been less worried about backing up, he might have noticed the wreckage included two running boards. He might then have reflected that a running board had been already ripped off the old Packard in the biffing along the old Montauk road. Instead he said into his radio mike, "Game's won! Let's move!"

Beside him, a girl replayed the end of a monitoring tape. "The name sounds like 'Fishhook,' " she said. "Mean anything to you?"

The driver got back over the ridge and negotiated his place at the head of the pack again. He shrugged off her question. "My English, she not so good!" he roared happily, his big shoulders heaving with the humor of it all.

6

The first news of General Massey's fatal accident drifted over the car radio like fragments of gossip at a cocktail party. None of it made sense to Sally, driving to the family estate in East Hampton with Talbott. She had only just recovered from her surprise at being summoned to see Grandpa Massey the day after she began to learn about the real Talbott.

"A fog covers the tragedy," said the radio. *What kind of jeezly fog?* Sally asked herself, angered by the sloppy language. "Most famous of spy masters . . . author of scientific books . . ."

They found a service station near the end of that interminably boring stretch of Highway 27 between Patchoque and the Hamptons.

"You call," said Sally. "I want to be sick."

She disappeared into the restroom and Talbott tried General Massey's unlisted number from a pay phone. There was no reply. He called the only other person he could: Sol Farkas. "Go straight to Fishhook's place," said Sol. "Save the questions—" He sounded confused, uncertain, not like Sol at all. "Your girl," he said, "phoned a West German number. Düsseldorf. Person to person for *Jake Cooke* . . . It's bizarre." What could be more bizarre than present events, Talbott did not find out. Sol cut him short as Sally reappeared.

That previous evening had passed with none of the tension secretly feared by Sally and Talbott. Their concern for Bronfmann was a topic that lasted through dinner. Later, Sally, as if it was something she had been brooding about, asked Talbott what he had meant by saying—after she confessed a loyalty to Jake Cooke—that he'd gone through the same thing himself.

"I understand the conflict when personal feelings intrude on journalistic judgment."

"I don't follow," said Sally, back on guard.

"Well, I was in Beirut when the Israelis invaded Lebanon. I knew some of the junior Israeli commanders, always admired their spunk. But I was there to report, and what I had to report didn't always make my friends' bosses look so hot. I finally asked to be taken off the assignment."

"Are you always so holy? Or was it moral cowardice?"

"Oh, cowardice, without a doubt!" said Talbott with a disarming grin. But she knew she had touched a sore spot. Later she tossed another dart at him. She couldn't see why he wasn't already in Düsseldorf looking for his missing producer. "Or isn't it a big enough story?"

"We've got people checking into it," he said, and this time he sounded testy.

She began enjoying this gentle provocation of a man she supposed was accustomed to being treated with reverence. She said Bronfmann had found it hard to adjust to Talbott's impersonal manner when he was not on camera. She only mentioned it, she said sweetly, because *if* she was going to work with Talbott, she needed to know his bad habits. "You cease to exist," she said, embroidering on what Bronfmann really had said. "You see the world only through the camera lens, he says. As if you're nothing more than a mirror of events."

Talbott eyed her. "Take a walk through my looking glass, then!"

"You're supposed to keep me locked up!"

"Not if you don't mind risking the streets," said Talbott, knowing the real purpose of keeping her away from the hotel had been achieved.

Outside, there was a cleansing chill in the air. She began to understand what he meant about his looking glass, his small world of reality, his village. It stretched to Central Park, down Broadway, along 42nd Street. These were real people he knew in the nooks and crannies, not electronic gnomes. He talked of them with affection. In the workaday whirl of Manhattan, they were so easily overlooked or taken for granted. Frosty smells cut through the lingering musk of summer. "Smells," quoted Talbott, "surer than sights and sounds to make the heartstrings crack."

Sally wondered what it was had cracked Talbott's heartstrings. The remark had been deeply felt and he seemed to be talking to himself. Most of the time, he amused her with stories of the street peddlers, the small shopkeepers and craftsmen who fought the battle against concrete and plate glass. He brought her back by way of the Roosevelt Island Tramway station and stopped before the prim Episcopal doors of All Saints on East Sixtieth. "Look," he said. "An all-Schubert concert. Tomorrow night."

"Will I be there?" she asked.

"Depends on your grandfather," he replied. "You know what he's like."

"You probably know more. How close were you to Quex?"

"Not very," said Talbott, surprised by the sudden question. "He once wanted me to come work with him in some outfit predating the CIA."

"And you did?"

"No. I was very young, with an innocent belief that freedom's best served by the free flow of information. Which means a free press."

"You don't think that now?"

"Yes, but I'm uneasy with high-flown sentiments. When the media gets shrill about giving the people the facts, I look to see where the people are getting screwed. When governments say they've nothing to hide and spread out their hands, they're likely to be up to some sophisticated deception."

"So what you really want is to be free from any institution, either government or media?"

"Yes, I guess you could say that." Talbott laughed. "Sometimes makes me feel like a loose cannon."

The doorman was holding Sally's bags. Someone had delivered them from the hotel. "Sol Farkas was right," Sally announced after checking. "Nothing taken. Just research notes all jumbled up. I wonder why?"

Talbott was tempted then to tell her.

Sally, it so happened, was close to confessing the whole story of Jake Cooke; but she was still afraid. Afraid, she supposed, as Talbott must be afraid. He clearly didn't trust her yet, even if he needed her. He had been standing in the doorway of the spare bedroom while she emptied her bags. He looked unexpectedly forlorn.

Later, in her narrow bed, she thought how self-isolated he was. Under street or studio lights, he seemed nothing more than a mirror, reflecting history back at the little people who made it.

Sometime before daybreak, she had heard the telephone ring; and then Talbott had come to tell her Grandpa Massey was ready to see her.

". . . No, don't ask questions. Just go!" Talbott heard the words as Sally walked slowly back from the restroom. It had taken an age to contact Sol Farkas. "Don't go *near* the Massey property!" the network vice president insisted, and broke the connection.

Talbott stepped out into the light drizzle. Sally avoided looking at him. She was waiflike in an old belted raincoat he'd lent her. She waited until they were back in the car before she asked the unavoidable question: "Is Grandpa really dead?"

Talbott summed up his effort to get information. "Sol wouldn't say more," he concluded. "He was afraid of being overheard."

"Blast Sol Farkas and his frigging intrigues!" Sally sat up. "You're all sodding scared." She let go with a string of imaginative obscenities learned in London. "Didn't you call anyone who *knows?"*

"I couldn't—"

"Then, stop the car!"

Talbott put out a restraining hand, "Trust me."

"The way you trust me?"

"I'm sorry." Talbott inched cautiously onto the highway, fearful she might grab at the wheel, yet admiring her grit. "It's Bronfmann—"

"I don't give a fuppenny tuck about Bronfmann right now!"

"He was *never* assigned to the Mother application," Talbott said swiftly, shocking her into listening. "Did you know that?"

"No!"

"Did *you* talk to the Russians?"

"No!"

"Okay," said Talbott. "I have to believe you now. Yesterday, I couldn't."

She fell silent, hugging her knees, watching the rain bounce off the road ahead. The radio was still playing softly. Another news bulletin made her snap it off. "What kind of a lousy journalist are you—or Bronfmann—to get sucked into Grandpa's bloody games?"

"I wish I knew" was all Talbott said, and she fell to brooding again. Then, without prompting, speaking at first in the whisper of a timid child, Sally began to talk about a General Massey that he had never known. "He raised me as a child," said Sally. "My parents were dead. He'd no children of his own. My grandmother and the general had what's called a sensible marriage. They set more store by loyalty than love. Self-control was the mark of superior worth. He was part Cherokee and part Scot, or so he boasted. He'd always wanted a son. I was a big disappointment. I did my best, but I couldn't turn into a boy, could I?"

There were tears in her eyes. Talbott concentrated on his driving.

"He was always so *certain* of anything he said. He prided himself on accuracy and dispassionate judgment. He was *never* wrong. Until he was dragged along to some reunion of old wartime spooks. Not the Oh-So-Socials. A bunch of European resistance men and women. They met in Vienna."

She broke off as Talbott turned onto the Sag Harbor turnpike. Then she resumed: "He was upset by things he heard. Documents he'd never seen before. He came to me. Said he'd been fooled."

"Then, he must have regarded you as something more than a disappointment," commented Talbott.

"Also as part of the family, too loyal to gossip outside."

"Why do you put yourself down whenever you speak of yourself in relation to him?"

"Do I? Sorry. Anyway, I hadn't yet gotten into journalism. I was working part-time at CBS and doing free-lance research. He sent me to dig into the wartime archives in Jerusalem. You know"—Sally brightened—"I really was the one person he trusted to go there. He'd never treated me seriously that way before. Like, I really was the son he'd always wanted. That's how I met Jake Cooke."

She peered out at a pair of huge iron gates as Talbott slowed down. "Hey, isn't this the Fishhook Sherman property?"

"You know Fishhook?"

"Well, of course." Sally was back in the present. "He's just about my favorite person. He was Grandpa's *nicest* friend." Her next words, Talbott dismissed as wild talk prompted by having to confront her grandfather's violent death. "Fishhook," she said, "never brought up Citadel, never accused him of deliberately killing Jews. He's loyal." Then she pressed the back of her hand against her mouth as they emerged from the winding driveway to where Fishhook towered in the open doorway of his house.

Talbott had last seen Fishhook at a reunion of the Veterans of the Office of Strategic Services, the wartime OSS, forerunner of the CIA. An old FBI man, Fishhook at the reunion stood out like a sore thumb among the sleekly tailored. Yet he was one of the wealthier men there. Fate had made him the sole heir to properties built up by a succession of ancestors. Fishhook never gave up an austere style, rattling around alone in the vast and windy old manor house whose library was witness to his obsession with books. His independent spirit was reflected in the words carved on a gravestone under a great oak in front of the house: "In memory of Captain Sherman of the Privateer Merlin. During the American Revolution, he was one Long Islander who never could be forced to take the oath of allegiance to King George of England."

Fishhook came down the steps to greet Sally. He was a big, loose-limbed, handsome man in his mid-sixties. "Brace yourself—" he began.

"We've heard," said Sally. "The radio."

Shock distorted Fishhook's features. *"Radio?"*

But the girl was already running past him into the black void beyond the great doors. Fishhook turned helplessly to Talbott. "It should never have reached the media," he said enigmatically. "Good God!"

Talbott began to run. Something was wrong. He left Fishhook, still looking dazed, and raced through the paneled hall to the library. At first he saw nothing but the tall, uncurtained french windows overlooking the ornamental gardens on the far side. Then he saw a woman reclining on the carpet. She was illuminated by watery sunshine that brought out the rich colors of the carpeting and touched the diaphanous folds of the woman's summery dress, outlining the sensuous curves. The woman was looking back over her shoulder at Talbott, her face half in shadow. He thought of

34   ECLIPSE

the Turkish concubine in Ingres's *Grande Odalisque*, that painting of rare voluptuousness.

Finally he saw Sally. She was kneeling in deep shadow in front of a wheelchair, where General Quex was propped up like a dummy.

7

"What a cruel, stupid trick!" Sally got to her feet. "Is this a *joke?*"

"My dear child . . ." began Quex Massey. He rose, then toppled forward so that Sally had to catch him.

Talbott watched in stunned disbelief. General Massey alive? Yes, and kicking! The wily old bird had just converted Sally's rage into a tearful embrace.

Talbott turned from the intimate scene.

"Don't cut and run *again*, Talbott!" said the reclining woman.

He stopped in the act of withdrawing to look for Fishhook. "Rinna? Rinna Dystel!"

The woman rose with languid grace. "We had to do it this way."

"We couldn't warn you," said Fishhook, entering the library. "The news reports got out before we were ready."

"We didn't make a wrong step, other than that," boasted Quex, disengaging from his granddaughter.

"Other than scare me to death!" Sally accused him.

"The general's life is in danger," said Rinna, her smile blunting the harsh edge to the words. "It seemed best to kill him off ourselves."

"An extravagant deception," Quex assured Sally, who was pink now with anger instead of grief.

"Deception!" Talbott studied Rinna Dystel with open admiration. "I

should have recognized your handiwork." He saw Sally's eyes flash and hastened to explain: "Rinna was a movie set designer. Back in the thirties, Hollywood called her the mistress of deception. She was still barely out of her teens. She was recruited to deceive the Nazis—fake tanks, secret war plans that were phony, airfields that didn't exist . . ."

Rinna had moved to the fireplace and was kneeling to light tinder under the piled logs. The leaping flames confirmed the durable beauty of an intelligent woman. A warm glow lit the cavernous room. Quex was relaxed again in his wheelchair, Sally at his side. To Talbott, the two belonged in a family portrait. He wondered if Sally had decided upon a truce. Just then she lifted her chin in renewed impatience as Quex said, "What did the newscasts say about me?"

Remembering Sally's description of the general as a vain old coot, Talbott jumped in hastily. "Nothing!" He glanced warningly at Sally. "Just vague conjecture—"

"I think you're all mad," Sally interrupted. "Mad hatters!"

Quex's face hardened at the last two words. Nobody spoke. A soft-footed young man appeared from the hallway, cuddling a machine pistol.

"No weapons in daylight!" Rinna pounced upon the boy.

"Apologies." The gunman ducked his head in embarrassment, spoke rapidly in another language, then drew back.

Rinna said to the rest of the room, "I'm sorry about that. He was reporting the monitored newscasts. Well, we know all about those now, don't we?" Her smile was strained.

Sally said, "It's obvious he's not a Hat Man."

Fishhook began banging about the liquor cabinet. "Time for a drink!"

Sally forged ahead in the ensuing silence. " 'There's a hat—black, huge . . . You put it on, and then no one on earth can see you!' That's the way Ibsen put it, right? 'At the next masquerade I'm going to be invisible.' What's the masquerade this time, Grandpa?"

Quex winced and reached gratefully for the long-stemmed glass of champagne Fishhook brought him.

"God! Doesn't anything change?" asked Sally. "Champers and oysters for the general. Health shattered by narrow escapes, General Massey lives on a diet of Rockefellers and Dom Perignon . . . Who writes the press release this time?"

"That's unfair," protested Rinna. She joined Quex, and there was an intimacy in the way she rested one hand on his shoulder.

The gesture seemed to offend Sally. "What do you know about it?"

"My dear, we're only trying to protect your grandfather."

"Against what?"

"Six or seven other governments, to begin with," said Quex with evident relish. "All fighting each other to rub me out."

"You flatter yourself!" Sally exploded.

It was Fishhook who restored order. He put an avuncular arm around the girl's shoulders. "Let's leave this until dinner. I'll show you to your rooms." Sally turned to Talbott. He nodded quickly, thinking that if her grandfather piped up now with the same suggestion, she would resist it. Her life with the general must have been an unbroken contest of wills.

"But—" she began.

"This way," said Fishhook, taking her firmly by the hand. He never had been much of a one for chitchat.

"I'm not exactly grace under pressure, am I?" said Sally when she was alone again with Talbott. She stood in the doorway between their bedrooms.

"Not everyone has a dead grandfather who pops up alive."

"If he's officially dead," she said slowly, "he can't get official protection, can he? His enemies can't be accused of murdering a man already dead. It's a dangerous game you're all playing."

"All?"

She looked up at him with eyes that, reflecting her mood, had changed to aqua-green. She was ready for a fight, but frightened. She said, "All of you Hat Men."

"What," Talbott asked, "do you mean?"

"Wartime buddies. In peace, ordinary men and women with a sense of honor. Grandpa's bedtime stories were about Hat Men when I was small. I saw them as office clerks perched on Dickensian stools. If one got in trouble, far away, the others got down from their stools, donned their hats and slipped out to the rescue." She gave a small, nervous laugh. "After a time, each returned to his stool as if nothing had happened. Stuff and nonsense, but romantic enough for any kid. Then I realized it might be true. Is it?" She saw the conflict in Talbott's eyes and added, "You can't *afford* to be mixed up in such silly, schoolboy heroics. The American public trust you, more than any reporter I know."

"You're assuming a lot," said Talbott and walked away.

Dinner was in the cavernous basement kitchen. Fishhook, to maintain his local reputation as an austere recluse, was keeping tight control over the hydro bills. Candles replaced electric light. Rinna's mysterious guards lived off their own resources and were quartered in cellars rambling under the big house. In the kitchen, such ingenuity faltered. It was left to Rinna to whip up a tolerable meal from Fishhook's uninspired hoard of canned food.

Quex savored the makeshift supper, the smoking fire, the dripping candles. He had been an aviator in the First World War. His memories reached back to the muddy fields of Flanders and squadron bivouacs on French farmland. To him, Sol Farkas's arrival from the network news center was like the sudden appearance of some shell-shocked dispatch rider.

"They've got Bronfmann alive, the bastards!" Sol Farkas announced without preliminary.

He took a place at the long oak dining table and turned to Sally. "The 88 Movement. Know it?"

"Neo-Nazis," she replied promptly. "Take their name from the alphabet. Letter number 8. For *Heil!* and for Hitler. A tricky lot, because they seem to get funding from the East."

The network executive nodded heavily. "They want Talbott in Düsseldorf at once, or they'll kill Bronfmann."

Talbott scraped back his chair.

"Don't panic." Sol raised a paw. "Your secretary's booked the first available flight. I'll drive you to Kennedy. Meanwhile, eat and—"

"And listen to me," said Quex.

Sally listened, her heart heavy. Grandpa's pride would get him killed yet.

"Some of you know some of the facts," said Quex, peering at each of them in turn through the candle smoke. "None of you know the whole.

"I did something unique. I dug into my own past as an intelligence chief. Historically, spy masters don't do that. Their secrets are torn up and thrown away, their agents silenced. All that remains is the agreed version of events.

"But after years of conventional wisdom about World War II, I've been shown evidence of things concealed. I've had to ask for new answers to old questions: Why didn't Hitler invade England when it was so easy? Why did he turn instead on Russia? Every military man knew that was suicidal. Did the invasion of Russia signal the real start of the Holocaust?"

Sally felt Sol Farkas's eyes on her. His earlier hostility seemed to have turned into puzzlement. She turned her attention back to Quex. She was afraid of his ego. Did he want to blow open some frightful conspiracy before the facts emerged in some other way, making him look less than infallible?

Quex was saying, "Only the State of Israel wants the truth out. I don't have the unfettered power of wartime dirty tricks. But I do have my memory. And I have Sally, here, who did early research in Jerusalem. My other resource is what Sally as a child heard me talk about as fantasy. My Hat Men."

Again Sally stirred uneasily. Now she was the excuse for Grandpa to recapitulate the Hat Men's history. How he did love the spotlight, as if to make up for the years of concealment. He had a captive TV audience: two of the most powerful men in the industry. Still, it was a good story.

The concept is born after 1940, when nearly half a million fighting men are snatched "out of the jaws of death and shame," in Churchill's phrase, by hundreds of small boats. Amateur English sailors cheat Hitler's blitzkrieg to rescue the armies from Dunkirk. A naval flier who is there writes: "Never in maritime history, throughout the centuries, in any country in the world, has such an armada put to sea, spontaneously . . . *No need for a clarion call.* Men who owned boats put down their office pens, put on their hats, and set forth . . ."

Quex, as President Roosevelt's personal observer, marvels. Those who work for him later in cloak-and-dagger inherit the symbol of Dunkirk. All the amateurs in Quex's war become . . . Hat Men.

"They did what they had to do," Quex now said. "When one Hat Man died, another stepped from the shadows to take his place.

"I need what's left of you Hat Men today. Another rescue operation. To rescue the truth. We mustn't let Jerusalem do it alone."

"All we want are facts," Rinna interrupted. "We're not paranoid. But too many Israelis feel isolated. The mood's dangerous. Nobody else asks the awkward questions."

"Did Hitler let the British escape from Dunkirk deliberately?" Quex supplied. "Did he cancel the invasion at the cost of the Jews?"

"It makes for good soap opera," said Sally. "It'll get good play in the *National Enquirer.* It'll goose our ratings."

"We're not chasing ratings," growled Sol Farkas. "As a network, we can help. Otherwise your grandfather's on his own—"

"Except for Rinna," said Sally. "And whatever she calls *her* hat men."

"She saved my life." Quex thrust out his chin. "You notice the radio said nothing about *her?* That's one small blessing. She faked that accident to shake off our opponents, whoever they are. I'd been under surveillance a long time. Rinna's people in Jerusalem had evidence I was marked, and they didn't want to lose me. Not yet. So Rinna conditioned the opposition to my daily habits. Including the daily drive in that old Packard I'm supposed to have kept in the stables ever since I got rid of the horses. What the opposition didn't know was, Rinna had stashed away an exact replica. It provided the 'wreckage' for the accident."

"And you'd have put out the phony story?" Sally pounced on Sol Farkas. "How could you justify using the newsroom that way?"

"Don't spoil my funeral!" Quex pleaded, heading off another argument.

"Funeral?" Sally sat back, aghast. "So the masquerade goes on?"

"Not for me." Talbott stood up. "I'm off to stop a real funeral. Bronfmann's."

"I'm coming with you," said Sally.

"Stay, child!" commanded Quex. "You're my only kith and kin. The locals will smell a rat if you're not at my burial. Stay, if only for the pleasure of dancing on my grave."

"You're too hard on the girl," Talbott said later, when Sol took him to the airport.

"She's still said nothing about calling Jake Cooke?" asked Sol, unwilling to challenge the accusation.

"No. I don't propose to probe, either. She'll talk when she's ready."

Sol pulled at his ear in frustration. He had been a news-bureau chief abroad in places where Talbott had been a correspondent. That created a bond. Both men had deep-dyed beliefs: a reporter must set aside personal prejudices; only facts led to the truth, and even if the truth wasn't what you'd like, publish and be damned!

"I heard *you* talk of the network supporting Quex," said Talbott. "That's off limits."

Again Sol looked frustrated. "He's digging up dirt," he began cautiously. "Institutional dirt. It threatens the agreed versions. Governments, even ours, want to stop him. He couldn't go to the CIA or the FBI for protection . . ."

Sol began to talk at last. Talbott listened carefully, because he'd never known Sol Farkas to even consider using the news to serve other ends than the public right to know. By the time Sol steered onto the ramp for the Kennedy terminals, Talbott was feeling distinctly queasy.

"Where will you start?" Sol asked him.

Talbott tapped the file of research notes. "Where the 88 expect to see me first. The war-crimes trial. That's where Sally's work for Bronfmann last took her. It's where Bronfmann was last seen in public." He added, as if he expected resistance from Sol: "I want Sally to join me, soon as she can."

"Well, don't drag a damn great crew around," Sol laughed, and the tension eased again. Both men knew the hazards. They had started in the news business with nothing more than pencils and pads. They had graduated into a multibillion-dollar industry. They mourned the early days of TV journalism, when the reporter worked with a single camera-and-sound man. Now the correspondent was "talent" and performed at the sharp end of a team of technicians, production assistants, directors and producers. Sol knew how Talbott rebelled against it. He'd be glad to get back to solo reporting, to what he'd always done best.

Sol pulled up outside Lufthansa. Talbott said, "Those aren't Fishhook's pals guarding Quex."

"Not with Quex rattling so many skeletons."

"So?"

"There's only one foreign government with its own army guarding its defense missions in this country." Sol raised his eyes. "The brass plates say import-export, but to see the manager you have to get past the guards from the Kyrya."

Talbott retrieved the overnight bag Sol had collected from the correspondent's office. It contained the essentials for foreign travel and reminded Talbott of the many times they had depended upon each other. "I could use one of those guards in my apartment," he said. "If that fake funeral's delayed, or Sally has to stay there for any other reason—well, I kind of like the girl, but alive, not dead."

Talbott didn't need to ask who were the guards from the Kyrya.

8

The man in black coveralls moved up the side of Talbott's apartment as if the surface were horizontal. He recited the drill in his mind. Revolve the obstacle through ninety degrees. Imagine it parallel to the ground. Will yourself to be drawn firm against the surface, as if by gravity. Don't look behind.

He carried a bag of tricks; coiled ropes of a new fiber; the lightest of precision tools. They had taken him safely through worse field operations than this one.

He had started from the fanlight over the street-level bagel shop. A plan of the building was engraved on his memory. He knew how to skirt the lighted windows, and how to locate Talbott's place by taking a fix on other lights burning through the night.

Few would believe he was window-cleaning at midnight, but he knew how to bluster his way out. New Yorkers were not disposed to push suspicion far if offered some explanation, however implausible.

Mandy Roberts let herself into Talbott's apartment. The black Jamaican doctor had flown up for an unscheduled meeting with UN officials. She had her own keys, Talbott's permanent invitation to use the apartment as she chose, and a message that Talbott was out of town.

She pressed the light switch inside the front door, and nothing happened. She groped her way to the kitchen and tried another light. Damn! She changed direction. Suddenly an arm cut across her throat. She felt a sharp prick in her neck, below the jawline, close to the top of the spinal column. A blunt instrument pressed up under her chin. She was unconscious in forty seconds.

Her assailant knelt and withdrew a long needle, tearing the skin. Blood sprayed him. He took out a flat-pack camera with optional light: invisible, flash or natural. Pictures would supply the confirmation required at the Karlshorst. It wasn't that they distrusted him. They simply enjoyed reminding Moscow of their efficiency now that they no longer ranked as the largest KGB complex outside the Soviet Union but came instead under the East German (DDR) Main Administration for Espionage in East Berlin.

The flash popped. He should have selected, for the most elementary security reasons, invisible light. But it was his solitary pleasure to see all his own work. He sucked in his breath. In that microsecond of orgasm, he had stared into a face darker than his own. He had killed the wrong woman.

9

The working day was just starting in West Germany. Talbott's tidy world was about to blow apart. Had he foreseen the shocks in store, he would have been less slavish in making the hasty transfer from the New York-to-Frankfurt flight to the Düsseldorf shuttle. But that was what the itinerary said he must do, and that was what he did.

The world began to tilt when the woman across the aisle reached out to him as if asking for a light. She held a cigarette between stubby fingers. The nails were broken, the hand the creamy texture of chocolate. Her spectacles sparkled under the brim of a felt hat. She had a husky whisper. "Rebecca," it seemed she said. "Remember Rebecca."

No other name had this power to shake Talbott. He had a dizzy impression that the airbus rolled over, but it was only the sunshine from a porthole shifting across the outward curve of the woman's glasses.

He took a grip on himself. He looked around. Law-abiding commuters drowsed in their cocoon floating steadily to Düsseldorf. The woman was lighting her own cigarette. She sighed contentedly and blew a thin stream of smoke at the back of the seat in front.

"Excuse me," said Talbott. "What was that again?"

He had to repeat himself before she swiveled round. "Pliz?" she said, glasses flashing so that he found it impossible to make out her face. "The English I am not spikkin so good."

"Sie haben doch jetzt gerade mit mir gesprochen!" declared Talbott.

"Nein! I haff not with you spikked."

"You said, 'Rebecca.' " He was half out of his seat now.

The woman looked down the aisle for a flight attendant. Then she reached for a call button. Talbott sat back. The woman seemed ready to accuse him of harassment. Instead, she ordered a beer. By uttering that name, however, she had rolled away the stone from a cave. An iron band seemed to tighten across his chest. He felt as if he were going through an earthquake, all the natural laws—like gravity and the substantiality of the ground beneath your feet—suddenly suspended. He had spent years guarding his privacy. It was only on camera, these days, that he fought the bad guys. People took that seriously sometimes, and tried to bring him their troubles. He'd learned to safeguard his privacy against random importunities. Now this total stranger had uttered, as it were, a code word to gain entry to his innermost being, only hours after Sol Farkas had told him how something almost as spooky had happened to the network executive himself.

Sol had been driving Talbott to Kennedy Airport. "I don't give too much of a damn about the story," said Sol angrily. "Bronfmann looked into the Hess case and saw things he shouldn't. *That's* the issue. There's a pattern of violence."

"Mmm." Talbott was noncommittal.

"Okay, I sound paranoid. But I had a visit early this morning from a man out of my past. The same man I got so paranoid with Sally about."

"What?" Talbott had almost jumped out of the car.

"That's how I reacted when they called his name up to my apartment . . . Jake Cooke."

"He came to your home?" This was startling too. Sol's place in Manhattan went under the name of his lady friend. The address and phone number were closely guarded secrets.

"Very early," said Sol. "Before daybreak. He said he'd flown directly from Europe. He would never have got past the doorman, only he mentioned Citadel."

Talbott's head had swum. "You've never told me Citadel meant anything to you. And why would Jake Cooke—" He stopped for a moment. "That's impossible! Jake Cooke was in Düsseldorf when Sally spoke to him. You told me yourself."

"We don't *know* it was Jake Cooke she spoke to," said Sol. "And he could have flown over in the interval."

"Did you ask him about Sally?"

"He never gave me time for questions. The name Citadel established his credentials—"

"How? Goddammit, Sol, you've got a lot to explain!"

"But I won't. Not yet." Sol had clammed up about Citadel. "He had

reports showing systematic acts of terror against Jews, so widely scattered
that the pattern escapes the concern of governments other than Israel.
That's all he'd come to show and tell. Then he was gone. Like the rabbit in
a magician's top hat."

"What are you afraid of, Sol?"

"For myself, nothing. But I'm a Jew. I can't ignore the danger. Each
isolated act of terror against a Jew merits no more than a local news squib.
Each Jewish counterblow gets headlines. Israel could find itself someday
judged guilty by the media, and hanged as a mad dog."

Talbott had found this line of reasoning hard to follow. Where did
Bronfmann come in? Or Hess?

"Decoys?" suggested Sol. "To suck you in? You must know something.
In some way, you hold a key."

And now this strange woman dug up a name from Talbott's own past.
He wondered who planted the idea that he held the key to some mystery.
Was it this Jake Cooke, who seemed able to be in two places at once?
Maybe there were two Jake Cookes? It was no more unlikely than what
had just happened.

The weird thing was, Talbott could do nothing. The woman had spoken
a name she *must know* had the power to shock him. But who'd seen her
address him? And what had she done wrong, anyway? He could hardly
complain to the management: *Please, this woman is torturing me with
things buried long ago.*

Just before the descent, she lurched into the aisle, swinging her handbag.
He leaned out to follow her uncertain progress to the forward toilets. She
was an odd fish; belted red raincoat over black trousers, the red felt hat,
and brown flat-heeled shoes. If he followed her, if he tried to question her,
she would assuredly make a scene.

She did not return. As soon as the airbus touched down, Talbott shot
ahead of the other passengers, ignoring their protests and the admonitions
of the cabin crew. He was first off, and stood aside to scrutinize those who
followed. It was uncanny. The flight terminated here, but the woman was
not among those who disembarked.

The waiting taxis were sleek and expensive. The orderly trees marched
across the parking lot. The impeccable rain fell from the olive-drab sky.
The song of an unruly thrush intensified a sense of regimented gloom.

He slumped into the back of a Mercedes. A blue neon light flickered: the
airport Sex Shop, opening for breakfast. Faint images teased his memory.
Another shop with a blinking blue light. Rain drumming on flattened soil.
Stark trees like gallows. A thrush squandering its notes into the silence of
Rebecca's tomb . . .

A man at a pay phone near the taxi stand said in German, "He got the message."

The man wore a reversible raincoat, black side out to match his trousers. He carried one of those Dunhill bags that fold inside out from handbag to carryall. He felt through his pockets for a cigarette, groping past the red felt hat in one and the wig in the other. He watched Talbott's taxi glide away and he spoke again into the phone, juggling the cigarette between scarred chocolate fingers. "He's all yours now," he said.

In the hotel, Talbott checked the bag Quex had produced for him. It contained a new minicamera system. The general had once backed an engineer to develop it for medical research: the buttonhole lens could be floated through a patient's arterial system on its fiber-optic tether. The line could be woven just as easily through Talbott's suit.

"Cameras are banned in the Düsseldorf courtroom," Quex had claimed. "I'd defy anyone to spot this one. Here! Just in case you need it." Talbott doubted that he would. He certainly saw no reason for taking it into the courtroom on a first visit. He turned to notes Bronfmann had shipped back to New York:

"War-crimes trials seem odd, after all this time. It's only Bonn, prosecuting a few small-fry Nazi camp guards. The trials are a great bore to citizens of this capital of North Rhine-Westphalia. They've stopped reading about them because their newspapers have stopped reporting them.

"Düsseldorf once had a large Jewish population. Now there's only the solitary synagogue left. Guarded by the West German Army! The twenty accused Nazis are defended by lawyers who make the Jewish witnesses sound guilty for bringing such outrageous charges.

"The trials have become political theater. The Left wants to prove the slave camps served capitalism. Bonn wants to show the world it continues to crack down on Nazism. Now there's talk of some legal device by which Deputy Fuehrer Rudolf Hess can be brought to testify against the Jews. This would be sensational. The four powers would have to obey the law. Or kill Hess . . ."

Talbott was expected. He felt this from the moment he mounted the steps at 34 Muhlerstrasse and entered Courtroom L.111 after the mid-morning break. A gray-uniformed attendant led him to a chair behind the defendants. An old, silver-haired, rosy-cheeked woman leaned back and said, "They say I set dogs on pregnant women. Lies! You will hear the truth. When our deputy fuehrer speaks."

Talbott looked away. Wartime maps covered the walls. They showed European Jewish settlements linked by railroads to camps. Some camp names were now infamous. Others remained obscure. Every major city seemed to have the connection. There were far more camps than Talbott remembered. He saw, with a start, blowups of the same U.S. Air Force photographs he had himself displayed during the General Massey interview.

A brisk young defense lawyer was addressing the tribunal: "Our position is, these photographs confirm American complicity. They were classified by the U.S. Government to conceal the truth. American Communist pressures forced upon the German people these renewed trials. Those pressures have backfired. Classified secrets have started to emerge, telling a different story . . ."

A woman in a red felt hat brushed past Talbott and sat near another of the accused. Her glasses sparkled and her head bobbed in Talbott's direction. He thought he heard a whisper: "Rebecca." He tried to get a better view of the woman, but she rose again and left by the farther door. The ushers seemed to know her.

He sat paralyzed. Once again, he had fallen through a hole in time. Rebecca? Buried in a bombed house. All the memories entombed. What right had these people to disinter such things?

"Sometimes women and children were pushed alive in the ovens."

The speaker was a gray, formless figure in the witness box.

"Kindly keep to the point," said a defense lawyer. "I repeat, How did you know it was your wife and child who were executed?"

The formless witness said faintly, "The whole camp knew it."

"*You* saw this?"

"We—all of us, we smelled the burning of bodies."

"Yes, yes, yes." The lawyer hunched forward. "You told us already about the smell."

"I was speaking of the smoke from the ovens."

"We are speaking now of the smell, Comrade Orlowski."

The witness peered down at the court, bewildered. "We learned very well to know the smell of human flesh burning."

The lawyer flapped his black gown in a show of exasperation. "You are determined to play on emotions, aren't you? Not the smell. How could you recognize the smoke?"

The unsubtle attempt to confuse him made the witness straighten up. "Prisoners were burned. It is impossible *not* to know the smell of burning human flesh. One does not survive these things incredulous of such horror."

"Human flesh?" The lawyer smirked. "You eat well, comrade?"

The witness stood mute.

"Yes, the answer, I believe, is yes. We all know how well the workers eat in their Russian paradise."

The sniggers from the spectators caused the witness to tilt his head.

"Is it not a fact that the only witnesses to these so-called crimes come here with Soviet consent because the so-called death camps are now in Soviet-controlled territories?" continued the lawyer.

The chief prosecutor jumped to his feet. "I object—"

"I wish to establish the credibility of Comrade Orlowski."

"Objection overruled."

The witness in the box was swaying. He seemed to Talbott more form-less than ever. The defense lawyer was switching back and forth in a deliberately confusing manner. "Isn't it true the Soviet Union wishes to prolong these trials in the West to maintain the myth of German guilt and divide the Western alliance?—Can you tell us, Comrade Orlowski, how to distinguish between the smell of roasting pork and a burning human corpse?—Come, you have just told us how well you eat. Jewish? Of course, then let us rephrase the question. How did you know it was your daughter roasting and not a side of beef in the camp kitchens?"

The witness keeled over. Two court officials caught him before he struck the floor. One of the prosecutors asked for an adjournment. A defending lawyer protested loudly against the courtroom tactic of Jewish witnesses: "They weep and wail, and throw fits when the defense threatens to expose their lies."

"The court will adjourn for lunch," decreed the presiding judge. The chief prosecutor intervened.

". . . wish to obtain an injunction against defendants' move . . . ur-gent matter . . . cannot tolerate this legal maneuver . . . goes against the intent of this court." Words were lost in the bustle and stir as ushers flung open the doors. Talbott leaned forward, straining to hear. "It defeats justice for the defense to subpoena former Deputy Fuehrer Hess, Prisoner Number Seven in Spandau jail . . ."

"We will discuss the matter in chambers." The presiding judge pushed back his chair. "The court will rise."

Back in his hotel room, Talbott contemplated the ceiling. How could you capture this inversion of truth for young TV audiences? They had no direct knowledge of the reality. Many would sympathize with those an-cient camp guards with their innocent, apple-red cheeks, their white locks, their overwhelming self-pity.

The spectators packing the court were hostile to the Jewish witnesses. Suppose the local police had similar inclinations? Contacting them wouldn't help Bronfmann. New York must handle that. Talbott was here to wait for the neo-Nazi 88 to follow through on their threats.

He fell asleep. In place of the ceiling, he saw burning timbers. The hotel plumbing grumbled. He seemed to hear voices shout, "Come back, you bloody snotty, or you'll bring the lot down on her!"

The phone rang. He'd no idea how much time had passed. The caller spoke classroom English: "We expect you tomorrow with Miss Ryan. The details will be in your hotel mailbox. Remember Radzki."

"Remember who?"

"Remember Rebecca," said the caller and rang off.

Talbott stared at his hands. They were shaking. The caller had said "Radzki" first. Radzki? Christ help me . . .

He called the overseas operator and got through to Fishhook Sherman's house in Long Island, hoping to find Sally.

"Sorry," said a strange voice, "they're at the funeral."

He'd forgotten about Quex's damned funeral.

He tried Quex's unlisted number in East Hampton. The moment he heard Sally's voice, the trembling stopped. Her cautious response was a reminder of possible eavesdroppers. He said, "I'm sorry I can't be there. It must be very hard for you—"

"Poor, dear Grandpa," said Sally.

"There's a move to bring Jonathan here."

Jonathan was the wartime code name the British had given Hess. Sally responded swiftly. "I mustn't be late for the funeral. Say hello to the affiliate. I'll call you there in forty."

Forty minutes later, Talbott was in the Düsseldorf TV station. Its exchange agreements with his network roughly justified Sally's use of "affiliate." The editors in the newsroom knew Talbott. Yes, of course he was welcome to take a New York call. Then Sally came through. She was in a phone booth near the cemetery, worrying about time.

"Who knows I'm here?" he asked quickly.

"Everyone. I can see them assembling. A couple of newcomers from London. And of course, your office."

He groaned. Anyone, then, could have forewarned the court or the woman in the red felt hat. He said, "Can the court force Jonathan's release to give testimony?"

He heard the sharp intake of breath and then, "He's reported—Didn't you know? Jonathan's dead."

"Impossible!" He stared through the glass panel separating the assignment editor from the rest of the newsroom. Hess dead? It couldn't be true.

"It was a news flash," Sally temporized. "Already Voice of America's broadcast a denial. Look, I'm late . . ."

Talbott went over to the lineup editor. "Seen anything on Hess?" he asked.

"You soon got onto it!" The editor pulled up the agency report. "I suppose we'll make it the lead. If it's true."

Talbott read the item. "They don't rule out foul play?"

"The whole thing is foul," said the editor, "and it's all rumor anyway, isn't it? We trust the four powers to tell us what goes on inside that jail. They could turn Hess into a frog, flush him down the toilet, give him a castle in Liechtenstein, we'd never know the difference, would we? Not if they all agreed upon their story?"

"When have the four powers ever agreed?"

"Whenever Hess threatened to reveal something embarrassing."

"Like?"

"Memoirs," said the editor. "There's talk he wrote them on bits of lavatory paper."

Talbott looked innocent. "What can he possibly tell us now?"

"Something of which he was the only living witness?" suggested the editor. He shrugged. "It's ludicrous, really, this late in the twentieth century. Everything still gossip and rumor. Look at this." He showed Talbott another news item. "A Red Navy warship *might* have run down a Yankee submarine in the Baltic. But no confirmation. And when we *are* told anything, how do we know it really happened the way they say it did?" the editor asked glumly. "We won't be told the truth even if it leads to a third world war. The public knows that, so you can't blame the public for gobbling up any old rumor about Hess and Hitler's war, can you?"

10

Rumors, thought Sally. I live in a world of secrecy, gossip and rumors. I'm sick of it. *Shshshsh!* whispered the wind in the trees, following her progress through the Old Burial Ground at East Hampton.

No flowers, service private. It was what the townsfolk would expect. Anonymity. Swift burial. They knew all about the secret wars of General Quex Massey.

Could you fake a death without the help of some faceless agency? All this deception was dangerous. When Grandpa Massey declared himself dead, he passed beyond the law's protection. She felt the eyes of the gravediggers on her. How did she know they were gravediggers?

She shivered . . . A morning starts, wet and windy, with foreboding. A radio report of collision between American and Russian warships. Who knows where the fault lies? A submarine tracks the opposing fleet, surfaces incautiously. What does the average schmuck in Moscow know about it? How do *we* check our side's official version? The tensions have been building for months. Everyone lies. Is Hess really dead or did some intelligence bureaucrat have a disinformation brainwave in a period of frustration after his wife refused his conjugal rights?

Sally saw the heavily veiled figure of Rinna Dystel and felt a stab of resentment. Even Rinna's war, such ancient history, no longer seemed what it was. Well, they said her specialty had always been deception. Unauthorized onlookers would never recognize her in that funereal garb, and she must have disguised her presence from the locals during her stay with Grandpa.

Sally stared into the open grave, where the coffin, convincingly weighted with stones, made a jerky descent. You had to presume Rinna was in love with the old coot supposedly down there. It had given him a new lease of life. She smiled in spite of herself. New life for a fake corpse.

Drops of rain plopped onto the box from which the body was missing. Nobody could wish Grandpa Massey in it. Nor was he ready. His wits were as quick as— She stole a glance at the rotund figure opposite. At the Reverend Canon Marcus Furneval, some kind of chaplain to the English Queen. Or one of many honorary guardians of royal conscience. He looked far from royal now, flinging up against the gusting rain a peculiarly English brolly.

He'd come bustling into the cavernous basement kitchen of Fishhook's house that morning, shaking out his umbrella, dropping mud all over the stone floor. "Don't mean to butt in," he told Quex. "Heard the sad news. Decided to come."

Sally wondered how he'd gotten there so quickly. He must be one of the Hat Men from the way Quex had parried him. You couldn't butt in, Rev. It's *my* funeral. You can even get to say a few kind words."

"While the late-lamented celebrates in discreet concealment?" Marcus Furneval had joined them for breakfast. Suddenly he was pointing a fork at her grandfather. "Finished the memoirs, laddie?"

"Memoirs?" For a moment, the general looked like a schoolboy caught stealing apples. He glanced uneasily in Rinna Dystel's direction. "Ah well, what's documented is under lock and key."

The chaplain tapped his bulbous, oddly twisted nose. "Ha! Not forgotten a basic rule of deception, eh?" He, too, shot a quick glance at Rinna. "If you want a document read with absolute greed, make strenuous efforts to hide it."

"You," retorted Quex, recovering, "remember Occam's razor."

The chaplain snorted playfully. *"Non sunt multiplicanda entia praeter necessitatem."* Clearly, it referred to some obscure joke between them, sealing their comradeship. "You get lost in fantasy if you play with theories more complex than the facts justify," he explained to the others.

When Sally had helped Quex in the preliminary research, she'd turned up information on the Reverend Furneval. He'd been known as the palace parson back in the 1930s, and then as the Boxing Parson for his work among London slum kids. Old newspapers gossiped that his slum work was atonement for his indiscreet aid to a playboy prince. Furneval had entered the secret wartime world because of some quirky brilliance in code-breaking and his supposed knowledge of the Nazis from student days. Today, he was one of those elderly clerics dusted off from time to time to carry out delicate missions. He was reputedly a master of intrigue. He looked more like an old convict, and Sally avoided his eyes, because she felt in some way threatened by him.

"Earth to earth, ashes to ashes." Fishhook Sherman winced, not at the words, but at the hollow sound of clods banging down upon the cheated coffin. His back still ached from putting in the stones: they were the right weight, but too compact. Thus the telltale echo. A shock for the old biddies, watching from across the pond, if they guessed he was conniving in a mock funeral. It carried him back to those wild wartime wheezes with Commander "Izzie" Nelson of Scotland Yard, now billowing beside him in wind-inflated raincoat, an expression of false solemnity plastered across his wicked old mug.

Fishhook had renewed the friendship cautiously, waiting to meet Nelson at the Tinker Alley Tavern in Sag Harbor. There was no mistaking the man when he rounded the corner of Rector Street, arms swinging, a lion's mane of white hair flying, big feet slapping the sidewalk with a London bobbie's beat. Nelson of the Yard, a legend too big for his detractors, yet fighting now to keep his reputation. Fishhook's mind had gone spinning back to the 1940s, when Nelson was on "cargo-protection" duties in American ports. Nelson had strangled a seaman who was selling information so that U-boats knew where to intercept the arms-laden ships. "Cheaper than a trial!" was Nelson's comment, but the law was the law. On the other hand, the FBI had been directed by President Roosevelt to give clandestine aid to British security, and so Fishhook had quietly smuggled Nelson out of the country.

Now Nelson's enemies were leaking such stories, and accusations that he regularly abused his authority—even that he covered up secret Soviet operations. Officially, he was on leave pending an investigation. Unofficially, the Yard backed him against enemies in M15 and M16, the secret services.

At their reunion, Nelson reminded Fishhook of an ancient formula that allowed for "disposal of a body under protection of the Crown." It had been the unwritten law under which Nelson, back in Britain, escaped punishment for executing the traitor. Fishhook wondered if it still applied in these days, when heroes could be turned into traitors by a twist of the headlines. Nelson had said, as they followed the coffin, "Looks like we're disposing of Quex's body under protection of the Crown," nodding over at the Reverend Canon Furneval.

Fishhook assumed he was joking. He had little time for royalty and less for the palace parson.

The wind was rising. The graveyard trees trembled and shook down water on the tomb of an early settler, showering Red Crombie, too.

"You'll see some of the old-timers there," his Washington chief had promised. "Hat Men. The originals took their name from some Ibsen rot about the big black hat, you put it on and nobody can see you." The chief noted his incredulity and said, "You kids missed something when you missed that war. There was no confusion about which side was good and which was evil. The good guys were part of Quex's family. You didn't get born into that family. Quex requisitioned you."

Red Crombie supposed he was on requisition now. He leaned against the tomb, with its stone knight recumbent. Funny sort of an Old World relic for a pioneer family to choose: perhaps in their loneliness they had felt the need for some symbol of tradition. The idea of knightly chivalry, Crombie quite liked. The old stone knight protected family honor, provided a shield in the struggle on a new frontier. No such shield would guard Crombie's honor if things went wrong. He was long ago told, "We disown you if you get caught."

What he was getting now was most awfully wet. He wondered if it was sacrilegious to open up his tattered umbrella. His former chief had been so starved of funds, covert action had adopted the dirge: "The rain it raineth every day/upon the just and unjust fella. But more upon the just because/ the unjust's got the just's umbrella." The former chief's name was Walter Juste.

Crombie saw the funny English parson putting up his own umbrella and so he shook open his own. "We don't have the umbrella of diplomatic privilege for what you do," the former chief had also said. Crombie looked up into the weeping sky and trusted God would not disown him too.

Quex had been waiting in Fishhook's library. There he watched the mourners troop back through the hedge at the end of the ornamental gardens, slapping their hats against their thighs, gazing up in wonder at the magically clearing skies. They had returned, as they had gone by way of the Massey estate, in a windowless van bearing the device REMOTE BROADCASTS and the network logo. Fishhook had let it be known among the neighbors that the network was shooting a TV movie, using his house as base. It explained the unusual traffic.

Sally was first into the library. "This report that Hess died—"

"Rumor!" snapped the old man. "Voice of America denied it."

Sally hid her irritation. It was vintage Grandpa Massey to know all the news, rising at dawn to skim it off the shortwave radiocasts, serving it up with breakfast and his analysis of world affairs. "Well," she said. "Here's something you don't know."

Quex waited with a show of modest contrition.

"Those Nazi lawyers have found a way to get Hess out of jail."

"I know," Quex said. "By court order."

Sally compressed her lips.

Quex grinned up at her. "That's all right. Somebody will stop it."

Sally felt like a small girl again, fobbed off with candy. Then Quex's eyes shifted. His face lit up. "Ah, Rinna!"

Rinna Dystel swept into the library. "What a ghastly ordeal!" She sat on the footstool and reached out to him. "I had to keep telling myself it wasn't real. Then I rushed back to make sure."

Sally felt furious with herself. Why could she never voice affection for Quex this way without spoiling it the next moment with some snippety argument?

She saw Red Crombie hesitate in the doorway. She walked over, openly displaying curiosity. Crombie wasted little time on introductions. "You have an exciting job, Miss Ryan," he said. "Let's hope it won't get you into hot water." He had an all-American smile that concealed an infinity of complexities. "For instance, your application to film Hess inside Spandau—"

"What of it?" asked Sally, startled.

"You should renew it." He glanced round.

"They say Hess is dead."

"Oh, that!" He dismissed it with a flap of one hand.

"Who are you with?" she demanded.

"DI. Defense Intelligence. I'm a photoanalyst."

Photoanalyst, my sainted aunt! thought Sally. With those muscles and that tan?

He cocked his head. "You find that hard to believe? Well, now . . . those aerial photographs you think came through us from wartime archives. Not so."

Sally stared at him in bewilderment. Sol Farkas was moving in their direction and she bit off the questions suddenly crowding her mind. Crombie moved away. She thought, if he's here, he's party to the masquerade. Yet he shouldn't know about the aerials. She had a nasty sense of something astir, out of view, as if she had disturbed the sleeping dogs of an old war. Let sleeping dogs lie, they said. Crombie's masters certainly believed that. So what was he trying to tell her? Once, she might have enjoyed coaxing indiscretions from such a man. She couldn't play that game now. Talbott was too much in her mind. Other men, in the romantic sense, had suddenly lost appeal for her. In a few hours, she'd be with Talbott again. The prospect blotted out the agreeable Mr. Crombie. With that reddish hair and wolfish grin, he was uncannily canine, a huge Irish red setter, a dog disturbed and hungry.

Quex, the ghostly host at his own funeral supper, avoided the hefty sandwiches Fishhook had ordained as suitable for a sober country mourning. Rinna had whipped up a fluffy omelet to go with his champagne. One good mark for Rinna, thought Sally; Quex had never before diverged from taking his eggs scrambled.

He tapped a glass for attention. "As the specter at the feast," he began to a chorus of groans and laughter, "I thank you for coming . . . Our immediate concern is to prevent a real funeral for a young colleague."

He was tyrannical in that wheelchair, as Sally knew too well. The tyranny of the infirm, she thought. The sick tyrant who knew how to get his way. He said, "Our missing friend is Jewish. This house is protected by Jewish volunteers, because Israel has decided any Jew anywhere must have its protection—and so must those who help . . .

"Hitler got away with mass murder because there were no such forces to stop him. Yet intervention would have been possible. *Nothing* was done! Because of a failure of intelligence . . ."

Nice and abstract, thought Sally. Not *his* failure. She winced when he said the good Lord intended him to stay alive until he'd rooted out the truth. Was he requisitioning the Almighty as well? She caught Red Crombie's eye, and his smile flashed on and off.

"You've all played your parts since my search began," said Quex. "Thanks to Mr. Crombie here, I can confirm that thousands of feet of film shot by American fliers—in bombers we said couldn't reach the death camps—are safely stored under the green Maryland pastureland . . ."

Sally saw Crombie's face turn crimson. She sympathized. It was just like Quex to build up the importance of his allies to magnify himself.

Then Crombie interrupted. "Those death-camp pictures may well be fakes . . . sir."

Quex's eyes glittered.

"Those particular prints came through Europe," Crombie insisted.

"I expect opposition from Washington," snapped Quex. "But Mr. Crombie is on loan to the Suitland archives as a technician." He made Crombie sound like an office boy. "A *specialist* in computer enhancement of wartime negatives worked on the camp reconnaissance pictures." He glowered at Crombie. "Tell them to feed the Auschwitz coordinates into the national photo-interpretation center. We'll soon see if we don't get back the same pictures."

Crombie folded his hands in mock humility and said no more. Already Parson Furneval was jumping in. "This might be the right moment," said Furneval, "to raise another aspect. We do our own computer enhancement in England, of course." He paused.

Quex gave a resigned nod.

Parson Furneval clasped his plump belly. "We put through some old photographs from German sources . . . Rudolf Hess beside his aircraft just before flying to England, taken by his adjutant. It is quite clear the machine Hess parachuted from isn't the one with which he started out!"

Quex asked reluctantly, "Where did these pictures come from?"

"Bronfmann." Furneval saw their surprise and added, "Not that he came to me, nothing like that! He saw some of our chaps in the ministry. I gather he thought Hess wasn't the pilot." The parson searched their astonished faces. "If Hess wasn't the pilot, who was?"

Sally, quicker than her grandfather, glimpsed what Quex missed: a look that disturbed for the fraction of a second the cool surface of Rinna's face: a fugitive glimmer of fear briefly beyond control.

Sol Farkas repeated for Sally the service he had done for Talbott: he drove her out to the airport. "I feel," he joked, "like a wartime dispatcher."

"I thought you were one of the dispatched," she said.

"Where'd you hear that?" He was genuinely astonished.

"Quex," she lied. It was useful sometimes to have a grandfather who claimed to know everything. "Is it true?"

"I was only thinking I covered this same stretch with Talbott—"

"The clockwork mouse? Sending agents into the blue?"

"Clockwork mouse? Where'd you learn that?"

"Old OSS types, I expect."

Sol crouched over the wheel, beefy and square, lost in the nostalgia of another time. "What did you do in the great big war, Daddy? We used to joke about that. What would we say? That we dangled from parachutes, dropping into nothing, on nothing missions that accomplished nothing? It was all secret. All wiped from the records. Nothing."

"You did nothing," she echoed. "No names. No pack drill."

"Oh-So-Secret," he said. "Now it's the Old Soldier's Society. What's left."

"What about the new ones? What about Crombie?"

"I know nothing of Crombie."

"Nothing, always nothing!" she mocked. "Deny everything, disown those who get caught. Know-nothings, the lot of you." She simulated anger. "What *do* you know? What do you believe, all you nothings?"

He sat in injured silence, eyes on the road.

"You Hat Men," she pursued. "Don't you cling to some shared belief?"

He still wouldn't budge.

"You put a news organization at my grandfather's disposal," she accused him. "Yet, in your bio, you quote Adolph Ochs, who became publisher of the New York *Times* and promised 'to give the news without fear or favor.' "

"You can't give the news if you're not free," Sol said softly.

"So *that's* what the Hat Men do? Guard freedom?"

Stung at last, Sol retorted, "They do today what they did yesterday and will do tomorrow, I hope. Keep an eye on things."

"Is that why you took part in Operation Citadel?"

He almost drove off the road at that.

But he said nothing.

And Sally had her answer. Or at least a part of it.

11

Talbott surprised himself. It seemed a long time since he had felt such pleasure at seeing someone again. He told himself it was the relief of escaping from his second day at Courtroom L.111.

Sally came swinging toward him down the corridor, her hair buttercup yellow in the dusty shafts of sunlight, her face glowing with an innocent beauty that brightened an atmosphere otherwise oppressed by the wrinkled masks of the defendants and the closed expressions of their victims. The hostile groups hovered in the passageway, waiting for the morning session to resume.

"You got here fast!" Talbott took the girl's arm. "A chip off the old block. They used to say Quex arrived before he'd left."

He drew her away from the curious stares. An usher bellowed, "Court's in session!" In German, it sounded like a call to arms. Talbott said, "I've seen enough. Let's get coffee."

They sat in wintry sunshine outside the Gasthaus Schroeder. There was so much to say. Neither, though, was in a hurry to talk business. As if each knew there would be no more quiet intervals like this.

"I had nightmares on the plane," she said.

"Twitched up. We're all a bit twitched up."

She understood too well what he meant. Grandpa Massey used to say a touch of the wartime twitch was always good for a few days' medical leave.

If they'd been suffering from combat fatigue now, it might have been easier to handle. This was another kind of heartache.

He wanted to talk about his own mid-flight nightmare. Yet he could not bring himself to speak about Rebecca. Not in the same breath as the woman in the red felt hat.

The sun was unseasonably warm. The coffee had a special flavor. The pleasure of each other's company held them in comfortable silence. The moment soon passed. A courtroom messenger had tracked Talbott down and dropped a note on the table between them. The youth had gone before Talbott could question him.

The note said: "Bring your companion to Ratingerstrasse 2200 hours tonight to see your Bronfmann again."

"The red-light district," said Sally.

"Then, you don't go."

"But if it means Bronfmann's life?"

"We can't act under that blackmail all the time."

"Just what Grandpa Massey said when Rinna tried to prevent me coming here," said Sally. And then she told him what had happened.

The argument had broken out just before Sally left Long Island.

"You can't let the child go back into danger," protested Rinna.

"It's vital to Bronfmann, vital to all of us," said Quex. "She'll have protection. And she's good as any man."

"You're *primitive!*" Rinna accused him. "A tribal chief, sending the youngest to save the honor of the clan. You'd sacrifice her—"

They sounded to Sally like actors shouting their lines. There was no audience except herself and the palace parson, Marcus Furneval, who had intervened unctuously at one point: "We all make sacrifices. God told Abraham to sacrifice his only son, Isaac."

"God was testing the father's faith," said Rinna.

Quex quoted in support of the parson: "God said, 'Take . . . your only son Isaac whom you love . . . Sacrifice him as a burnt offering.' "

"That's diabolical!" said Rinna.

"It's *your* Old Testament!" retorted Quex.

Sally had the sense of hidden meanings. She had no intention of letting anyone stop her from returning to Düsseldorf and the whole argument seemed silly. She could not imagine why Rinna was so opposed—a woman who had taken terrible risks in her time.

Luckily, Sol Farkas had joined them. "We're late" was all he said. "Let's move it, Sally."

Then Quex had reached out to her. "You'll have plenty of backup, child. You're on assignment, nothing more. But keep in mind, Talbott's caught between two sides. One wants him to learn the whole truth. The other wants to see what he finds out and then bury it."

Sally had surprised on Parson Furneval's countenance a smug and pious smile. She now told Talbott: "I thought suddenly of the little red tramway swinging between Manhattan and Roosevelt Island, with yourself the pendulum."

Talbott brushed aside the pit-and-pendulum image, but he was secretly disturbed by the foolish banter about Sally being Quex's sacrifice. He took her back to their hotel. They both had business to transact. Mercifully, it took them away from the war-crimes trials. An old dread was creeping out of his bones: the fear that he still carried the infection of violence, going back to when he contributed to Rebecca's death.

A call from New York startled Sally. It was their executive producer, Tom Middleton, reporting that for the first time in his experience, there seemed a chance of that interview with Hess in jail. The authorities seemed eager to shoot down reports that Hess was dead.

For Talbott, there was some personally shocking news. He took it in the privacy of his own room. Mandy Roberts had been found dead in his apartment.

"The killer seems to have gone into a frenzy," Sol Farkas said on the transatlantic phone. "Police say he could only be a psychopath. She was already dead when he violated her. I'm sorry, but you'll be hit with these details sooner or later . . . entered her . . . savage mutilation . . ."

Talbott could not absorb the last words. Mandy! Beautiful, intelligent, resourceful in serving society—and black. Black! The killer attacked in darkness. Did he, then, find he'd killed the wrong woman? Was he after Sally?

"A porter found her," Sol Farkas was saying. "The guy who waters your plants. He told the police you were gone, but they still want to see you."

Talbott lowered the phone. A professional killer might well go into a vengeful frenzy after discovering he'd hit the wrong victim. Or he could have been hired precisely because he was sexually deranged. Suppose the target was really Sally . . . ?

He ought to carry a leper's bell. "Unclean!" he should cry, an untouchable.

He said nothing to Sally. She was a professional colleague; Mandy had been a companion. He stood waiting that evening for the limousine he had ordered for the 88 rendezvous.

"You didn't contact the police, I hope," said Sally.

He shot her a look of guilty apprehension, thinking: so she already knows.

Sally added, "About the Bronfmann message."

"No," he said in a small explosion of relief.

"Because if they think you talked to the police, the bastards are capable of killing Bronfmann."

They were standing under the hotel porch. She added as further explanation, "I know this territory. There's always a watcher. Like the one over there, under the tree."

Talbott peered into the night at a man in a crumpled homburg. The figure was too jaunty to be sinister. He reminded Talbott of a London wartime cartoon showing an American bomber crew under a Berlin plane tree. They trailed parachutes, waved cigars, and shouted, "Taxiiii!"

He told Sally the story after they settled back in the rented limo. "Your 'watcher,'" he said, "looked more like some Hat Man." Then he added, "Funny word to use, *watcher?*"

"It's what"—she caught herself—"what they call each other here. The spies. West Germany's full of them." She concentrated on the passing streetlights, the shopwindow displays along Koenigsallee, covering her near blunder. She had almost said *Jake* called them watchers. Sometime soon she'd have to tell Talbott about Jake. He was out there now, watching, waiting.

At the foot of Ratingerstrasse they left the limo and Sally led the way through cobbled lanes. "Welcome to the artists' quarter. The arts of the 1980s, that is. Patronized by the rich. The arts of corruption."

"Come, my darlings!" A bearded giant absurdly robed as a Russian cossack bore down on them from under a sickly green light. "You keep good time." His massive belly nudged them down steps. His fat fingers dangled like sausages brushing Sally's neck. "Tell us your preferences," he pattered. "Dildo, fist, whip, mask? The Discipline Sex Club caters to all. Golden showers? French? Greek? Whatever your hearts desire, my lovelies." Sally sensed Talbott's rising anger and caught him in the act of grabbing at the doorman. "Shouldn't drink champers on empty tum, darling!" she slurred, hanging onto Talbott.

The doorman ballooned in an effluvium of grossness, tiny black eyes squinting from a jungle of greasy whiskers. He shoved open a door, releasing a burst of martial music. Inside the anteroom, amplifiers blasted out the din of a brass band. Tattered banners hung over a trestle table strewn with bits of German winter campaign uniforms, and a pile of peaked caps.

A falsetto voice pierced the taped profundo. The drums and trumpets died. ". . . at your service. Obergruppenfuehrer Spiess!" Light flooded up beneath a figure, tall and vaguely ludicrous, in the far doorway. The face was yellow like papier mâché stretched tight over a plastic skull. "Follow Madame Obedience!" said this apparition, and led the way through a corridor lit with imitation torches.

"Call me Madame O," invited the woman who brushed up against Talbott. A bared breast offered him a lipsticked nipple smile. She moved ahead, each step parting the curtain of her gown behind. The twin globes of her buttocks were dimpled and yellow like Swiss cheese.

The procession wound through plastic timbers buried in cardboard walls, under a low ceiling of compressed newsprint. Talbott stopped dead. Sally caught his arm: "Don't pick a fight!" He stumbled and stopped again like a mule. "For Bronfmann's sake!" she urged. He hurried on, glimpsing posters enlarged from porn magazines. Ersatz sex shone in the sickly light of the ersatz torches. OUR DONG STRETCHER MAKES HER SQUIRM . . . DOLLY OIL FOR BACKWARD ENTRY . . . HARD-ON PILLS GIVE ENDLESS RHYTHM. A gallery of sick illusions. Light and shadow. Substitutes for human love. Hitler's erotic appeal revived.

They came to a dance floor. Columns of light supported nonexistent arches. The architecture of flashy promises and empty ideals. Nuremberg again. Phallic zeppelins thrusting through pillars of searchlights. Nothing but vulgar dreams and a little dictator's prostatic hysteria.

"It's easier to kill with aerial bombing than with a knife," shrilled a voice from the floor. Sally and Talbott were marched to a booth. A leather-coated figure held the spotlight. "You think it easy to be a good SS officer? *No!* A strong man is needed to look into the eyes of the child to be sacrificed for humanity."

Talbott was hypnotized by the knife, shocked by the reference. Was he hearing the words of Jung, or only an echo from his past? *"You destroy yourself in youth to fulfill ambition, but the person destroyed will return to destroy you, knife in hand."*

The fool on stage was brandishing the knife over a pigtailed girl in a pushcart. The cart was pushed by the woman in the obscene gown.

"We gaze fearlessly at the challenge of racial poison!" declared the leather-coated man.

Talbott hunched protectively in front of Sally, remembering how he'd failed to shield Rebecca. He felt as if the whole performance had been constructed to bleed out memories he'd sealed off. His own damn-fool impetuosity had killed Rebecca.

"Personal responsibility is our creed," said the man with the knife. "Moral stamina is required to kill in the course of duty."

The figure on stage reached out and jerked the girl by the hair. Talbott jumped up. Men stepped from the shadows to block him. The man with the knife slashed at the frail child dangling from his raised fist. Instead of blood, sawdust oozed from the decapitated torso.

"Sieg Heil!" shouted Spiess.

"Sieg Heil!" responded men lining the walls with truncheons or guns, their presence announced by a magical flaring of concealed lights.

The woman bent over the broken doll and exposed her naked rump. The man opened his leather coat and flexed a massive hose of black corrugated rubber. Other figures joined them, to an amplified military march performed to a slower, sensuous rhythm. The lights started to fade. Sally forced Talbott back down. A projector whirred in the sudden quiet. A sober voice said, "In the spring of 1941 was the first step taken to build the Anglo-German alliance behind the façade of war." The clean-cut features of a German general shone from the cinescreen, seeming to speak from a Nazi newsreel of the period.

The sudden contrast with the earlier pornography made the film seem almost reasonable. "The Hess Command was created to carry out the Final Solution." There were scratchy shots of Hess in flying kit. "The secret agreement saved Britain from losing her empire."

Titles rolled over the noisy bombast from old wartime newsreels: *The Hess Command—with Actuality Film 1938–45. Production 88.* It opened with scenes at an Anglo-German Friendship Society dinner before the start of World War II. There was footage of King George VI with narration: "He hears that Jewish refugees try to enter British Palestine and he voices pleasure that steps are taken to prevent them leaving their European places of origin."

There were scenes of war leading to the Battle of Britain. "America is not yet in the war. Only by cooperating with the Third Reich can the British survive. This is the message brought by these Englishmen." Blurred images of men moved jerkily in and out of luxury cars over the subtitle *Lisbon: 1940.*

"It is not Germans who flood into British possessions abroad," said the narrator. "It is Jews and Bolsheviks. This is Hitler's reply." Maps and charts appeared on the screen. "On the eve of war, where had Britain committed its chief military strength? Palestine. Why? Because Palestine is the key to Suez, and the canal is the empire's jugular. It must be defended against World Jewry."

Hess was back on screen, joking with Hitler, taking salutes, climbing in and out of aircraft. "It is 1941 and the Hess Command will extend from the Baltic to the Black Sea, spreading behind the armies of the Third Reich as they sweep to Moscow. His command will liquidate the blood poisoners. But first, at the invitation of British ruling circles, Hess flies to guarantee the Fuehrer's side of the bargain . . ."

Talbott tuned out the propagandist's voice. The film had been cut with skill and moved too fast for an audience to think. Original newsreels had been cleverly matched with counterfeit film, the whole transferred to raw stock, producing a seamless, sepia-tinted "documentary." Hollywood had the sophistication for such a production. Who else? Talbott could only think of the porn-movie industry, fed by Mafia millions in need of laundering and fattened on petrodollars and hot money looking for sheltered, untaxable investments.

A giant screen obscured the first, dropping from the ceiling and picking up the next sequence, of Hitler proclaiming, "Our duty to the Creator is to rid humanity of poison germs." Talbott recognized the words from Hitler's so-called last will and testament. He was certain the speech was faked and then edited into old stock footage of the prewar Nazi rallies. A younger generation might suppose the orgiastic crowds were responding to the Fuehrer's proclamation of the Hess Command.

American officers strode arm in arm with Nazis along trenches of corpses in camps where, said the narration, "these parts of Europe are still not at war and remain friendly to the Reich, cooperating in the Final Solution." Allied officers were shown turning away when SS guards shot women and children. "The blood purge is not easy. We alone are judged worthy to carry out orders . . ."

The war scenes gave way to a final segment: *The Great Betrayal*. The words were printed over D-day newsreels and the retreat from Moscow. Stalin and allied leaders at Yalta appeared. "Bolsheviks seize control over decision makers in London and Washington," said a new voice. The first pictures of Hess after the 1945 defeat almost pulled Talbott out of his seat. "The deputy fuehrer is secretly returned to Germany. Anglo-Americans substitute a look-alike." A beetle-browed Hess faded into the prisoner in the war-crimes dock at postwar Nuremberg: "This is the Hess who is presented for 'justice.' See the insanity? It is characteristic of lunatics that they hold, indefinitely, postures awkward and unnatural. Marshal Göring testifies this man is mad. Other Nazi leaders, improperly on trial, declare it is impossible to recognize in this victim of an Allied conspiracy the habits of mind and manners normal to Hitler's coauthor of *Mein Kampf*, a man accustomed to mix in the highest social circles and who launched the first great German offensive against Poland by his 1939 decree . . ."

The lunatic Hess began to speak. The projectionist killed the sound, leaving the lips flapping wordlessly.

"Sound!" shouted Talbott.

"All in good time, professor!" roared the bizarre doorman, back at his side. "Stripteasers do not show it all at once."

Talbott was on his feet. "Stop wasting our time."

"Time no longer exists," called back Spiess, caught in the spotlight as the screen vanished. "You've seen time destroyed. *Spiess* makes past present."

Spiess. The German word for . . . what? Knife, dagger? Talbott began to swear.

"Ah, yes," shouted Spiess. "You'll have your Bronfmann. If you tell the world our truth."

More lights flowered. Exits were blocked by men cradling weapons. Talbott lunged out blindly. The doorman chopped at him. If Talbott had been less charged up, the tremendous blow might have felled him. He was lost in the isolation of blind rage. Sally cried out, "The pendulum . . . Stay the course!"

Talbott gave his head a violent shake. He called out, "Just give us Bronfmann." He was breathing heavily, but he was back in control. "No deals. Just deliver—"

"You'll get him," Spiess promised. He began to walk backwards in step with Madame O, followed by the man holding the mannikin's head, and the cloakroom attendants. Mechanical devices clicked softly. Lights died. Everything was nothing. It must have been this way when the Nazi rallies ended. The architecture of searchlights collapsed. All that remained was darkness, and hate masquerading as love of the masses.

"Follow your Uncle Feelie!" cried the doorman from the passage. "Fifty minutes we allow . . . Come, my darlings, for the lively pleasures we give you fifty; for the grave, five. No more, no less. Mollycoddles or masturbation, the time's the same, massage or micturation."

Sally felt his sausage fingers graze her face. She caught Talbott's arm again, but he was staring back into the black pit of the club. It had become a cavern filled with the odor of rusting waterpipes and the rustle of tiny claws.

Under the green streetlight, a Mercedes waited with its door flung open.

"We'll take our own!" snarled Talbott.

"Nonsense, professor!" boomed the doorman. "Hop in. Dispose your carcass before the 88 dispose of you." The odd slang hid the menace of the cloakroom attendants materializing out of the rain, closing on Sally and Talbott, while two of them held up a drunk.

"Go fetch!" ordered the doorman, and the drunk tumbled or was pushed into the back of the car. "Good doggie!" the doorman said, and flung a package after him. "Uncle knows best."

Talbott was frozen with horror. There was something familiar about the drunk . . . The doorman shut the giant umbrella over their heads with a vicious snap. Rainwater cascaded over Talbott and Sally. Caught off balance, they were propelled into the car.

The drunk had fallen sideways to the car floor. The rear door slammed shut. The carbuncled face of the doorman in his cossack rig leered through a window. Then the Mercedes shot forward, so fast that Talbott and Sally were flung back. The stereo sound of Wagner's *Tannhäuser* blasted their eardrums. Talbott forced himself forward to pull the drunk upright. Sally turned away.

First, she hammered at the thick glass partition. The chauffeur's cap in front was unmoving. She knew, without consciously thinking it, what Talbott would find if he wrestled the drunk face up. She could not handle this fresh horror. Not yet. She felt for a window button. There was none. The window was locked tight and could be opened only by the driver. She groped for the door release. None.

They were trapped inside a *berline* brothel-on-wheels whose spacious rear converted into a *lit de plaisir*. The speakers could relay piped music, or the threats of the pimp at the wheel when clients turned nasty. The glass was bulletproof. There were windows the driver could black out automatically, and doors he could unlock after the client had paid. *Berlines* toured the sex-club district after dark and were ignored by the police. That final recollection struck Sally at the moment she confronted the truth she had been subconsciously trying to deny.

The limp body stared up into the pink light of a concealed lamp. The face was frozen, the eyes filled with a mute appeal.

"Curare!" The name of the poison jumped out of Talbott's past. "He's not drunk. It's poison."

"It's Bronfmann," said Sally, touching the pink face in horror.

The eyes began to slide around in their sockets. "Oh, God!" groaned Talbott. He shook Bronfmann's shoulders but the head only flopped higher and wedged itself between Sally's legs and the panel in front. "Curare," Talbott repeated.

He knew the poison. Another name nagged him. *Ricin?* He slapped Bronfmann's face in a vain effort to get a muscular reaction.

The brain cries for mercy, but no organ responds.

The sentence surfaced from submerged memories. Drugs. Wartime experiments. A report for Quex, so long ago that if Talbott had been asked to recall it a few seconds earlier, he would have looked blank.

The limbs lose motion. The voice goes. The eyes function longest. No more horrible suffering can be imagined. The will, the sensibility, are not affected. Indeed, the poison heightens the brain's perception as it freezes the flesh.

Bronfmann uttered a faint sound. If the poison had just been injected, would he have some lingering control? Talbott leaned closer.

"Motherla—" Bronfmann's mouth was open. It seemed full of bloody fiber.

"Mother?" demanded Talbott.

Negative. Pink spittle bubbled and burst from Bronfmann's mouth. The effort turned Talbott's stomach just to watch.

This death is accompanied by the most dreadful, drawn-out agonies that cannot be voiced.

Talbott gripped the dying man's shoulders. "Motherland, is it?"

Light blazed in Bronfmann's eyes. "Hess." The name came out like the hiss of a snake.

Hess? Or a hiss? Talbott said, "Deputy Fuehrer Hess? And the Fatherland?"

The eyes separated, converged, and for a moment held in coordination. "Hess . . . Mother!!!!!"

The last word emerged like a scream from under water. Bronfmann's mouth blew bubbles and slowly shut.

Perception heightened. Completely alive but unable to reach out of the imprisoning corpse.

Talbott's fingers dug like talons into Bronfmann's neck. Locked in that brain was an answer desperately needed. But there was no response. The eyes slowly rolled back until only white gleamed in the sockets.

The Mercedes had shifted into high gear. Music blared. Bronfmann's body rolled with the new syncopation, *why, why, why?* Why kill Bronfmann? Why Hess? Why Mother?

Talbott ran through the sequence from the moment he thought Bronfmann was a drunk. Something the drunk had said as the club bouncers hustled him across the sidewalk. Something like . . . Radzki.

And the dying Bronfmann had groaned, and perhaps the groan was a name: Radzki.

It wasn't possible. Talbott reached down to search Bronfmann's pockets. The air was suffused with a stench from bowels and bladder out of control. There was a sudden silence before the driver's voice reached them: "I will tell you when to touch the body!"

They were trapped with a corpse in a wheeled prison. The *berline* glided to a stop. The driver said, "Do only as I say."

12

In the Kremlin that same evening, the KGB conspired with the CIA. That, anyway, was Secretary Nick Kerensky's view of it. He kept a record from behind tasseled red draperies, Mother's insurance against future distortions of this conference with Walter Juste, U.S. Vice President, and director of central intelligence before the current crisis. The meeting had taken painfully long to negotiate; to cancel it now would have been to give the crisis more significance that it had already.

The crisis was over the collision in the Baltic between Soviet and American vessels. An East German admiral, the first ever to hold such high command, was screaming blue murder, demanding action because the incident took place in East German waters. What a laugh! thought Kerensky. *Our* waters. But it was typical of upstart satellite self-assertion these days. He hated to think what the satellites might make of this secret meeting. Between Mother and Juste, just about every secret in the whole wide world was known, *including each one's plans against the other!* Kerensky shuddered. But even if he had not been devoted to Mother, his life and career depended upon his discretion.

Walter Juste had returned to his hotel before tonight's late banquet. Now it was the turn of that upstart German secret service prick, Helmuth Henkell, to consult with Mother. Once, in the old days when Berlin was the spy's paradise, Kerensky had quite liked General Henkell. Now the chances were Henkell would come blustering in, full of piss and vinegar. Odd to think that the American and the Russian had conversed at least like civilized men. While Henkell, the German ally, was out for blood. He'd already refused to cancel the Hess Command project.

"These American contacts won't change anything," Mother said when the tall East German spy chief joined him in the Green Room.

"There's nothing left to change," retorted General Henkell. "You've already switched the line to soft."

"A revolution proceeds in zigs and zags," Mother recited tiredly. He made Henkell sit by the elegant windows overlooking the Alexandrovsky Gardens. The Soviet leader held out a scrap of Sovtel paper with the teletyped words TARGET ECLIPSED.

"Eclipsed in his own backyard." The Russian struck a match and lit a corner of the message. "The end of General Massey." He let the paper curl and the ashes fall into a metal ashtray. "You wouldn't call that 'soft,' would you?"

Henkell kept his counsel. He had his own ideas about who had eliminated Massey. The German poked a finger into the ashes and said, "Who spread the story Hess was dead? Disinformation of that quality is *our* responsibility. German responsibility. Or must I remind you of the Warsaw Pact protocols?"

"Hess is *our* concern, a matter of Soviet history." Mother's amiability was gone. "Hess represents German evil. Hess reminds us of twenty million Russians slaughtered by German treachery. You tamper with Hess, comrade, and the Russian people will have your balls for breakfast."

Henkell blew out his cheeks. He was not ready yet to openly challenge the Office of Crude Bandits, *Kontora Grubykh Banditov*, the KGB. You moved against that vast estate only when you were fully prepared. So Henkell made a small puffing sound and said, "Naturally we assume the Hess death report was to block the legal steps being taken to bring Hess into the Düsseldorf dock?"

"Hess will never go before that court." Mother removed the spectacles that put dark circles around his eyes. "His good health will be attested by the American journalist Talbott. His network regularly asks to interview Hess. This time we have said yes."

"You can't—" began Henkell.

Mother's growl pulled him up short.

At a signal from Mother, attendants appeared at either end of the long room. "I hope for your sake," said Mother, turning his albino eye on Henkell, "you will mind your language when we gather at Igalo." The eye was empty of all emotion, sucking up information and betraying nothing, the unblinking orb of a circling shark.

Henkell knew when to leave well enough alone. He bent stiffly and submitted to a chaste Soviet kiss on either cheek before he withdrew.

Nikolai Kerensky stepped out of the shadows.

"A dangerous fool," said Mother. "Was he always more German than Communist?"

"What German isn't?" countered Kerensky. "They say they invented Marxism and we stole it. He won't make the same mistake twice."

"What mistake?"

"Wrestling with you in private. He'll take his arguments onto the floor wherever he can. He'll quote party dogma like holy writ to bless his petitions."

"Don't we all?" Mother commented sardonically. He limped back to the small table. His old leg injury was acting up again: he took it as an ill omen, for age and danger had made him superstitious. He stared at the charred remains in the ashtray: General Quex Massey's ashes.

Kerensky misread his thoughts and said, "Can't we take active measures against Henkell?"

"It would precipitate things with the DDR." Mother watched the secretary. It would be wrong to discourage Kerensky's enterprising spirit: he'd set up ECLIPSE. The Russian acronym translated loosely into Extremely Confidential Liquidations Involving Personnel and Propaganda Serving the Enemy. He chafed in his current harness as chief of Mother's personal secretariat. But these cross-postings were vital to young Kerensky's progress to the top. He was learning that power was best exercised without violence. "I'll deal with Henkell in open debate," Mother said finally, "*after* Talbott's encounter with Hess."

"Ahhh!" Kerensky responded, seeing at once the direction of strategy.

"I shall want a full visual report," Mother continued. "You know the conditions: No recordings. Talbott's questions to be submitted beforehand. None to refer to the Nazis or to the present, or to politics . . . How Talbott behaves will tell us more than any other source. Then I'll be ready for Comrade Henkell. You can start now getting some appropriate quotations. *But no Karl Marx!* That's the fucking German I'd like to have eclipsed!"

Walter Juste thought the banquet went splendidly, except for one jarring incident. Yuri Gorin was new in the saddle and needed a period of relative quiet abroad while he won satellite confidence. That gave the Americans some leverage. There had not been a banquet like this since Stalin, with drunken toasts into the wee hours: long live U.S.-Soviet friendship, long live Russian caviar, long live Hollywood and cooperation in space. You'd think the Baltic crisis was a fiction.

Then this tall, blond East German proposed an end to secret warfare. "We know who your agents are," he declared, "and you know ours. So let us drink"—he bowed to Juste and then to Mother—"to the last of the spy-heroes, the German code-named STIRLITZ, who worked for all of us!"

Walter Juste glanced at Yuri Gorin and the Soviet leader got up. "Our guests may not be familiar with Soviet culture," he said. "STIRLITZ is our *Soviet* James Bond on television. Better they fight on the screen than in life!"

Everyone cheered.

Later, in a bug-proof part of the U.S. embassy, Walter Juste had a farewell drink with the ambassador.

"You saw Mother's face when that East German toasted STIRLITZ?" asked the ambassador. "We're on a tightrope, Walter. Mother's got too many other enemies waiting, like jackals, for the goddam Jerries to strike the first blow."

"We'll learn more after Igalo," Juste promised. *"That's* when he must confront the rebels of East Europe. It's never been done before."

Never? The ambassador kept his thoughts to himself. There was a hundred percent fatality rate among Soviet leaders who tried to run the KGB *and* the satellites. Walter was preparing Mother for the executioner if he pushed too hard. The Russian would soon face, at Igalo, the real test of his ability to bring back under control the weapons of deceit. It already looked as if East Germany's disinformation experts had distorted the Baltic crisis, almost as if they had manufactured it to sabotage the Washington-Moscow talks.

"By the way," said Vice President Juste with one of those winning smiles that aroused an even deeper apprehension, "there's a small hiccup in the schedule. I'd be obliged if you'd discourage any sensational guesswork by the media."

The ambassador heaved himself up from his chair and moved with studied casualness to the liquor cabinet.

"I'm joining Mother on a boar hunt," said Walter Juste.

"I see." The ambassador rattled the ice tray, and thought he'd better mind what he said from here on. Mother and Juste had been hunting one another when they directed CIA-KGB warfare. Now they were hunting *together?* Who'd be the prey? Not a wild boar, that was sure.

They slipped into Britain: men with unobtrusive bags, sober suits, impeccable passports. They did nothing to draw attention to themselves; no sandals, no long hair, no torn jeans. Some stepped off boats at Harwich, Liverpool and Dover. Others landed at Heathrow, Luton and Gatwick. They all made their way to London by bus or train.

Not one had the bad luck to spark the interest of an immigration officer, so he'd open his big black book and look for special codes beside the name. That was because security was overwhelmed by special notices.

Such as: *Urgent Attention to S T. DOB 1.6.25 US National. PA reservation ex-Berlin optional flights . . . Alpha Omega Alpha.*

The last three words indicated the category reserved for someone in extreme danger or of great national-security concern; someone under close surveillance who must not be made aware of it.

13

Talbott was locked inside the limousine with Sally and the dead Bronfmann, surrounded by darkness. There was a mild percussion. A new voice came over the stereo: "Your driver just left. This is a timed recording. You will be released automatically." Rain hammered on the roof. A dim interior light came on. The dead man stared up. "There is a large package with Bronfmann," the metallic voice resumed.

Talbott remembered the doorman throwing it in. "The package is a copy of the Hess Command on video." The voice paused expectantly.

Talbott reached down. Almost at once, flashguns popped. They came from behind thick glass panels. Talbott broke a fingernail trying to wrench the panels open.

"These pictures will not be used for criminal proceedings," said the taped voice, smug in its programmed assumption that Talbott would trigger the inaccessible cameras. "Not unless you make a false move."

A false move! Talbott's revived nightmare. He'd just made another one.

"In sixty seconds police will be directed here, the scene of murder. They cannot locate those flashgun pictures without the 88's help. We shall withhold that help for as long as you cooperate. In thirty seconds from now, the car doors will unlock. You must run. Don't forget the Hess Command package."

The door beside Sally clicked.

"Ten seconds," hissed the tape.

A siren under the *berline*'s hood wailed. Talbott grabbed Sally's hand. Together they tumbled onto the rain-slick macadam.

They were pursued by the sound of the siren and the responding klaxons of the police until they found refuge in an unfenced park.

"Flashgun pictures!" gasped Talbott, collapsing against a tree. "I'm the original village idiot."

"You reacted like anyone," said Sally.

"No. I'm properly framed." He waited until his heart stopped pounding, and then he told her about Mandy Roberts, murdered in his apartment.

Sally could find nothing to say. In her mind's eye lingered the image of Talbott embracing the dead man, just as he would look to the police. The distant death of a Jamaican girl she had never met was only an abstract horror.

Headlights of a car gleamed between the trees. The car was joined by another.

"Good God!" Talbott was genuinely shocked. "Cops! Snooping in a public park."

His civic outrage was so completely unexpected, she began to laugh. "They could be lovers," she said.

Her giggles were infectious. There was nothing hysterically funny in their situation, but suddenly everything seemed laughable. There was no other outlet for pent-up emotions in the aftermath of tension. The fingers of light probed, waggled and shriveled. Another set of lights sprang up behind Talbott. "They're cops all right," he said. "Peeping Toms in blue."

"We'd be safer giving them a show, then." Sally pulled his head down and kissed him. There was more passion than theater in that kiss, and perhaps at this stage more pity than passion; but the sweetness of it was not easily surrendered. Their bodies clung while the branches were set afire around them by a wide beam of light. The wet grass turned a foggy yellow and the light swept unconcernedly past them and was gone.

"I hate to break this up," Talbott said after a while, "but they *were* looking for us, not for lovers."

Sally sighed. "I think I knew that all along," she said. The sound of prowling cars had died away. Her voice became businesslike. "We're near the old yacht club. I recognize those tower lights. Head in that direction. You'll hit a road and a taxi rank—"

"It's not such a hot idea to split."

She considered. Well, it had to happen sometime. "Look," she said, "there's a . . . a place. The Lido. All-night porn shows." She was uncomfortable now. "I'll meet you in the back row of a cinema called Movies Blau. In, oh, forty minutes."

But it took him less than ten minutes to be driven there. He wondered how she could have been so far out in timing. Movies Blau seemed to be empty. He was juggling the 88's package. His mind was too busy to pay attention to the screen.

"Talk dirty to me," said a woman over the sound system.

He opened his eyes. He must have drifted off. He stared at enlarged genitalia in gorgeous technicolor. A man sat beside him and touched his arm. Talbott balled his fist and the man said, "Sally sent me, don't be difficult."

Talbott tried to see the face in the light from the screen. It was narrow and long, like a face in a medieval painting: long gray beard, long thin nose, long silver hair.

"My name is Jake Cooke," the man said. "It's time we met."

Talbott bent down to retrieve the 88's package from between his feet. He could have sworn the man jumped.

"Go through that door under the red light," said the man calling himself Jake Cooke.

Up the back stairs, in an office, sat a woman under a poster: The Lido Porn Palace. "In there," she said disapprovingly. She had a gun in her out-tray.

Talbott sat where he could watch her from the inner office. A youth crossed his line of vision and picked up the gun. Like the woman, he wore a khaki military-style blouse.

Jake Cooke reappeared. "Sally's safe back at the hotel." He put up a hand to ward off Talbott's angry reaction. "Please. We've given her protection for some time."

"The way you protected Bronfmann?"

Jake Cooke peeled off a black fur-collared topcoat. "In Bronfmann's case, God save us, we could do nothing." He spread out his arms. "You have the package."

"Not for you."

"Maybe for both of us." His eyes sought out the parcel and seemed to be held by it. "Let my boys check it for booby traps."

"I don't know you. Why should I trust your 'boys'?"

A disarming smile lit the man's face. "You will remember me by my true name: Jacob Slominsky."

"Slominsky!" So Sol Farkas had been right. "Your face—all over British Army WANTED posters!"

"In those days, we were all wanted, dead or alive. The live ones became premiers and foreign ministers. Half Israel's leaders had been condemned to hang, one time or another, before we kicked our British friends out of Palestine."

A bizarre reunion in Tel Aviv came to Talbott's mind. "Hell," he said, "if anyone knows about parcel bombs, it has to be one of the men who used to make them. Go ahead."

Jake Cooke leapt to his feet and called through the open door. Men appeared. Talbott suddenly understood why the girl at the desk had seemed poised for flight. He bent down automatically to pick up the package and Jake shouted, "Don't touch it!"

In a corridor, safely distanced from the package, Jake said, "I was afraid you'd argue. Some of those parcels are booby trap upon booby trap. A favorite is triggered to explode not on the first jolt, but the twenty-first . . ."

There was a muffled bang from the other side of the wall.

"That's nothing," said Jake. "Just a punching device. If the contents are papers, you'll see a couple of small holes."

He was moving like a cat, along passageways, up iron stairs, stopping suddenly to listen or speak. A lot of half forgotten memories from Mideast days were coming back to Talbott. Slominsky. Alias Kooke. Cooke. The man who promoted to the position of foremost importance to Jews "a 614th commandment to add to the other 613 biblical precepts: 'Thou shalt not allow Hitler a posthumous victory!' "

Talbott had glimpsed him once at a reunion party of the Stern Gang, while filming in Israel. Menachem Begin had been there; it was before he became Prime Minister, and Begin had pointed out Jake as being close in spirit to Abraham Stern. Stern had fought the British during the Second World War, claiming they were more dangerous to Jewish aspirations than Nazi Germany.

Now, in the Lido's loft with the marquee lights shining through grimy windows, it was difficult to recognize this Jake Cooke as the scruffy figure at that Tel-Aviv party long ago. Jake said, "You find it odd, Slominsky's here in a sex emporium? But a good masquerade, right?"

"I'm more puzzled about Sally."

"She's safe. The police won't pick either of you up. Not until the 88 decide. It's the threat they'll hold over you."

Talbott watched the shadows between cardboard scenery stacked against bare brick walls. "You seem to know," he said.

"We have our 88 contacts," Jake conceded. "Even the devil has his uses. You'll want to televise the Hess Command, of course."

"Under threat—?"

"No, as a public duty."

"Crap!" Talbott exploded. "Dangerous, vicious, obscene crap!"

Jake waited until the anger had spent itself. Then he said, "Remember who wrote this? *We were kids, but we knew what Hitler was doing to the Jews.*'"

Talbott blinked. "I did."

"Forgive me if I don't quote accurately."

Talbott shrugged. "I was protesting against those postwar professors who said we didn't know why we fought, didn't know about the final solution."

"So. It's a story. And here's the story you wanted to tell. Remember when—"

"A good deal too much remembering has been asked from me lately," Talbott snapped.

"Boardman," said Jake Cooke.

Talbott rejected the name. His head twisted this way and that. But the name hammered away inside his head, and refused to go away. He peered at the parts of a fretwork village, piled where the garish outside light fell upon a church, an inn, one-dimensional cottages. All fantasy.

"Boardman was shot down in front of you," persisted Jake.

"Better for him. He didn't have to survive and learn the truth."

"Ah! How easy it becomes to kill those already dead!"

"You don't know what you're talking about."

"How's it feel," prodded Jake, "looking at those death-camp pictures, knowing you could have bombed them?"

"If we'd known, we'd have bombed."

"Like the pilot court-martialed because he fired his rockets at a locomotive taking Jews to Dachau?"

"He abandoned his designated mission," Talbott began. He was shaking his head again like a fox cornered by the hunt. "He disobeyed."

Someone climbed into the loft and said, "The package is clean, Mr. Talbott."

Talbott broke away. He grabbed the package from the man at the head of the stairs and began to make his descent. Jake stood above and said, "Keep in touch." He sounded amused. He called down, "We'll repay any favors, you can rely on that."

Talbott paused at the lower level. His flight had been unreasoning, rude. Above him stood Jake like a nagging conscience.

"For example," said Jake, "you'll find your Hess interview is fully authorized. It should jog your memory."

Talbott stared up, lost for words.

"You'll find an unlisted number penciled on the package," said Jake. "Call us, day or night."

"Thanks," Talbott jerked out. "But no thanks."

He went straight to her hotel room. Sally had changed into a blue robe, tied loosely at the waist. Before he could start the questions, she turned to the messages under her desk lamp. "This one was under the door," she said. "The 88 demand the network transmit the Hess Command. Otherwise those flashgun pictures of us with Bronfmann will be released and we'll be wanted for murder." She paused. "That's an old *East* German trick. A murder charge makes us Priority One fugitives. Descriptions are automatically sent over the teleprinter linkups. There's a better chance a murderer will be turned in by the public, in the East or West. That's why the DDR cooks up murder charges if it wants you badly enough."

Talbott gave her a strange look. He dropped the Hess Command package onto the bed. "Get this off to Sol Farkas tomorrow. I don't want *anyone* to see it except Sol and Quex's crowd."

Sally said, "There's another message. Washington's okayed the Hess interview."

"How the hell did Jake know that?" Talbott sank onto her bed.

"*Jake* told you the interview was on?" Sally tightened the belt on her robe with an angry jerk.

"He seems very close to the 88, too."

"He's a Jew. They're Nazis."

"Living under the same Lido roof, happy ever after?"

"I couldn't explain that before. Perhaps I was afraid. Maybe you never gave me the chance," said Sally defensively. "The Lido covers his work. International money, hot money, goes into porn. It's a big source of the hardest foreign currency, dollars. The police never look closely. It's a way to move the large funds Jake needs—"

"So the Stern Gang can ride again?"

"They're not terrorists! They follow Jake's hard-line policy, to protect Jews anywhere."

"They slip in and out of countries with terrorist ease. Are their loyalties just as flexible? I mean, isn't this what the Kyryan guards are supposed to do for your grandfather? Protect him?"

Sally leaned against the bedroom wall, puzzled by his hostility. He was gray with fatigue. He seemed to expect no reply to his last questions. Instead he leaned back on the bed and said, "Ryshnikov. Radzhnikov. Radzki. You'd find it easy to confuse those names, wouldn't you?"

"Yes." She stood with her back to the wall, looking down at him.

Suddenly his eyes opened wide and he asked, "Were you and Jake lovers?"

She pulled the robe closer round her neck, suddenly conscious of her nakedness underneath. She had no idea how to answer the question.

"I'm sorry!" He got up abruptly. "I'd no right."

"You do have a right," she said slowly. "You have a right to know if it's you or him I work for."

"I wasn't thinking of work."

Sally caught her breath. She spoke with care. "I love Jake. For his old-fashioned loyalties. For his passion in a cause. In Israel, doing Grandpa's research, his 'guards' even taught me to handle weapons. Surprised? Well, you didn't see what I saw in the archives. I realized then the wars weren't over . . . But as to Jake being my lover?" She took Talbott's hands. "You and me pretending in the park was more real!"

Talbott retreated to the door. Suddenly he laughed in embarrassment. "Dammit, Sally, I really think I'm jealous."

To help him, she joked, "The newsroom stylebook should warn against romance on the road."

"What it *does* say," he rejoined, "is . . . watch the clichés."

"Why? Because they cover true feelings?"

He groped behind him for the doorknob, and pondered. "There's no cliché to cover what I've been through tonight. Top and bottom. More than you know."

She was taken aback. And more surprised when he added, "You're a great girl, Sally Ryan!" At this, he seemed ready to bolt. "That's a platitude," he added hastily. "Not a pass."

She stopped him from opening the door. "You can't dismiss emotions because they sound trite." She brushed her head against his shoulder. "You're pretty great yourself. And here's another truism to fit the case: two heads are better than one, right?"

"Right."

She let him go then. They were both being careful, and each knew that about the other.

In the corridor, he whirled round. "The schedule! What's our schedule for Berlin?"

"Day after tomorrow we meet with Hess's jailers."

Talbott groaned. "Cops?"

"No, military."

Talbott nodded and moved off down the passageway, a gray shadow swaying with fatigue. Sally had a vision of him pursued by police on both sides of the Atlantic, and she thought: My God, we've got to be even more careful. Don't phone New York, for example. Let them call us.

She was asleep before she fell into bed. Nightmares followed. Talbott was burying two people. The earth heaved and threw up meatless bones. He cradled two shining skulls and sang from *Carousel* that, for figuring things out, two heads are better than one.

14

They flew to Berlin through the East German corridor, their only airway into the former capital. They picked up a Volkswagen camper from a rental agency. Talbott drove in silence until the dirty red-brick jail came into view. "What a slaughterhouse!" he said, at last voicing his thoughts.

"You've been here before?" Sally asked, surprised.

"In imagination. We studied models, to blast the place open from the air."

"But you flew navy?"

"Yes, and mighty brains said if you could fly into the confined space of ships, you could winkle your way down city streets to plant a bomb on Spandau's doorstep and release its anti-Nazi German prisoners."

"So why didn't you break open the death camps—?"

Talbott's response was to make an unnecessarily sharp turn off Heerstrasse. They were climbing the final slope to the old battlements before he replied. "Hitler kept German bigwigs here for torture. All we had to do was smash down the walls." He knew it wasn't any kind of an answer at all. He began to say something more but had to brake as soldiers swarmed across his path. American soldiers, thank God! The Hess interview had been approved for the period that Americans guarded the jail. Hence the urgency. The guard was due to be changed within days.

Sally remained with the van. Talbott walked down to the interview cell under escort. He was shaken to discover how well he knew each step of the way: the chambers for torture, the guillotine room. From crime to punishment—from Nazi thumbscrews to the punishment of the last Nazi, Hess.

Hess had seen nothing of his wife and son during the first thirty years of incarceration here. Now what served as social intercourse for the prisoner was the periodic changing of the guard between the four powers—an occasion for lavish banqueting and a booze-up. Each country's honor was at stake while Hess crouched in solitary confinement, surrounded by 599 empty cells, listening to the boisterous noises of national one-upmanship, the rival jokes. "What do you think of the French penis?—It is like a rumor, passing from mouth to mouth. And the American? Up and down like a theater curtain. The English? Always stand in the presence of a lady." The American garrison would polish such jokes, leaving to last the ones about the Russkies.

Talbott concentrated on the American commander, who read a formal statement while the other nationalities listened: ". . . no touching of the said prisoner, no passing of materials through third parties . . . All questions to go through four languages . . . No pictures . . ."

He was acutely aware of the minicamera system woven through his suit. He hadn't used it at Düsseldorf. The rehearsal would have been handy. But then, he hadn't known this was about to happen.

The American finished the litany and raised pale eyes with a pretense at severity. Earlier he had told Talbott in private, "It's like a zoo here. Behind the bars is the man who keeps the whole industry going."

Waiting for Hess now, wondering if Sally had got the equipment running in the camper, hoping she'd be getting sound and picture transmissions already, Talbott glanced around the interview cell at the senior officers present from each power. Which feared Hess most? Feared his capacity to blow the gaff? Explode myths? The British were behaving with painful correctness. Talbott remembered the penis joke. An elegant Frenchman had lowered his long frame into a chair and was yawning up at four bored colleagues. The Americans bustled about like wardens at an execution.

There was no doubt who really ran the show: the Russians. How did the last joke go? "The Russian prick is like the revolution, you never know when it will strike from behind."

The chief Russian delegate occupied the head of the table and stared unblinkingly at Talbott through rimless spectacles with lenses like the bottoms of vodka bottles. He was balding, dumpy, wore a threadbare commissary suit, and with him, you just would never know.

Sol Farkas had called from New York the previous day. "We never got to first base with Hess before," he said. "State would always refer us to the Pentagon, who pushed us onto the Russians, who sent us to their mission in Berlin, who referred us to the Brits, who said to go to the French . . . Talk about runarounds."

There wasn't a news organization in the world that hadn't undergone the same frustration.

Talbott had to interrupt. "Bronfmann's dead."

There was a silence and then questions. "Not on the phone," pleaded Talbott. He'd already written a full report and Sally had shipped it out before breakfast with the 88 package of Hess Command video.

For once in his life, things had seemed to move too fast that day. New York had arranged for him to fly over Berlin with a British air patrol asserting the right of access. Talbott's pilot was not the sort to look for trouble. "We fly the flag to remind the Russians we share the occupation. But it's a game of chicken." He waggled the wings of the old prop-driven Chipmunk for emphasis. "The Russians have two hundred thousand troops ringing the city, tanks, artillery and super-jets. And then there's me and me Chipmunk."

The game was played according to rules laid down when the occupiers had carved up Berlin. Each power drove through or over the Berlin wall. If the Russians were testy that day, their jets would exercise so close to the civilian air corridor, passengers imagined they felt the jet blast.

That was one reason Talbott's pilot declined to fly over Spandau. "If the Reds thought we were trying anything with Hess, they'd start another blockade."

From his seat behind the pilot, Talbott expressed skepticism about Russia imposing another Berlin blockade.

"It's the bloody East Germans now," said the pilot. "They're blowing up this Baltic affair out of all proportion."

It turned out to be more informative than your standard thirty-minute joyride. Talbott hadn't realized how badly the situation had deteriorated. The Russians were being blamed for bad seamanship, and the Americans for trying to sneak a nuclear sub into East German waters. Suddenly the events in Düsseldorf seemed to dwindle.

"These things blow over," his pilot breezed on. "But I'm not hanging around to see. Me for Blighty next week. I don't want to be a death-and-glory boy." He made a tight turn over the dreary East German landscape, unchanging since the war in its hostility. "No charge of the light brigade for me, chum!"

Nobody spoke while he waited for Hess. Lost in thought, Talbott was startled by the sudden arrival of armed men. A figure shuffled through their ranks. The American colonel, with instinctive compassion, leaned forward when the newcomer faltered and seemed about to fall.

"Stop!" The chief Russian delegate stepped in the way. "It is contrary to the Nuremberg agreement to have human contact."

The prisoner stopped in front of a plain kitchen chair, then locked into this bent position, waiting for permission to sit.

So this was Rudolf Hess. Conscience of the Nazi Party. Author with Hitler of the plan to destroy World Jewry.

Talbott let out his breath. "Please sit!" he said in German. Nobody else appeared to want to say it.

The old man's baggy bottom hovered. He looked around him.

"Sit!" commanded the Russian. Then Hess sat down.

His companions judged most villainous had been hanged here by the neck until dead. Seven comrades, villains no doubt, but still useful for what they knew, were jailed instead: and one by one, those were freed. Only this Prisoner Number Seven, code-named Jonathan by the British and said to be Hess, lingered. It must be twenty years since the last of his fellow prisoners, Hitler's armaments chief, Albert Speer, had left him to the tender loving care of the armies of four nations, forty-eight cleaning women, a chief cook and seven assistants, a doctor, a pastor, and a German staff costing Bonn U.S.$670,000 a year.

With each passing year, the world found it harder to comprehend the Nazi madmen. Here was the last live specimen. Today there were questions shrieking to heaven for answers; questions not thought about in the stunned aftermath of the Third Reich; questions arising from fresh knowledge, changed perspectives, and greater insight into the demons in man. And nobody could put those questions to this last Nazi. Not even Talbott.

Instead, he had been ordered to limit the questions to nonsensical, harmless stuff that could offend nobody. He disposed of a couple: do you sleep well, and are your bowel movements regular? Mostly, he just wanted to give Sally a chance to adjust the receiver to the signals pulsing from the antennae woven into his clothes.

Each exchange wound through four translators and back again. At this rate, he'd never get a usable reply within his allotted thirty minutes.

He took the plunge.

"Did you fly to England alone?"

There was an immediate uproar in the small cell, even before the words passed laboriously into Russian, French and German. The British major barked: "Out of bounds! Most improper! No notice of the question!"

But Hess had already lifted his head to look directly at Talbott. The lantern jaw was underhung with bristly dewlaps. Only the famous gray-green eyes betrayed a sense of self, a flaming of curiosity; and although the question had been arrested in its passage, Hess quickly shook his head.

Sally, behind the camper's sliding doors, watched the tiny monitor and saw Hess almost imperceptibly shake his head. *No, he had not flown alone!*

She hugged her knees in surprised delight. Nothing else mattered. Here was a clear picture of Hess, undeniably revealing what had never been disclosed, never even been considered before. What might have escaped his jailers was perfectly clear in video close-up.

She was entitled to a second's self-congratulation. So many difficulties had plagued the equipment. The tiny, unfocused eye in Talbott's necktie had been feeding back images of faces stretched absurdly. He had forgotten not to fidget, and the fish-eye lens collected wildly dancing, crazy, panning shots. Then, magically, she heard the key question just as Talbott remembered to think of himself as the camera and leaned forward for a perfect full-face closeup of the prisoner.

Now, suddenly, a shrill squeal was followed by the shrinking of the picture to a pinpoint. She ran through the trouble checklist. The recorder was silent, the plastic window dead. Yet nothing was wrong. Except: the transmission had been jammed!

Before wiring Talbott, she had discussed emergency procedures. She squinted through the camper's curtains. The same armed men lounged beside the same sleepy guardhouse. She turned off the power to avoid detection. We're in the proverbial *merde*, she thought. So what? We've got a scoop.

Talbott had expected they would terminate the interview. The Russian surprised him by shrugging. "Let's go to the next question." More chick-enfeed produced the answer, "I read nineteenth-century novels and space books."

It was obvious that everyone in the cell had instructions to play it through to the end. Hess had used body language to break their rules. The jailers could not know that, God willing, the silent reply was on record. Talbott mouthed another banal question. If he'd had all the time in the world to study Hess, it still wouldn't have been enough. One way to prove his identity would have been to examine an irremovable lung scar, but his guards had always prevented this. What *were* they hiding?

The Nazi Party's official organ had proclaimed in 1941: "Our Fuehrer's deputy directly initiates all government measures. His work is enormously diverse, it covers everything and cannot be outlined in words." A week later, Hess had flown to the enemy.

Talbott readied himself. Hess was looking up at him with the obedient expression of a fawning dog.

"Did you carry to England the plans for the Hess Command . . ."

Before Talbott could complete the abrupt question, there were angry growls around him. Talbott was afraid Hess had missed the words. But again the eyes lit up and before anyone could stop him, Hess said, "Drugs. In England they put drugs, poison, in my food. To stop—"

The words vanished in the British major's explosion of rage.

"Let the prisoner answer," decreed the Russian.

But the prisoner had become mute.

"I think, old boy, your time is up," said the major.

Then Hess lifted his long chin in a gesture almost of defiance. He seemed to draw the next question out of Talbott by sheer willpower.

"Who was Radzki?" Talbott's whisper was penetrating, as if he had hissed it, with the major already gripping him by the arm.

There was a brief flicker of response at the back of the dark eyes, a tiny signal of recognition. Then pandemonium broke out. The major's face, purple with rage, blocked Talbott's view. Another voice in a fierce groan repeated, "No more questions, I say! No more!" The French were talking rapidly among themselves. The Russian shouted, "This is not in the spirit of the convention!"

The prisoner ignored them all and rose swiftly to his feet. He glanced neither to right nor to left, but bore himself with unexpected dignity to the door. There he turned to stare directly at Talbott. The look was conspiratorial, as if Talbott had confirmed the preservation of a secret. Then an overanxious guard knocked Hess out into the corridor.

"Nice try!" murmured the American garrison commander to Talbott. "That's the biggest reaction from Hess I've ever seen."

"Someone jammed us," reported Sally. "You can't celebrate that . . ."

But nothing would dilute Talbott's sense of triumph. He was driving the camper back through the British sector, and he was laughing. "I knew something was wrong when they delayed me, after Hess had gone. First, the Brits lectured me on good manners and unsporting behavior. The French were intellectual about rules. I think the Russians were torn between wanting to kill me, and hanging me by my thumbs until I confessed what I knew."

"Whoever did the jamming can't have told the others." Sally reached to remove the minicamera lens from his lapel.

"Is the cassette okay?"

"What I could get was fantastic. You see Hess cheating the jailers, saying nothing, just shaking his head."

Talbott hummed to himself, broke off, and said, "Then, you lost audio, as well as picture?" He was thinking of his attempt to get a response to the name of Radzki.

"I'm afraid so . . . Did you think he was sane?"

Talbott added a tiddley-pom to whatever he was singing under his breath. "Sane? He played the old jailbird's trick: 'I've said nothing, you can prove nothing!' He wants the truth out. It's there in his eyes . . . Maybe the 88 sold him on a Nazi revival . . . maybe they somehow got to him."

"If the 88 work with the East, the Russians could make the contact."

"The Russian boss man, come to think of it, seemed almost to encourage me at the end."

Their thoughts were bubbling along now.

Sally said, "If Nazi bogeymen are raised again in the West, it would keep Germany divided a while longer."

"Which would suit Moscow. I wonder if Hess was secretly coached? Or is he suddenly more willing to take risks?"

"What's he got to lose?"

"His life, what's left. He must know they can bump him off without the outside world ever knowing what happened. Anyway, he showed there really are reasons why he's treated with such inhumanity. That seems sane enough to me."

Sally had unzipped her briefcase stuffed with research notes. "The last psychiatrists' report"—she pulled out a folder—"here, says Hess had no psychosis, only *hysterical amnesia* which can in time transform itself into *voluntary amnesia.*"

"He forgets what his subconscious knows he'd better not remember," said Talbott.

Sally gave him a strange look.

A roadblock appeared ahead. A police officer directed Talbott to the side of the road. Talbott's mind was still on the story. "What's incredible is how Hess stayed silent all those years."

"The way you did?" asked Sally.

He glanced at her, perplexed.

"One keeps one's sanity," she continued, adopting a neutral tone, "by becoming a voluntary amnesiac."

The police officer stuck his head through the open window. Talbott displayed his press card, and while the officer inspected it, asked Sally, "What are you suggesting?"

Sally's eyes slid past him and widened in fright. Talbott felt cold steel against his neck. "Step over here, Herr Talbott." The policeman's voice was that of a bully. For a split second, Talbott thought he had strayed into the Soviet sector.

He leaned forward as if to switch off the engine but released the hand brake instead. He twisted his head and locked eyes with Sally. They both had the same thought. If these were West German police, then the Bronfmann flashgun photographs must have been released. "Go with the tape!" Talbott hissed, and pulled the choke out a fraction.

The sound of the revving motor agitated the policeman. "Out! Out!" He emphasized each word by thumping on the roof.

Talbott flung open the door. "You should be chasing criminals!" he shouted in English. "Not holding up law-abiding citizens—*Go! Sally! Go!*" He blocked the policeman's gun, moving down on him, forcing him to fall back as he slammed shut the door and resumed his outraged protest, ". . . red tape, rules, regulations, how the hell does one get any work done?" He sensed Sally's hesitation and knew nothing would move her but professional duty. "The tape, for chrissakes!" He heard her gun the engine, heard gears grind and tires squeal. The West German police, unlike those of the DDR, would not open fire. Then he realized his mistake. These were not policemen.

Sally crashed through the barriers. Two men in gray leapt into a battered green Renault. Two more boarded a blue pickup. The man with the gun tossed aside his jacket and took the wheel of a dirty gray laundry van. There was not a police vehicle in sight.

Talbott had thrown himself into the roadside ditch. He raised his head as Sally disappeared around a curve in the road, traveling faster than her pursuers. He stood up. There was nobody left to shoot at him. He felt cheated. Dry grass and thistles worked under his clothing, and he began to itch. He vaulted onto the road. It stretched between flat fields, empty except for the slow procession of fake police led by the green Renault. He began walking in the same direction. He knew Sally would give them the slip. He was only put out because they'd abandoned him to chase her. After a while, he began to laugh—at himself.

Sally saw in her rearview mirror a green bug, a blue pickup and a gray van weaving in her wake. She had glimpsed the absence of police vehicles as she crashed through the cardboard barriers. If her pursuers were not police, who were they?

She was hurtling along that unfortunate wedge of land between the Wall and the Tegel Forest where small farms and allotments lie surprisingly close to the heart of Berlin. Glossy new luxury cars stood among the mud-caked tractors across the fields. The shabby rattletraps chasing her seemed misplaced, as if they'd missed a turning out of the Russian sector. She would shake them off in back streets she knew well, dump the camper, grab a cab for the airport. She held reservations with Talbott on Pan-Am leaving in about an hour. If they missed that? She ran through the alternatives. Lufthansa was forbidden from flying the East German corridor under the old four-power agreement reached with a Soviet gun at Western heads. Dear God! she prayed, the image of a Soviet gun flashing through her mind. Keep Talbott safe! I love him.

What a damn silly time to decide you're in love! Think of a place where Talbott would expect you to go. The airport's dangerous. The 88, or the fake cops, will look there first. Or the real cops, if the 88's given them those compromising flashgun pics!

Her mind raced. Her heart jumped. Talbott's chief concern is the Hess interview secretly recorded on microtape. One man can get it out of Berlin . . . our network stringer. He filmed the Spandau "wallpaper" footage. He's got his own studios. Talbott sooner or later must check in with him . . . If Talbott doesn't check in his chips altogether.

15

Talbott hitched a ride with a Berlin doctor who was enchanted to help a television personality he recognized. "Do our German stations try to censor your programs?" the doctor wanted to know. "Are the translations accurate?" Talbott's courteous replies reinforced the doctor's resolve to get him to the airport in time.

Talbott checked at the Pan Am desk. No, Miss Ryan had not shown up yet. He found a pay phone from where he could watch for her and placed a call to Sol Farkas.

"Sol? Thank God! I'm boarding in ten— Listen!"

"No, you listen!" Sol cut in. "The fuzz is out. The telephones are not safe . . ."

Talbott clapped a hand against his other ear to shut out the airport noise. His heart jumped. There she was! Red raincoat. Blond hair. Moving to the ticket counter.

"Go to Henry's place," Sol was saying. "Same place, same time where we always met . . ."

Talbott was too impatient now. Nothing could go wrong. Sally was here, the plane was leaving—

"Don't try to contact us," said Sol.

"Got you!" Talbott replaced the phone and ran to catch up with the woman in red. He came up behind her, expecting to see those aqua-blue eyes blaze up with relief when he touched her shoulder. But the woman who turned to face him had creamy chocolate features and pebbly black eyes. He stammered an apology. The woman shook her head and walked on.

He stood staring after, Sol's words still echoing. Did they mean that the Düsseldorf police now had those flashgun photographs? In that case, all airports were being watched.

Something about the woman in red seemed familiar. He caught up with her at the security barrier. She dumped a large handbag on the conveyor. He glimpsed blunt fingers and scarred nails. She moved through the metal detector without looking back.

Talbott turned, irresolute, and saw two men in gray uniforms thread their way through the crowd and converge upon him. He walked hastily through the security checkpoint and headed for the Pan Am gate. Once, he glanced back and saw the two men arguing with a security officer.

The woman had walked straight onto the aircraft. He waited until the last passenger boarded. Then he walked casually back along the corridor until he spotted an airport mechanic entering a washroom marked STAFF. He dodged inside behind the man. "It is forbidden!" the overalled German said sternly. The door locked shut behind them both. Talbott clutched his stomach, bent over double, groaned and stumbled in the direction of a cubicle. "Of course!" said the German, hastily pushing open the toilet door. When Talbott returned, the corridor was empty, the aircraft gone. The men in gray must think he'd caught it. He scurried to find a taxi. "Kurfürstendamm," he instructed the driver. "I'll direct you."

He went through his pockets. Passport. Traveler's checks. And finally, the card of the stringer Sally had asked to film establishing shots of Spandau.

"Frig it!" said Sally. "I forgot my raincoat."

"Let me get it," offered the stringer.

"No! No, thanks all the same. The correspondent will pick it up." She could hardly say she'd left it in the camper; that she'd dumped the vehicle after a chase. "Talbott'll bring it."

"He will wish to approve my film, naturally?"

"Well, if he phones, put him through," Sally said tartly. "But I'll decide if the film's any good. Just give me time to go through these notes."

The stringer, unconscious of treading on toes, glanced proudly around the editing room. He understood about secrecy. He'd broken rules to get aerial shots of the prison, though forced to circle the complex at an extreme distance. He stole away, leaving Sally jabbing at her notepad.

Talbott must call here, she told herself. She just had to be patient. Shouldn't have bitten that poor stringer's head off . . . When the extension suddenly rang, her pencil bored a hole through the paper. Her eyes closed in relief.

"I got a ride—" Talbott began.

"No need for you here," Sally cut in.

He was prepared for the obfuscation. "Fine!" He hesitated, formulating some innocuous phrases.

From the cubicle next door, Sally could hear the sounds of an antinuclear demo. Someone was doing a voice-over. Someone with a frightfully British accent.

"I heard from Sol," Talbott said cautiously.

"Do what he says," she advised. She picked up the pencil and broke it in two, hugging the phone against her ear, miserable from the need to communicate in this oblique way. She wanted to say: O God, thank you! Talbott's alive! She wanted to say: I love you, Talbott, but we'd better stay apart until we know how much trouble we're really in! What she did say was, "Everything's under control this end. Next time, call Jake. No, definitely, it wasn't his boys did the"—she searched for some euphemism for roadblock—"were at the checkpoint. Please trust Jake. Trust *me*, then."

She sat trembling for a long time after. She began to gather her things together. Again the extension rang. She snatched it up, ready now with all the phrases she'd belatedly worked out to convey something deeper than logistics. But it wasn't Talbott. Of course there was no reason why it *should* be Talbott. Irritated with herself, she let the irritation show in her voice.

"What's wrong?" asked Jake Cooke.

"Jake?" It hadn't sounded like Jake. But then, she hadn't expected to hear from him, had she? "Nothing's wrong."

"I'm glad. Because it couldn't be worse here." Now the guttural accents did sound familiar. "Talbott's in terrible danger. I've spoken to your boss in New York. Yes, Mr. Farkas. Do exactly as I say."

Sally stared at the blank wall through which the plummy BBC voice-over intermingled with screams and explosions. She couldn't believe what Jake was telling her to do. If only she could reach Talbott. But he hadn't told her where he was going, and she hadn't dared to ask.

Henry's place . . . What was Sol trying to say? When Sol had been bureau chief, and Berlin was in his parish, there'd been Das Maître, run by a French Jew with outstanding taste in wine and good food. It had become Sol's favorite watering hole, the place where he held court. The French Jew was Henry Levy.

The moment Talbott was back in the neighborhood, he knew his way. Nothing had changed. He went straight to the bar and ordered a Pernod, something he hadn't done in years. He brooded over his drink. Sally didn't want him bumbling around the stringer's studio. She did want him to keep to Sol's veiled instructions. If someone was to meet him here—*who?*

He was suddenly aware of a substantial presence on the adjoining stool.

"Crombie," said the stranger. "Red Crombie. I was at Quex's funeral." It seemed as good a reference as any.

"I make travel arrangements," said Crombie. His whole manner was vaguely irritating to Talbott. It wasn't that the newcomer had offensive mannerisms; he simply filled up more space than his body required and his assumption of authority whispered a warning. "We're working with Quex," said Crombie, and the unconscious adoption of that royal "we" was to mar an evening gastronomically memorable. The "we" was to Talbott's ear an affectation, a bureaucrat's way of dodging responsibility for what he said.

The dining room was packed, but the mention of Sol Farkas had been enough to conjure up Henry himself. "I should be honored to direct the meal myself, personally, in memory of such a great gastronome," said Henry, ushering them to a private corner where Talbott almost expected to find Sol's name enshrined. The scene should have put Talbott in good humor. Then Crombie made it clear he was paying. Talbott stifled an urge to say he'd gladly verify the bill for whatever Washington agency examined Crombie's expenses. It was a churlish reaction. Talbott knew it, but he had a deep distrust of intelligence bureaucrats who used patriotism to justify excess.

"We felt," said Crombie, "it was time to get together. We think you're being framed. Nobody wants you dead. You're too useful to them as a puppet." To follow Crombie, you needed to be familiar with a certain kind of American idiom. His lips moved without always releasing sound, so you needed practically to lip-read. "Incidentally," he said, "go careful with Sally Ryan. She's with Jake Cooke's crowd. Dangerous to you." Talbott felt himself slipping from bland politeness to silent hostility.

He wondered where they dug up guys like Crombie. He wore granny glasses which he probably didn't need. They disguised shrewd, lidless eyes. The reddish hair noted at the funeral by Sally, unknown to Talbott, was more of a frizzy blond in the soft light. He wore a gray flannel suit bought off the peg, Talbott felt sure, from Raleigh's, clothiers to Washington politicians and diplomats. He used the Georgetown University word *really* with a peculiar Georgetown emphasis and he seemed to wear the Georgetown varsity tie more as a recognition signal than to serve any sartorial purpose. He switched topics without breaking stride when the waiter submitted for his approval a 1933 Millésime Rare champagne from Laurent-Perrier to go with the first offering of *foie gras*. He told Talbott it would be unwise to leave Berlin by air—at least from *West* Berlin, he added. Then he turned to the Baltic crisis. The crisis was integral to the thesis he would unfold. It struck Talbott that the precautions against being overheard were needlessly droll. When the waiter was out of earshot, Crombie abandoned the crisis and said, "This man Cooke's background is entirely violent. Keep that in mind before you reject our theory he's hand in glove with the 88."

"They're neo-Nazis," Talbott replied evenly. "Jake Cooke's Jewish. I find what you say not only offensive but criminally stupid!"

"Really?" was Crombie's only response.

They paused. Talbott gravely acknowledged the wisdom of a choice 1953 Château Pétrus red to go with Harry's rare roast beef. For a time, the two men devoted their attention to what Crombie called, again with that curiously self-confident air of patronage, "your beer and vittles." He added, "God knows when you'll eat properly again." He did not appear the least disturbed by Talbott's earlier outburst.

"I can't imagine any circumstances where a devout Jewish nationalist would have dealings with the new Hitlers," said Talbott, returning to the subject.

"Churchill said he'd deal with the Devil to save his people," Crombie retorted. He dabbed his mouth with a napkin. "Jake Cooke might have pushed things too far, though. We can't afford that risk."

They both looked up as Harry came back with a Nuits St. George as the proper companion for his own selection of rare cheeses. "Frankly," Crombie said later, "I expected more questions from you."

"I have one," said Talbott, crumbling a piece of bread as if it represented something that he understood and valued for its simplicity. "Who the hell are 'we'?"

Crombie frowned. The evening's warm ambience had been spoiled by the crudeness of the question. "Well, right now, I'm sort of an honorary Hat Man, I guess."

"And you came all this way to see me?"

"To help," Crombie corrected him gently. "We've a safe little *pension* where you can spend the night while we arrange to get you out of Berlin."

The CIA's own little pension plan, Talbott joked to himself, sitting alone in the bed-sitter where Crombie had left him. The room was over a studio where an amateur string quartet practiced, not untunefully, most of the night. Crombie had said he would pick him up for breakfast. For bedside reading he left a report, *The Holocaust Revisited: A Retrospective Analysis of the Death Camps*, openly stamped with the CIA's eagle and compass.

Before reading it, Talbott reviewed the evening's artful conversation, searching for trigger words intended to lead him to conclusions authority could disclaim if things became embarrassing.

He could assume Sally was safe. He was not disturbed by the idea that Jake Cooke would be protecting her, even if Crombie's masters considered the man potentially dangerous. Crombie had harped on about Sally's part in militant Zionism. "We're worried about the switch in East German propaganda, the old Nazi drumbeat about Jews starting a world war to serve Jewish ends. We see a young woman of Sally Ryan's sensitivity being outraged into swinging the other way. She's with a terror-against-terror outfit that goes to such extremes it unwittingly feeds Communist lies."

What Crombie didn't talk about was the Hess Command, or the bootleg interview with Hess.

While the musicians below sawed away at something by Haydn, the trills long and trembling with portents, Talbott read the report. It was really an appeal to legislators for more money to fund photo interpretation. To show how much this had advanced since World War II, experts had retrieved the old aerial photos of Auschwitz and subjected them to modern analysis. It was the CIA *today* that had labeled the gas chambers, the burial pits . . . The photographs, fed through Sally, treated these identifying labels as if they'd been made *at the time.* The report inadvertently exposed the fakery of the photographs Quex had brought along for the filmed interview in New York!

So Crombie was discrediting Sally. Or her sources. Other parts of the official CIA report, though, supported the argument that Nazi death camps could have been bombed. Almost 3,000 U.S. bombers were recorded as striking at targets near Auschwitz during mid-1944. In that period, some 450,000 Jews had been transported to Auschwitz from Hungary alone, and 150,000 were gassed.

If the CIA photographs showed the Auschwitz mechanism for mass murders had not been identified at the time, they nevertheless proved the camp had been well within bombing range, despite U.S. War Department denials. The report also made clear the pictures were never made available to Jewish agencies, nor to the Jews in Operation Citadel, launched under cover of such raids. Citadel had been a desperate operation by a few Jewish volunteers to halt the death traffic. The details had been supplied, not by aerial reconnaissance, but by couriers! Jewish couriers. Escaping from the camps. Reporting to London. And going back in again!

Remember Radzki! A courier? Talbott recoiled from the name. It was almost dawn. He fell into a deep slumber and awoke in a cold sweat. He'd seen Sally trapped under debris, and when he'd reached her, she'd turned into his mother, Rebecca.

He was in no mood to play games when Red Crombie returned. "We can get you out through East Berlin," Crombie announced.

"You think it's easier to cross the lines?" asked Talbott in disbelief.

"We've friends in the DDR who'd love to put one over on the West German police."

"Very cozy." Talbott had made up his mind. "Had breakfast?"

"No, but—"

Talbott held up a hand. "No buts. Breakfast."

"We haven't much time."

"I'm sure you don't. There's a place right opposite." Talbott stood in the bay window of the room and pointed. "Order me the closest thing to a real American breakfast, huh? I'll meet you in ten minutes."

Talbott waited until he saw Crombie cross the street, and then he went in search of the boarding-house *Hauswirtin* and a telephone. There was one place left to call. The number was answered by a girl with a Bavarian accent. She knew nobody by the name of Jake Cooke. Her voice lost its detachment when Talbott volunteered his own name. "One moment, please." She had the pinched tones of virtue Talbott remembered in the girl who wanted to be disassociated from the Lido's pornography. When she came back on the line, her voice was warmer. "You have been reserved seats on the following flights, sir. Please take whatever's most convenient." The flights were timed out of West Berlin between noon and late afternoon. "On arrival, please check the noticeboard for a message under the name of Radzki. I'll spell that . . ."

Talbott felt a bead of sweat trickle down the side of his face. The parlor seemed to shrink around him.

"Shall I repeat that, sir?"

"No! No, thank you." He forced a smile as the landlady returned. Radzki again. It was only when he reached the street that he felt a sudden relief. Of course! Radzki was the name Sally would quote because it meant nothing to eavesdroppers. She must be in London already.

He found Crombie contemplating the enormous breakfast he had ordered. "I hope this will do?" Crombie asked, raising reverential eyes.

"Looks great."

"You're all set. I'll escort you to Checkpoint Charlie, where someone else will take charge. You'll be on your way tonight, Polish LOT flight to London."

"*London?*"

"Gets you back into our territory without disturbing the local yokels."

"I don't like it."

"Really? We are a travel service, you know. We know what's best for our clients." Crombie coughed apologetically. "That roadblock yesterday was the work of Sally's friends. The 88—"

"Suddenly you know a lot you didn't last night," said Talbott, dropping his knife and fork.

"I was waiting for you to ask."

Talbott resumed eating.

"You mustn't let personal feelings color your judgment," said Crombie.

The patronizing tone began to irritate Talbott again. He said warningly, "Sally's a complete professional. That's how I judge her."

"You guys pretend to be so tough," said Crombie, "but you're pushovers for a sob story."

"Your job teaches you to expect the best in people?"

"The young are so easily led astray."

Talbott took a deep breath. "Is this more professional guesswork?"

"We can never be identified with guesswork."

Talbott stood up abruptly. "When *your* guys grow up to take responsibility for what they say, call me."

Crombie's face darkened.

"Thanks for dinner, Crombie. I'll pay for breakfast myself."

Crombie rose awkwardly. "You're out of your depth—"

Talbott grasped his hand. "Let's behave like little gentlemen, shall we?" He waltzed Crombie to the door, certain the last thing he'd want would be a public scene. That, beyond doubt, would be bad tradecraft.

Crombie was on the phone ten minutes later. "I botched it, frankly. Talbott's got too much loyalty. You'll have to try and put a tail on him."

He put his next call in to the Bonn internal-security bureau. You could keep your fancy scramblers and the channel-hopping transceivers. Public phones were still the most secure method of communication, provided you kept moving.

Talbott simmered down only after he was back at the airport. Then he began to wonder if he might have judged Crombie too harshly. The man's mistake had been the veiled attacks on Sally. There might be good reason for distrusting Jake Cooke, of course. It was too late, anyway. Talbott had put himself in Jake Cooke's camp because he believed in Sally. Still, Red Crombie had a good, strong handgrip. Even if he was misguided, he seemed like someone you could depend on in a tight corner. Talbott's cautious return to a kind of remorseful goodwill evaporated in the events that followed.

Talbott picked up his tickets for the third flight offered by Jake's girl. No questions were asked.

He presented his passport at the control desk with greater apprehension. This would be where the police, if they were looking for him, would act. Still no questions.

No bobbies awaited him in London, either. Talbott fumed. Hadn't he been nearly panicked into bolting through East Berlin because Red Crombie claimed all Western border points were being watched?

"Nothing's ever what it seems," Quex had warned him. The old spy master had spoken of powerful government agencies who might wish to wipe him out if he persisted with his investigation. "They'll knock you off too," Quex had said, almost with relish.

Talbott stood in the central concourse at Heathrow and fought off the fear. London was sane, safe, sensible. He stopped to pick up his bag and felt the bulky CIA death-camp report in his inside pocket. How did he know that wasn't fake too? Along with Crombie's portrayal of police on every continent searching for Talbott and Sally?

Then he saw two large London police officers heading his way. He turned his back to them and hastily scanned the message center. Yes! A note under the name of Radzki. He tore it open, anticipating Sally's handwriting. Instead, there were typed *orders*. Perspiration trickled down his spine. Was it going to be Bronfmann all over again? Arrive overseas, follow orders, find a dead body? The two policemen were breasting the tide of bags and passengers, still moving implacably toward him. This wasn't the time to call Sol Farkas, even if the bobbies were looking for nothing more dangerous than a cup of tea. Talbott sought the anonymity of a square, boxlike, turn-on-a-dime London taxi.

"Gorblimey," said the cab driver. "Never 'eard them kind of directions before. Cum from a foreigner, I'd reckon." The driver was a black Jamaican and gurgled at his own joke.

Talbott tried to share the driver's humor. The acquired cockney accent could not hide the musical lilt of Jamaica. The echo of Mandy's carefree spirit sent a cold chill through Talbott's bones. "Go to Wapping High Street," began the army-like orders. "Then downriver along the Thames, past Execution Dock, to the old charity school of St. Luke of Shadwell . . ."

These were not the directions given by a foreigner looking at a map. They came from someone who knew Talbott's early life, and wanted Talbott to know he knew.

"Bin 'ere before, then, guv'ner?" yelled the cabbie.

"A long time back."

"You'll see some changes, then. Like us cockneys. Different color, same rhyming slang."

Talbott looked in the direction of the cabbie's jerked thumb. A conductress scrambled up the outside staircase of an Edwardian double-decker bus resurrected for tourists. She was an olive-skinned Chinese, with delicate features and a shrill Billingsgate voice to chivvy the passengers.

So much had changed; so much was unchanging. Other cities had repaired the damage of the Second World War. London had rebuilt bomb-devastated areas in what was vaguely called the East End, and yet pockets remained, as if a blasted heath here and there kept up the traditional association with slums. Old bomb sites survived to taunt the returning traveler. But how many travelers, Talbott wondered, had ever bothered to return? Tourists might penetrate as far as Wapping, but travel guides would never encourage them to go farther east along the Thames, to Stepney Green and Mile End, to West Ham and Poplar; or to the East India Docks, emptied of ships since the decay of empire. The East End had seen many sudden violences in the passageways between huge prison-like warehouses and clamorous dockyards. It was a place where exuberance and vitality were exhibited in Jewish open-air markets, in pubs, in streets where children learned before their time the many ways of survival. It was a source of crime, a source of genius. Few Londoners who did not live in the East End cared to know about it. Few Londoners today had much idea of the appalling conditions still prevailing east of the Tower, not in the extensive housing development schemes that covered many of the blitzed

areas (though many had become slums too), but in intervening neighbor-
hoods like Cable Street. Talbott had tried to cling to the romantic wartime
images: a king and queen inspecting bomb damage at Buckingham Palace;
the dome of St. Paul's Cathedral rising above a sea of fire. He had avoided
the lesser-known London because he did not wish to cope with the personal realities behind the legends.

"You sure this is where you want, mate?" The cabbie broke into his
thoughts. "Don't reckon there's bin nobody 'ere since the Blitz."

But where Talbott had instructed the taxi to go was not where Talbott
would be finally going. He suspected a journey into his own past, a journey
he had avoided. The message itself had said someone would give him guidance, and you didn't have to be neurotic to read different meanings into
that. All he must do is walk through the massive doors guarded by statues
of a boy in knee breeches and a girl in mobcap and apron.

It had grown dark. The abandoned school stood alone. Talbott dismissed the cab and listened to it chug off into the gloom. Radzki had risen
from such a twilight, to walk into the life of the boy called Talbott, son of
Rebecca; a boy later sacrificed by the man he'd grown into; sacrificed by—
what had Sally called it? "Voluntary amnesia." The boy seemed to wait
behind those doors, knife in hand.

Part II
The Boy from Yesterday

16

He was a small boy again, school cap flat on the back of his head, the ground-hugging fog swirling around his bare knees, the doors of the charity school huge and forbidding.

Inside was dark and smelled of classrooms unaired for generations.

"Remember old man Scroggins?"

Talbott whirled and the doors closed behind him. "Who's there?"

"A friend. You delivered newspapers for Scroggins, right?"

"The newsagent at the corner? Yes."

"Good." The male voice was rich with approval. "Reckon you can find your way, then?"

"To Scroggins? He was bombed out."

"The place is still there. Fixed up as a dockers' caf' now. No dockworkers, of course. The docks that once were busy, they're empty and silent since you were here. The fleets of commerce, all gone. Gone with the empire." The voice was schoolmasterly, and vaguely familiar. "They're waiting for you, though."

"Who?"

There was no response. Talbott heard a movement on the old stone staircase to the assembly hall. *"And make earth better for our presence . . . "* The old school song. The lines were about all that stayed with him after war ended. "Make earth better . . ." It had been the least he could do. The price of his own survival. He'd worked later to forget thing; worked hard to make others forget this was where he once belo not native-born, but for a time deeply rooted.

His fingers felt inky. He could almost smell chalk dust on his jacket. backed away from the memories, backed out into the dingy streets and familiar darkness. Sure, he could find his way. He'd learned to deliver newspapers here in the pitch black of the blackout, in the first year of war, in the sixth hour of each new day . . . *Daily Mirror, Mail, Express, News Chronicle, Herald, Telegraph, Times*. There were so many different papers. He had to memorize which house took what newspaper; and he found each letterbox by feeling his way and counting his steps, the sack of papers hanging from his neck. Hanged by the neck? His mind stumbled over the garbled words and he shoved aside a memory seeking to intrude. Delivering the morning papers was not easy in the blackout. If he missed a house, the rest of the papers fell out of sequence. He got to know the papers by weight, by texture. They were all skimpy from wartime rationing. The *Daily Worker* was skimpiest of all. The *Worker* went to the Reds, waiting to spring out on him, with hammers and sickles. Small and gullible he'd been when Hitler delivered the blitzkrieg in place of papers.

He was astonished to see the greenish flare of gaslights. They'd gone out in 1939, with the start of Hitler's war, two years after his father had brought him here as a small boy from New York. The dockyards had been his father's political soil. They were also the first target of the Nazi Blitz. And now the gaslights flickered again, unexpected, anachronistic, preserved no doubt by some obscure historical society. The macabre light disoriented him. The streets he'd memorized so carefully had been flattened by bombs, and the gaslight glow lost itself in empty spaces. He shivered. Early twilight, when he was a boy running home from school in gloomy expectation of winter, had always given rise to strange fancies. The boy of yesterday would see this will-o'-the-wisp glow of the gas lamps now and shudder, thinking it was the burning of some marshlike effluvium released by corpses buried long back in the Blitz.

Talbott's legs found their own way. They, at least, remembered Kim's Game. Once, Talbott had identified with Kim, hero of Kipling's tale of the boy who'd learned the memory game in preparation for espionage in India. The newspaper delivery route was a slum substitute for the challenge of the jungle. "No better way to train your memory than popping the right rag into the right letterbox, laddie!" The stentorian voice of the Boxing Parson echoed out of the past. "Kim's Game with a twist. It'll turn you into a bonny fighter, laddie!"

How the parson would have gloried in the challenge of this new jungle rising from the old craters! It was removed from all civilizing authority. Blitz-weeds luxuriated, blurry and sinuous, like maidenhair underwater. London under the Blitz, Churchill had said, was like "some huge and prehistoric animal, capable of enduring terrible injuries, mangled and bleeding from many wounds." That prehistoric animal had shrunk. It crouched here, mangled still, in a modest no-man's-land east of the Bank of England. These enduring ruins made a painful contrast with West German prosperity. It was better, thought Talbott, to be bombed flat by the democracies than by the Nazis. Better to be a bombed banker than a bombed docker.

He moved like a somnambulist into the carcass of time. Here, he knew, had been the corner of Kitchener Grove and Marlborough Avenue. The names of military generals had never really meant much to the inhabitants who now lay dead and buried under the wartime rubble. They were the wrong class to rise above sergeant in the First World War; too stubborn to move to safety in the Second. The place where he had lived was here, with nothing to distinguish it from the other lumpy mattresses of clay and weeds rising from uprooted homes.

He stopped. This was where it had happened. This was where Talbott had killed Rebecca. Others blamed the bombing, of course. But try telling that to a son so distraught he does all the wrong things, and *brings about* the killing of his mother! How little he'd really known about her! Her stories were all about Father's struggles to unionize New York wharfies, and then the dockers here. Here, the union-bashers said he was a commie Yankee rabble-rouser. The son got into fights at school defending him. Then Hitler invaded Poland. Father went away. The barrage balloons flew over these streets and gave meaning to the warning, "Look out, mate, the balloon's gone up!" France fell. Suddenly Father'd been gone a year. Gone to build an underground resistance, Rebecca said, because of his left-wing contacts. Gone. Never to be seen again.

Where they had once lived were now two rows of burial mounds and then a neon sign NO-MAN'S-LAND TUCKSHOP above a solitary boxlike structure. The sides were shorn. The steeply-pitched slate roof had been blown away by the bombs of long ago. He pushed inside, half expecting to see Scroggins blink up at him from between the glass jars of gob-stops and bubble gum. But there were no racks of magazines, no tins of tobacco. Steam hung under a naked light bulb. An elderly Chinese came through the swing doors and seemed to expect him. "This your place?" Talbott asked.

The Chinese smiled. "Camp. Very good." He waved a bottle of Camp Coffee concentrate in the cloudy light, unscrewed the top and poured the thick syrup into a chipped enamel mug. He squirted scalding water into the mug from an urn. "Drink!" he commanded. "Good for—" He gave an imitation sneeze. "—for ah-tish-oo!"

Talbott cupped the mug. He hadn't seen the name Camp since boyhood. This stuff was an air-raid warden's brew. He heard the German bombers again, their unsynchronized motors singing, "Where-are-you? We'll find you! Where-are-you?"

The hole in which the No-Man's-Land Tuckshop now sat had been made by a land mine slipping noiselessly on parachute cords into Scroggins's backyard. All was blown apart except the bottom section of Scroggins's store. Gone was Scroggins. And with him to kingdom come went the outside lavatory where he had been sitting.

Talbott hunched over the counter, defeated by the past and the sense of betrayal. Sally's perfume announced her presence before he saw her. She had slipped onto a stool as noiselessly as the German land mine sliding silkily out of a black sky. She seemed remote, a figure in a dream. The only familiar thing about her was the perfume.

"This wasn't my idea," she whispered. "This goose chase."

"No?" Talbott frowned. She seemed to be wearing a bush jacket over dungarees. She pushed what looked like a toy machine gun across the linoleum-covered counter. He said, "What the hell is that thing?"

"It's German."

"But what is it?"

"A Heckler and Koch . . . MP5. The Special Air Service use it here."

"Damn who uses it!" He stopped, appalled. "Why have you got it? Protection against me?"

"No, no, of course not!" Her reserve crumpled. "It's in case—" She stood. "Oh, God, I was so scared for you."

"You chose a funny way to show it."

"Jake made me come here. He said—well, it's like I told you. The East Germans get everyone's help, even the West's, if they trump up a murder charge."

Talbott thought of Crombie's effort to lure him into the Eastern sector. He thought about the absence of questions when he came through the control points in Berlin and London.

Sally said, "There wasn't evidence of a police lookout, was there? Not for me. Not for you . . . A false alarm."

"Or a neat trick to get me here."

"No." She removed a scarf from her head, shook out the blond hair, took a step closer. By these small actions, she became more herself. There was an urgency between them. He had an impulse to take her in his arms. Then his eyes strayed back to the gun.

She said quickly, as if to show she'd been a good girl, "I shipped the microtape interview with Hess from Heathrow."

She saw how he shrugged this off. It would be the first time Scott Talbott put work second. She said, "This is the safest place to be. The wasteland's empty and free of police."

"In my day, it was overcrowded and the cops always found us."

"The police were after you?"

"We were kids then. I lived here."

"Jake told me. I didn't know."

"We committed serious offenses. Tied front doorknockers together. Shot out streetlamps with our catapults." He wondered why he was telling her all this. "My life of crime."

The kitchen doors swung open. "Talbott?"

This time he was sure it was old Scroggins. The figure was wrapped in steam or smoke. The pungent mist curled and crept along the shelves where Scroggins had kept the tobacco tins, Golden Nugget or Player's Navy Cut; or piled the comics that were swapped at school: *Wizard* and *Boys' Own, Magnet* and *Dandy, Beano* and *Hotspur*. Now there were only red packets of Shanghai noodles.

He stared at the deeply shadowed face and expected to hear Scroggins's catarrhal cough. But it was Jake Cooke. "You're right to be cross about the melodrama," said Jake, as if resuming a conversation. "How else could I get you here, out of danger?"

Talbott wrenched his mind back to the present. "I'm a coward about things that have gone before," he said.

"Not a coward where a good story's concerned?"

"What story?"

"The truth. The truth about the Hess Command. The truth about Operation Citadel."

Talbott saw the nervous twitch of the hand Sally rested upon the counter. "More jiggery-pokery?" he asked.

"You'll know if the stuff's genuine." Jake spread his arms like a welcoming host. "First, you must settle in."

"I'll talk now, or leave."

"You can't go." Jake's face hung between Talbott and the yellow glow from the kitchen. "You're one of us now. Like Sally, stuck for the duration."

The word struck an archaic note. Duration of the war, thought Talbott. He hadn't heard the expression in years. He took Sally's arm. "We've work to do."

She resisted. "Jake's men have the place surrounded."

Jake said, "Unlike the Berlin crowd, mine shoot to kill."

"You set up the roadblock?" demanded Talbott.

"No. That was amateur stuff. This is serious." He dipped a finger in the dregs of Talbott's coffee and traced a circle on the counter.

"These are the streets of your youth." Jake drew sticky trails within the circle. "A wasteland now. Under my boys."

"And girl?" Talbott interrupted. "Is that Sally's job? Playing umbrella girl between you and Quex?"

"Quex!" Jake's face remained in shadow, but his magpie eyes glittered. "The days are gone when Quex could put up a protective umbrella for *me*. The roles are reversed. A lot of roles have been reversed." He had turned the tables on Talbott, too. Talbott was no more the master of the interrogating camera's eye, reinforced by the studio directors swishing their cable tails and the studio space-maidens with antenna-like rods emerging from earphoned heads. Talbott was alone, dragged here by the boy from his past. All this shone in Jake's dancing eyes.

Talbott turned away. "Then, exactly what *are* you doing here, Sally?"

"Please," said Sally. "Please listen to him."

"You're poisoned bait, Talbott," cut in Jake.

But Talbott was still watching Sally. She was clearly frightened. Not for herself. Quite plainly, though, this was no time for a showdown.

"Bait," Jake repeated, and Talbott shifted his gaze to the countertop, where Jake had both hands around a mug. "The poison is whatever resides in your memory," he said. "No fault of yours, Talbott." He was gazing into the mug like a fortuneteller reading tea leaves. "No poison for you, either." He put the mug dead center of the circle. "It's deadly, though, Talbott. That's why I got Sally to bring you here. To save your life." Jake looked up sharply, and Talbott saw how the man's features remained indistinct: the beard, the seamed face, the brooding eyes, they were all somehow ill-defined. A trick of light, perhaps . . .

"You don't believe me, do you?" said Jake, not unpleasantly. "In a way, you're right. I'm not interested in saving you. I'm interested in what you know, and in the people who want to find out what you know."

"I've nothing to offer."

"Except your memories."

"I remember nothing of importance to anyone but myself."

Jake cocked his head. "What about notes? Notes written and concealed in the confusion of the Blitz. By a man called . . . Radzki?"

Talbott froze.

"Don't pretend you never heard of Radzki," said Jake. "You asked Hess about Radzki."

Talbott moved slowly back from the counter. He stared accusingly at Sally, but said nothing. He turned and walked to the door, its curtained windows shining in a ghostly blue light from the neon sign outside. "I need some air," he said.

Jake put a detaining hand on Sally's arm.

"Let him go," said Jake. "He'll be okay."

The door gave a faint jingle as it closed behind Talbott. So something of old Scroggins still survived. That little bell on the coiled spring above the glass-paneled door was another of the sharp little memories, along with the smell of tobacco and pulp magazines and the tang of the first wintry wind blowing off the Thames. He waited outside until his eyes adjusted to the night. He wished Sally would join him. She had a lot of explaining to do. Well, she hadn't shot him, anyway! Sold out? Yes, perhaps. How else would Jake have known about his question to Hess?

Under his feet, the old macadam felt broken and soon dissolved into mud. Puddles reflected the stars in a clear sky. He caught himself searching the horizon for the blue flashes of double-deck tramcars picking up the power from overhead cables. The huge flashes, it was said, guided German bombers better than their own parachute flares, and soon the trams had to stop running. Nobody, though, could stop the Thames from shining. The bombers had followed the river's reflection to the target: the dockyards: cockneyland.

The cockneys had gotten in the way of Hitler's plans, like the Jews. Many *were* Jews. They were all riffraff to be blown away. Nobody held memorial services for the cockneys broken and burned here; there were no cockney museums around the world to stir the conscience; the empire they and their ships had served was now destroyed, though not by Hitler. The Fuehrer could have saved himself a lot of trouble and the British could have saved their colonies if there really had been a deal offered by Hess, and accepted.

Talbott's feet followed again in the tracks of his old delivery route. He'd carried Scroggins's newspapers through a neighborhood of zigzag lanes and alleys. It had required Nazi bombing to show him how really small the neighborhood was. Take out the terraced housing, the hole-in-corner shops, and the neighborhood shrank to the size of a death camp.

That's what this bit of cockneyland had become. Five years as a bull's-eye for bombers, with a climax of buzz bombs and Vengeance rockets falling from space. And now forgotten. A death camp with different horrors, where incendiary bombs incinerated the innocent, and others were gassed when gas lines were ruptured, where children were torn from their mother's arms and mass executions were carried out from above. Everyone knew about the Holocaust. Did anyone today care about cockneyland? Not much. Not here. Perhaps there was a poetic justice in it, thought Talbott, remembering how wartime propaganda had praised the cockneys and ignored the camps.

"Suppose he tries to walk away?" demanded Sally.

"He can't go far," said Jake.

She stood at the door of the No-Man's-Land Tuckshop, resenting Jake's certainty. "It's cruel, what you're doing to him," she said over her shoulder.

"Then, join him. Explain."

"You mean that?" She spun round.

"You'll find him over there, where his home used to be. Make lots of noise. My men tend to shoot when startled."

At moments like this, Sally could almost hate Jake Cooke.

She found Talbott at the edge of a shallow depression, near an embankment overgrown with weeds. The nearest streetlights were so far away, they seemed to shine from another galaxy. Trees lifted tortured limbs against the sky-shine of the metropolis. Hitler had drawn the First World War trenches this way, before he became the great dictator. A landscape like this, thought Sally, would drive any young man off his rocker.

"Jake give you a visitor's permit?" asked Talbott.

She was shocked by the rancor. "Jake's not my keeper!"

"Then, who is?"

"Please . . ." She took his arm. "His men are all around."

"You want to pretend we're lovers again?"

"It might be friendlier."

"I'm not in a very friendly mood," said Talbott. "The human race just now doesn't strike me as something to write home about."

"This is hard on you." She knew the words must seem insincere.

"I feel like all survivors. Guilty." He peered at her face, white in the dark. "What do you know that makes you so . . . understanding?"

"Only that you lived here once."

"But I was born American," Talbott said with a kind of defiance. "My old man's idealism trapped me here. His dreams—" He broke off and made an odd, jerking motion with one hand. "It's always others who pay for your dreams. My mother died in this place. I ran from here as far and as fast as I could."

Sally had never seen him so agitated. He was asking for her sympathy, and rejecting it. She sensed he would welcome a fight. She said carefully, "There's something different about Jake—"

"Jake, Jake . . . Always Jake?" He was becoming angry. Sally drew away. "I'll be here when you want me," she said.

Talbott shivered and scarcely heard. He told himself his small patch of blitzed London hadn't stayed this way simply to torture him when he returned. Tomorrow, he would see these ghostly remnants for what they really were: a new industrial site probably, or a park, or a cemetery.

Or a cemetery! Talbott turned, prepared to see the man who had been sitting with his mother here, in the house now gone. His mother had been pleading, "You mustn't go back. Here, you can bury yourself in some university . . ." And Samuel . . . Uncle Samuel, Szmuel in the original spelling, unaware of the young man's presence, had growled, "The only place I can safely bury myself, Rebecca, is a cemetery."

Talbott had been on active service when he was informed, officially, that Uncle Samuel had hanged himself. Here, in the yard behind their small terraced house with the slate roofs, Samuel had put an end to his life with a loop of rope. Talbott rubbed a scar bisecting one eyebrow: a scar more readily felt than seen, the result of banging his head against a cockpit stanchion after a clumsy deck landing. That accident had happened at the time "Uncle Samuel from Berlin" committed suicide.

Now, in appropriate darkness, Talbott shied away from these relics in the wilderness of memory. He seemed to wear a blindfold, as if once again asked to recall objects scattered across a tray. Kim's Game. The boyhood game taught him by the Boxing Parson. You studied unfamiliar objects and then, blindfold, you tried to recall them in sensible order.

Talbott shivered again, like the bare-knee'd boy he had once been, in a raw November wind of yesterday. The war had consumed his youth. He'd always been terrified—there was no other word—that coming back here, he'd be sucked into the old, familiar quagmire. It was a place of doom. After the house was bombed, he'd kept on going, afraid to look back, like Lot's wife, afraid of being turned to salt. Sodom and Gomorrah. Sod 'em. *Sod the whole effing lot of them!* He'd said that then, and yet here he was. Back! With Jake Cooke strewing objects higgledy-piggledy across his vision.

Was it Kim's Game that Jake was playing? Talbott broke into a sweat despite the chill air. "The way to remember," the Boxing Parson used to say, "is by association" . . . Bronfmann . . . death camps . . . Quex in wartime . . . Objects in a tray. Twenty was the limit of a boy's memory until that boy learned the trick of association. Then one thing led to another.

Talbott turned away. He had lost more than youth in that war. Time had been compressed. You did in a week what took a year in peacetime. Dates meant nothing, and events were squeezed into obscurity.

He was surprised to see Sally, a shadow moving in the deeper dark. She touched him. She was trembling and her first words set him back. "How could Jake have known," she asked, "about that question you put to Hess? The one about Radzki. There was nothing recorded on the Radzki question. Not on audio. Not in pictures . . . Nothing on the microtape. So he could never have got it from there."

"That still leaves you," Talbott said roughly.

"And the others in the interview cell. The Russians, say!"

Talbott stiffened. He cocked his head, straining to recapture a sound. There it was again! The distant clank of an anchor chain. A boat on the river. In this barren land, the sound carried so clearly, it might have been that of a man's steel-tipped boot striking a stone.

He knew he was using the distraction to avoid the issue. It was a form of self-deception from another time. But definitely he didn't want to face Radzki!

"Jake slipped up," Sally insisted. "It changes things for me." She was still shaking. There was another metallic sound, sharper and closer. "Play lovers," said Sally, clinging tight.

He kissed her full on the mouth. Relief and a fresh awareness flooded through him. Of course it could not have been Sally. Whoever had reported the key Hess question to Jake *must* know about Radzki.

Radzki. A man out of the darkness of occupied Europe, with strange connections, with access to Communist guerrillas fighting fascism. A man Talbott had known as Uncle Samuel?

He gently disengaged from Sally. "I think a man called Radzki died here," he said reluctantly. "We knew him as an uncle from Berlin." He was

talking to himself. "But maybe he didn't die." Suddenly he was quite
certain. "He *couldn't* have died here."

"Stop!" Sally was shaking. "Let's get out of here. Please?"

"And get shot?"

"I've a terrible feeling you might get shot anyway, if you talk too much
about the past."

Her fear, Talbott realized, had been all along for him.

"Grandpa warned me," she said, " 'Talbott knows but doesn't know he
knows. Our enemies want him to remember and tell them what he remembers, but they'll stop him from remembering too much.' "

"If it's that important to them, it's important to me." He took her arm.
"Look here."

He walked her along the embankment. It was overgrown with grass and
weeds and raised a shaggy profile against the city's glow.

"We hid in here when I was a kid. We're not hiding now, Sally. But if we
have to . . ." There was a manhole cover where he dug the point of his
shoe. "It leads into an access tunnel to an old sewer."

He stopped. This time, they both heard the same sharp sound. Out of a
clump of bushes stepped a figure whose stance had become familiar in the
world of inner-city warfare: the matchstick man whose body and limbs
present as skeletal a target as the gun he carries. Any fool can become a
matchstick man once you make his head inflammable with a cause, but
only a fool would provoke him to strike. Talbott tugged Sally away from
the forbidden zone. The guard said nothing.

"One of Jake's," whispered Sally.

Talbott had a terrible urge to throttle Jake for turning home territory
into a tray for Kim's Game . . . objects uncovered by association lead to
deeper secrets. If Uncle Samuel didn't die here, Talbott had to rethink
lifelong assumptions. Already he saw the impossibility of his alleged uncle's
dying at the time and place stated in the death notice delivered to him on
board the baby aircraft carrier *Thunderer*. He was Midshipman Talbott
then, a miserable "snotty" in ancient Royal Navy parlance, from the supposed habit of wiping one's nose on one's sleeve—for the prevention of
which, midshipmen wore brass buttons where men old enough to be officers wore gold braid. *Thunderer* was just back in Scapa Flow from a
murderous Russian convoy to Murmansk. Two thirds of the ships had been
sunk. Talbott had little appetite for brooding about an uncle he'd hardly
known.

Now he suddenly understood! This so-called Uncle Samuel "hanged"
himself in the house *after* it was bombed. So the death papers were falsi-
fied!

The nightly bombings had always been recognized as good cover for
murder. But an official cover-up meant something else. To provide a new
identity for a secret agent, a man could be conveniently "killed" by the
Blitz. Talbott had accepted this man as his mother's brother. Others might

have seen him as material to be sent back into the Nazi territories from which he'd fled.

Talbott was thinking aloud, the words stumbling out. "That death notice came to me as next of kin. I couldn't be the nearest surviving relative unless the rest were dead. And Rebecca died when the house was hit. That's more proof the notice was bogus . . . Unless someone figured I'd never return."

"How monstrous!"

"But plausible. Life expectancy was a month for boys flying from Woolworth carriers in arctic seas. I'd been on operations four months straight. It was a reasonable gamble—the official death notice pigeonholed, bureaucracy served, a mission protected . . . laddie."

Laddie! What had made him use that expression? He thought at once of the Boxing Parson. The name popped out. "Boxing Parson! I'd forgotten him! Well known in the East End. Went into wartime intelligence and vanished from the headlines . . ."

Sally picked up the last phrase. "You told me this slum preacher picked you to bomb Spandau . . . I asked you what kind of a parson, and you said the naughty kind that gets his name in the papers."

"Naughty society vicars sometimes worked among slum kids for penance."

Sally resumed walking. The No-Man's-Land sign was suddenly upon them. She was afraid to push Talbott too hard. Still she had to know, before Jake pounced.

"Why would this parson bring you in?" she asked.

"To keep it in the family."

"You're related?"

"No! Family in the sense of a cozy circle. All in the family of old school ties, the club. It seemed safer that way."

Sally took a deep breath. "Was this naughty vicar's name Furneval?"

"How on earth—?" Talbott stopped dead.

"Parson Furneval came to the funeral after you left." Sally described the visit. By the time she had finished, she was standing very close, her face tilted. She glimpsed a movement of the curtains at the coffee shop and moved back. She sensed Talbott's annoyance and she said hastily, "I don't think Jake should—"

"—suppose we're lovers?"

"No, it's not that!" She saw the first warning signal of misunderstanding. "I— I want us to be lovers, Talbott. In our own time. Not because we're being manipulated—"

"Into bed?" He laughed softly. "Even Jake can't make that happen if your popgun goes with you."

She remembered the gun on the counter. "It's Jake's," she said. "Though I *have* learned to use it."

Where? Talbott wondered. In Israel? Under Jake's instructions?

Then the door opened and they both saw Jake's face, suspended under the light like a mask, the rest of his body invisible.

Sally said softly, "There's something different about him. More bitterness. Perhaps hate. It actually alters his appearance . . ."

Talbott listened, puzzled.

"Let him do all the talking," she whispered as they drew closer. It sounded as if the advice was meant for herself. "Remember *nothing* for him. Nothing!"

17

"I remember!" barked General Quex Massey. "I remember very clearly! That *is* Rudolf Hess!"

Quex stared defiantly over the counterpane of the big bed. Serenely, Hess gazed back from a display screen in the penthouse suite of Fishhook Sherman's house. It was midafternoon in New York. On the other side of the Atlantic, Sally was urging Talbott to keep silent about his reviving memories. Here, her grandfather proclaimed the infallibility of his own. "Watched Hess every day at Nuremberg! He hasn't changed that much—"

"But you never saw him in captivity in England," Rinna reminded him.

"Churchill was satisfied it was Hess. Told Roosevelt so."

"You're dodging the question," said Rinna, and a deep silence followed.

Quex had been startled from an after-lunch nap by Fishhook delivering the microtape of Talbott's interview with Hess. Now they all studied the freeze-frame on the screen.

"While you're thinking about it—" ventured Fishhook.

Quex would not let him finish the sentence. "I don't have to think about it. That is Hess."

"I was going to say," Fishhook said mildly, "some troubling news came along with the tape."

Quex's head rose off the pillows.

"Your granddaughter and Talbott haven't been in touch with the network since yesterday. They're in London, but nobody seems to know where."

"We expected something like this," said Quex. "It's normal."

"Commander Nelson hasn't left for London yet?" interrupted Rinna. "His old Scotland Yard contacts would know . . ."

There was no need to complete the thought. The ex-FBI man was already heading for the door.

In the library, later, Quex wheeled himself across the room with Rinna in disapproving attendance.

"Please!" she said. "You'll overdo it!"

"Nonsense!" roared the old general, braking. "Watch!" He levered himself upright. "I really can walk. It's only a start, but I'll get there."

Fishhook, unnoticed, stood in the doorway.

"You're hopeless," Rinna complained.

"You've got it wrong." Quex, half crouched over his cane, grinned up at her. "Not hope-*less*. Hope-*full*. Full of hope. The hope you've given me, my dear." He was shaken by a fit of coughing and lost balance. Rinna caught him without making it obvious. He gave her a debonaire peck on the cheek. His face only flushed when he saw Fishhook.

"Didn't mean to intrude," said Fishhook.

"Just, ah, practicing my foxtrot," Quex called out. "Better come in before I wear out this poor girl's gams."

"Quex thinks he's going to London," said Rinna. "Talk sense into him, will you?"

"It's Nelson who goes." Fishhook stood aside as the Yard man bustled in.

Nelson had his own way of handling stubborn old generals. "Did you have Sally research *amnesia?*" he demanded.

Quex slowly collapsed back into the wheelchair. "No, sir."

"Notes," said Nelson, waving sheets of paper at him. "Torn up, thrown into the garbage." He had become as miserly with words as Fishhook.

Fishhook said, "None of the garbage compactors work, because I removed the fuses."

Nelson had taped the pages together. His big fingers were remarkably dexterous. "What it says," he offered, "is that '*voluntary amnesia*' has become much better understood lately." He flipped through pages. "The quacks haven't lacked for raw material in recent years. 'Voluntary amnesia' pops up wherever ordinary people are suddenly confronted with horror."

Fishhook took up the pieces from a newspaper clipping. "Listen to this. Concerning a death-camp survivor, now a successful Washington lawyer. To qualify for West German compensation to victims, she had to prove 'mental anguish.' She couldn't. Even with compensation money at stake, she couldn't remember anything from the camps." Fishhook read from the

Washington *Post*'s report: "The medical board and psychiatrists' final statement says, 'The victim was consciously determined at all costs to put her previous life behind her, being unable to come to terms with the horrible ordeals of the past.' "

"Let me look at the handwriting," said Quex.

"Most of it's typed," said Nelson. "There are pencil notes in the margins. Here—"

"That's easy," said Quex after a moment. "This is Furneval's research."

"The Reverend Marcus Furneval?" asked Nelson, frowning. "He's flown back to London."

"Correct. See this word here? *Confabulation.* It's in Furneval's handwriting: *a medical term to do with filling gaps in a disordered memory.*'" Quex shrugged. "He said he'd been digging into some newly released material."

"But why *amnesia?*" persisted Nelson.

"He's an absentminded old codger," said Quex, sounding not a little smug. "He's also too proud to go to doctors about a failing memory. I expect that's why."

Quex knew very well that wasn't the reason why. He said as much to Rinna after Fishhook had taken Nelson off to pack for the London flight.

"You don't trust the parson," said Rinna.

"No, not any more I don't."

"It must be something very serious made you change your mind?"

"I'd rather not discuss it just yet."

Rinna shot him a worried look. Nothing hurt Quex more than personal disloyalty. She hoped the parson had not betrayed Quex, because if Quex should turn vengeful, she pitied the parson.

Her apprehension grew with the return of Nelson. "I'll take my leave, then," he told Quex. "Don't worry about that grandchild of yours. We'll watch her."

"I'd better come along to help you," said Quex.

Nelson took the remark as a joke. "Dead men don't travel."

"That's what gives me shock value," retorted Quex. "Shock! Surprise! The best of weapons, when you don't have any of your own any more, Commander."

"He's still got Scotland Yard behind him," said Rinna.

"No," answered Quex. "He hasn't."

"Oh?" Rinna looked at Nelson.

He rewarded her with a broad wink. "The lads know I'm no traitor. They'll give me the helping hand, under the table."

"Talking of traitors," said Quex, "you'll be back in London well before Guy Fawkes' night."

Nelson buried his nose in a large handkerchief, blew a trumpet blast, and surfaced. "When I was a nipper, we'd sing *'Remember, remember, the fifth of November . . . Gunpowder, treason and plot!'* "

Quex laid a hand on Rinna's arm. "These cockneys celebrate Guy Fawkes"—he said—"because he blew up parliament, or tried."

"When a traitor's safely dead," muttered Nelson, "he's an excuse for a party." He stowed away the handkerchief and said to Rinna, "Your lads'll get me out of here, right? Soft as leopards. Like they did for Parson Furneval?"

Rinna touched his face in sudden affection. "Take care. Don't give any Guys the matches, Commander."

"I'll be there quick as a wink if he does," announced Quex.

"Over my dead body," said Rinna.

Nelson busied himself with buttoning up his old black mackintosh. In his ears, her words had an unpleasantly prophetic ring.

Quex really wanted very badly to fly to London. He argued this with Rinna until the poor woman was in despair. She had never before let personal feelings conflict with duty. "I love you too much to let you have your way," she said.

"I want to nip something in the bud."

"It's all too dangerous. Self-indulgent. Irrational. But yes, you're right!" she conceded. "Things are coming to a climax in London." By then, she had coaxed him back to their suite and was leafing through papers brought up in a box by her guards. "See here?" She passed over a printout spattered with odd-looking script and digits. He glared at it. He had tried not to resent the clatter of the machines behind the kitchen, spitting out words no longer meant for him. It bothered Quex, even after all these years, that he couldn't barge into any communications center and tear off the incoming bumf himself.

"You see, a Hess Command story is being offered the print media," said Rinna, settling on the bed. "The 88 play this cleverly. It'll make the network hungrier for the film."

"But we knew this would happen," objected Quex. "That's why we had the house searched."

Rinna leaned back, shocked. "You mean, Nelson rummaging through the garbage . . . ?"

"Specifically, through Parson Furneval's garbage. He left in haste. Why? Because Lord Swithin, who owns the *Daily News*, offered our parson a substantial fee to say the Hess Command seems authentic."

"He'd betray you to say this?"

"Oh, no, he wouldn't regard it as a betrayal," said Quex. "He'll say Swithin can't stop his competitors from writing wildly speculative nonsense on the basis of material offered to all newspapers in open auction. He'll say—ah, he has a *duty* to see the thing handled responsibly in Swithin's *Daily News* . . ."

"Nice allies you've got," said Rinna.

"That's why I'm needed in London." Quex returned to the attack. "The one steadfast supporter I've got is said to be a traitor."

"Nelson?" Rinna met his eyes. "We've got people in London to back him."

Quex waited. The seconds ticked by. "Very well," he said finally. "Explain."

"If you make me a promise."

Quex folded his hands over the top of his walking stick. "There. Even my fingers aren't crossed."

"You promise."

"Not to go to London. Unless, as you say, over your dead body." He grinned up at her.

"No qualifications. No escape clauses."

Quex sighed. "My dear girl, it's like one of those meaningless clauses in a life-insurance policy against which you write NA for Not Applicable. If you were dead, I wouldn't want to go on living."

If Rinna had been paying attention, she would have scrutinized that last sentence more closely. But she was trying to decide if she should give Quex the whole story. It was undoubtedly a breach of security: yet if Quex pigheadedly insisted on this London trip now, it could have disastrous consequences for Israel. She weighed one danger against another and threw into the scales her personal relationship with Quex. Then she gave him the facts she believed, for once, he did not know.

18

If Quex had been granted a bird's-eye view of London early next morning,
he could have confirmed Rinna Dystel's description of the square mile of
wasteland around the No-Man's-Land Tuckshop as a sort of Bermuda
Triangle where even taxis went missing. It remained a neglected desert
beyond the London Docklands Development Corporation project to revi-
talize what had once been the warehouse of the world. After Hitler's war, a
quarter million East Enders vanished from the docklands, which slipped
into dereliction. The Tuckshop wasteland was still abandoned, though
careful examination would reveal the presence of young men in nonde-
script fatigues. Some were Jewish defense volunteers who lived in London
except when Israel faced another war, when they quietly boarded commercial flights to Tel Aviv. This time they had been called out by Jake Cooke,
to fight another kind of war on home ground. They were reinforced by the
men who had drifted in quietly from abroad.

Nelson was unofficially aware of their presence. He had cooperated with
Israel in antiterrorist work; ironically, his earlier police work had required
him to chase Jewish "terrorists" like Jake during their struggle to create
Israel. Nelson's conversion to a pro-Israel stand got him in trouble, and the
nickname Izzie. When he began investigating certain political murders
committed under cover of Nazi bombing, though a great many years later,
he was warned to stop. He refused. A campaign to discredit him began.

Still he had support from old colleagues who saw him as the victim of some obscure war between departments. Most of this Quex knew. But not all.

Talbott woke that morning in London with a violent start. He saw it was five o'clock. At that hour, Scroggins had expected him to start his daily paper rounds through what was now no-man's-land. Some trace of Scroggins must linger in the coffee shop to have aroused Talbott. He tried not to disturb Sally as he got to his feet. They had chosen to sleep in the front of the store, using sleeping bags supplied by Jake. Nobody had disturbed them until Scroggins's ghost padded by.

Talbott made his way to the kitchen.

"Breakfast?" asked Jake, as if he'd been waiting there in the shadows to make just such an offer.

"If our Chinese chum's got more than noodles."

Chinese Lum looked up from the stove with an uncomprehending smile.

"He's feeding a small army," said Jake. "Eggs, and that ghastly coffee concentrate, and noodles. He's practicing for when he opens Chinese Lum's Snackies. We got him the franchise. He's just aching for us to go."

"What customers could possibly replace you? It's bare as the Tibetan tablelands out there."

"But earmarked for public housing."

"Then, Lum's earmarked for bankruptcy. Nothing's better preserved in London than bomb ruins."

"Slums," Jake corrected him. "Most blitzed places were rebuilt. Some have turned into slum ganglands. Nelson must have told you."

"I don't know who you mean."

"He was at Quex's funeral."

"Perhaps. But I wasn't!"

"No, of course not!" Jake gave him a strange look and hoisted himself onto the big table which occupied a dark corner. He was wearing faded khaki trousers and an open-necked shirt. He reminded Talbott of the Israeli Army rabbis he had encountered in the desert night, commanding an authority that drew upon the men's own piety.

"I knew Nelson when he was less exalted," said Jake. "He chased me round London. He was with counterintelligence. I was printing Zionist pamphlets and distributing the Irgun's underground newspaper, *Herut*. It became the name of Begin's party, later." He smiled. "I guess you and I were both newspaper delivery boys at one time." Jake's smile vanished. "It was against the law then to plead for a Jewish national home. The death camps had just been entered by Allied troops, but by God none of those left alive were going to get to Palestine if the Grand Alliance could stop it!"

"You weren't just printing appeals," Talbott objected. "You were hanging British soldiers from lampposts."

"That was Jerusalem. The British jailed and executed our men for military activities, refused to treat them as soldiers—"

"Because soldiers don't blow up hotels full of civilians, like the King David!"

"Another exaggeration!"

"You can't exaggerate your assassination of the British minister, Lord Moyne."

"By that action, extremists hurt our cause." Jake stroked his beard. "There's such hate, isn't there? What was the point of antagonizing the British, who could have been our best friends?"

"Your best friends then were the Russians."

Jake shrugged. "Things change. Now I'm upholding the law and Nelson is chased by others." Jake broke off as if he had said too much, and turned to address Chinese Lum with a few words of Cantonese and many gestures.

Talbott thought, he's become accustomed to the role of the conspirator —the sudden flights, the sense of high purpose, the game of wits, the risks. He slips into another language as easily as he dons a fresh disguise.

Lum returned, carrying a tray.

"Your breakfast," said Jake. "Bit messy, not American. Wouldn't blame you for losing all faith in me." He wore a sad smile and gestured at a sheaf of notes, folded like a newspaper, on the tray. "Read that. Maybe you'll see my point of view."

He walked to the kitchen door and stood there for a moment, brushing away the condensation on the glass like a man dispelling the cobwebs of a bad dream. Then he walked out.

There was a small room off the kitchen. Talbott remembered it as Scroggins's parlor. Lum took him there. In front of a makeshift table, a dirty window looked out into what had been Scroggins's backyard, now a wilderness of frosted weeds, surrounded by a tall, new fence. The table was an upturned crate. There Talbott hungrily consumed Lum's watery eggs and greasy toast.

He unfolded the papers. The first page was numbered 129. The printing was the smudged violet ink of an old-fashioned Gestetner duplicator. The strangely printed words leapt out of the past, and the moment he began to read, Talbott's morning sense of well-being vanished.

. . . Watch was kept on the Wendell Talbott residence from day of Szmuel Radzki's arrival. On night 29th May stick of bombs wiped out neighbouring street and damaged Talbott house seriously. Rescue workers began to dig at approx. 0215 hours after reports Rebecca Talbott, 37, buried under debris.

Talbott massaged his throbbing temples. The report came from M15 counterintelligence, he supposed. In 1942 it would be normal to keep watch on Radzki, a refugee from Nazi Europe. He'd come under routine suspicion as a possible spy. But he might also be under consideration as a courier in the secret wars against fascism.

In the afternoon, voice contact was made with Rebecca Talbott. Word had been sent to Midshipman Scott Talbott of the Royal Navy Air Service. This young man (ST/01/RNAS-1523 refers) technically underage, hence Midshipman rank in accordance RN regulations. Midshipman Talbott's ship was in port. He had been flying in stressful conditions and allowance must be made for subsequent events . . .

Talbott swallowed his distaste for the anonymous, know-it-all author.

Midshipman Talbott ignored salvage squad warnings. He had been told his mother was alive but pinned down by heavy timbers easily dislodged by impulsive action. He tunneled into the debris. Rescue operations were brought to a stop.

A man in a black raincoat entered the danger zone, having apparently told air-raid wardens he was friend. This was about 1900 hours. Unexploded and delayed action bombs had now been reported in the neighborhood. There was argument among rescuers about advisability continuing excavate rubble on this site since more urgent situations were being reported minute by minute.

The night's bombing had recommenced. Several adjacent terrace cottages fell in. New flames spurted from remains of the Talbott house. Black Mac, the name used by official witnesses who did not get the man's identification earlier, emerged at 1937 hours, followed by Midshipman Talbott. . . .

Talbott's hands shook as he turned the page. This was himself they were talking about!

Sometime later, workers learned the woman, Mrs. Talbott, was crushed to death by collapse of structure. It was noted Talbott's uniform was badly torn. Black Mac had taken him to former boys' club. Both were clearly seen by light of several big fires. Talbott stood at attention while Black Mac threw rubble. Talbott had back to remaining wall of club. Several witnesses to this (see below). Black Mac later left. Talbott then collapsed. Navy medical examiners attested boy could not recall events when questioned at Queen Anne's Mansions . . .

Throwing pieces of rubble? At a midshipman, rigidly at attention among incendiary bombs? Talbott stared through the grimy window. It could not be true. Yet the description disturbed some early memory of a game played with a hard leather cricket ball.

The next sheet was typed on a different kind of official notepaper. It was an autopsy on Rebecca Talbott. It was impossible. An autopsy on his mother, when so many were dying from the bombs? The medical and other services were strained to breaking point by the bombings; and autopsies were carried out only in rare circumstances.

Which was why murders were committed under cover of the Blitz!

The report showed an abnormal quantity of morphine in her body. It had been recovered three days later, in a bombing lull. The fires had not burned down that deep. She had been extricated whole. The list of broken bones and internal injuries was horrifying. In such conditions, the report noted, anyone administering morphine could miscalculate.

Yes, thought Talbott, an overdose was not uncommon. Sometimes it was given for humanitarian reasons to bring easeful death. The humble often played God during the Blitz. Still, the stark fact seemed to be that Rebecca was killed by morphine. Not by bombs. Not by her son's hysterical defiance of the rescue experts.

He had buried the guilt, and with it all remembrance.

He need never have felt guilt. Yet the facts, the autopsy, had been concealed from him, and he had been sentenced to a lifetime of guilt.

His body felt drained of strength. It had always been like this when he tried to recall his last hours with her. He had never been able to cry about it. He had never again believed in anyone's God. He had never again found it possible to love anyone. He had come to believe that such a love as he had for Rebecca was always paid for in pain.

If he hadn't killed her, who had? Not the Germans. They had broken her body with their bombs. But only the morphine could rob her of will-power. She had struggled against her injuries *to keep her mind clear*. To tell her son something! He knew this with sudden clarity. The rest was a fog. Black Mac. Somebody had known who he was, to admit him into the smoking ruins. Talbott himself must have recognized the man, to allow him close to Rebecca. It wasn't something you permitted a stranger to do, like a strange priest administering the last rites. *Priest?* But Rebecca was Jewish. It couldn't have been a priest. An old friend? Szmuel Radzki?

The name, when it came to him, somehow caused no surprise. Then he saw it printed on top of the final report, from Churchill's wartime intelligence adviser. "*Source:* HM Public Record Office, PREM 3-352/14Z-06984-B." It said:

Subject Radzki.

Radzki reached England in 1941 with details of what he claimed was a Nazi death camp in Poland near German industrial development at Birkenau-Auschwitz. He also claimed to have arrived via certain escape routes already known to us, including *Base Anna* in Stockholm. This exit would not have been possible at the stated time. He came under the VIIth Bureau for liaison with the Polish government-in-exile.

Radzki was able to give, however, a complete history of these Nazi concentration camps, starting with Buchenwald in 1934 when it was planned to hold 100,000 (by middle of war, the figure was near 800,000 of which 51,572 exterminated).

Talbott glanced at the foot of the report and saw it was dated May 1945, three years after Rebecca's death. The Public Record source had been added. The paper was a summary of some other document, and was typed on modern stationery.

Radzki was kept under observation because of suspected links with Soviet intelligence networks. It is now believed he soon realized he was under surveillance but continued with his declared mission to place before war leaders in the West an appeal from Jewish inmates of death camps that the Allies should bomb those camps, railroads and other means of mass murder.

Radzki had spent long periods in Nazi police jurisdictions and seemed fearful of betrayal and arrest. He is thought to have concealed plans, eyewitness reports and technical details concerning the camps all over London.

Radzki failed to catch interest at any high level. He was reported in official documents to have committed suicide in despair, allegedly at the home of Rebecca Talbott, said to be a distant relative. There was talk Rebecca Talbott took possession of files listed by Radzki under Hess Command.

Talbott felt ill. There was no evidence of when this last paper had been written. The 1945 date could have been stamped on it by Jake's own intelligence people. The final paragraph read:

The original documents have been removed from declassified files now in HM Government Public Record Office. The Radzki suicide, however, is reported by M15 in separate file as covering the return of Radzki to Occupied Europe as a courier whose ultimate loyalty later discovered to be Soviet military intelligence.

There was a sudden knock on the door. Talbott heard Sally ask if she could come in.

"Yes! Please . . ." He was grateful for the interruption.

Sally joined him at the table. "Jake suggested we take a walk before the rain begins." She stopped, shocked by his expression.

"Clever bastard," said Talbott softly. "He knows now I won't run."

She glanced at the papers. "So he finally hooked you."

Talbott shook his head. "We can talk outside."

The light of dawn drained through a thick overcast. The air was electric with the approach of thunder. Talbott summarized what he had just read. He was brief about his mother. The guilt simply weighed upon him more than ever. But Radzki! He'd wiped out all memory of Radzki, and now Radzki overshadowed everything.

"I'm scared," said Sally, taking his arm. "Jake must know much more than he's told you." She sounded bewildered, as if her own words were taking her by surprise. "I had a loyalty to him, and it's hard to shake that off. But . . . something has happened to him."

"What does he want from me?"

"Radzki's papers. He must think you know where they are."

"What do you know about them?"

Sally shook her head, as if she would reveal no more. Perhaps, thought Talbott, she had nothing more to reveal. He looked away, and instantly recognized an old, shameful habit of glancing the other way when confronted by something unpleasant. He first caught himself doing it while piloting a Seafire, the naval version of the Spitfire, through the antiaircraft fire of a German harbor. He was flying near sea level and was confronted with the gaunt skeletons of dockside cranes. It was too late to haul back on the stick or twist away. Above him were cables. On either side were masts and gantries. He could only fly straight on and hope he'd squeeze through. And so he'd turned his head as if to admire the damned view, blocking from his mind the impending disaster.

His thoughts were distracted by the spectacle of a small boy on a pile of earth with one sack over a shoulder. A boy who might be himself years ago. He saw another boy and then another. "Gor blimey!" Talbott said. "Bleedin' mud larks."

Sally could only see three small and unprepossessing boys straggling away from the river and the rising mists.

"We mudlarked here when the tide was out," said Talbott. "We dug up treasure, Roman coins mostly, out of the river mud."

The boys were peering into a shallow hole. Two carried short-handled spades. With a sudden chill, he saw they must be digging for treasure from the Blitz! *Relics.* Of what?

He tugged Sally in their direction. "Bits of German incendiary bombs instead of Saxon silver, that's their treasure!" He sounded torn between anger and despairing laughter. This, he thought, must be modern history's first civilian combat zone. Now the kids shot each other in every big city. Beirut. Belfast. Barbecued boy bonzes in Bangkok. He said, "These kids think it's all ancient history, Nazi bombs against cockneys."

The boys' chatter carried on the damp air. They were arguing about a corroded object sticking out of a hole. Their leader caught sight of Talbott. The boy must have been all of ten years old.

"You carn't chase us orf, mister," he yelled. "Not this time!"

The trio took up attitudes of defiance. Talbott shouted back, "We're tourists."

They watched with thinly disguised suspicion as he took Sally by the hand. "Come on," he told her. "Come and take a look at myself when young."

"You're not wiv that other lot, then?" asked the same boy.

"What lot?"

"Nah, it don't matter!" interrupted another of the ragamuffins.

Talbott picked a way around an excavation of sorts. "Did you dig this?"

"Yus. A long time ago."

That, thought Talbott, could mean a week. He peered into the newly dug hole and saw twisted handlebars. A buried motorcycle. Must be Ted Morrison's BSA with its one-wheel sidecar, the only motor vehicle on the street. The handlebars were corroded to the point of disintegration.

"Know wot it is?" asked the first boy, with sharp perception.

"It's a BSA motorbike made in 1936, year of the Coronation," said Talbott.

"Cor' stone the crows! 'Ow'd yer know that, then?"

Another boy said, " 'e's bin 'ere before, Charlie. That's 'ow 'e knows. Bet 'e cum wiv them Germans."

"Nah," said the child addressed as Charlie. "That suit's a Yank suit, ain't it, mister. My old man's a detecative," he added proudly.

"We're the Blitz Kids," one of them said finally.

"Shut up, Candlestick!" he was ordered by Charlie.

"That's a bit fancy." Talbott laughed. "Blitz Kids dye their hair, paint their faces. They're older than you lot."

This provoked Charlie. "Maybe they don't let us in the Blitz bars," he said. "Don't mean we ain't got the right. See, *we* took the name first, from the real kids of the real Blitz. Them other ones, they're more like Nazis. Not us. We'll fight anyone says we can't call ourselves the original Blitz Kids. You watch out for us, fireworks night."

"Penny for the Guy?" asked Talbott.

"See!" shrieked Candlestick in triumph. "Told yer 'e's bin 'ere before."

"We're making a Guy," said the middle boy. "Got any clothes, mister?"

"Shut up, Ginger!" warned Charlie.

It had started to rain. Thunder growled. The boys sniffed the wind blowing off the estuary. It had the same gray, sad smell Talbott remembered. The boys in their gray shirts and shorts, their socks drooping around their boots, were like all the boys who had ever lived here. They were torn between curiosity and a need to run home before the storm.

"If you'd lived 'ere once," Charlie interrupted their unnerving silence, "you'd 'ave some things down there. That's 'ow you know about the mo-torbike." He glanced at the others in triumph. "Tell you wot, mister. If you want us to dig, meet us tomorrer. Just say when."

Talbott considered the offer. "You know the Embankment?"

" 'Course," Charlie said scornfully.

"I know where you can get into the pipe runs beside it."

"It's true, then, 'e did live 'ere!" cried Charlie. His flaxen hair was soaking up the rain and he danced to keep warm in the sudden rise of the wind. He turned to go. The others fell in behind. Talbott detained the boy called Ginger, who carried a sack.

"You a paperboy?"

"Yus," said Ginger, looking scared. "My route's a long way from 'ere."

"Got any papers left?"

" 'e's already delivered them," said Charlie. "All except Missus Sedgwick. Gets the *Mirror*, she does, but she's in the infirmary. Go on, Ginge', give it 'im. Charge special delivery."

"Will five quid do?" asked Talbott, offering a polite bribe. He had a feeling he might need the boys. He surrendered a five-pound note under their rapt gaze. Ginger fished out the tabloid.

Talbott's impulse had been to see what, if anything, had been reported concerning events in Düsseldorf. He was not prepared for front-page head-lines big enough even for Sally to read from where she stood. HESS SHOCK! DID HITLER'S AXMAN FIX UK DEAL ON JEWS? It must have been the first time in days that the Baltic crisis had not dominated the front page.

A flash of lightning was followed by a violent surge of wind. The boys fled. The rain became a slashing torrent. Sally slid into the shallow bowl where a house once stood. Talbott, ahead, had the paper open. " 'German scholars claim they've uncovered evidence Hitler used Rudolf Hess to ne-gotiate a secret agreement with the Western Allies.' " He turned the pages impatiently. "The 88 leaked this. A lot of old photographs and a text that doesn't support the headlines."

Sally took the wet pages. "They talk of the Hess Command and *'a newly discovered archive.'* Must be part of the buildup."

"Buildup to what?"

"Your part in televising the Hess Command." She began to dig her foot savagely into the ground. "I'm burying this before Jake sees it."

He stared at her. She was digging unwittingly into soil, compacted dur-ing the years, over his mother's tomb. But this had not caused his expres-sion to freeze. His mother had refused to die before telling her son some-thing. Then Black Mac had come to stop her. And then he, Scott Talbott, had run away, back into the forgetfulness of combat.

"Darling!"

Sally's voice reached him from a great distance.

"Where were you?" She sounded scared.

"It's nothing. Let's go."

"You're so wet," she said as he helped her climb out of the muddy basin. "You'll catch your death."

It was the kind of thing his mother would have said. She would have approved of Sally, sloshing through the puddles beside him, alive and warm. Neither of these women would run from emotional responsibility, the way he'd run. He hadn't been any hero that day, like everyone thought, running back to war. He'd been running like a common coward, away from domestic grief and its accompanying obligations.

It had become easier to close a fighter's cockpit hood against realities; easier to put the cameras between himself and personal commitments; easier to judge headline material than become involved with the tangled little problems that ordinary folk faced day after dreary day. He thought of the weightlessness of certain aerobatics; the removal of gravity under water; that lifting away of weighty burdens in the rapture of the deep. What was this great weight he'd been trying to forget? Forgetting what his subconscious knew he'd better not remember?

"What is it?" asked Sally, alarmed by yet another long silence.

"What's what?"

"I thought you—wanted to say something."

"Did I?" He stopped and found he was looking into a face that might, in this melancholy light, have been Rebecca's. And now it came back to him in a rush, her voice struggling against death to convey words so important to herself, so quickly pushed aside by her son: "Scroggins . . . papers . . . *The Daily Worker.*"

19

The Soviet leader was too old for high adventure. Still, the map across Yuri Gorin's knees excited him more than the unread file beside him labeled *"American TV Encounter with War Criminal Hess."*

He sat on the veranda of his Black Sea villa, far enough south of Moscow to catch the few remaining days of decent sunshine. He had driven into the Caucasian foothills that morning to see the former chief of U.S. central intelligence, Vice President Walter Juste, before he flew from Yalta to Washington by way of Bucharest. "We both have an interest in killing this story," Juste had said on parting. "If this Hess Command mischief goes too far, neither you nor ourselves will get the genie back in the bottle."

The details were in the file. The Little Mother of all the Russias sighed and put it aside. First he must indulge himself with the map. He was buoyed up by this evidence of his continuing duality. While hunting wild boar with Walter Juste, he had known again the thrill of guns and the chase. Now, granny glasses back on snub nose, rug warming knees knotted with arthritis, he was back to playing the master administrator.

The hunt had taken no more time than was needed for Mother to brief the ex-CIA director on his own. Neither man would survive any rumor that the CIA might be making cozy deals with the KGB. Mother traced the American's subsequent route: a modest hop, skip and jump through

East Europe long enough to be seen shaking hands with local party dignitaries. The press pictures would reassure Washington he was doing his job, quietly encouraging disaffection among the restless satellites. Then Walter Juste could return to his task of watching out for Mother.

The stubby finger of the supreme Soviet leader traveled down to the Adriatic town of Igalo. That was where Mother must soon begin *his* task. The setting was appropriate. At Igalo, the great dissident leader, Tito, had once plotted his break with Stalin, to bring Yugoslavia some independence from Soviet rule. There, at Igalo, Mother would start the process of reintegration, with the party leaders of every Soviet satellite to witness and applaud.

He shifted the rug on his knees. It grew cold out here, though the sun was brilliant in a clear sky. Below, he could see the guards move between the tall cypress trees. The villa was encircled by a ring of KGB steel from one of Mother's own regiments, each man loyal to Mother alone. It had taken years to lay the groundwork for such devotion. A moment's inattention could blow it all away.

He turned to the Hess jail report, studying it with that fierce concentration for which he was both famous and feared. His appetite for detail, his prodigious memory, his divinations, had carried him to the summit of power for a purpose he believed with a metaphysical passion would be fulfilled. The flow of self-satisfaction, rare in a life of unending struggle, dimmed as he read deeper into the report. He began to shuffle his feet. He removed his spectacles. He rubbed the shinbone of his left leg where the old war wound had started to throb. He put his glasses back on again. To the very few who knew him, these were ominous signs.

He read further, laid the report on his lap, took off the glasses once more and polished each lens with his handkerchief. He was not given to gestures. He could outsit any member of any committee without batting an eyelid. Only his closest intimates would have detected that Yuri Gorin was now in a state of extreme alarm.

He lifted his head and wondered what had become of the sunlit sky. He groped for the report again and held it close to his naked face, moving each sheet across his line of vision as if his mismatched eyes were separate lenses that recorded every line.

Here was Scott Talbott's first surprise question to Hess. It had elicited a reply without a word being said. Had the deputy fuehrer flown to England alone? No, Hess had replied by silently shaking his head.

What prompted the American to ask such a question?

Mother felt a terrible constriction of the chest. He forced himself to breathe deeply. Here, near the end, was another surprise question. *Radzki!*

Talbott had asked if Hess knew a man called Radzki! Why?

This time, there'd been no response from Hess, no body language, although Mother's agent had seen how long they stared into each other's eyes. But *Radzki?*

Mother threw aside the lap rug, gripped the report in one fist, rose and lumbered across the veranda to lean over the fretworked fencing and suck in the clean air of the pine forest.

If only he'd seen this report before Walter Juste's departure!

It was too late now. He would have to fall back upon the dangerous, dreary, awkward procedure he hated and dreaded.

It mustn't end this way.

Secretary Kerensky, summoned hastily from the adjoining villa, took the dictation. Everyone would be reading it the next day.

The article, signed Observer, would appear in *Pravda*. Of course, the central committee would be agitated. This, in the present circumstances, scarcely caused even a mild flutter in Mother's heart. He had done it before, conditioning the party for a return to Stalin's practice of publishing, at once, without time-wasting consultations, some necessary *Diktat*.

The sermon from Mother this time was on topics he had made his own: absenteeism, heavy drinking, abuse of party privileges. At regular intervals, the obligatory party phrases were inserted like raisins in a plum pudding. He concluded that the achievement of a socialist society would certainly not be delayed "by a measured release of those goods commonly associated with frivolity. Number Seven Toy Factory at Kiev is now engaged in worker-management talks, so that production may proceed with teddy bears, traditionally symbols of contented childhood. If Marxist-Leninism is not good enough to make teddy bears, then it is good for nothing."

Mother felt Nick Kerensky's eyes lift from the pad.

"That will be all."

"Thank you," Kerensky murmured politely and put away his notebook. Mother knew exactly what would be running through the man's mind. Why this urgency? What on earth was all this rot about teddy bears? Stalin had said, of course, that Marxist-Leninism was good for nothing if it couldn't develop heavy industry. Mao had said it about Chinese agriculture. But teddy bears?

"I said that's all!" growled Mother.

Kerensky jumped. In his nervousness, he became formal. Mother, watching him back away, was tempted to give a further imitation of Stalin and order him to dance like a Cossack. It was true, what Stalin had always said. The Russians needed a tyrant. They hungered to be kicked in the butt, like serfs. If Kerensky was rattled, well and good! Mother's enemies in the system would shudder too. The only language any of them understood was spoken by the whip.

With little time left, Mother would crack that whip, at Igalo.

He listened to Kerensky's boots thunder down the wooden steps. The article would be sent over a party teleprinter and picked up by the long ears of American electronics. Failing that, the U.S. embassy would copy it to Washington when it appeared tomorrow in Pravda. What mattered was not the diplomatic guesswork it would inspire, but the accurate combining of words to trigger those clever computer lookouts in Washington.

A woman's voice carried up from below. Mother leaned over the veranda. "Irina! Come here. Immediately." He returned to his wicker chair and closed his eyes. Irina was the closest he would ever come to possessing a wife. He had never slept with her, and she protected the secret of his celibacy.

Her high heels scraped on the top stair. She cursed cheerfully. Mother grumbled, "It may be chic these days for Soviet women to swear, but not in my presence."

Irina came up behind him and put one hand over his eyes, the other over his mouth. "See no evil. Speak none. Surely a virtuous comrade may listen?" She had hobbled from the stairway and now removed the shoe on which the heel had broken. "If not to cussing, to a dirty story? I have a good one from the central committee shop."

"Not now!" Yuri Gorin turned. Irina was still dressed for shopping. She was small, with a pouter-pigeon bust and jet-black hair. Her eyes danced with the quickness of her wits. Irina, who never acknowledged her Jewish background, was totally without fear.

"Here's another joke, then." She brightened. "Quite clean this time."

Gorin squinted at her, wondering what she really wanted to tell him. So many of their conversations were in a sort of code.

"Israel's going broke," said Irina, encouraged by his silence. "One cabinet member says, 'Let's start wars against both Russia *and* the Americans. Then we can get money from both sides.' Everyone says, 'Brilliant!' Except the Prime Minister. He says, 'Suppose we win? Then, what will it cost us?' "

He rewarded her with a bleak smile. "Not dirty. Not funny."

"Have I upset you?" She watched him anxiously. "It's only a silly joke."

"And inappropriate." He returned to the map he had studied so complacently such a short time before. In the twinkling of an eye, everything had changed. He had traveled so many roads in his time. He looked at the forking of rivers, highways, railways. How often had he stood at such crossroads? Never knowing which way would lead to disaster. Trusting only his sense of destiny.

"What are you thinking?" asked Irina. The question, from the wife of a leading party official, would be dangerously impertinent. From a housekeeper, it was nothing worse than a faint echo of that familiarity with which domestic servants treated the czars.

"That you should return to Moscow," he said without looking up. Irina would know he meant the *dacha* at Peredelkino, and also why he would want her there.

She was lost for a moment. Something was terribly wrong. She straightened her back. He wanted to get her out of harm's way. They had learned to communicate like prisoners. She needed to stroke his face, utter some consolation, for even a man trapped in evil deserves a little comfort. But it might be that her own survival now depended upon remaining calm. "Very well," she said tonelessly. "As you wish."

His attention was back on the map. His hand brushed over Hungary. Interesting to see how little the transport systems of Europe had changed since the death camps were sited at the hub of each steel web. Even the underground travel routes were much the same. Once, they had been evasion routes for Nazi agents; then Nazi ratlines for those escaping Allied justice. One Anglo-American line, run by Washington's MIS-X experts, had zigzagged all through Europe to Igalo. Such an obscure Adriatic fishing village it had been then. Jews had exited via Igalo in the great escape from the liberated death camps to Palestine. Now, very soon, Mother would be back again at Igalo, the scene of his coming showdown with the Soviet satellites. If things in Igalo had changed, geography never altered. Igalo was still conveniently close to neutral waters. And the guards from the Kyrya.

He withdrew his hand as if the map had turned suddenly to liquid fire.

20

It was midafternoon of the first full day of what Talbott regarded as his coffee-shop captivity. "Who gives you orders?" he demanded with calculated rudeness. "The Kyrya?" He knew the question would irritate Jake Cooke. But Talbott was irritated too. No iron bars. No bruises. Yet he was in a prison, as much of his own making as Jake's.

Jake refused to take offense. Talbott was rubbing salt in old wounds, pronouncing it *kyria*, having in mind that ferroconcrete complex squatting in downtown Tel-Aviv; that place sometimes called in a whisper The Kyrya, which sucks up knowledge of the world, vital to survival for a state under siege. It sounded too much like the Vatican curia to suit the taste of old Jewish underground fighters. That curia was the most ancient of enemies.

"I take orders from nobody," said Jake.

"Not even the Sayaret Motkal?" Talbott taunted him, naming the secret intelligence arm Israel had never officially acknowledged.

Jake would not be provoked. "Kyrya means supreme authority. It's not used any more."

Like hell it isn't, thought Sally. She was sitting at the coffee bar, watching the men explore each other's minds. Talbott sprawled by the street window. Jake, as seemed to have become his habit, chose to sit away from the light.

"I want everything the Kyrya's got on Radzki," Talbott said suddenly.

"I told you, there's no Kyrya."

"I knew Radzki when I lived here."

Sally jumped at the sudden disclosure. Hadn't she warned Talbott to volunteer nothing?

Jake said swiftly, "For that, the Kyrya might be revived."

"Then, tell me what's known about Radzki."

"If you play ball, I will."

They'd started to maneuver again. Sally leaned back, resigned. Over the top of the dirty curtains, beyond the rain-lashed windows, she had a view of the wasteland. It had the quality of a smudged photograph taken inside the concentration camps. Some of Jake's guards were out there, children of survivors. They'd grown up, like herself, sure of their rights. They knew so little, really, about what it was to face, unarmed, at every turn, a specific and focused hatred.

The afternoon darkened. Jake talked now as if Talbott's admission about Radzki had opened a door. Sally sat unmoving and looked out at a world full of decoys and death traps.

"Jewish boys out there will never understand," said Jake. "We weren't all led like lambs to the slaughter. Take me. I followed an MIS-X escape route out of Nazi territory the last time, so routine it was like taking the subway. But I'd first come to London out of occupied Poland. I envied the fighting Poles who'd also escaped to London. They'd got a government to speak for them, even in exile. They'd got a secret army fighting the Nazi occupiers. We Jews had no such voice.

"Then along comes Szmuel Radzki. A week after London's battered by the heaviest air raid known in history to that date. May 10, 1941."

"The night Hess flew here!" said Talbott.

"Well, that's when the documents say Radzki arrived," Jake acknowledged. "He was nothing more than another shabby refugee with a funny accent and a broken cardboard suitcase. London was an inferno. Who wanted to listen? He didn't have authority, represented no government, had neither money nor power. He was nothing. Zero."

His reports on the Nazi "work camps" in Poland are frankly disbelieved. They catch the eye of a British special-operations chief, Colin Gubbins, who argues that the Nazis can be undermined by irregular armies sustained from America, at that time still neutral. The American who subscribes to this view is General Quex Massey.

Quex is helping carry out President Roosevelt's secret instructions to give all support possible to the British, despite U.S. neutrality at this early stage in the war. Radzki is turned over to Quex in the greatest secrecy.

President Roosevelt's man, dressed anonymously in a British austerity suit, is to walk Radzki through the Soho district of London during the blackout. Each goes under a false name. If, after hearing Radzki's story, Quex concludes it is accurate, he will desert the maze of Soho streets and go to Oxford Circus, where a special-branch escort waits to take Radzki back to his lodgings. If Quex judges otherwise, he will direct their footsteps to Marble Arch, where counterintelligence can tuck him away with other "deemed suspect" Jewish refugees.

Quex first sees Radzki in the pencil beam of a policeman's lantern hooded for the blackout. The refugee looks like a starving anarchist. He is unshaven, thin as a rake, clothed in a moth-eaten sweater, cotton trousers and clumsy boots. Once they begin their strange journey on foot, Radzki betrays a military bearing. Despite a bad limp, he marches through the alleys and says what he has to say with precision.

Quex himself will soon help wield the greatest secret power in history. President Roosevelt has confidentially advised Churchill against the temptation to strike a deal with Deputy Fuehrer Hess, whose mission is already rumored around Washington to be a peace overture. "Hang on," the American President signals Churchill. "We'll soon be fighting at your side."

With so much on Quex's mind, he still finds something pretty impressive about Radzki. They strike into the jungle of Soho. Streetwalkers, wearing white rubber boots or raincoats to make themselves conspicuous in the blackout, pluck at Radzki's arms and once almost succeed in hauling poor Quex into a courtyard resonant with the murmurs of hasty copulation. This matches the obscenity of what Radzki is describing. He says nobody who has not lived inside the Third Reich can understand the sheer impossibility of committing to paper the information he has gathered on the Nazi camps. Instead, he is preparing "an index," a guide to the reports and drawings he has made from memory since reaching London.

"Why not hand the reports over to the authorities?" Quex asks.

Radzki stops and looks up into a sky lit by the first glare of incendiary fires. "When I get written guarantees that the Allies will bomb those camps," he says, "I might consider it. Otherwise, the index and the reports will be concealed until I return."

"Return from where?"

"From wherever else I must go to get help."

"Your best help is here."

"I wonder," says Radzki. "Hitler believes he has support here, just as he has it in other parts of Europe, for his extermination plans."

"You're a victim of Nazi propaganda."

"No!" Radzki gives Quex a wild, strange look. "The camps could be bombed now, but they are not. Even the inmates have pleaded for this. One bomb on one camp would be enough to stop Hitler. The monster is so ashamed and frightened, even he will not directly order the exterminations. A small but firm sign from here would make him hesitate. Just one week of hesitation would mean the postponement of thousands of executions."

The bombing grows closer. Buildings shake. Radzki refuses to take shelter. He feels safer aboveground. So they keep walking, deaf to shouted warnings, though the fires blaze more fiercely than before. Near Hyde Park, Quex makes a small detour to let Radzki see the girls in uniform who manage the elephantine barrage balloons, beside the artillerymen at the ack-ack guns. He wants the refugee to drop the notion that Hitler could strike a deal with such a people. But Radzki will not yield on his point, that Hitler certainly believes the final solution could have secret approval in London.

Apart from this fixation, Radzki is persuasive. Quex has no doubts about the man's intelligence and courage: it's now a question of coaxing Radzki to return to Nazi-held territories as an Allied courier. So far as Radzki's account of anti-Jewish actions goes, Quex is like so many Americans who cannot believe such a systematic slaughter possible. So while Radzki continues to plead the Jewish case, Quex is quietly assessing his value to special operations.

At this point in the narrative, Talbott had to stop Jake Cooke and ask: "What's your source?"

"Quex wrote it up for our archives," said Jake.

Sally noisily scraped her stool to remind them of her presence. "Grandpa needed the help of archivists at the Yad Vashem, so I went over to Jerusalem for him with the material they wanted there."

"So you knew all this?" There was more than reproof in Talbott's astonished question.

"Yes and no," said Sally. "When I was helping Grandpa Massey, maybe three years ago, I wasn't terribly clued in about your particular war. You lived through it. I didn't. So I'd no way of appreciating the value of the odd bits and pieces I collected." She glanced helplessly at Jake. "And all this material was part of a quid pro quo. I didn't have the right of disclosure to anyone else. It was confidential. Between Jake and my grandfather."

Talbott swung back on Jake. "Why didn't Churchill's own experts interrogate Radzki?"

"Some did. But I told you already, even Churchill didn't trust their judgment altogether, as we've since found out." Jake saw the expression of skepticism on Talbott's face and pulled over one of the files before him on the coffee table. "Here's what one Israel Prime Minister said, for the record . . .

"A few years ago, the British Government decided to shorten the period of secrecy. At the beginning of 1972 the minutes of cabinet meetings in the early 1940s were made public. Now we know.

"The International Red Cross had planned, according to one of these documents, to transfer 40,000 Jews from Hungary to Turkey to continue on to Eretz Israel . . . Another 400,000 Jews were sent to the gas chambers, be-

*cause Britain opposed their transfer lest they come to the Land of Israel . . .
Another document revealed . . . 'the British foreign office is concerned with
the difficulties of disposing of a considerable number of Jews, should they be
rescued . . .'*

*"An entire nation, six million men, women and children, sank into an
abyss, in a planned campaign of annihilation, which lasted five whole years,
because the Germans decided to destroy it, and the British decided not to
rescue it."*

That was strong stuff. It came from Menachem Begin, a Prime Minister
who had been in office during Israel's worst trials, when it needed all the
friends it could get, including the British. Talbott could find no adequate
response, and Jake took his silence to mean that he should continue:

Churchill is outraged when he hears that Jewish leaders still alive in
Europe wonder if they are being deliberately sacrificed. He doesn't know
reports such as Radzki's are held back from him. Whatever Quex did to
enlighten the political leaders is soon overshadowed by Pearl Harbor and
America's entry into the war. With so much to do, Quex does not again
confront the Jewish situation. He is in Washington when the Hebrew Liberation Committee makes yet another appeal. It quotes Roosevelt: the
United States will retaliate if Nazi Germany uses poison gas against human
beings. The Hebrew Liberation Committee writes: "Since hundreds of
thousands of Hebrew people are being asphyxiated through the use of
poison gas, we ask that unless the German gassing cease forthwith, retalia-
tion be ordered immediately to impress upon Germany that Hebrews are
also considered to be human beings . . .."

To this, there is no response from the U.S. Joint Chiefs of Staff. Quex
cables Churchill: THE HEBREW LIBERATION COMMITTEE CONCLUDES THAT
THE ALLIES DON'T COUNT JEWS AS HUMAN BEINGS WITHIN THE MEANING OF
ROOSEVELT'S WARNING.

Churchill demands to see all the relevant secret files. He thinks an anti-
Semitic cast of mind in his foreign office and its chief organ of perception,
the Secret Service, might be at work. He lets it be known he is signaling
President Roosevelt that if the Allies emerge victorious, "the creation of a
great Jewish state in Palestine with millions of Jewish inhabitants will be
one of the leading features of peace-conference discussion . . . We cannot
agree to the pro-Arab solutions which are the commonplace of the British
Armed Forces."

Churchill is resisted by his own bureaucrats, whose secret memos are to
be kept from public scrutiny for a further thirty years. But Quex glimpses
a sampling. "Jews have done nothing but add to our difficulties since the
war began," writes a British Foreign Office man, J. S. Bennett, "with their
unscrupulous Zionist sob-stuff and misrepresentation." A deputy Colonial
Office under secretary, Sir John Shuckburgh, reports, "In their hearts the
Jews hate us at a time we're fighting for our very existence."

There is a lot more in the same vein. "Palestine colors the views of the British advisers excessively," notes Churchill, and later the words would be made public. "Palestine seems critical to them because the Middle East seems crucial to our survival, and they think we'll lose the Middle East if we lose Palestine to the Jews. I'm all for the Zionist plan for a Jewish homeland in Palestine, but first we have to make sure there are Jews left to go there."

Sometimes, Quex glimpses an appeal from groups of Jewish resisters begging for arms drops. Then the mystery revives in his mind. Is there *nobody* to speak for the Jews in Allied war councils? Every other group of Nazi victims has a voice.

One message that gets through from the Warsaw ghetto is a declaration of Jewish readiness to fight. It again pleads for weapons of any sort. Quex is now up to his ears in subversion, sabotage, armed resistance and espionage against the Axis powers all over the world. The plight of the Jews is something that nags, but further and further back in his mind.

There is an increasingly urgent need, though, to think ahead to when Europe will be liberated. In London are gathered all the exile governments whose followers in Nazi-held territory can contribute to behind-the-lines operations. Quex thinks that surely the Jews, of all people, will provide the best anti-Nazi resistance. He goes to Polish underground headquarters at 18 Kensington Palace Gardens. The Prime Minister-in-exile is Stanislaus Mikolajczyk, a squat peasant, self-educated, industrious, and stubborn.

Quex mentions Radzki and the Pole says, "We have to protect such men. They lead dangerous lives."

"You mean he's back inside Europe?" asks Quex.

"Didn't Special Branch here tell you?"

"No, they didn't tell me!" says Quex. "That means he gave them the slip. I'm glad. I'd hate to see him caught by the Nazis because the god-damn paper pushers made him fill up their blasted forms, damn their bureaucratic little souls!"

This outburst delights Mikolajczyk, who hates officialdom. "Come to my home," he says. "We can talk more freely there."

In his flat on the Bayswater Road, the Polish Prime Minister is still more frank. He is surrounded by broken furniture, the windows are boarded up against bomb blast. He says, "We've got to convince you Americans we fight effectively. Otherwise, support will go to Stalin's stooges. Here, already, too many officials are ready to believe only the Communist underground kills Nazis. And some are ready to help Stalin take all Poland."

He pours Quex some vodka. "The best," he says. "Vodka from Poland. Courtesy of Radzki. He'll be back soon, if you wish to see him."

How can Radzki travel back and forth so freely?

"He's a natural for underground work." Mikolajczyk's blue eyes sparkle. "The British have him under some other name, totally divorced from his past. He was a radical student, before the war, a real troublemaker. It's proving good training for blowing up Fascists."

But why, Quex wants to know, did he run the terrible risk of coming so often to London? Why not use the secret transmitters now supplied in abundance to the burgeoning secret armies of Europe?

"He brings out drawings, even photographs and eyewitnesses," says Mikolajczyk. "He goes back with reports to boost morale in the resistance."

"So London believes him?"

"Oh, no," replies the exiled Polish leader. "His reports never reach the top. But we keep trying."

Perhaps he sees skepticism in Quex's eyes. He says, "My dear friend, here is an example. On his last journey, Radzki got back into Auschwitz— you must know the camp has its own underground among the working prisoners? He brought back pictures of the execution centers, of bodies piled high for the crematoria, and signed appeals from Jewish inmates. I happen to know none of this has been forwarded beyond British Foreign Office intelligence.

"And this business of the ghetto. There will be a Warsaw uprising, rest assured. But the Jewish Fighting Organisation will receive only a token drop of arms."

Mikolajczyk rummages under his kitchen chair and pulls out a battered suitcase. From this he takes out some papers, and skims one across the floor to where Quex sits on a folded army blanket with his back to the peeling wall. "That," says the Prime Minister, "is a telegram from myself to the leaders of the Polish Home Army in Warsaw."

Quex reads: "The British Staff express readiness to bomb Auschwitz . . . We would like to combine this with a mass liberation of inmates from Auschwitz. Your extensive cooperation is necessary to liberate them immediately after the raid . . . The operation is scheduled for . . . the longest night."

But the raid has never taken place.

"There was every intention to launch that and several subsequent raids," says Mikolajczyk. "Somebody at some high level put a stop to them."

If Radzki, a Jew, knows about these betrayals—no other word will do— why does he keep going? He must be driven by a fanatical faith. "Is he— ah—?" Quex begins, blows out his cheeks, and falls silent.

"A Communist?" Mikolajczyk laughs. "Maybe. All we know is what he tells us. He speaks fluent German with a Prussian accent. He knows his way round Europe. He could have served as a Comintern agent before the war. My opinion is, his experience in recent times has turned him back to his roots, to his Jewish beliefs. Why don't you study him again?"

"Can you arrange another meeting?" asks Quex. "But without going through official channels?"

"But of course," says the exiled Polish Prime Minister, who understands exactly what Quex is thinking.

Quex sees Radzki the next time because U.S. bomber forces are looking for ways to coordinate their daylight raids with the RAF's heavy night-bombing. There are arguments about which methods are most effective, and on-the-spot verification is needed to reinforce the claims made by analysts with their own particular axes to grind. It occurs to Quex that Radzki should be given a chance to ask, as well as to give. In exchange for target information brought out by Radzki and other brave couriers, it seems fair to let him put before the bomber chiefs the plea to bomb the camps.

There is little interest shown by Quex's American colleagues. Churchill, however, can get pretty much anything he wants out of his own people. He's fond of Quex, respects what the American has done for England, and cannot refuse one of Quex's rare requests. Churchill is too well protected by his own intelligence aides for Radzki ever to see him, but Churchill does arrange that Radzki be taken to talk directly with the air marshal directing RAF Bomber Command's mounting attacks on Germany. Quex has several pressing reasons for renewing his friendship with the air marshal, "Bomber" Harris, especially because the U.S. air forces now have their own ULTRA officers drawing on the intelligence derived from the systematic decoding of German communications. So he grabs the chance to take Radzki into the Buckinghamshire countryside where Harris has his headquarters. They travel in a limousine driven by one of Churchill's own staff, for security reasons.

Radzki has not changed much. The terrible risks he runs, of course, mark his face; but even to see the legendary Harris, he wears the same kind of ill-fitting clothes as at the first meeting with Quex.

"Is it true they call this Marshal Harris 'Butcher' because of the way he squanders airmen?" he asks.

"I wouldn't advise you to call him that," Quex cautions. "But that's what the aircrews call him when they're aloft and can't be heard."

"He shouldn't mind wasting a few of his bombers on Jews, then," says Radzki.

Air Marshal Harris receives them in Springfield House, a modest home within bicycling distance of the High Wycombe nerve center where he studies target intelligence, assigns that night's German city to be bombed, and sends out the orders to his squadrons now embarking upon a program to systematically destroy German factories and houses, block by block.

He is a gruff little man with a bulldog stance. It soon becomes obvious that Harris is seeing Radzki only because Churchill requests it. Still, Harris is also in Quex's debt. The RAF chief had been on a mission to Washington when arrested for reckless driving late at night. Quex, on the same mission, discreetly fixed things, then asked the police officer why on earth he'd clapped this important foreigner into the hoosegow.

"I started out warning him he could've killed someone," said the cop. "Then he said, 'Young man, back in England, I kill thousands every night.' I kinda figured then he needed cooling out."

Harris's manner to Radzki is cool. The first of his bomber streams roars low overhead when Harris sits down with his guests to an early dinner. "I've got seven thousand lads up there tonight," he tells Quex. "All heading for Berlin."

The bombers are so heavily loaded, their engines seem to scream across the peaceful English countryside as they claw for altitude. It has been a perfect spring day. Driving out, Quex has been touched by the winding lanes, with heavily scented hedgerows and trees bursting into bloom, blessed by the murmur of evensong from the ancient Norman churches. But he knows Radzki is oblivious to this and thinks only about the strange fact that here he is at the heart of the greatest concentration of air power in the history of the world and unable to get even a single small bomb for humanitarian use. A month earlier, he'd been near Auschwitz, trying to explain why neither the camps nor the railroads serving them had been bombed yet.

Harris usually catnaps after an early supper. The emergency phones are near his cot in the hall. When his bombers reach their target, he starts work again. This time, a phone rings before they have finished eating. Harris disappears. When he comes back, he seems elated. It turns out later that his so-called "4,000 Plan," to mass that number of bombers over a single city within a brief span of time, has been approved. He says, "Quex, come see what we're doing over there," and makes a gesture that encompasses Radzki.

Harris, once in his study, his "Conversation Chamber," makes Radzki peer into the stereopticon, where images of shattered German cities spring to life. "This," says the bomber chief, "is how we'll win the war. Not by wasting planes on secondary targets." An obvious reference to Radzki's mission, it shows that Harris has been secretly briefed.

"My plan," Harris goes on, "is to de-house all civilians within minutes by bringing over the selected city a concentration of thousands of bombers from all directions." He explains the complexity of guiding such a vast strike force through hostile skies to arrive together at a distant point. "No place is safe," Harris boasts. "German morale will break."

Radzki says, "You can't bomb a nation back into the Stone Age. But you can put a stop to that nation's attempt to destroy another nation by mass murder. If nothing is done, my people will cease to exist in two years."

"In two years we'll have won the war," growls Harris. "That is the way to save lives."

"By bombing open cities?" demands Radzki.

Harris turns in the doorway to his study. "Civilian morale is a legitimate target," he says. "More to the point, what information can you give my Target Intelligence officers?"

"In every death camp there is a well-organized underground. We smuggle out precise details as to location of the gassing and burning chambers, the worker-slave quarters . . ."

"That's not target information," replies Harris.

Radzki ignores the interruption. "The exact plans can be provided of torture cells, theaters for surgical experiments, the warehousing of wedding rings, children's crutches, human hair."

Harris asks Quex if he cares for some brandy.

"The railroads," Radzki persists, "carry cattle wagons packed with human prisoners. They work as slaves until they are killed. The German economy needs those slaves. The Nazi munition makers would lose half their manpower if you destroyed those railroads."

"It's impossible to disrupt rail traffic by bombing," Harris intones. Later, he will write that his bombers made the D-day invasion possible by disrupting railroads carrying German troops to meet the invaders.

"You've bombed prisoner-of-war camps," Radzki says, "with less information than is being offered by me."

"And killed our own prisoners."

"Some. But you gained the release of secret army leaders. And killed their torturers."

"Those raids were based on military orders."

"If the concentration camps were bombed, and the survivors armed from the air, they could become centers of resistance, and tie down German troops."

"A Jewish resistance?" scoffs Harris. "There's none now. Why should there be one then?"

Now it's out in the open! Radzki stays calm. He says, "Jews, sir, fight where they are given the chance."

"And who do they fight for?" Harris demands. "Zionism? Bolshevism? Or the right to open black markets *outside* our cities after they're blitzed?"

Still Radzki keeps his self-control. "Jews fight *when they can* for humanity. For mercy. Love. Things of the spirit."

Harris's eyes glaze over. "I am able to burn Berlin end from end." The bomber chief stands aside, indicating Radzki may leave. "It will cost me a few hundred aircraft, but it will cost Germany the war."

"Have you considered what it will cost my people?" inquires Radzki.

Quex is not surprised later when Radzki, in a last, brief encounter, tells him, "I shall deal with men of power one day again. And they will listen. They will go down on their knees to listen. Because the next time, I shall have greater power than all of them combined."

It seems an idle threat. A solitary Jew cannot be heard. The sixty-three days of the Warsaw Uprising merit one small paragraph in the London press.

When Quex hears Radzki has killed himself, he's absentmindedly sorry. He doesn't even inform himself on the reasons why. Radzki's wife and children had been in the Warsaw Ghetto when Jews fought almost bare-handed against Nazi storm troopers. The official Jewish Fighting Organisation, after repeated appeals by radio, received one light machine gun, ten rifles and ninety pistols. That was their total allotment out of the twenty thousand weapons dropped to partisans in Warsaw by Western bombers. "The world of freedom and justice," the ghetto transmitter protested in its dying broadcast, "is silent and does nothing."

The episode passes Quex by. The rush of great events is sweeping him into preparations for victory. Soon he altogether forgets the refugee whose identity fades into the blur of so many code names.

Jake Cooke told the story well. He raised no objections when Sally and Talbott said they needed some air. The two Americans stood outside the No-Man's-Land Tuckshop. Night had fallen. Sally said, "My grandfather seems to have known a lot more than he's admitted. Do you suppose all his talk about a massive, tragic intelligence failure is cover for something deeper?" She studied the reflections of light in the muddy water at her feet. "It's funny he never reacted to Radzki's name when I noted it from the Jerusalem files."

"Even I'd forgotten it," said Talbott. "And I was closer to Radzki for longer."

"You've been sucked into something unspeakable," Sally burst out. "You know more about Radzki than anyone. If Grandpa Massey isn't pulling the strings, who is?"

But Talbott was off on another tack. "If Radzki came the first time to England on the same day Hess flew here, they could have come together."

"In a single-seat fighter?" She shook her head. "I'd like to forget Hess and worry about you."

"Don't dismiss Hess. He's just given us the bargaining chips."

"For what?"

"Scooping the world. And turning the historians on their heads." The words sounded more like the Scott Talbott of popular legend. "That's our bread and butter. A goddam big scoop!" But his voice was flat and regretful.

"You seem depressed by the prospect."

"It's one story I'd rather not break."

Sally pondered. "Secret armies were raised among the French, Danes, Dutch, Belgians, Czechs, Yugoslavs, Norwegians . . . even German rebels . . . Only the Jews were deemed suspect and detained here under DORA—"

"Dora?"

"Defense of the Realm Act," explained Sally. "I remember something else from the Jerusalem archives . . . written after the Jewish Fighting

Organisation was wiped out in Warsaw . . . You know, a courier did commit suicide. Here. In London." She stared into the black night. "The man's family had died in the Warsaw battle. He left a note before hanging himself. He'd been a deputy with the Polish National Council in exile. His note went along these lines: . . . 'The responsibility for this crime, this assassination of the Jewish people in Poland, falls indirectly on the Allies, who failed to help or intervene. I could not die with my family, nor with my betrayed people, but I belong in their common grave. Let my death become a cry of protest against the world's indifference.' You see?" Sally faced Talbott. "There was a famous suicide. Radzki must have used that tragedy in some way to cover his own disappearance."

"There are lots of ways to commit suicide," said Talbott. "You can hang yourself. Or you can spend the rest of your life strangling your personal feelings. The second kind of suicide frees you to serve an idea, a dogma, an obsession."

"He hanged himself symbolically?"

"Physical suicide at the time would be a terrible waste."

"You sound," said Sally, "as if you'd been there."

Talbott was looking directly down at the small puddle of rainwater as if he'd seen someone new in that oily mirror. "Perhaps," he said.

His tone startled her. His face, a white oval, seemed in the faint light to be as vulnerable as a schoolboy's. Something warned her to stay silent.

After a while, he said, "Suppose all those sacrifices were in vain? Suppose we were betrayed? When I was a boy, we knew war was coming. We knew why. We knew what was happening in Europe. We knew something had to be done to save the weak and helpless. There's been such a hell of a lot of brainwashing since, everyone's convinced we knew nothing about Hitler's extermination plans. Christ!

"Even I forgot just what it was like until I came back here. We'd walk home from school talking about what was bound to happen. The kids in my class all knew we'd have to do the fighting. It put an end to our dreams. It makes me goddam angry to think Radzki didn't understand that about us, and Jake evidently still doesn't . . ."

"Historians," said Sally, "now say the programs of extermination were 'a terrible secret' concealed from the public."

"It wasn't concealed where I came from," exploded Talbott. "I not only delivered newspapers, I read them. Three whole years before America came into the war, a year before it began in Europe, the old German Kaiser wrote one of his relatives, the Queen Mother in England, that he was for the first time in his life ashamed to be German. How'd I know that? Like ordinary people, I could read it in the papers, dammit!" He faced the stuttering light over what had once been Scroggins, Newsagent. "The London *Times* reported plans for a Nazi extermination center as early as 1939. It was before the first wartime Christmas. My mother said it was ironic, to get the news in the middle of the Jewish holidays. She got me to scrounge a copy of the *Times* from Scroggins. There was a map showing this special 'area of concentration,' and a report from Poland of a Nazi death camp."

Talbott continued after a pause: "It was the general opinion among the kids in this neighborhood that if the world was so bloody awful, the least you could do was take a couple of Nazis with you on the way out."

"You talked about suicide?" Sally sounded shocked.

"Boys don't voice these things. But boys before they're ready to shoulder arms are generally sensitive, romantic, often tragic. Radzki should have known."

As if the name was a cue, Jake appeared in the doorway. "Radzki," he called out to Talbott. "Want to see a photograph of Radzki?"

Damn Jake! thought Sally. Another twist of the knife!

But Talbott was eager now to resume the game. He was like a compulsive poker player, desperate to see what new hand Jake would deal him. Under the eerie blue light, he gazed at a black-and-white print, badly worn.

"You recognize him?" asked Jake.

"I think so. I'm not sure. Perhaps it's Radzki."

"Perhaps? Maybe? It is him, isn't it!" Jake challenged.

Sally held her breath. Yesterday, Talbott would have pounced on anyone who talked that way to him. Now he seemed lost in a daze.

"He was photographed," Jake persisted, "just before the Russians reached Berlin in 1945."

"Radzki was officially dead by then," said Talbott. He returned the picture. "This man looks different."

"He looks different because this time he was *needed.*" Jake shoved the door so savagely that Scroggins' bell jangled madly. "He wasn't begging for help, see? He wasn't coming cap in hand. The generals this time had to listen—"

"How to bomb Spandau!" Talbott said suddenly. "Oh, Christ!"

Jake let him stumble back into the building, and then he said, "You remember the briefing? You were among the pilots, trained in precision work. You were to hit the jail, break out certain inmates."

"German anti-Nazis." Talbott guessed it all now.

"For a bunch of turncoat Germans, they let you fly such a mission." Jake smiled bitterly. "But not for Jews."

Talbott went to bed early. He had no need to excuse himself. The bedding was already made up on the floor, and Jake took Sally to forage in the kitchen.

When Talbott was alone, he stared into the darkness, seeing the passport-size portrait again. It was the face of a man who'd been introduced to the flying crews as a resistance fighter. His face was in shadow, but now, in retrospect, Talbott felt he must have sensed or seen eyes blazing with a fanatical resolve. The agent had spoken with forceful authority, standing outside the fierce illumination beamed upon the target models. Everything had to be memorized. The man spoke from memory. It was a prodigious feat. He seemed like a superman to the kids who diced daily with death in clean blue skies.

He must have hated us. The sudden certainty struck Talbott like a whip-crack. That was why he had never for one second connected hangdog "Uncle Samuel," who lived for a time at home and then was reported dead, with the man who briefed them on Spandau and who radiated, not courage, but hate. Who could blame him? He had asked for airmen to deliver his people from German slaughter. Now he was called upon to instruct those airmen instead on how to liberate Germans from Spandau, where there were no Jews.

Radzki, thought Talbott, must have committed a spiritual suicide, killing in himself the love and the mercy, the things of the spirit, which he had once seen as the complete justification for a Jewish state. He had said his people would fight for those values, given the chance. They'd not been given the chance and most were dead.

Radzki loves only the dead. Talbott put the sentence into the present tense without conscious thought, as if Radzki still lived.

All night, at regular intervals, Talbott was shaken by violent tremors. He kept seeing a reborn Radzki, his back no longer stooped, his face alive with power.

21

The monster face loomed out of the London gloom, fangs bared.

Peled "Steely" Pamir, founder of what he privately considered the world's best tactical air force, sprang back in mock horror.

"Penny fer the Guy, Mister?" The ancient appeal came from a small boy pushing the scarecrow in a creaking perambulator.

"Okay, sonny," Commander Nelson intervened, tossing a coin into the urchin's upturned cap. "Now then, 'opit!" He turned to his companion. "Welcome to Guy Fawkes, General!"

"Mad!" groaned the Israeli. "Mad dogs and Englishmen. Who else makes effigies of their enemies?"

"We generally make them prime ministers," grunted Nelson. "Gandhi in India, Kenyatta in Africa . . ."

Like two grumpy old gentlemen repairing to their club for a bracer before lunch, the pair resumed their stroll along Piccadilly. There was, however, a regular twitch of impatience in General Pamir's magnificent handlebar mustache, souvenir of his flying days in the wartime RAF before Israel was born. Like Nelson, he wore a crumpled business suit; but the black glove on his left hand hid another war-service souvenir: a steel claw.

"So what's the griff?" he asked when they had turned into the relative peace of Green Park.

"The 88 want three hours' live transmission, globally, of the Hess Command." Nelson spoke calmly, as if reporting the weather. "They sound crazy but they're moving to a precise schedule. Scattered acts of terror first, then attention focused on one or two prominent targets. A flurry of alerts to selected editors. Planted rumors. 'Insider' stuff on the Hess Command. They're plugged into the local grapevine now with fresh gossip."

"What kind of gossip?" Pamir asked sharply.

"About a blockbuster operation. It's all over the docklands." Nelson paused, yawned, looked longingly at a park bench. "It's been a long night." He had visited all the usual criminal haunts, and at dawn surveyed the wasteland where Sally and Talbott were thought to be. Then he had boarded the London Underground at Whitechapel. Now, eight stations and one change later, he was gasping for a mug of tea.

Steely Pamir sympathized. Before Nelson's fall from grace, he would have taken him to the Israeli embassy, in Kensington. Now Pamir could only utter an encouraging "Yes?" and try not to be too offensive in his tearing great hurry.

"Action Remembrance, that's what they call it." Nelson reluctantly plodded on. "I talked with all my old mates. Coppers' narks. Glib con merchants. Even with old Johnnie Quick—remember how we sprang the safecracker from jail to be dropped behind the lines? None of 'em want London taken over by *foreigners.*"

Anyone was a foreigner who resorted to guns in that underworld where both sides still kept respect for Nelson of the Yard. The woolgatherers of C13 discreetly helped Nelson: they were the antiterrorist branch, where he kept an office though he lacked the formal authority even to order paper clips. The woolgatherers were an immense resource. They moved expertly through the staging areas of terrorism, weaving their patterns.

"They know something's planned," Nelson said wearily. "They say Jake Cooke's a diversion."

It was then Pamir asked a strange question. "Have you seen this Jacob Cooke with your own eyes?" He asked it very casually.

Nelson noted the emphasis on *this,* as if another Jake Cooke might exist. "I last saw him when he was a fugitive Zionist."

"Not more recently?"

"No, nor wish to. It'd be better all round if you'd get him out of here, him and his lads."

"I don't control him." Steely Pamir turned their footsteps back toward the roar of traffic. "Nobody does, right now."

Nelson drew his shaggy head back inside the upturned collar. "There's a danger our counterterror chaps might attack him. Then everyone would assume the danger's over. Leaving the 88 to get on with their plans."

"Can you do something? Unofficially? 'Desperate diseases demand desperate remedies.' "

Nelson's head shot out again. "You really do know your English history."

"I know Guy Fawkes said that to explain his gunpowder plot." Pamir led the way through a park gateway facing the Athenaeum Court Hotel. "I'm only quoting Guy now to enlist *your* help." He tugged Nelson's arm, plunged through a gap between double-deck buses, paused, then cut through more of the slow-moving traffic. "I've got Fishhook Sherman already," he yelled above the screeching brakes.

"Fishhook?" Nelson perched on the opposite curb with a small explosion of relief, a taxi missing his coattail by a whisker. "Between Fishhook and myself, you couldn't do better. Now, where's me cupper tea?"

The Athenaeum Court was the haunt of Israeli intelligence officers "declared" to the British. It provided a convenient rendezvous when meetings at the embassy might seem undiplomatic. Pamir kept a suite there. Since taking charge of Israel's official counterterror bureau, he spent increasing periods in London, the financial haven for bomb throwers.

A couple of young workmen on Pamir's floor nodded when the pair arrived, and disappeared into adjacent rooms. Inside the suite was an overalled plumber who did not take it amiss when Pamir told him to brew up some tea.

"Clean as a whistle," said Steely Pamir when they were alone. "The exterminators guarantee it. A thousand pounds for any bug we find."

"Make it dollars," Nelson said morosely. He had his hands around a steaming mug; his stockinged feet were up on the coffee table. "Anyway, you're the one who's talking."

Pamir gave a quick little nod. "Right," he said, and proceeded to deliver a briefing that was short and, to Nelson's ears, sweet. Retired from the Israeli Air Force, General Pamir held the diplomatic rank of minister at the London embassy. By a special arrangement, unwritten, he flew back and forth to Israel using his own Phantom jet, which he parked (unofficially) in the NATO corner of the nearest RAF fighter base. Pamir had a special dispensation to move goods and individuals in and out of England. All these informal arrangements depended upon an old-boy network that in turn required him to keep the goodwill of his British counterparts. His diplomatic immunity would not give him much protection if he lost that goodwill—say by interfering in a matter that, when it became known to the local authorities, would involve the touchy subject of sovereignty.

"When we went into Entebbe to rescue the hostages," said Pamir, "Israel's enemies screamed blue murder, said we'd trespassed and injured the territorial integrity of Uganda. We can't afford bad publicity like that. It's no good my going to the usual departments here, because I can't trust anyone, not so long as that mangy dog Marcus Furneval's free to piss in our soup."

Nelson found it ironic that Steely Pamir nevertheless put trust in him, Nelson, the suspected traitor. He listened while Pamir outlined his needs, and then he said, "Don't feel too badly about our bloody sovereignty, old son. All my life I've broken the law so we'd continue enjoying freedom under the law."

Later, Pamir stood in the window overlooking Piccadilly and watched Nelson stride out between the billowing Arab cloaks always sailing through central London and crowding every other luxury hotel. The Athenaeum Court seemed, like Israel, to be a tiny Jewish island in hostile seas.

But we mustn't live as if we've no friends left, thought General Pamir, holding back the curtain with his hook hand. That was the mistake made by Jacob Cooke, Irgun, the Stern Gang, and their descendants. Although who could blame them, when you considered that Commander Nelson down there was only one of many whose work for Israel had made them MISFIT targets? MISFIT was a weapon in the campaign to isolate Israel's supporters, discrediting the victim with a series of accusations. MISFIT was an acronym. You began with M for Money, and spread gossip that the target could be bought. If that didn't work, you went on to I for Intoxication and said he was drunk on the job. If *that* didn't work, S for Sex . . .

They hadn't ruined Nelson's reputation until they got to the very end: T for Traitor.

And still there'd been no formal charges made, only an internal investigation with results so inconclusive that Nelson stayed on the payroll, though neutered.

Pamir let the curtain fall. If he was wrong, then God help a lot of people. Still—desperate diseases demand desperate remedies. Guy Fawkes had said it four centuries ago, and England recalled it annually with gunpowder and bonfires. The cause had been Papist, the plot was against King and Parliament, but there was nothing wrong with the sentiment. Terrorism, thought General Peled Steely Pamir, is a scourge demanding desperate remedies. What London needs now is a match, a flame, a rocket and stars to illuminate the heavens and the minds of all good men.

22

"Guy Fawkes!" Talbott breathed the brisk air from the open doorway of the No-Man's-Land Tuckshop. He'd been here less than two days but already the time blurred into a past when he would have been making the "Guy" with newspapers stuffed into old clothes. And by tonight, there'd be such a whizzing and banging, such a scatter of stars as the rockets sizzled and soared while effigies perished on a thousand bonfires.

Sally saw how his mood had changed since the violent nightmares. She had watched him fall into a deep slumber at dawn, when the guards changed shift and men moved stealthily into the cellar below.

They went outside for greater privacy. There was a dusting of frost on the wasteland. Mist flaked off the river. Patches of wintry blue sky appeared directly overhead, though mist still clung to where the ground fell away to the river. There seemed not a soul in this world, but they could feel the unseen presence of Jake's men.

"When the weather turned crisp like this, old Scroggins would lock up shop," said Talbott. "He'd a great urge to chase the rabbits on Wanstead Flats. But on *this* day, he'd lock up so we couldn't pinch his papers to stuff our scarecrows. That's what he *said*. It turned out what he really did was take advantage of all the distraction and noise to hold his 'annual party meeting.' "

Sally had been forming a mental picture of Scroggins the shopkeeper. "Scroggins a Communist?" The idea shocked her.

"Well, he pushed the party's *Daily Worker*. I doubt if he got more than half a dozen half-baked intellectuals." Talbott halted. *"That's* what my mother meant."

He stumbled forward again. Sally told herself: He's here because he wants to be, not because Jake's forcing him. He's as patient as Jake, groping his way to some moment of dreadful enlightenment.

He had stopped once more and was staring into a square, brick-lined hole with weeds growing out of the sides and a natural garden of wildflowers and grass around a muddy pond at the bottom.

"Jimmy Boardman lived here," said Talbott. "When Jake made that crack about rescuing Germans before Jews, he forgot something."

"Jake forgets a lot of things," Sally said. "Sometimes he doesn't seem the Jake I knew at all."

But Talbott was completely lost now. "Boardman was killed on the Murmansk run. I should have been. Was it planned? Christ, it's madness to think like this." Talbott stopped speaking and drifted among the images.

Midshipman Scott Talbott sits in the cockpit of a Sea-Hurricane. The fighter is perched on a catapult rigged forward of the bows on a rusty freighter. The ship dips and rises. Here at the extremity of the catapult, the pilot freezes. The baby Woolworth carriers were bad enough. You had to land on ice-sheathed decks pitching and rolling through as much as forty degrees. This Catapult Aircraft Merchant ship, though, permits no return. Once launched from a CAM-ship, you jump or ditch. And death in these waters is quick.

He is defending vessels bringing supplies to Russia through a thousand miles of enemy-dominated waters. He has watched the ships go down, victims of U-boats and aircraft working out of Hammerfest, Narvik, Trondheim, Kirkenes . . . Norse names to fear. The Russians take the few shipments that get through as if they suspect a capitalist trick.

Talbott has been brooding here, on and off, through hours of the arctic "white night," waiting for German shadowing aircraft to fly within range. But the German pilots have learned to stay beyond the reach of the British suicide pilots. They are never called suicide pilots, of course. Everyone goes to great lengths to play down the danger. The Royal Navy has even issued a cheerful handbook by the medical director-general: "No great harm is likely to be suffered," it promises, "from a Brief Immersion." No sailor survives three minutes in those freezing waters, but "a pilot should find the risk acceptable if he adjusts his flying clothing to keep out the cold water . . ." Hence the briefing-room admonition, echoing the sign in London public lavatories: "Please adjust your clothing before you leave."

The control stick jerks between his hands. A deckhand is banging the aircraft elevator to get his attention. The German Focke-Wulfe FW-200's still hang over the horizon. Then Talbott sees the spread of Ju-88 torpedo bombers threading his way. He lifts a gauntleted hand to signal the freighter's captain, an old Merchant Navy mariner who has the customary disrespect for the pukka Royal Navy and a certain astonished sympathy for the pimply-faced schoolboy who has this sudden authority to make him change course. He swings the tramp into wind, and hopes it won't take long to punch the Hurricane into the air. Time out of convoy is time exposed to U-boats hungry for stragglers. "It's a bleeding expensive way to kill the poor, perishing little snotty," mutters the uneasy first mate. "Might as well toss the fucking sod over the side, stark bollock naked, and keep his marvelous flying machine for the sodding museum."

What *was* it all in aid of? Talbott wondered. Jake had taunted him: "Why didn't you bomb the death camps?" Did any of us have the right to weigh one sacrifice against another? We flew impossible missions to float tanks to Russia, because it seemed quicker to save the innocents of Europe by ending the war quickly. We covered many times the distance from England to Auschwitz. It wasn't as if we didn't know. But there were "operational necessities." Impossible choices. What kind of captain would willfully expose an entire ship's crew to submarine attack by pulling out of convoy to yank a pilot from the water? What bomber chief felt he could endanger a single aircrew to ground fire purely on a mercy mission?

Jimmy Boardman is launched from another freighter's catapult. He catches a pair of Ju-88s, sees them explode on the water, climbs after a Focke-Wulfe FW-200, pumps his shells methodically into the control cabin, killing the pilot. Standard tactics. Always go for the pilot.

Talbott is chasing more of the Ju-88s when he hears shouts break the R/T silence. Boardman is suddenly in a steep dive. A fighter-direction officer guesses Boardman's oxygen line has jerked loose, and against all regulations is shouting to try and bring Boardman back to full consciousness. Before Talbott can see if it works, he is jumped by two long-range Me-109s. Lead thuds into his instrument panel. The whole aircraft shudders. Pickled in salt after rotting on the catapult for days, it is no match for land-based fighters. He throws the Hurricane into a tight turn. The newest breed of Me-109 has poor radius of turn near sea level. Talbott tightens his own turn by putting down flap. His wingtip skims the waves. His windscreen is covered in oil and spray, but he sees he is banking inside the Germans. The lead Me-109 will fully extend his flaps, tighten his turn, and then throttle back to keep a bead on Talbott. It can't be done. The German is making the wrong moves to prevent himself overshooting his quarry. His first burst of fire shakes the Me-109 airframe just enough to fatally disturb the airflow. It goes into a high-speed stall and flips over. At that low altitude, there is no hope of a recovery.

Boardman regains consciousness in time to pull out of his dive. He sees the first Me-109's spectacular cartwheel. The second skids out in a flat turn, trying to get back onto Talbott's track. Boardman, with plenty of speed in hand, is perfectly placed. The Me-109 stops dead in the air, blossoms into flame, and disintegrates.

The two friends are low in fuel and ammunition. Talbott has no desire to ditch. The hump-backed Hurricane has a lethal habit, when striking the water, of tipping tail over nose, trapping the pilot in his cockpit under a topsy-turvied, sinking hull. So Talbott claws his way back to two thousand feet. Boardman has done the same. Before his eyes, Boardman's propeller stops turning. There are still enemy aircraft in the vicinity, and Talbott delays his own jump to cover his friend. He watches Boardman safely exit. He loosens his own safety harness, then sees with horror that another Me-109 has pounced on Boardman dangling helplessly under the huge silk canopy. Talbott rolls into a diving attack, too late to save Boardman, whose body is already riddled with bullets. The Me-109 has high-tailed it home.

Talbott shifts around in his bucket seat. He has ignored the fate of other crew members in the FW-200 crippled by Boardman. The FW-200 is burning. The crew has bailed out. Three are still in the air, their parachutes an easy target. Talbott goes for the closest German airman, balancing him at the center of his gyro-gunsight, not even obliged to make a curving approach and not required to allow for deflection, just flying straight at him, taking cold and careful aim, squeezing off no more shells than are absolutely required to kill the bastard. Later, he will offer excuses and reasons: there are U-boats waiting to pick up the airmen and learn what they've seen of the convoy's movements, and so on. The truth is, though, his only thought is revenge. He kills the second man with the same economy. The third hits the water and vanishes under the collapsing folds of his parachute as it is dragged under. Just to make sure, though, Talbott expends what little remains of his ammunition in a single pass, and then his own fuel runs out. He hits the water with one wing, which unexpectedly saves his life. The wing breaks off, the machine slews round and digs the remaining wing into a creaming wave. Talbott rattles around like a pea in a pod, his elbow banging through the emergency side panel. Somehow, he is freed of oxygen and radio lines. The machine begins sliding under the waves right side up. "I left her like a gentleman," he reports later. "My clothing was properly adjusted." He deserves a medal for not creating an operational necessity, because he lands in the path of an escorting frigate. The skipper has no tough choice to make. He scoops up the snotty on the run.

Talbott stood on what had once been Kitchener Grove and wondered what those two schoolboys, Midshipmen Boardman and Talbott, would make of him now, this man who lived through the television camera, who came alive when the red light blinked. This entertainer!

He'd learned early to dodge reality. Jimmy Boardman's nerve test. It taught you not to flinch before oncoming disagreeabilities. The old Seafire Syndrome of turning your head away from trouble. But the nerve test preceded that bad habit of his flying days. He remembered standing on this selfsame spot while Boardman with his school cap on the back of his head hurled a leather-bound cricket ball as close to Talbott's face as possible without hitting him. The boxing parson had asked what the devil they thought they were doing and Boardman said, "Please sir, it's a test of nerves, sir."

Talbott jerked his thoughts back to navy days. "A bloody war and a sickly season!" was the toast they drank at sea. The bravado fended off the ugly reality. It failed to do so now. He could not get rid of that picture of a small boy standing at attention. A leathery missile. Don't turn your head, but dodge the danger with your mind. Clamber out of the house where your mother has just died . . .

He heard Sally say something. Whatever thread had snagged itself on the unwilling fingers of memory was suddenly lost.

He must have been telling the Boardman story to Sally. He must have said something about guilt, because she was saying with that fierce intensity he was beginning to recognize, "But *they* did it to *you! They* machine-gunned Boardman after he'd bailed out!"

Talbott looked startled. "Yes," he said slowly. "But don't you understand? What matters is, *I* did it to *them.*"

He looked back into the hole where Boardman had once lived. What a betrayal it all seemed! Other schoolmates had been thrown into Bomber Harris's onslaught against Germany. He remembered something written by a member of RAF Bomber Command who later won fame in the United States as a physicist. Freeman Dyson. "The Command . . . invented by some mad sociologist . . . to exhibit . . . the evil aspects of science and technology . . . dedicated to burning cities and killing people, and doing the job badly . . . Harris was as indifferent to the slaughter of his own airmen as he was to the slaughter of German civilians . . . Secrecy pervading, not so much directed against the enemy as against the failures and the falsehoods of the Command becoming known to London . . ." Secrecy to conceal mistakes at home. Self-protective secrecy to cover up shameful deeds.

And Samuel Radzki had had to plead with Harris! One insignificant refugee without visible authority having to negotiate . . . of course he was doomed to failure. The overheard conversations between Radzki and Talbott's mother began to make sense, and so did some of her last words.

"Give me your courage!" she had said, struggling to remain conscious under the bomb rubble, desperate to give Talbott the message from Radzki.

And Talbott had forsaken whatever courage he'd had, and set out to forget everything.

He heard Sally beside him say, "Blame the old men who loaded children with such responsibilities! You grew up *after* the war ended. Of course you put it behind you."

But Talbott stopped listening to her again, and turned his attention to the shallow crater that was the Boardman family tomb, decorated with Blitz-weeds in place of flowers. After that catastrophic convoy to Murmansk, he had returned here to tell the family. He'd thought of the Earl of Northumberland, on learning his son was killed in battle: "Why, then, God's soldier be he! Had I as many sons as I have hairs, I would not wish them to a fairer death . . . They say he parted well and paid his score."

But the parents were themselves killed by the bombing, and Jimmy's sister was shell-shocked. Her hair, once black, had turned completely white.

He looked into the lake of muddy rainwater and imagined Jimmy's white bones gleaming between the ribs and stringers of his rotted aircraft. The Jews were denied Boardman's and Northumberland's solace, that a man died well if the wounds were in his breast and not his back. Jews were denied the choice. "You talk of courage and resistance," Radzki had once said. "You think of courage as a resistance, armed by air drops, trained by agents. In the concentration camps, resistance is a modest matter. If a scrap of food is smuggled to a dying child, *that* is resistance. Courage is passing along a fragment of outside news, substituting a broken woman for a dead patient in the camp hospital, saving some possession from the camp guards robbing the condemned . . ."

What a coward I proved, thought Talbott. "Give me your courage," pleaded Rebecca. And all I did was retreat from one moral position to another until I had no moral position at all. Boardman, myself, we *were* idealists. We wouldn't kill innocent civilians, we said when we were schoolboys, foreseeing the war. We wouldn't fly bombers. Then came the time we had to protect unarmed ships. When we saw them torpedoed, we did the same to the enemy . . . German rescue planes? We shot them down despite the hospital markings. We would argue that otherwise their rescued airmen might fly and fight again. Soon it doesn't matter who you are killing.

Rebecca doesn't know all this when she begs God for her son's courage. She needs all her strength now to whisper one final, urgent message. "His papers," she tells Talbott. "Written in his own hand. With Scroggins. Among the *Daily Workers.*" And then a bulky figure comes wheezing through the tunnel Talbott has dug to reach her side. Black Mac? Snuffling and grunting prayers beside Rebecca and . . . *then insisting on consolation—not religious, though that is there too—but the consolation and the blessing of morphine.*

Talbott almost jumped with the shock of recognition. The last rites of a killing overdose! The scene was vivid, as if he had discovered a color slide long lost and quite forgotten. There had been only one Black Mac. One man always present when Talbott was up for new flying duties. One man who knew the convoys, the later raids in support of covert actions. One man who remembered Boardman's "nerve test."

One man who clearly knew nothing, though, about the secret conceal-ment of Radzki's papers. What Rebecca had confided with her dying breath to Talbott was passed on to nobody else.

Talbott was half running. He had forgotten Sally, forgotten caution. Scroggins had always kept the controversial *Daily Worker*s hidden in his basement. "One copy for history," he'd say optimistically. And being an orderly if eccentric man, he would have kept them in dated order.

Dated order? As Talbott banged through the shop door, he made a rapid calculation. *The Daily Worker* had been banned in January 1941, when British Communists were still agitating against the war that rained bombs on their own homes. He pulled up short. He'd been so sure of discovering the final clue somewhere in the old *Daily Worker*s. But if publication had been suspended . . . ?

Suddenly Jake was confronting him. "Down with you, quick!" The Is-raeli pointed to the cellar.

Footsteps thudded from the back of the building. Two guards fell in step beside Talbott and Sally.

A beam of light washed over the front of the No-Man's-Land Tuckshop. Talbott heard the grinding of gears and clipped masculine accents. His last thought was that all of them were fugitives now.

Part III

The Radzki Secret

"For quite six years the English admirers of Hitler contrived not to learn
of the existence of Dachau and Buchenwald . . ."

GEORGE ORWELL, May 1945, *Notes on Nationalism*

23

The call from General Pamir for Rinna Dystel came over the secured
telecom system where Rinna's men were bivouacked in Fishhook Sherman's house.

She returned to the library, her face a mask, her body trembling. Luckily, Quex was absorbed in watching the screen set up near the french
windows. She sat beside his wheelchair and tried to concentrate again on
what was being said.

"It's brilliantly faked," Sol Farkas continued. "As the expert in deception, Rinna, you'll appreciate this . . . ."

Rinna felt Quex's eyes upon her. He squeezed her hand. "Anything
wrong?"

"Just a routine problem . . ." she lied.

"This so-called Hess Command documentary," said Sol Farkas, "would
have been a logistical nightmare to produce. The cinematic trickery is the
stock-in-trade of a very small handful of cinematographers.

"The producers had to get authentic newsreels. Here, for instance, you
see American officers seemingly observing Hitler's invasion of Russia. The
illusion's done by superimposing new images with optical devices called
mattes." Sol waited for several changes of shot on screen. "Here, newly
shot film's mixed with vintage stock. The illusionists mimick the old news-

reels by putting the new footage through chemical baths. Sometimes they film new shots through lenses from the wartime era—not easily found, but essential to give the proper 'feel.' These close-ups of an American general with Nazi camp commanders at Buchenwald is really an old American newsreel superimposed on captured German footage."

Sol stopped the copy he had videotaped of the Hess Command film.

"Can't this trickery be exposed?" asked Quex.

"Not quickly enough," said Sol, with the confidence of his own experts to back him. "The 88 will exploit the first impact when it's televised—"

"*If* it's televised," growled Quex.

Sol fished out a piece of wire copy from his pocket. "They're preparing to panic the networks . . ."

"How, for the love of God," demanded Quex, "can they panic you?"

Sol flourished his piece of paper. "This came over the wire from Paris. One more turn of the screw. Interpol requests all media to give publicity to this 88 message. It follows the bombing of a Paris synagogue, the disappearance of a rabbi . . ."

Another synagogue would be bombed if the 88's message was not circulated. The message required the listed radio and TV networks to begin promoting the Hess Command, "time of transmission to be announced." With the rabbi's life also in jeopardy, the media wouldn't stop to argue.

"They've got the Devil as their publicist," said Quex.

Sol shot him a quizzical look. "Only one cinematographer is capable of this fakery. He's in East Germany. As to the publicity genius, he must have enormous resources that only the state can muster."

Sol fed a new cassette into the video player. The familiar pictures of Auschwitz taken from the air jumped on-screen. "We were told these were originals," said Sol. "These labels identifying gas chambers, crematoria and so on were supposedly printed *at the time* by our intelligence analysts, right?"

Another aerial image, a kaleidoscope of colored dots, replaced the wartime shots.

"I got these through EROS," Sol went on, naming the U.S. Earth Resources Observation System. "Our latest Landsat satellite penetrates the earth's surface with radar sensors. Its new multispectral scanners build up images of old earthworks, architecture, former rivers . . ."

"You didn't go straight to EROS for *these!*" exclaimed Rinna.

Sol stopped in mid-flight.

Quex gave a warning cough.

"How much have you told the CIA?" Rinna tried to keep her voice under control.

Sol hastily stopped the machine. "I transferred everything to tape," he said, "including a CIA report on how we can examine old wartime aerial surveys to learn new facts. The 88 somehow got hold of these CIA treatments, lifted the printwork and transferred it onto *these* photographs."

Another set of Auschwitz aerials appeared on the screen. "They *look*," said Sol Farkas, "just like U.S. Air Force pictures taken in the middle of Hitler's war. But they're not. They were filmed recently, from the same altitude. Only Soviet aircraft fly in this area. Now, watch carefully."

Quex leaned forward, entranced by the technology. He supposed Rinna's sharp intake of breath expressed a similar fascination.

"Here's what our Landsat satellite reports Auschwitz actually looked like in wartime," said Sol. "I've laid, over the color image, the *faked* American bomber pictures. You see, they're different!"

"Well, maybe the Landsat sensors misreported—" objected Rinna.

"No!" Quex intervened. "I'm familiar with the way they work. What we're looking at, in color, are the foundations of the original Auschwitz buildings."

"After the war," explained Sol, "the Polish Government turned Auschwitz into a museum. They restored buildings, consolidated others, put in different access roads. The Poles had no intention to misrepresent, but the restoration did alter how the camp now looks from the air. See?" He had transferred to the same tape a final set of Landsat imagery, genuine and fake aerial photographs, and finally the Polish blueprints for the museum.

"Such an elaborate deception," said Rinna. "Faking the Hess Command has obvious propaganda uses. But old aerials . . . ?"

"They provoked Quex to go public," Sol pointed out. "And Jake Cooke's confirmed in his belief about betrayal."

"Jake's no fool."

"But he knows there were wartime couriers to London who could pinpoint the gas chambers, the execution walls." Sol rose. "In the notes with the Hess Command film, there's reference to papers taken to London by a courier named Radzki."

"You know about Radzki?" demanded Rinna, turning white.

"From Talbott. When I got him in Berlin and warned him—"

"*Warned him!* Why?" Rinna was trembling.

"Because I'd had a call from Jake Cooke."

"You're *sure* it was Jacob Cooke?" demanded Rinna.

"I think I know his voice," Sol said indignantly. "Our paths *have* crossed, you know." But he found he was talking into a vacuum. Rinna had gone.

She broke every one of her own rules. The rules of many years dodging death. She told nobody her plans. She took a car without notifying security. She gave way to panic.

Only to a bewildered Quex did she say she had to go to the Israeli liaison office in Manhattan. She drove at breakneck speed. She wanted to get well clear before she found a pay phone and made the request El Al could not refuse: an A-level priority on the evening flight to Tel Aviv, even if it meant flying as crew.

The more distance she put between herself and Quex, the less hurtful it might all be. She kept seeing him, so full of life, with legs that refused to obey. What irony! The man of will was powerless, the mistress of deception unable to disclose the ultimate deception. She had no choice. The knowledge she shared with only three men in the world, she could not share with Quex.

General Pamir's call had made her see the 88's real aim. Everything Sol said subsequently had only served to confirm what should have become apparent to her sooner. Someone, not part of her small circle, knew Radzki still lived and wielded secret power. One man could accidentally lead the 88 to Radzki's papers and thus to a truth Israel risked everything to protect. That one man was Talbott, spurred by Jake Cooke. She could not guess Jake's motives.

A silver sedan came speeding alongside Rinna's car. She paid it no heed. She was thinking about duty while weeping inwardly at the separation from Quex. Duty! She'd once accused Quex of letting duty blight his life. Quex was so frightened of emotional pain, he'd done what so many did, and closed up his armor against the love of one person. Until now . . .

The silver sedan edged closer, but Rinna noticed nothing. She was whipping herself back into the line of duty. Radzki had fashioned himself a crown of thorns to make sure he never forgot duty. She had experienced some of those thorns. The "mislaid" study, for example, showing that death-camp bombings were feasible. A study ordered by Churchill, "in view of the appalling slaughter reported out of Auschwitz." Radzki had obtained Churchill's original order: "I want an investigation into how we can bomb the railways leading to the death camps and the camps themselves with the object of destroying the plants used for gassing and burning . . ." Nothing had been done. Radzki set down such things for history to judge. And Radzki had written them *in his own handwriting!* The thought made Rinna swerve, and for the first time she saw how close the silver sedan had drawn alongside.

The sedan scraped her front fender. She braked gently, and cast an angry glance at the driver. But he was invisible behind flush-mounted, tinted windows. She was tempted to clip his beautiful, long, low profile, the goddam son of a bitch! A German Audi 5000. She'd only to veer a couple of centimeters. It wouldn't be the first time she'd shocked some bullying road hog.

Instead, she pushed up her speed. The Audi promptly matched her acceleration. She braked. So did the Audi. The damn fool thought he was a flying circus. She braked again, this time making the tires squeal. She felt a thump behind. In her rearview mirror she saw another vehicle. Out of nowhere! Goddam kids! Picking on an old lady! She'd show them.

Then the rear window turned into a spider's web. She thought she heard a *plop!* Yet surely the glass was shatterproof? The Audi slid ahead and crossed into her lane. This time the *plop!* was quite loud, like a fall in air pressure. Now a tightly woven spider's web spread across her windshield, too. A pellet device? She could see a sort of liquid plastic divide into tiny filaments and harden. And then it was all she could see, front or back.

She took her foot off the accelerator, felt the car slow down, sensed the grass verge under the nearside wheels, told herself to stay calm. Already, the spider webs were breaking up. Designed, probably, to dissolve. *Before the police arrive*. The car lurched and she fell forward as it began a near-vertical plunge down the embankment. God help you, Radzki! You're really on your own now . . .

24

The intruders had come out of the night. The growl of their vehicles could be heard even in the cellar of the No-Man's-Land Tuckshop, where Sally and Talbott waited. Men's voices rumbled overhead. Someone shouted down the steps. The off-duty guard, still half asleep, rolled out of his cot. The moment he clattered from sight, Talbott seized the man's rubberized flashlight and moved swiftly to the crawl space where Scroggins in wartime had squirreled away party literature and copies of *The Daily Worker*.

Talbott shone the flashlight into the narrow gap and levered himself around a brick pillar, praying he wouldn't disturb any part of the old structure weakened by that land mine whose silken arrival had blown away Scroggins. He was certain this was where the old radical hoarded each *Worker*, as prudently as the contributions to help keep it going. How those appeals for money had sucked up the resources of comrades like Scroggins and other true believers! The *Worker*'s fighting fund, it was called. Moscow kept the paper short of cash as a matter of policy. Revolutionaries were supposed to make their own sacrifices . . . Churchill had been unable to stomach the hypocrisy, for of course the Soviets subsidized the party; and dictated a party line, preaching peace in that first winter after Hitler had overrun Europe and Britain stood alone. Finally Churchill banned the

Worker for trying to demoralize the country. Then Hitler invaded Russia
and overnight turned the comrades into anti-Nazis.

Talbott sneezed from the dust stirred up as he squeezed under worm-
eaten beams. It would all be here, he supposed: in the headlines; between
the yellowing sheets. Rebecca had said so. Now her words came back to
him, nothing would block them out again. He stretched full length on
layers of brick dust and mortar, and reached out towards the past, towards
neat stacks tied with rotting string.

He had forgotten how thin the newspapers were in those days. After the
fall of France, newsprint was tightly rationed. Yet the *Worker* then still got
its ration, though it increasingly tried to sabotage Britain's solitary fight
against Nazism.

He ran the significant dates through his mind while he tore at the string.
Hitler's "peace offensive" . . . launched while German bombers tried to
break morale. Hess, arriving in May of 1941, when London got its worst
pasting. Then Rebecca suddenly talking about *Nacht und Nebel*, a diabolical device, she said. A man was arrested by the Gestapo at night, and fog
swallowed him up.

Rebecca must have told Scroggins, who would tell his grim-faced comrades the following Guy Fawkes Day, when the old conspirator held his
"party conference." By then, Germany's invasion of Russia had turned
them into fervent warmongers.

Talbott leafed swiftly through 1940. There were no *Worker*s for 1941.
Here was the gap eloquent of Churchill's contempt. And here? Hardly
daring to believe his own deductions, he carefully approached the flimsy
onionskin sheets compressed between the pages of dry newsprint. Talbott
extracted the precious sheets and held them one by one under the flashlight. A crabbed handwriting; charts and sketches; line after line of a
strange script alternating with English. He was startled by the abundance
of material.

The red cloth-and-board diary fell out of the space between two string-
tied bundles. He knew what it was before he opened it. Perhaps he had
seen his mother writing in it when he was a child. He flipped through it
quickly, almost afraid to recognize his mother's flowing handwriting, the
generous, leaping loops, the mid-European style.

He turned back to a page on which five words had been printed: Der
Peter Yiuv <u>bei</u> uns.

The date was entered in Rebecca's hand: January 10, 1941.

On the opposite page she had written: "This is the entire message in a
Red Cross card from Poland, smuggled through Geneva. The Yiddish
means: 'Uncle Yiuv is with us.' I know nothing of any Uncle Yiuv. I
consult a friend who consults rabbis. They say Job is Yiuv, so I look in the
Book of Job. <u>Bei,</u> being underlined, must be code also. The rabbis say the
number 16 corresponds. Verse 16 of the book of Job reads: 'A fire of God

has fallen from Heaven and hath burned the sheep and the servants and consumed them, and I only have escaped to tell thee.' "

Rebecca had added: "Szmuel will come to bear witness that these dreadful reports are true . . . 'I only have escaped to tell.' "

Talbott lay compressed between the weight of bricks above and the fathomless depths of the earth below, his face pressed against Rebecca's diary. So early in the war, it had been, and already she had known.

Sally's voice reached him. "They're coming! Please hurry!" He jammed the diary into his jacket and gathered up the sheets of paper. He inched back a few feet and stopped. His mother had been trapped, had died, in such a space. Someone had joined Talbott at the last moment, perhaps to kill her. He had been sure, moments ago, that he knew who it was. He closed his eyes, trying in vain to reconstruct the scene.

"Talbott!" That was Jake. The next words were lost in the noise of men crowding into the cellar.

Talbott took another hasty look at the remaining papers under the flashlight. Many were held together by old-fashioned filing laces threaded through a corner of each sheet. Quickly he removed what looked like Rebecca's personal letters, and folded these inside his jacket with the diary. Then he snaked back out of the space, thrusting the Radzki papers behind him, thinking how Jake and his Hebrew Liberation Committee in Washington could have used this evidence, and shouting in excitement, "Here, Jake, these might have sent America to war much sooner. No wonder so many wanted the evidence suppressed." He tumbled out onto the cellar floor.

"Shrewdly said!" another's voice replied. "Always said you were a shrewd fellow-me-lad!"

Talbott stood up.

"A rare treat, after all these years," said the Reverend Canon Marcus Furneval. "To meet again." The palace parson took the Radzki papers from Talbott's loose grip and folded them inside his cape.

Sally was standing slightly behind him. She began to edge away, putting herself closer to the guards' card table, with the German HK submachine gun lying on it. Around her were the newcomers, young men with ruddy English faces.

She saw Talbott reach instinctively for the papers he had mistakenly handed Marcus Furneval, and then stop as if afraid to draw further attention to them. She had no doubt this was the Boxing Parson, from Talbott's boyhood, and she felt the same irrational apprehension she remembered from the odd way he'd turned up at General Quex Massey's fake funeral.

Parson Furneval was holding out his free hand. Talbott ignored it. The parson gave a furtive smile and said with a slight flourish, "Meet Mr. Grimweather of the SAS."

Grimweather wore his civilian clothes like a uniform: cavalry twill trousers, roll-brimmed trilby and soft brown shoes. He was tall, thin, elegant, slightly bored. He spread himself before the wood stove. "This is not a military operation," he said. "My men wear civvies. Still, they draw fast and shoot straight. We'll all live longer if we can sort things out with civility. Let me put you in the picture."

Talbott felt little need for the explanations. He knew the British 22nd Regimental Special Air Service, the SAS, to be killers. This unit of young men who now crowded into the cellar looked harmless enough in sweaters and jeans. They represented a fraction of the elite antiterrorist force which had started life striking terror behind Nazi lines. Their dead were now strewn from the Malay jungles to the burning Arabian Desert and the shabby streets of Belfast.

Talbott had been invited once to observe an SAS operation. It had scared the devil out of him. They were secretive, avoided publicity and tolerated him only because he was awaiting demobilization and serving with Quex in the aftermath of the war.

Grimweather's group had infiltrated Jake's wasteland. "No reflection on your chaps!" Grimweather reassured him. He glanced over at Marcus Furneval, who remained near the stove.

Furneval took the cue. "Ticklish business," he said. "As a man of the cloth, I felt it best to negotiate, avoid rumors about some sort of religious conflict. The gossip was going the rounds we'd got full-fledged Jewish extremists running some paramilitary action here. There's been a lot of sensational nonsense in the press about Jewish TNT groups, terror-against-terror . . . People get nervous." The chaplain was wearing a tattered tam o'shanter, which he removed and replaced repeatedly. His cape covered gray flannels and rubber boots. He added, rather unnecessarily, "We're all dressed in civvies."

"Like proper gents," put in Grimweather. "No military stuff. Minicabs and police Pandas."

"And your personal jeep," Furneval pointed out.

Talbott decided both, to some extent, were bluffing. If this operation had been fully authorized, would there be such gentlemanly restraints? He remembered that the SAS could operate inside Britain only in support of the civil authority, the police. There was a procedure to be followed: a formal request from the local police to the Home Office, which in turn required a request to be made to Defence, which in turn approached the Director of Military Operations. "The Regiment" could be activated swiftly despite the cumbersome machinery; and there were occasions when the initial call for help came from the local police after most forceful and formidable "advice" from on high. He also seemed to remember, traditionally, SAS officers did not take part in urban combat; that was left to noncommissioned officers and troopers. So it appeared most likely that Grimweather was not expecting to lead an assault; and that this entire approach to a potential problem was tantamount to a copper on the beat settling a dispute with the few well-chosen words: "Hullo-hullo-hullo! What's all this, then?" Nevertheless, someone at a high level of government must have contrived this very British solution.

Talbott took the chance that he was right in guessing Grimweather was on thin ice. "I'll have those papers back," he said to Furneval.

"Sorry, dear boy," huffed the parson. "Government property."

"You're not the government!" burst out Sally.

"In this he is. Official Secrets." Grimweather spoke as if in capital letters.

Sally took another two steps closer to the card table.

Talbott caught her intent. For a diversion, he called to Jake across the cellar: "If you lose those papers, you've failed!"

Heads turned. Sally snatched up the Heckler and Koch gun. "The papers," she said quietly. "Give them to me, Reverend."

Furneval spun round. A look of blank astonishment creased his plump face. Sally was aiming the HK at Talbott.

"If anyone so much as *twitches*," she threatened, "Talbott's *dead!*"

She sounded as if she meant what she said. Talbott stared at her, thunderstruck.

"The papers," she repeated, reaching out her free hand.

"But, Miss Ryan . . ." Furneval choked, and his dentures clicked with frustration. The parody of a smile dawned, flowing from one scarred corner of his mouth to the other, lighting up gold teeth, pink gums, purplish lips. "Your grandfather. These are his—"

"The papers! Give them here, where they belong."

"Where they belong . . ." The false dawn faded from Furneval's face. He withdrew the papers, made a distracting gesture at Sally and then lunged at the gaping mouth of the stove. Sally jerked back against the wall behind her, recovered, took calm aim, fired. The single shot crashed and echoed through the cellar. The parson clutched his wrist. She swung the gun back onto Talbott, freezing Grimweather and his men. The papers fluttered through the air, and Talbott scooped them away from the stove. A few pages fell at Jake's feet.

"Up the stairs!" Sally ordered, moving with her back still to the wall. Talbott obeyed, watching her and the gun like a mailman edging past a ferocious dog. "Jake!" said Sally. "And you," she added to Grimweather.

Outside, the stuttering coffee-shop sign cast a fuzzy light in the riverine fog. Grimweather's Land-Rover crouched at the door. Here, Grimweather hesitated.

"Make your men give way," said Sally. "I'll shoot his head off if you don't." She jerked the gun in Talbott's direction for emphasis.

Grimweather vaulted onto the Land-Rover's hood. "Now hear this!" His words echoed into the night. "Hold your fire!"

Talbott was aware of muffled bangs like the erratic beat of drums. The kids were setting off their fireworks. A rocket sizzled into a clear patch of sky and sank back into the fog. He heard Sally say something about "safe-conduct." He thought angrily that he didn't need anyone's safe-conduct here on his own territory. From these slums had gone the men who fought in the First World War trenches. And then their very homes became the trenches too. Here, the zeppelins of the 1914–18 war had aimed the very first aerial bombs against civilians. It had been called a cesspool of humanity. The sacrificial slaughter of its young people in war after war had never been reckoned such an offense against humanity. So who the hell needed Sally's patronage or Mr.-frigging-Grimweather's safe-conduct?

The gun jabbed Talbott in the back. "Stop right there!" ordered Sally. She cast her voice at Jake: "Now *your* men. Tell them, No funny stuff."

Jake looked up at the stars in a broadening patch of clear sky as if to mourn the months of wasted planning.

"Tell the men!" Sally ordered again. "We're passing through. Because *you* come with us."

Jake took a deep breath. His voice reverberated across the wasteland. The words sounded harsher in Hebrew.

"Good," said Sally at last. She waved the two men ahead of her.

"Shoot them down!" shouted the Reverend Marcus Furneval.

The three figures were dissolving into the thickening ground mist.

Grimweather looked down at the parson and thought: Bloodthirsty little cockroach! But all he said was, "No bloodshed, sir. Those are *my* orders."

Furneval struggled with his own frustration. He had wrapped a handkerchief around his wrist where Sally's bullet had nicked him. He held it up. *"They*'re bloody shooting!" He got no response. "What about self-defense?" he snarled. Nobody spoke. His face blotched with rage. In the gruesome neon's light, he looked like some apoplectic old man. He threw back his head and screamed, *"Killers of Deir Yassin!"*

Grimweather understood the parson's purpose. Such a shrill cry at such a tense moment could trigger a firefight. The words were aimed at the Jewish guards as well as Jake Cooke.

The SAS commander wasted no time. He slugged the parson with such economy that he caught the man before he had even slumped to the ground.

Sally had a vague sense of the direction she must take. She prodded her charges ahead, across the muddy wasteland. Two men materialized out of the mist. They were armed with stubby new SA-80 rifles carried horizontally across the body. They wore earplugs, and when Sally shouted, "Stand back!" they cocked their heads and tuned out their transceivers. A third man, their leader, came up behind and spoke with a throat mike. Before he could finish, she had the barrel of her gun under his jaw. "Disarm them, Jake!" she said quietly. "Smash their radios."

They encountered two more groups of men. All had heard the shouted orders and readily gave way. Jake's men were easily identifiable: each wore slantwise across his chest the same HK short-barreled 9-millimeter sub-machine gun with an up-and-over folding stock; and each had that mis-leadingly casual stance of men trained to jerk into action in half a second. They were alien to the landscape, yet stood as if reborn out of this bomb-plowed soil.

"Do you know what you're doing?" Talbott muttered, stumbling into another pocket of ground fog.

"No," said Sally.

Talbott stopped dead. "Then what—?"

She lowered the gun. "It was the only way to get you out." She turned to Jake. "Don't try anything!"

"How can I?" Jake shrugged. "If my men take action, the British out-number them. I'm better with you."

They kept their voices to a whisper. Even so, Talbott felt naked, vulner-able. He was thinking quickly. There was only one reason they were all here. The Radzki papers.

He turned to Jake. "You must have vehicles somewhere?"

Jake took a moment to reply. "Yes."

Talbott turned to Sally. "The embankment—?"

She said quickly, "I know."

He handed her the Radzki papers. "Jake," he said, "give her the rest."

"You're mistaken," said Jake. "I haven't any."

Sally was almost certain Jake was lying. There wasn't time to argue. She had the gun, and the bulk of the papers Jake still badly wanted. If Talbott wanted her to go, alone, to the schoolboy hiding place he'd shown her, what would Jake do? He couldn't follow her while she held him off with the gun. Therefore he'd stick with Talbott until they were all together again.

"Go," said Talbott to her.

She backed off, then stopped. The mist had parted. The soaring rockets cast a leaden gleam upon their faces. "Be careful," she pleaded. "Both of you."

After she had gone, Jake said, "Where now?"

"Your car," replied Talbott. "We could use some of that old Irgun touch right now. But hurry."

Talbott had guessed right. Jake had concealed emergency vehicles in the empty sheds along the dockside where billboards advertised a nonexistent housing development.

"We only need one set of wheels," said Talbott. "Enough for a diver-sion."

Jake asked no more questions. He took out the keys to a battered French Renault, still carrying European plates. On Talbott's orders, he got in and started the engine. One of Jake's men, drawn by the noise, ran up. He was little more than a boy. Talbott told him to get into the car, and then explained what he wanted.

Grimweather was speaking on a field radio when the Renault chugged into sight.

"They can't get far," he was saying. "No, sir, the opposition seems to be withdrawing." Then he saw the car. "Hang on, sir!" He gave an order to the man beside him in the jeep, and a beam of light sprang out to meet the oncoming car. "This seems to be them now. We'll try some bluff." He shouted more orders and four SAS men ran and spread out across the broken road.

The searchlight followed the car as it approached the impromptu barrier.

"Fire over their heads!" shouted Grimweather.

The rattle of gunfire punctuated the night. The car appeared, was lost in another bank of fog, then reappeared, gathering speed. "Keep firing but not to kill!" roared Grimweather, now using the loud-hailer. The men dropped to their knees, shooting independently. The car swerved and then raced down upon them. Grimweather saw three heads silhouetted in the searchlight beam. He spoke quietly into his lapel microphone: "It's them all right, sir." He paused. "God knows what they're doing. The car seems out of control." A voice squawked back at him. "Yessir, it was at my discretion. I take full responsibility." He broke off to shout to his men. The firing stopped. The lights of the car could be seen, a dancing will-o'-the-wisp.

"They're heading for the docks, sir!" called one of the men.

"Give chase," said Grimweather. "No firing."

Parson Furneval climbed shakily to his feet in the back of the jeep. "That was a stupid thing to do," he said.

"Sorry, Rev. No choice."

"You never heard of the Jewish massacre of the villagers at Deir Yassin?"

"Perhaps not." Grimweather watched the gray streak of light above the river. His original dislike for Furneval was intensified by that last remark. The tragedy of the Arab village was a subject for study by British antiterrorists: Grimweather used it as an example of how reaction to terrorism could be twisted to hurt the true victims, in this case the Israelis themselves.

Where Grimweather looked, the sky suddenly blossomed red. Then one of his men rode up on a motorcycle. Grimweather listened to the man's report. "Guess you got what you wanted, Rev," he said to Furneval. "They blew themselves up."

But what Furneval wanted was not the Radzki evidence exploding in a getaway car as it struck a dockside crane and then hurtled into the Thames.

Talbott picked himself up and began a search for the others. The young guard had stripped off his shirt before they rolled out of the car. Jake punctured the gas tank and sent the Renault coasting along the dock with the petrol-soaked shirt wedged between the exhaust and the chassis. The eventual blaze covered the river where the car had plunged from sight.

"I did what you wanted." Jake's voice made Talbott jump. He whirled to face Jake's young guard, gun at the ready. "Now it's our turn," said Jake, emerging from behind a wooden pillar.

"You kill me, you'll have lost Sally," Talbott said steadily. "She's got what you're looking for."

"Right," said Jake, and spoke quietly to the youth. "He won't shoot if you don't frighten him," he said to Talbott. "Let's go."

Sally stood at the foot of an iron ladder, her gun aimed at the manhole cover above. It had been moved recently and shifted easily. The Blitz Kids had said they used the old embankment just as Talbott once had done.

There was a loud hammering above. It reverberated through the pitch-dark tunnel. Her grip tightened on the gun.

The steel cover was moved aside again. She caught a glimpse of stars, and the perfect target of a man's head.

"Who's there?"

Sally made no reply, though she recognized Jake's voice. All her misgivings about Jake were beginning to crystallize. She would do nothing now without Talbott.

"We're coming down," said Jake.

"Stay where you are!" She took steady aim.

There were whispers from above. Jake's head vanished and then returned. "We've got Talbott with us."

"Let him speak."

"He can't," said Jake.

Can't? Sally asked herself. Is he hurt? For a split second, she felt panic. She steadied the gun. She was not going to budge until she heard from Talbott. She listened. The whispering stopped.

She was sure Jake had some of his guards up there. She braced herself. She'd shoot Jake if he'd hurt Talbott.

"Sally, we've got to come down!" That was Jake again.

"Not until I speak with Talbott."

"Sally, it's . . . dangerous."

"Then, you're in trouble," said Sally.

Lying flat on the ground above, Talbott listened but could do nothing. There was a gun at his head, held by an extremely nervous young man who said he would blow out Talbott's brains if he made the smallest sound. The young man was from the Jewish Defense League's London motor-mechanics' division, and the burning of the Renault from his car pool had confronted him with the reality of what he'd got himself into. He did not know Jake Cooke personally, only that Israelis came and went with impunity. For himself, his family and his job were here. He was loyal to the league, but that was supposed to require fighting in Israel, not violence at home, unless to protect Jews and their property. The flaming car had seared his mind with one clear message: he could get back in good standing if he turned in this American.

Talbott sensed the Londoner's rising fear. The youth had enough sense not to want to add murder to the crimes committed tonight; but his extreme nervousness also made it possible he would shoot if suddenly threatened.

Sally's voice broke the silence again. "Where's Talbott?"

"He's here. He can't talk directly with you."

"I need proof you're not lying."

Talbott tried to wriggle forward. The gun was jabbed savagely against his temple, and he grunted with pain.

"Perhaps he can give you a message," said Jake desperately. He whispered to the young guard, but the boy kept shaking his head.

Sally called up, "What's an eight-letter word for the Roosevelt Island Tramway, Talbott?"

Talbott stifled a groan. Crossword puzzles! What else, from someone who started out in research? Then he thought: Research? Objectivity. Looking at both sides . . .

"Nothing will happen to you!" Jake snarled at the young guard.

"Shut up!" The boy's eyes rolled in the direction of the noise of engines groaning and car doors slamming.

Talbott's body stiffened. His mouth felt dry. He said softly, "Pendulum." The boy's arm trembled.

Jake caught the word, scarcely more than a sigh. He waited long seconds. "You've done nothing wrong," he said in English to the boy. "But if you use that gun—!"

Sally was poised on the edge of action. The manhole cover was only a third open, but she could hear the renewed rumble of SAS vehicles. She had given a message for Talbott to which nobody else could possibly respond.

She moved up the rungs, bracing herself with one foot against the opposite curve of the tunnel.

Jake heard her shoes scrape. He guessed what might be in her mind. Risking all, he called down, "Pendulum."

The boy said, "I told you—"

Talbott saw the boy's hand jerk up, and he grabbed the wrist as he rolled sideways, forcing back the boy's gun. The two struggled on the ground in silence, limbs intertwined so that Jake was afraid to jump in.

The boy's gun glistened, vanished, shone again between the writhing bodies.

Sally lifted the manhole cover. She heard a single shot ring out, and saw one of the two bodies go limp.

Jake slid down the bank to where Talbott and the boy lay. The perverse night had changed with the drawing back of the mist. Starlight shone upon the boy, spreadeagled on his back, eyes wide.

"In the head," said Talbott. "My fault."

Jake looked up from the body. "Here, help me!" Together they lifted the dead youth to where Sally waited, and then they lowered the body from sight, inside the tunnel.

The reaction set in later. They were sitting on their heels, their backs against the tunnel wall. The youth lay beyond a curve, near stagnant water. Nobody felt like talking.

The Embankment. That was what Talbott had called this place as a boy. Like a Roman burial mound, it ran for miles, part of Victorian England's biggest sewage system, but also linked with ageless waterways beneath London, a city of underground streams known to few. The maintenance tunnel where they now sheltered could be entered by widely spaced manholes, also little known.

"They won't find us here," said Talbott. "It hasn't been used in donkey's years." He was beginning to shake.

Jake put a hand on his arm. "It couldn't be helped."

"He was hardly more than a schoolboy."

"Old enough to fight," said Jake.

"This isn't a battlefield," protested Sally.

"That boy believed so." Jake's voice was matter-of-fact. "If the fighting had been in Israel, he'd have gone there. It just happened the war shifted here. He's the first casualty—"

"Truth," said Sally. "That's the first casualty."

"Truth? As in Hess?" Jake asked with renewed harshness.

There was silence. Deep in the earth, they seemed to be, burdened by layers of ancient, corrupting soil.

"The truth and Hess turned things rotten for Radzki," said Jake.

The air was muggy and smelled of old, decomposing metals. There was no light, now they had replaced the manhole cover.

"We had to bring our Jewish war to London," continued Jake. "This is where Radzki left the evidence."

Then even Jake ran out of words. All anyone could hear was a distant drip of water.

Talbott crouched with his back against cold concrete. He seemed to hear the gravelly voice of the Boxing Parson shouting, "Pull yourself together, laddie . . . The nerve test!" It must have been the feel of the concrete, the graveyard smell, the knowledge that a boy's dead body lay close by. The whole episode returned vividly to his mind. Parson Furneval descending into a dark and oppressive place like this with murder in his heart where mercy was expected, and Talbott retreating, climbing out of the rubble with perhaps no more than a vague sense of what had happened. And then—and then Furneval pushing him against a broken wall and throwing rubble at him. Why? That was how you got a shell-shocked sailor moving, by playing on his disciplined reflexes. Where had he read that? In some navy first-aid instructions, which also warned: "The expediency can be harmful if it wipes out recollection of preceding events."

Suddenly he could hear Furneval, the Boxing Parson, asking him, accusing him: "What have you done, laddie?" The guilt for his mother's death had been planted right there, reinforcing the self-accusation of a midshipman whose nerves were obviously strung out. Furneval had thrown rocks at him. If the boy moved, he lost a point, that was the way the game was played. "What have you done, laddie?" The taunt was delivered with every rock. And a half-demented midshipman had run back to the warfare he understood, and looked away from any murderous consolation Furneval had given Rebecca.

Jake's shoes scraped in the dark. "It's time we all showed our cards," he said.

Talbott felt Sally's hand brush his knee. He remembered her warning: Tell Jake *nothing*.

"I've no more cards to show," said Talbott.

Sally rustled the papers Jake wanted. In that lightless tomb, where every sound was exaggerated, the rustling exploded like crackers in a Chinese temple. The papers even gave off tiny sparks. "Then, it's up to you, Jake," said Sally. "You know the connection between Radzki and Hess."

"Very well," said Jake. "Radzki was Stalin's spy when he came here with Hess."

25

Yuri Gorin was up to his neck in mud. Millions who feared him would be surprised to learn he was also up to his neck in trouble. He smiled grimly.

The Igalo nurse caught the smile. She had seen all kinds come to the health spa. It perched on the sunny side of the Communist empire, separated from the frivolous Italians by no more than the Adriatic Sea. She did not approach the Mother of all the Russias in awe. He had none of the mystical carnality of statehood found in a monarch, no *corpus mysticum* of divine right. What enthroned a man such as this was hunger and ambition. He could never rise before her with the majestic indolence of royalty.

She dangled her hand in the warm thermal ooze filling the trough-like tub where Mother stretched naked but mostly submerged.

"The mud is not too hot?"

"No," he grunted. "Not hot."

She let her hand drift. In the body of the monarch were said to reside the identity and liability of the body politic. The nurse, like so many Yugoslavs, still had an instinct for monarchy. She saw nothing here but a piggish bureaucrat. She said experimentally, "President Tito was often here. For his sciatica. We cured him."

"So what killed him?"

The nurse gazed into the mismatched eyes and saw a glint of amusement. "Old age. He killed himself with it." She saw the bushy eyebrows fly up. "When a man no longer takes pleasure in himself, he decides to die of old age."

Mother examined the nurse with renewed interest. No fool, this one. Her name was Vesna. Spring. "Yugo-red" dyed hair. A shapely though doubtless muscular body which would certainly be naked under the hospital gown. One more temptation to be resisted. He felt himself growing erect. He concentrated on mental arithmetic: How many temptations resisted? Say, two a week since he'd struck out for real power? One hundred emphatic temptations a year for forty years. Ah, but what about the years before that? His mind grew dizzy with the calculations, but at least he was flaccid again.

Vesna saw the slight hardening around his mouth, and ever so gently withdrew her hand. She'd been around powerful men long enough to have a quiet contempt for those who pretended to serve the people while hogging the perks. This specimen *must* be different. He had to be tough, to preside over the ten members of COMECON, the Council on Mutual Economic Assistance. In truth, he was their king. There was no majesty in this hairy, bearlike body; although in the face, a certain nobility. She got off her knees, smoothed hands over hips, and fiddled with the thermostat. She had given him the routine opportunity for sex, very discreetly, and he'd rejected it with equal discretion. She wondered what he did for it. One heard so many stories. But then, look at what they said about Tito.

Mother reflected on the radioactive mud. Very tranquilizing. The mud burst up from the bowels of the earth, volcanically propelled to the adjacent seabed. For centuries, men had piped it from the bay into these bathtubs of Roman dimensions. The eccentric Communists of Yugoslavia, tainted with Titoism, revered the Simo Milošević hospital as a shrine for the miracles it had performed on Tito. Now it had been cleared for the party leaders from more orthodox bastions of communism. The purpose of the conference would have made Tito spin in his grave, considering Tito had done the impossible and defied Stalin. Well, Mother reminded himself, lots of things were *said* to be impossible.

He lifted his leg against a weight of mud, surfacing a large foot. Mud dribbled between the toes; sickly gray mud, flecked with silver and gold. His toes betrayed him as a peasant. What else might they betray? Frostbite? Torture? All the nails had been removed from this one foot by torturers. The big toe was deformed as the consequence of a badly executed parachute jump. The toes poked up from the mud, symbols of his submerged self. He had confided his last secret to another man long ago. The subsequent betrayal taught him a lesson. Now he communed only with his toes. Flat, carbuncled, bent and ugly though they might be, they were his sole confidants. Down there, they listened to Mother arguing that now was the time to bring Yugoslavia back into the fold, and they nudged each other and wiggled with glee. They knew better.

Mother felt an onrush of good humor. It was quite remarkable. He had stored up big trouble for himself by setting in motion certain emergency procedures involving former CIA director Walter Juste. So why was he so pleased with himself? It must be the adrenalin. It was like the old days, keeping one jump ahead of the Gestapo, out to torture and kill him.

"Hardening of the arteries," he said to the nurse. "That's what kills old men."

He peered up at her, his head barely visible above the mud lapping around his snout.

Vesna thought she detected all the signs of thermally inspired content. "Be careful," she warned Mother, and plunged her hand deep into the concealing sludge. She groped along the bottom of the tub, her face close to his, her china-blue eyes resting speculatively upon his blurred features. "What finished off Tito," she said firmly, "was that he got bored."

"Would you believe"—Mother's chest heaved under the mud—"that he was anything other than a locksmith?"

Vesna's eyes widened. Her hand located the big plug and she jerked it sooner than she intended. "You tease?"

"No."

She kept a cautious eye on him while she stirred the mud around the plughole. "I am going to change your bath now," she said.

Mother shook his head. "I have a meeting shortly. So no, not this time. Now then," he added quickly, "did you hear that Tito was a Polish Jew who played the piano like a maestro?"

She pretended to be shocked. "Gossip is not *Kulturni,*" she said virtuously. "It is without culture."

"Gossip repeated becomes truth." Mother heaved himself into a sitting position. "A dangerous thing, gossip."

If you say so, thought Vesna. She had uncoiled a rubber hose. "Permit me," she murmured.

The first jet of sulfurous water caressed his shoulders and chest. His mind was on the old Tito rumors. He would use them to make a point at the conference. It was obvious this woman had heard the gossip. Then he saw her breasts pendulous inside her gaping coat. She had wide hips. She leaned away from him to do something with the giant taps, and he was distracted enough to consider the phenomenon of Slav bums. She had the kind of magnificent bum only a Slav could love. His toes curled.

Vesna returned to uncover him with the jetted water as if the mud were a cloak peeled from a statue. It excited her to think how nobody ever saw this torso. She sluiced him down to the thighs, chasing the mud along fleshy channels leading to his groin.

"That," said Mother, "will be enough. I'll finish it off myself."

Vesna twisted her head up and round. She licked her upper lip, catching the perspiration. "You want to finish it off yourself?" she said. "Of course." Her smile, although only Mother could see this, was one of pity.

Mother lumbered into the huge dining hall on the hospital's first floor, the familiar bearlike gait evoking the usual rhythmic applause. He knew what the East Europeans said in privacy. The Poles joked about his bullet-proof corsets. The Czechs said he was vain as a dowager. The Bulgarians whispered about his opposition to the new military technocrats. Romanians and Hungarians chattered about his patchy mending of a Soviet economy inferior to their own. The East Germans—ah, the East Germans! They accused Mother of drifting from the true path. But wait until he growled in their direction. Then they would jump to attention. They all did, in the end.

Except the Yugoslavs. Their security was notoriously lax. The other delegates felt perilously close to heresy in a Communist neighborhood where the crack of the Kremlin whip produced nothing but "the donkey effect": every Yugoslav refusing to budge.

The way Mother lowered his rump into the presiding chair was eloquent of a similar, mulelike obstinacy. He made a small throat-cutting gesture and the applause stopped. Someone began to speak. Mother sat motionless, resigned to the unrolling of the carbon-copy speeches, his eyes masked by the tinted glasses, and his mind entirely free to look inward.

Hitler had educated him in the art of control. Hitler postured and blathered and let the Gestapo gather up the reins of power through its infiltration of the bureaucracies. Of course Stalin, even earlier, understood this: he had controlled the *nomenklatura* lists, the names of thousands who fed on the civil services. But when Stalin employed the technique, Mother had been too green to be aware of it; whereas Hitler had shown quite openly that it wasn't mass hysteria that commanded obedience in the end: it was the prospect of a safe, perhaps even a cushy, job.

There isn't a Russian soul, thought Mother, who today doubts that his family's existence depends on the files held by the secretariat; and that the *nomenklatura* is ultimately controlled by the general secretary. The ruling elite is the top circle of the *nomenklatura*. And the *nomenklatura* today is me!

The Adriatic sun streamed through the long windows. Mother sat in an attitude of rapt attention while the delegates droned on.

A mile away, Red Crombie kicked stones along an Igalo beach. In summer it would have been covered in nude bodies. Crombie nursed an embarrassing memory of this beach many summers ago. He had walked innocently through a door in a fence here, to find himself hopping and tripping over nude lobster-red sun worshipers. He had lifted his eyes to the sky and blundered back to the fence, dancing and twisting to avoid bodily contact with those horrifying mounds of sagging gray flesh, pursued by cross German accents. The strip that year had been the exclusive domain of West

German trippers claiming government benefits for Igalo's medical treatment of their imaginary illnesses.

The nudists had unwittingly led Crombie to a phenomenon more fascinating than nudists. The Igalo hospital collected West German marks for undervalued Yugoslav dinars. The German "patients" bought the dinars at a grotesquely favorable rate while submitting their claims to the Bonn medical service in marks. Everyone, except the West German exchequer, was richer.

Crombie saw a way to trouble the consciences of Igalo officials. The result had been an escape route woven into legitimate tourist traffic between the nearby airport of Dubrovnik and West Germany. The rudiments of such a ratline, or "snake," had been left by the OSS after World War II, with extensions into territories like Bulgaria. Red Crombie had finally taken over travel arrangements for hunted men to leave the hard-nosed regions of the Soviet bloc and become vacationers returning to the West from Igalo. The system, running with quiet efficiency now for two years, depended upon politely blackmailing local officials and bona-fide West Germans whose invalidism would be exposed as fraud if they refused to cooperate. It was no trouble getting a West German out later, after his identity papers had been used by a much needier traveler.

Crombie crunched across the beach to the second fence and back again. He saw a distant figure. It ought to be his contact. But from the way it hopped and hesitated, he feared that here, braving the November chill, came the first of the winter's fanatic nudists. He hadn't reckoned with beckoning blue skies and the hot concentration of sunshine between the arms of the bay, powerful lures for West Germany's medicare malingerers. He'd have to strip, or risk being thrown off the beach. Shit! He had been nicely settled in for Berlin's cozy winter. Blast the twit in McLean, Virginia, who switched him at such short notice. May the crazy bastard's house soon vanish under snow, its pipes burst, its central heating freeze!

Crombie found the place where the pebbles ran out into grayish volcanic sand. He dumped his gear. Slowly, savagely, he tore off his clothes.

At the clinic, the minister for East German security held the stage. His Stasi agents were whispered to be more efficient and ruthless with "administrative measures" than even their nominal bosses of the KGB. They had certainly cut off the balls of the Afghans, thought Mother, pitying the poor eunuch who represented Afghan "association" with COMECON.

Mother was bemused by the East German minister's obsessions. The man simply went on and on about how pleased the DDR's Stasi had been with Soviet communications equipment in rugged Afghan terrain. He called on the Yugoslavs to standardize upon it, instead of buying cast-off American stuff. There was some subtle message Mother suspected he was missing. Probably the Soviet equipment was made by the fornicating East Germans.

Mother moved his head back. The slight change of position electrified the rows of gray faces above the green-baize tables. He looked past them at the windows, half curtained by vertical red banners. Sitting with his back to the sea, Mother's view between the scarlet stripes was of blue sky and sun-capped mountains. Thousands of small birds danced outside the windows. He supposed them to be house martens or swallows. The din they made caused one or two speakers to falter. Security men made futile efforts to drive them away with smoke pots in the street outside.

Mother felt a tired contempt for the dummies who couldn't even silence a bunch of flycatchers. The twittering inside the building was more easily controlled. The party could manage human nuisances. The party failed when it tackled any real lust for life. However . . . He roused himself sharply. He had survived by never, ever, betraying what he really thought of dummies.

He pretended not to notice the stiffening of attention as he stirred to life. He did not return the sycophantic smiles. He ignored the busy revolving of pencils, the hands trembling for the cue to jump apart and begin the ritual of rhythmic applause. He wondered how he had endured these instinctive lickspittles for so long. Still, if the revolution had not made power available through their toadying, he would be dead by now.

"Comrades!"

His speech was a symphony. Each delegate played a part, never too loud, never too long. He conducted them together like an orchestra, emphasizing those sections of the grand theme suited to his purpose. Socialism first in the U.S.S.R. means obedience to Mother. Opposition to Mother means betraying the revolution to the encircling aggressors.

He displayed his gift for languages, drawing bursts of sycophantic laughter when he punctuated his generous references to bloc members with jokes drawn from their own culture and in their own tongue.

Then, with sudden gravity, he said he detected some slight differences, disharmonies . . .

These were code words. *Detected disharmonies?* Mother sensed the instant rise in tension. Dear God! How well they answered the classic description of a colony of ants, each separate, yet bound to one another by nervous impulses. Whatever ant functioned as the excitement center might send the worker ants scurrying to the production chambers and the soldiers ants marching to the ramparts with pincer jaws agape!

He had them trembling on every word. "Truth," he said, "is whatever serves the party's aims. We must use such truth to fight the lies of our enemies. But it must be done in concert."

The tall figure of East Germany's General Helmuth Henkell stiffened.

"No single one of us can fight their lies with lies of his own," said Mother. "The wisdom of the central committee in the Soviet Union is absolute. The judge of party truth does not reside in Budapest, nor Sofia . . . nor," added Mother after a suitable pause, "in East Berlin."

O what a cunning bastard! thought the East German. What a fork-tongued hypocrite! Shitpot!

"Cult of personality hurts in the end the one who makes the error . . . History teaches us . . ."

The words that followed took the delegates by surprise. "Consider the case of Comrade President Tito, victim of foul rumors . . . deviationist tendencies . . . in the end a target of disinformation, that he died in the counterattack of 1943 and was secretly replaced by Stalin's man, the Polish Jew Walter Weiss . . ."

The delegates exchanged quick, covert glances. Was Mother saying that Moscow's own disinformation agency had taken revenge?

"It is not necessary here to repeat what all of you will have heard of these attacks . . ."

Mother could see their antennae waving, frantic to pick up the correct signals. They would be unable to recall when a Soviet leader had flaunted the reality of his power so blatantly. He continued in the convoluted language of the faith, but his message was uncommonly clear. The intelligence services of fraternal governments must suspend, immediately, all operations not directly approved from Moscow. He talked as if the Baltic crisis was the cause of stringent measures. He had concealed his true concern: that if he was ever going to use all this power, it was now or never.

Vesna, the nurse named Spring, stretched lazily in the November sun, glad to be naked and free from the sulfurous odor of the mud baths. Wisps of white cloud blew off the mountain peaks, a reminder that this balmy weather was the freak result of warm winds and could not last long.

"Spring comes early," said the man lying close by.

Vesna almost giggled. The cue was correct but untimely in the circumstances. It also struck her as sexually ambiguous.

"It's never really cold." She gave the prescribed answer, her eyes fastened modestly upon the esplanade above.

Red Crombie rolled over. He'd always had trouble taking passwords too seriously. In Vesna's case, her decision to pose as a nudist sunbather only made her more readily recognizable. For he knew her well.

"What the hell's that bunch of characters there at the far end of the beach?" he asked.

Vesna turned onto her side. This gave her a close-up of the most fascinating aspect of his firm male torso. Loyal to duty, she looked beyond to study the intruders.

"Seven secretaries and middle managers from Hamburg," she said blandly. "All suffering nervous breakdowns."

"They can't be staying at the clinic?"

"No, they're parked in the annex, up the hill. Our doctors go there to sign forms and keep things legal. The clinic's stiff with security."

"Yours? Or Mother's?"

"Ours."

"Good," said Crombie. "Okay."

Crombie began his briefing. There was nobody else on the beach except the seven Germans timidly exploring the distant rock pools. Vesna absorbed every word while part of her mind caressed the muscular form beside her. It was an agreeable change to the fatty, ashen corpses dumped upon her to slap back into life under the hydro-jets and mudpacks.

"It is very dangerous for me," she said when Crombie had finished.

"We'll compensate accordingly."

"No," she said. "You would have to get me out of here."

He rested his head sideways, studying her. This was one of the curses of the job. No sooner were they paying their way at last, than they wanted to escape. Still, Vesna was a special case. She would *need* to run when this was over.

He sat up and stared past the Germans at a point beyond the last spear of rock. There would be equipment lying on the seabed for a third traveler, which was either luck or premonition, since Vesna would have to be added. He turned and studied the woman again. She was in good shape. She could manage.

Vesna shifted uncomfortably. She felt she was under a meat inspector's scrutiny, to see if she was fit for export. She remembered her pubic hairs were not dyed to match her loosened Yugo-red hair. The situation was just too aggravating. She said with angry impatience, "I'm not asking for money."

"Of course you're not," Crombie said soothingly.

She twisted to face the sun again. The thick tuft of black hair in the triangle of her thighs glistened, but she no longer cared.

Crombie casually shifted his bag closer to Vesna. "What you need immediately is in there," he said, and tossed a pebble down the beach. "We'll guarantee you safe exit. Resettlement in the area of your choice. Funding, if you want to start a business."

He had long ago learned to make that kind of an offer sound convincing.

Mother had finished speaking. The delegates rose to their feet and applauded in rhythm. Even the East Germans were up, bosoms and chests swelling operatically. But Mother had seen the Stasi chief angrily doodling. The doodles would be retrieved and analyzed. *That* was power.

Mother spread his arms. There was a sudden silence. That was power.

He recited the proper litany of mutual congratulation and then he began to clap again, and lumbered offstage to another rumble of hands beating together. The drumroll was like the thunder of blood in his ears, and he had a brief vision of a scarlet fountain that balanced upon its apex a celluloid ball. It came from some childhood fairground memory. He was like the ball, sustained only by the uplifting force of all those molecules. Outside the system, he did not exist.

The thought made him stagger slightly. It was a momentary loss of balance that would certainly not pass unmarked.

He came out into the rotunda, his vision mysteriously blurred. He saw the white-coated nurse by the elevator. She had an appointment with him. Mud or physiotherapy? He wasn't sure, but it would be welcome while the delegations worked through the housekeeping agenda. It was known that Mother had suffered a mild stroke this past summer.

He headed into the elevator at his normal stolid pace. The big Montenegrins assigned as bodyguards tried to follow. The nurse stubbornly blocked the way. Something warned Mother to intervene. "Peter the Great," he said, "made the first alliance between the vast Russian empire and tiny Montenegro." His voice—never mind the words—commanded silence. "The Montenegrins said, *'We and the Russians make 200 million men!'*"

He grinned. The Montenegrins began to smile back. Theirs was one of the six republics making up the Yugoslav federation, and Mother's implication flattered their ego.

"Surely," said Mother, "we millions of men should yield to this one Serbian woman, eh?"

They laughed with him while the elevator doors slowly closed. Alone with the nurse, Mother gave her an inquiring look.

"The schedule," said Vesna, "has been changed. Hydrotherapy first."

The elevator began its slow descent.

Mother peered at the white card in Vesna's hand. "Aerobics," he said. "It seemed to me the program called for aerobics."

"You are mistaken."

Mother scrutinized her, and glanced again at the card. On one side was his therapy timetable. He turned it over. The tip of Vesna's fingernail intruded and came to rest beside a vivid red X crayoned over a floor plan.

"There," the nurse said softly, "a traveler is waiting."

He raised his eyes. Her face was blank.

The elevator bounced gently to a stop. Doors squeaked. Steam hissed. Every sound was now an exaggeration. Mother saw the whirlpool vats with fresh vision, and the hydro-pipes snaking over white tiles that sparkled under blinding arc lamps.

"The section has been swept clean," said Vesna.

So the moment had come at last! Mother emerged, blinking. He made a pretense of stumbling. Let them think he was old and suddenly frightened! He peered about him, while his mind juggled with what he knew.

They must have decided upon the old MIS-X escape route.

Mother restrained a smile. His own KGB travel experts had watched Western intelligence lovingly restore MIS-X after the war. Then Tito had split with Stalin, and it had become a KGB special project; unknown, of course, to the other side or to the Yugoslavs. The KGB observed who went into the pipeline, and where they went when they came out. He racked his brains for the name of Washington's best travel agent: Red Crombie, that was it! How thoughtful of Walter Juste if he had sent Crombie in person.

"Take the turn to the right," said Vesna. She prodded him, because he seemed to be paralyzed, perhaps with fear. She had seen it happen before.

Yuri Gorin, whom Russians called Mother in a spirit of awe reserved once for the czars and the deity, smiled. A simple nurse was telling him to turn right.

26

Sol Farkas faced Quex in the library of Fishhook's home. It was several hours since Rinna Dystel's car had been found.

"We can't hope it's one of Rinna's deceptions this time," said Quex. He sat stiff and stoic.

"She was deliberately driven off the highway," said Sol. "By the same people, I presume, who wanted to kill you. The technique's the same. They must have discovered you'd both escaped by deception." He stood holding another report behind his back. His legs were numb after the headlong drive from the news center. If only Quex would break down. Instead, he just sat, demanding more punishment.

"What else do you have there?" the old man asked.

Sol postponed the evil moment when he would have to display the macabre report on how, precisely, Bronfmann had been killed.

"More 88 threats. Now it's about some violent act, next Sunday."

Quex stared into the blazing fire. "That's the anniversary of the war to end all wars."

"Yes?" Sol wondered if the general was handling his loss by escaping into the past.

"We signed an armistice. Called it Armistice Day. But then we had more wars and too many armistices. We kind of backed into naming it Remembrance, then Veterans' Day. The Brits do these things rather well. Brass bands, battle hymns and cavalry. Monarchs and marching men. All gathered around that incredible mountain of carved white stone they call the Cenotaph."

Suddenly Sol no longer worried about Quex's ramblings. "Of course!"

"What's of course?"

"The need to remember the old alliance against the evils of fascism . . . It was all in a think piece AP put on the wire. But that's the *Second* World War," Sol added, seeing his newly minted theory already collapsing.

"We celebrate two world wars," Quex said dryly, "to date."

"Well, wait a moment! The AP piece was about American participation. The President's going. A reaffirmation of the aims of the Grand Alliance. There was some White House statement about what Remembrance Day means. An appeal to all who fought together then to stand together now for peace. Seemed theatrical."

"Hard times," said Quex. "Theatrical gestures."

"Big parades won't end this crisis."

"Nothing wrong with parades." Quex's voice quickened. "They make us remember the sacrifices that make us what we are. All around that ceremony in London, the entire nation halts for two minutes of silence. Every solitary thing comes to a stop. You can almost hear the beating of men's hearts."

Sol contemplated the possibilities for terrorism when a great industrial nation suddenly stops ticking.

"In the middle of the morning," Quex persisted. "It's most eerie. You've got all those leaders assembled, naked as the day they were born."

"Naked!"

"A figure of speech." Quex waved aside its triviality. "Under an open sky, they gather, so lacking protection they might as well be stripped bare. You know the English."

"Eyes closed? For two minutes?" Sol shook his head.

"Including the armed forces!"

"God help us!" Sol raised one hand and began ticking off his outspread fingers. "Tomorrow's Tuesday . . . four, no! *Five* more days. And then what happens?"

Quex became still again. His eyes were fastened on the report in Sol's other hand. The network executive quickly hitched up his jeans and smoothed the sweater over the gentle curve of his belly.

"What *is* that thing?" asked Quex, and Sol saw that he had no choice but to hand over the chilling doctors' story.

While Quex read through the autopsy report, Sol went down to the improvised kitchen. He talked with the men responsible for Quex's safety. He sat at the long oak dining table and scribbled notes. He made telephone calls.

When he returned to the library, Quex appeared not to have moved.

"I think this situation's out of our control," Sol said gently.

Quex looked down at the floor where he had tossed the report. "I can't stop now."

"I didn't say anything about *stopping*. We need outside help."

"I've got Hat Men everywhere."

"It's a very romantic notion. But you're not King Arthur and they're not knights of the round table."

"What would you have me do?"

"Go back to old friends at Langley."

"Can't trust 'em, politically."

"You were glad the CIA exposed the faked death-camp pictures."

"That's the tradesmen's entrance," said Quex. "If you go through the back door, you're liable to get slung out the same way when things get hot."

Sol saw the old man's head profiled like a perpetual question mark. Such insatiable curiosity deserved better, from allies, from Quex's own disabled body. So much of Quex's relish for life would be gone with Rinna. The pain had yet to be felt. Until that pain overwhelmed him, though, Quex would settle for distraction.

"I've used the back door myself in extremity," Sol said tentatively.

"Same here," said Quex.

"You can't have gone any higher than my boy."

"You couldn't go higher than mine," retorted Quex, color rising.

They stared at one another.

"Nobody is higher than the former director," said Sol.

"On whom the rain it raineth every day?" asked Quex, showing the faint glimmer of a smile.

Sol felt a surge of affection for the quixotic old cuss. "Yes," he said. "Because the unjust's got the just's umbrella."

So they had each been taking a little over-the-back-fence help from Walter Juste! And neither had known what the other was doing. That left a large question mark in Sol's mind. He looked Quex dead in the eye and saw the same question there, too. How many others had been getting help from Vice President Juste?

27

London, England

Squatting there in the black hole of his boyhood, Talbott wondered how much of Jake's story could be true.

"Why didn't you tell me all of this before?" Talbott asked at one point.

"I told you enough. You remembered what I needed you to remember—where the Radzki papers were. Unfortunately, you have them at the very moment I cannot demand them. Not while Sally holds a gun on me. She really needn't."

"But I am," Sally assured him. She had sighted on Jake's wristwatch. The dial was an illuminated target in that profound darkness, jumping with each of Jake's gestures.

"All I want," said Jake, "is Radzki's version of the Hess Command. Just the summary, in his own handwriting."

Sally caught the wheedling tone. It wasn't like the Jake she'd known in Israel. She stared at the dancing wristwatch and thought: My God, I've never set eyes on *this* Jake under a bright light: we're always underground, or sheltering in shady coffee shops!

She was startled by Talbott. "Let's see if what you want is here. Don't we have *any* light at all?"

"Matches?" suggested Jake. His wristwatch circled the air.

"Light up if you've got some," said Talbott.

The scratching was uncommonly loud. Sally winced. The flare of the first match was blinding. She saw Talbott turn out the papers from his own pockets. She heard him invite her to do the same. She wanted to refuse: to tell him there was something dreadfully wrong about this Jake Cooke and his need to see the papers. Then she thought the eerie tunnel, the proximity of the dead boy, the prolonged separation from normality, were all making her absurdly suspicious.

Jake struck match after match while they thumbed hurriedly through the documents. Did they represent all Radzki had snatched out of the flames of Nazified Europe? One skimpy folder registered on their minds. *Proposal for submission by Hess in London 07.5.41.*

"That," said Jake, "is what I must have. I'd tell you everything I know just to get my hands on that one."

"Then, you'd better tell me everything you know," said Talbott. He waited in the black silence. A New York detective had told him once, "You can concentrate best in the dark. The suspect's voice gives him away, if anything does."

Jake's opening words put him on guard. "Radzki led a life of conspiracy under various names, but I'm sticking to Radzki to keep things simple . . ."

Radzki comes from that part of Poland where, to survive under successive foreign conquests, it is natural to adjust to the wishes of alien authority, disguise your origins, be multilingual. But already when he is ten, Radzki wants to find his roots, although the family name seems impeccably Prussian. He joins relatives on a farming community in Palestine, carrying papers to fool the British administration. This is the 1920s. Britain is whittling down the promise contained in the Balfour Declaration that Jews should have a national home. Eretz Israel is viewed by Jewish idealists like Ahad Ha'am (Asher Ginzberg is his real name, they all seem to have optional identities) as the spiritual center to nourish national unity. A true Jewish state, it will reject the use of brute power in a brutal world.

Radzki draws inspiration from Ahad Ha'am, whose fame will spread far and wide as the advocate of a clean, sweet, moral Zionism. He sees Palestine as the spiritual core of a Jewish renaissance. Power will be exercised as moral pressure. No physical violence. Just sweet reason.

Radzki returns to Europe, a Zionist of this school. His young friend, left behind in Palestine, is Jacob Slominsky, later known as Jake Cooke. Jake's faith in a cultural rebirth is shaken in 1929 when British police intervene to support Moslems in a clash with Jewish worshippers at the Western Wall, in Jerusalem. Soon, Arab gangs move against the Jews in all the neighboring settlements. The oldest Habad community, at Hebron, is destroyed, making the city of Abraham uninhabitable for Jews, who had lived there for thousands of years.

The president of World Zionism, Chaim Weizmann, voices concern to the British colonial secretary, whose wife observes that she doesn't "understand why Jews make such a fuss over a few dozen killed in Palestine. As many are killed here in London in traffic accidents."

Jake, as Jacob Slominsky, concludes that the dream of a Jewish homeland is possible only if Jews fight for it. Power comes out of the gun. When he is twelve years old, he becomes a courier in the underground of Zeev Jabotinsky, and so begins a career in what later becomes the Irgun. Their first newspaper is *Ha-Metzuda*, the Citadel . . .

Talbott cut in. "Is there a connection with Operation Citadel?"

"Yes," said Jake. "We'll come to that."

Radzki has vanished behind the walls of Hitler's Germany. He is an angry young man. While still in Palestine, he has been exposed to Marxist-Leninist ideas at weekly "Circle" meetings, part of a Zionist socialist youth movement. He decides socialism, like the Eretz Israel dream, won't work on moral platitudes alone. He is quickly, discreetly, contacted by Soviet talent spotters.

He is the right age. He has features allowing him to pass as a north German. It is the heyday of Russian espionage in Germany. Moscow transforms him into a certified non-Jew, with church records tracing his mythical family all the way back to the Crusades. He takes up gliding, a permissible sport that evades Allied limits placed on German rearmament. Glider pilots are sent secretly for powered-aircraft training in Russia. This is Stalin's payment for Germany's help in breaking Allied sanctions against the Soviets.

Radzki becomes a German flying instructor inside Russia. He is an outstanding aviator. Moscow boosts his credentials to guarantee he will catch the eye of the Nazi hierarchy. Hitler, now in power, is the first leader to use air transport as others use trains. He needs a good all-weather pilot. Moscow aims to put Radzki into Hitler's stable, but accomplishes instead a very good second best: Hess.

Hess, vain about his own prowess as a flier from World War I, takes a shine to Radzki. During many well-publicized Hess flights, it is Radzki who often takes over the controls. He discusses with great enthusiasm the deputy fuehrer's part in writing *Mein Kampf* and is especially interested in plans for disposing of the Jews. Hess is flattered and delighted by this bright young Nazi's perception of the practical side to the final solution of the Jewish problem. He encourages him to study the system of concentration camps, those in existence and those to come.

Hess already has his own intelligence service, under his exclusive control. It happens, however, to have been built up with secret Soviet help. It is a dictator's ideal instrument: a spy agency run, and paid for, by the enemy; but surrendering the entire product to yourself, in this case, Stalin.

It is easy for Radzki to feed Stalin details of the Nazi plans for a final solution to the Jewish problem.

The Nazi invasion of Poland heralds a wave of mass killings. Jake (Slominsky) Cooke is now in London, having quarreled with the faction of Zionists who say the British are the first enemy. He argues this is the chance for sensible Zionists to win over the British. They would never forgive Zionists who undercut the British struggle. Jake Cooke works with the exile Polish Government to set up courier services inside Nazi territory.

"That's when I ran into Radzki again," said Jake. "He was in Warsaw, in German uniform, looking for a girl who'd been with the Polish Communist underground before the war. Her communism evaporated with Stalin's occupation of half Poland after his deal with Hitler."

Jake hesitated. "The girl, Talbott, was your mother's oldest sister."

Talbott stirred in the darkness. "I never heard she'd got a sister."

"Her name was Frieda," resumed Jake. "She finished up in a Birkenau-Auschwitz work camp. They were called work camps then. That's why Radzki was so often in Warsaw. It was a center for gathering camp intelligence, and he could always find some excuse for flying there. Agents slipped in and out of the camps."

"It's funny I never heard of this Frieda," said Talbott.

"There are many things you were never permitted to know." Jake waited, and then added: "I can go into that, if you want."

"Let's get back to the main narrative," Talbott said brusquely.

Then Radzki is suddenly called on to fly Deputy Fuehrer Hess to neutral Lisbon. The exiled Duke of Windsor has fled there from Paris following the fall of France. Hitler is convinced the Duke is regarded as rightfully the King of England by a "thinking plutocracy" eager to reject Churchill's "war-mongering" and make peace. The Duke has already told Hitler he's "hundred percent German". His wife, that woman from Baltimore, wants to recapture the throne of England, under Hitler's patronage if necessary.

It is July 1940. The Battle of Britain has begun in the air. Invasion has been decided on, in principle, by Hitler. A portion of the British public, to its everlasting shame, has declared it is time to negotiate. Any talks the Duke has with Hitler's emissary could undermine Churchill's resolve to rally his people.

Hess learns that the British Secret Service plans to kill the Duke for treachery. True or not, this information is passed along to the Duke. He agrees quickly to Churchill's appointment of him as Governor in the Bahamas. It is about as far as Churchill can remove the Duke from action. It is about as far as the Duke can get from danger.

The Duke continues to stay in touch with Nazi Germany, even from his

Caribbean shelf. Meanwhile, Hess has been provided with what purports to be a pipeline directly into London.

All this, Radzki duly notes. Then an invitation arrives, via Lisbon, proposing Hitler send a trusted and high-ranking negotiator to Britain. The suggested emissary is Hess.

Jake was interrupted by a clawing sound. It made Sally think of rats. She said, rather breathlessly, "There's nothing in public records to substantiate that story—"

"Tchah!" scoffed Jake. "By the time those records at Kew are declassified, they've been weeded, sanitized, laundered. I *know*. I'd get back from courier runs and report not only to the exile government here but also to Churchill's intelligence advisers. What I told the British about the progress of the 'final solution' *does not appear in declassified records today*. But you'll find my reports in the archives of the formerly exiled governments!"

The sound like rats' claws resumed, and grew clearer. A series of sharp explosions, *tak-a-tak-a-tak*, rattled through the tunnel.

Voices could be heard, the words muffled. Sound stretched as it bounced along that enormous tube, and reached the three fugitives in a distorted fashion. Torches seemed to burn just out of sight. Talbott had time to register that they were not approaching from where the dead boy lay. Then an apparition stood in front of him, holding up a sparkler in front of a face shaded to putty gray, with green-dyed eyebrows and red hair backcombed upright. The dwarf wore a taffeta clown's suit of flaming red and continued to chant, "Gunpowder, treason and plot!"

Another voice squeaked, "That's 'im . . . The bloke wot knew King Edward!"

There was another ear-splitting bang. Under its cover, Jake retreated deeper into the tunnel and Sally shifted position to obscure her gun. Talbott said, "Charlie! I knew we could rely on you."

"Yus, well, we cum down the other 'ole, see," Charlie said.

"The cops weren't the ones wot did it," said Ginger, holding up a canister gas lamp.

"Shut up!" said Charlie, too late to prevent the boy named Candlestick from starting to say, "The soldiers dun it."

"Done what?" asked Talbott.

"Put out our bonfires and sed we mustn't let off more fireworks," completed Candlestick.

"Wasn't me dad's lot," chimed in Charlie hastily. "Me dad's a detecative," he repeated. "The cops don't push us arahnd like that."

The boys huddled closer. "Wot 'appened to the bloke wiv a beard?" asked Charlie. He set light to another squib and turned to toss it along the tunnel.

"That's enough!" said Sally, grabbing the squib and squeezing out the sizzling fuse.

A lot less put out than the squib, Charlie said, "We bin lookin' for 'im. Promised us a speedway, 'e did. But 'e's gorn, scarpered."

"What were you supposed to do in return?" asked Talbott.

"Keep digzee," said Candlestick.

Talbott almost laughed. It was clear Jake Cooke had used the boys all along.

"Digzee?" asked Sally.

"Dick's eye. From Dick the Highwayman, who kept an eye open for strangers," said Talbott, buoyed by this echo from his boyhood.

"This bearded geezer sed 'e'd get the local council build us a real speedway," said Charlie. "We went lookin' for 'im tonight at the coffee shop, 'cos we race our bikes there, see? Only, there wuz nuffink but soldiers. And then Commander Nelson—"

"Nelson?" queried Sally.

"Famous, 'e is. Picture in the papers every day until 'e got in trouble wiv the politicians."

While he spoke, Charlie was edging round Sally, who moved to block his vision. He must have sensed either the presence of Jake or the corpse behind her. She said hastily, "Go find Commander Nelson, show him this, tell him I'm here." She took out one of her business cards.

"It was the commander told us to find *you!*" exclaimed Charlie with deepest scorn. " 'E's not stupid, like them others! 'E knows when that car blew up, you wouldn't be in it . . ."

Sally glanced at Talbott's face, pale in the smoky glare from Ginger's lamp. She said, "Then, get back to Nelson, quick as you can! Tell nobody else."

"We don't snitch," interrupted Candlestick sternly.

"In return for your help—" Talbott began.

Charlie pounced: "We don't need no bribes. Not now. Not even from the bleeder wiv the beard. You and the lady stick arahnd 'ere. We'll get the commander. 'E don't never snitch neither!"

The boys had left them one of their lamps. Sally lifted it so the rays caught Jake moving cautiously out of hiding.

"The bleeder wiv the beard!" said Talbott.

"Don't joke." Jake rubbed his face wearily. "I dragged the body deeper into the tunnel. Those kids are too nosy . . ." He shuddered. "Well, now we've got some real light to shed on the subject, I want to see those papers."

Talbott made sounds of agreement. He knew now how to keep Jake's appetite whetted.

They squatted in a narrow circle. There were handwritten copies of the original orders known as the Hess Command. One copy was in English, the other in Hebrew.

Jake scanned the Hebrew. "As I feared—"

Talbott reclaimed the papers. He hated to haggle over the past. Yet Jake had to be forced to tell all the truth. It might not be objective truth, but it would be Jake's truth.

Jake said: "You remarked on the coincidence of Radzki and Hess arriving in England on the same day. What I never told you was, they also arrived in the same aircraft." He savored the effect of this bombshell and then exploded another. "Stalin knew all about it."

Sally objected, "Stalin can't have known or he wouldn't have risked looking foolish with his questioning of Churchill."

"Read Churchill's account more carefully," cautioned Jake. "He writes that Stalin said even in Russia 'our Secret Service doesn't necessarily tell me everything.' Stalin was having a little fun on his own, twisting the old lion's tail."

"How did Stalin know, *if* he did?" interrupted Talbott. "And how did Radzki come to fly on the Hess mission?"

Radzki in Hitler's Berlin has discovered his Jewishness with a vengeance. He knows now that Stalin sees only practical advantages to letting Hitler go ahead with building this bizarre machinery for killing the Jews of Europe: it will take up huge resources of German manpower, transport and administrative services, and military hardware. Stalin is still at this time Hitler's ally, but he wants to be sure the Nazi war machine finds other things to do than turn on Russia. The British, on the other hand, are now fighting on alone and say they will continue to defy what Churchill calls the monstrous Nazis. Radzki believes Churchill represents a genuine struggle for international justice. He is convinced he need only confront the leaders in London with the evidence of Hitler's mass liquidation program to get action. And Hess gives Radzki the opportunity.

For five or six months after the secret talks regarding the ex-King of England, Hess takes lessons in flying the Messerschmidt 110-D, the Zerstörer, or Destroyer. Radzki is his instructor. Each flight is filed as a solo "familiarization" exercise.

Finally Hess confides that an invitation has been accepted for the deputy fuehrer to fly secretly to England. To ensure success, Radzki must go as pilot. The Me-110, even with extra fuel tanks, cannot make a return journey . . . Radzki proposes he should parachute separately, and go underground to continue serving the Third Reich as a spy.

Radzki reports all this to Moscow, and also asks for Russian intelligence contacts in England so that he can resume his trade as a Soviet agent there! Impudent? Reckless? You have to remember by now that Radzki feels he must be the chosen of God. A solitary and secret Jew, he has been granted access to the very core of the machinery designed to destroy his people. And now he is in a unique position to talk directly with those who can stop that machinery. Meanwhile, he wants to keep unblemished his remarkable record in the Kremlin, where Stalin depends on him for each detail of the Nazi peace bid. He feels he can do anything, not an uncommon belief among archconspirators with the Lord on their side.

The flight takes off before dusk on Saturday, May 10, 1941. The official records say nothing about Radzki as pilot. No provision is made for a flight that extends into the North Sea and then follows a pattern that will puzzle experts later.

The leader of German fighter squadrons, Adolf Galland, is telephoned that evening by his chief, Marshal Göring: "The deputy fuehrer has gone mad and is flying to England. He must be shot down!" Galland searches the area and finds nothing.

That is part of Hitler's plan to make it seem Hess acts alone. Galland has been sent deliberately to search in the wrong area. The mystery still remains of where exactly the Me-110 has gone. There will be speculation later about the impossibility of its staying aloft for the five hours' duration of the mission, and the discrepancy between numbers identifying the aircraft which took off and the one that crashed.

"Radzki injured his leg when he parachuted," said Jake. "He linked up with Zionists in London and invented some story about escaping through Sweden. Six weeks later, Hitler invaded Russia, and then Göring ordered preparations for the final solution. To Radzki, the two things were connected."

"Can you *prove* that?" asked Talbott.

"Look at who benefited," flashed back Jake. *"Eighty* percent of German first-line military power became tied up in building and operating the death traffic."

Boots clattered, the noise eerily magnified. This was not the scuffle of furtive feet, but the implacable plod of a constable. A pencil of light crept along the curved wall.

"Nelson of Scotland Yard." There was a hint of self-mockery in the voice as the light came to rest on Jake. "Jacob Slominsky, I presume."

"Cooke. I'm Jake Cooke."

"Come on, me old china. To me you'll always be Slominsky. Caused mischief then. Causing it now." Nelson unburdened himself of a kit bag. "There's hot grub in tinfoil, hot coffee in flasks, groundsheets, some newfangled astronautical wrappers for kippin' down in . . ." He set down the lamp. "Now then, Slominsky, you're on record saying, 'One man can hold off an army if he fights his battle in a tunnel.' It won't wash here."

Jake drew back from the light. "The Nazis lost their last battle in a tunnel, in Berlin."

"Smart lad," said Nelson. "So move yourself along, and take your gangsters with you." There was an odd joviality in his voice that took the edge off the harsh words. "You're lucky it's not the Russians firing an artillery piece down the tunnel at you, like they did in Berlin. The SAS and Grimweather have kinder hearts."

"You mean they don't want political trouble," said Jake. "Everything's political, isn't it, in the end?"

"Sorry, but it's for Jake's own sake," said Nelson after Jake had scrambled up the ladder. "I had to get him out fast." The manhole cover fell back into place with a clang.

"You succeeded," Talbott said dryly. "And buggered up our negotiations. Why?"

"His gang's always been marked as terrorist. I don't want more screams about Jewish thuggery. He knows I'm doing it for his own good."

Nelson was tugging a thick envelope from his pocket. "In a few hours, a sewage-disposal truck will pretend to pump water out of here. The men will give you gear to get into, so they can trundle you away."

Talbott shook himself. "We can't creep around forever like hunted criminals."

"You won't want to get arrested, neither," said Nelson. "Not after you've read this."

Talbott stared at the envelope. Ominous black letters were stamped upon the brown paper: ON HER MAJESTY'S SERVICE.

Sally said, "We'd better tell Nelson about the dead—"

"Dead letters?" Nelson interrupted loudly. "No! Dead letters go to a special post-office department. Deals with letters where the addressee can't be found, eh?" He was booming at them, and they both stared back at him in astonishment. He seemed to have lost his senses. "Best, sometimes, not to find *dead* letters, eh? What you don't know won't hurt you."

Then it dawned on them. Nelson knew about the dead boy but chose to remain officially ignorant. He was in trouble enough, without being accused of complicity in violent death.

"Well, I'm going back the way I came," said Nelson. Again he thrust the brown envelope at Talbott. "It's the facts on the Bronfmann murder." He backed away, and his bulldog face seemed to lengthen. He became formal, like a constable breaking bad news. "Digest it, sir. Try to keep things in perspective. I shall have to ask you, later on, sir, if you think—from what you know—if your mother, Rebecca Talbott, might have died in the same manner."

28

Yuri Gorin had just received a copy of the same report from the director of the KGB's Department V, Tolya Petrov, arriving from Moscow that same night.

The Soviet leader was in residence at Tito's old villa above Igalo. He stood in a bay window, looking down to where three Yugoslav patrol boats swept the calm sea with their searchlights. Mother hoped they were not looking for the American traveler.

He turned back to Petrov. "Explain this!"

The soft growl warned Petrov to tread with care. Mother was not easy to anticipate. He proceeded like a grizzly bear on a date with a destiny known only to himself, shuffling and snuffling down some private path. Perhaps it was the only way a former KGB boss could progress through the treacherous politburo marshlands, but it made him unpredictable. He was notorious for sudden, savage diversions to catch out suspected opponents and crush them.

Petrov had flown to Titograd, then motored to Igalo. The ancient ferry at Kotor had delayed him. It was ludicrous that he should take the blame for arriving late. The fault was that of the lackadaisical Yugoslavs. Fraternal brothers of the Soviet Union they might be, but a pestilence nonetheless. "In Russia, I would have that ferryman in jail. But here—"

"Here we walk on ice!" Mother warned sharply. "Never mind Tito's wonderland. Explain this."

Petrov shot a frightened glance at the Bronfmann report suddenly waving in his face. "The first tests were made by the West German chemical-defense establishment at Weissenburg," he said hurriedly. "What they found made them turn for help to Porton Down, where the English have facilities—"

"We know about Porton Down."

"Their conclusions were photocopied there by one of our—"

"No!" roared Mother. "I don't want to know the nuts and bolts." His shock of iron-gray hair stood straight. The spectacles gleamed dangerously. *"Your part. Explain that!"*

Petrov tried to read beyond the mask. If he guessed wrong, he would soon stand against the Lubyanka's Black Wall. If he told the truth, he might wind up in the Mordovian crematorium, alive but not for long.

"I knew nothing about it," he said, his vision dimming in a moment of sheer terror. When he could see Mother's face clearly again, the iron teeth were showing in a smile. "That is what I have been told," said Mother. "Lucky for you. Now leave me."

The Bronfmann report was full of the wherefores and whereases that Mother supposed were like a pox in every secret agency. Bureaucrats were all alike. He spread the report out on a cloth-covered table and stood over it, reading. The pellet had been injected by needle, hidden in the umbrella, triggered by the handle. The 1.52-millimeter pellet was made of 90 percent platinum, 10 percent iridium. The contents were released through pin-tip holes sealed with wax that melted with body heat. The poison was ricin, derived from the castor-oil plant. The report went on:

British experiments in World War II, under code W, indicate this most effective mass poison (see Ministry of Warfare report MEW/W Chemattack SOE-5041-a: Proposal for Eliminating Staff in Dachau Rescue Op). Ranks alongside botolinus, tetanus, gramicidin and diphtheria as world's most toxic element. It is estimated a single gram of ricin will kill 36,000 adults. The assassins were still taking no chances. The ricin seems to have been mixed with bacteria of the type involved in gangrene. There was evidently no desire to make this appear to be death by natural causes.

Point of entry: Prostate gland. If the umbrella hypothesis is correct, victim would have been attacked while bending over, or while lying on back with legs spread in the air. However, the samples of tissue and fabric sent with the missile indicate victim was fully dressed at the time. This suggests the use of an unusually long, reinforced syringe-type injector, permitting the pellet to be fired after clothing and outer skin had been penetrated. *Re:*

*your requests for comments vis-à-vis physical and mental dis-
tress:* Extreme pain followed by rapid loss of muscular and nervous control is normal in such cases. The advantage of this poison is that the victim is rendered immediately speechless,
incapable of physical action. He usually dies in prolonged silent
agony. Judged from purely humanitarian viewpoint, this is a death
involving almost indescribable psychological pain . . .

There was something beyond sadism in this use of ricin. Mother sat at
the desk and permitted himself a moment's weariness.

The manner of Bronfmann's death would certainly drive Talbott to
desperate action. And wasn't this what that wooden-top, Helmuth
Henkell, would be counting on? The East German was more reckless than
the religious heretics of earlier times. The trick was to turn that recklessness to Mother's own advantage.

Mother took a deep breath. The plan he had been formulating for some
time had finally taken shape. He felt an almost orgasmic relief. He knew he
had been guided once again into making the right decision.

The villa had been equipped for Marshal Tito to conduct private affairs.
Behind a green padded door, Tolya Petrov was back at work on the routine stuff of Department V, the thirteenth section, identified only by the
letter F, the *taini otdel* (secret division) responsible for KGB liquidations.
It now ran the special Moscow school, at the corner of Metrostroevskaya
and Turnaninski Pereulok, whose Cyrillic name made the acronym for
ECLIPSE . . . Extremely Confidential Liquidation . . . Petrov hated
to run the words through his mind, because eclipse was not confined to
foreign territories; indeed, an eclipse order was more often directed against
enemies at home. The Blowaway Department, a few jokers called it; but
that was within the safety of the Moscow office, where Petrov himself
could draw reassurance from the surrounding fortress of files.

He trembled as Mother lumbered through the door, expecting the old
man to be still furious. Petrov, like the boss, had served as an illegal
abroad. The shared experience should be a bond; but it often left a lingering suspicion that one had been subverted: Stalin's old paranoia. To Petrov's joy, he caught from Mother the brief wink of comradeship and the
rare wintry smile. Some of the emptiness in Petrov's belly vanished. He
jumped to his feet and joined Mother with the quick footsteps of a priest
summoned to a private audience.

"Where is Shifrin?"

The sudden question brought color to Petrov's cheeks. Shifrin was head
of INTERINFOR, the department of international information, associated with the better-known Department for Disinformation, now called
Active Measures, all under the First Chief Directorate of the KGB. Active
Measures concerned the greatly expanded work of forging documents to

misrepresent Western, and especially U.S., policies. It looked as if Shifrin was the one who would land in the shit, not Petrov.

"Shifrin?" No point in making a meal of it. "Shifrin's still in Berlin."

"*Still?*"

Petrov breathed more easily still. "His task, you recall, was to coordinate work in his field among our allies. He hasn't progressed much beyond the German Democratic Republic."

"With Shifrin, we'll deal later. What, personally, do you know about the Hess Command?"

"Only what's in those folders." Petrov pointed with his chin in the direction of the desk.

"I'm not surprised." The response was not unfriendly. There was no hint of sarcasm.

Petrov brightened. He was trusted. He moved to the door.

Mother raised a pawlike hand. "Wait! I'm in need of your most proficient killers. None of your dumdum and piano-wire thugs." He ambled to the window and back. "Oxford accents. Good at small talk in a diplomatic setting. Some of the English brolly-and-bowler plus a dash of red-blooded American, yes? It would help if these young gentlemen sported expensive suntans from the ski slopes."

"Ski slopes? It's early for skiing, comrade."

The Secretary-General of the Communist Party of the Soviet Union laid a heavy paw on Petrov's shoulder. "You mustn't take me so literally, my dear fellow. It's the suntan that matters."

Later, in Tito's old study, Yuri Gorin gazed through the windows at mountains silvered by the moon. Skiing had been in his mind since the Hess Command had finally exploded into this personal crisis. He stared up at the snow-covered peaks, their expression as aloof as that of Hess on a memorable day at Garmisch, near Munich. The deputy fuehrer in his all-black skiing outfit had sniffed the alpine air that winter of 1938 and promised, "Soon, we shall smell only the spilled blood of the Jews. The Fuehrer himself has told me, 'The day of reckoning has come . . . We are going to destroy the Jews.' " And then, before pushing off down the slope, Hess had added in a matter-of-fact voice: "But of course the Fuehrer will never put his name to such an order. He's too clever for that."

29

Talbott was jerked from a deep sleep by Sally shouting, "Didn't you hear me? Jake went off with the papers!"

"*I*'ve got the papers," grumbled Talbott.

"Not the Hebrew translation!"

Talbott sat up. He'd no idea how long they must have slept in the tunnel, warmed by Nelson's rum. He groped through his pockets. Sally said, "I *know* he's got the Hebrew material. I had this dream. Jake was reading it, then Nelson distracted us. Only of course it's not only a dream!"

Talbott turned on the lamp and stared at her, appalled.

"You know how this will look, to Jake and his men?" Sally persisted.

Talbott was searching for the English copy. It was Radzki's account of what Hitler had proposed to a group of influential Englishmen, through Hess. If the Hebrew version reached Jake's men, they would visualize the ardent Zionist struggling against frightful odds to preserve the damning evidence. Just the survival of his handwritten notes alone packed an emotional wallop.

He rose and began his familiar pacing, back and forth, back and forth. Within the small circle of illumination, his movements constricted, he seemed to Sally to be slipping into his former mood of self-recrimination. "I've been dancing like a puppet," he muttered.

"But Jake's not pulling the strings," Sally said quickly. "He can't be."

Talbott paused. He distrusted his own judgment after reading how Bronfmann had died. Death by injection. It could be the way Rebecca died, even if the fake autopsy recorded morphine. He couldn't face the implications.

Before going to sleep, he had talked to Sally more frankly than he had ever talked with anyone in his life; had blamed himself for wiping out the past; had spoken about his ghost coming after him now with a knife . . . The ghost bit struck Sally as balderdash, even when he quoted Jung about our younger selves returning in vengeance. What the hell did Jung know? Sally had asked herself angrily.

Now Sally asked no questions, not of herself, not of Talbott. His nerves were raw. He must have been like this in war. He was in a class with Grandpa Massey, with Sol Farkas and Jake Cooke . . . They were . . . ? She settled on jargon from her own trade: they were out of sync in their private lives. Action and sound were out of synchronization. They were disjointed in their reactions at certain moments, as if they had trouble matching civilized behavior with the way they met violence in war. That must be why Talbott liked to keep on the move, though he claimed to hate the vagabond existence.

She saw him take out Rebecca's diary. His hands were trembling.

"The month before Szmuel—that's Radzki, of course—made his appeal for bombing the camps," he read aloud from one page, "the Germans announced the greatest raid of all time on London—100,000 bombs spread across London. The Mother of Parliaments burned. Westminster Abbey, St. Paul's Cathedral, the British Museum . . . one by one, the great landmarks were struck. The people were driven to shelter in the Underground . . ."

There it was again. Underground railroad, the tube, the subways buried deep under the city, a maze of rabbit warrens. The word had come to mean so much. Underground resistance, underground terrorists . . .

She wished she could get him out of the tunnel. It was too much like the Henry Moore impressions of London women and children sheltering from bombs. They resembled slave workers stacked like cordwood. The artist, even then, had the vision to see they were all innocents trapped in the underworld of camps and concentrated bombing.

The only way to stop Talbott lacerating himself was to push him into action. She was startled when the thought was followed by a blinding shaft of daylight from above. A man yelled, "Watch yer 'eads!" Two bundles tumbled through the manhole. "We're Nelson's garbage men. Get that gear on fast and shove your own stuff in the empties. Got it?"

"Got it!" Talbott shouted back. He turned. Sally stood in the beam of light, face uplifted, like a figure from a religious painting, struck by a vision. He called her name.

"That translation!" She came alive. "Jake must be familiar with Radzki's handwriting. Suppose Radzki's . . . alive?"

"He can't be. And handwriting changes." But even as he spoke, Talbott felt trapped in new misgivings.

"Some people never can disguise their original writing style," Sally persisted. "And what Jake would recognize is the old Radzki style. I mean, suppose Radzki's undercover? Look, it's no more bizarre than our trusting Nelson. Where can he take us? He's an outlaw himself."

"Not an outlaw . . ."

"Get a move on down there!" The booming voice ended their speculation.

"Coming!" Talbott called out. He emptied the sacks: rubber Wellington boots, white coveralls, peaked municipal caps. Sally refilled the sacks with their discarded clothes. Then they climbed into the dazzling light of morning.

A man in a garbage collector's outfit said, "Get in! We ain't got all day!" There was a blur of men jumping onto the back of the white sanitation truck. Talbott and Sally were directed to the driving cab. Someone hammered on the roof. The driver already had the diesel running. He swung the truck through a smashed fence and onto the paved road skirting the wasteland.

The wasteland seemed suddenly small, peopled with so many exhumed figures. In the perpetual twilight of the past hours, the gray shadows of Jake's men and the SAS had lent it a nightmare dimension. Radzki's strange life had woven into the tapestry of their imagination such richness of drama and conjecture that Sally and Talbott were shocked to see the wasteland as less than a vast battlefield. It was just another of those many abandoned estates where the dockers had lived, serving the busy yards, until the Blitz and then economic blight spread scars like a leprosy.

The gaunt No-Man's-Land Tuckshop passed by. Someone, after Scroggins' unpremeditated departure, at least had enough sense of humor to name it that. The place stood alone again. The gunmen were gone. No smoke curled out of Chinese Lum's kitchen.

And then they were snatched up by the novelty of speeding through the morning London traffic in a giant garbage truck. It rolled up the East India Dock road like a specter symbolizing all the trucks and trailers once grumbling and rumbling up from Woolwich and the dockside warehouses, belching fumes into the sooty air. It drilled a path through the crush on Commercial Road, wove between side streets below St. Paul's Cathedral, and swung round Ludgate Hill. It plunged into Cheapside, ancient flashpoint of sudden and bloody violence. It doubled back and emerged where the City and Westminster meet at Temple Bar. It tore along Fleet Street, contemptuous of outraged honks from swaying double-deck buses.

Through the Strand it thundered, and around Trafalgar Square. The menacing grind of its outsize gears sent the small English cars scuttling, as if their drivers expected to be stamped on, compressed, and served up as square meals of metal.

"Get a good dekko, mate!" the sweating driver said, directing Talbott to look down Whitehall from where Admiral Nelson stared stonily from his column. For an idiotic moment, Talbott thought he meant Commander Nelson of the Yard, for Scotland Yard was down there, still the home of the great detectives. And then he saw the Cenotaph. The Cenotaph! Assembly point for that vast yearly congregation of those who mourned the millions who died in two world wars. The Cenotaph stood bang in the middle of Whitehall, the Prime Minister's No. 10, the Queen in her palace, Parliament, the War Office . . . and Scotland Yard. "Parliament proposes," went the adage Talbott had learned in school. "Whitehall disposes. The Yard keeps the peace."

"Is that where we're going?" he asked the driver.

The man turned a scornful eye on him, as if the question was too stupid to be worth answering. Then he said, "No, but it's where your Yankee President will be standing, come Sunday."

Talbott caught his breath. Suddenly a lot of things made sense. He had forgotten the special arrangements to bring together the wartime Western Allies, here, for the first time standing shoulder to shoulder with leaders of the still-far-flung British Commonwealth. He glanced over at Sally. She was staring at the Cenotaph as if her eyes would pop.

The Cenotaph gleamed in the November sunshine. The sculptured stone rose like a snowy mountain peak. "Remember us, the dead!" it seemed to demand. And the demand would be met, just as it had been when Talbott was a schoolboy, year by year drawing the great crowds. Only, this time— in five days' time!—an American President would obey that command as well. Remember.

The barracks of the Household Cavalry spun by. Along the mall to Buckingham Palace, they overtook a column of black Daimlers. The lead car flew the royal standard. Talbott had some faint recollection that nobody overtook royalty. It didn't seem to matter. The garbage truck assumed a special dispensation, lurched in a wide circle to bolt up Constitution Hill, and finally rocketed round Hyde Park Corner after setting up reverberations along the high wall, armored with iron spikes, protecting the Queen's parkland. And now, as if out of breath, the truck slowed to a crawl, sucked into the treacle of traffic heading west through Knightsbridge and so along the boundary of Hyde Park to Kensington Gore and . . .

Embassy Row! Recognition jolted Talbott when the truck shot forward to make a sudden, sharp turn into a gated side street. Along this private highway, vast and windy Victorian mansions had been converted to foreign legations. As the driver leaned out to maneuver past a policeman on duty, Talbott said to Sally: "Soviets are at the top of the street. Israelis at the bottom. Want to bet where we'll end up?"

"I'd bet on Nelson," she said, thinking it was Nelson of the Yard got them into this, and it was Nelson who was accused by some of being a Soviet agent.

The ambivalence of her answer was not lost on Talbott. The Russians were at the far, Bayswater end of this gated road known as Palace Gardens. The Israelis were at the foot, here, at Number 2, Palace Green, below the old kitchen gardens of the rambling, modest, middle-class palace where the Queen's relatives lived.

The driver hung halfway out the cab, negotiating the narrow entrance past the Royal Gardens Hotel. The policeman held up his hand. "You know better than this, cock."

"Special instructions, mate!" The driver flourished a grubby piece of paper.

The constable read it slowly. "Request to remove trash? Diplomats! Always asking for special treatment. You've got a big bunch of lads for shifting dustbins, you 'ave." He hoisted himself up onto the running board. "Okay, move along, I'll come along for the ride." He glanced inside at Sally. "Funny bloody work for a lady, mum," he said before she could turn her head away.

The truck took a sudden lurch left. The heavy-duty tires crunched on gravel. The bobby jumped down as the big truck drew up behind bushes and trelliswork concealing the embassy from public view. The windows were heavily barred. Anyone approaching the entryway had to come by foot, under scrutiny of the security cameras. Talbott sagged with relief. The discreet brass plaque announced they were in the grounds of the Israeli embassy.

One of the men clinging to the back of the truck appeared on Sally's side of the cab, unwound a scarf concealing the lower half of his face, and said, "You look a mite sick, Miss Ryan."

The tension had turned Sally's face white. Now the color rushed back. She jumped to the ground and threw her arms around the garbage man's neck. "Steve McQueen! Straight out of *The Bounty Hunter.*"

Talbott joined her. "Fishhook!"

The former FBI man grinned.

"I hope you didn't bring handcuffs," said Talbott.

"Don't worry. You're both said to be missing in that dockside car crash." Fishhook Sherman spread out his long arms to encompass them. "But get under cover fast, before anyone sees you."

He swept them along a driveway cleared of all obstructions, giving the embassy security men a wide field of fire. Hefty young Israelis loitered among the laurels or faced the narrow lane into Vicarage Gate. From a turreted mansion across the way, advertising itself discreetly as the embassy of a Soviet satellite, a pair of binoculars reflected back a brief flash of wintry sunshine.

General Steely Pamir introduced himself. He had never entirely lost the understated, throwaway style of his youthful RAF service. Sally thought him a romantic, ageless figure. She also noted the line across his forehead separating the bronzed features from a patch of white where a peaked cap kept off the desert sun. She concluded he spent as much time in Jerusalem as here. She thought him a man unused to evasions, to judge by the candid eyes, the flamboyant mustache, the rather dashing way he waved the leather-gloved hand to make a point.

"Hope we didn't scare the bejabers out of you," said Pamir. "We'd no choice. London's on a full CRW alert. You'd better understand what that means. Counter-Revolutionary Warfare. One step down from a Black Alpha state of readiness. CRW teams are made up of SAS commandos and SPGs, Special Patrol Groups. CRW takes command authority over everything else in a London emergency. If Parson Furneval finds out you're still alive, he might find a way to seize you."

A boyish grin softened Steely Pamir's warning. "We'll keep the bastard guessing as long as we can. They've dredged up the car, but frogmen still have days to search those muddy waters. We just can't risk losing you. You've got something Parson Furneval desperately wants."

Talbott saw what was coming. This man would ask for the Radzki papers. He would have heard details from Nelson. He would also know better than anyone the significance of Radzki. The last time Talbott had seen General Peled Pamir was after the preemptive Israeli air strikes that saved the country in the Six Day War. Today, Pamir's office was an austere cell reached by narrow passages through clever security traps posing as sharp corners and unexpected steps. Steely Pamir was now sitting at a kitchen table in front of the single barred and frosted window, under a light from the only bulb, strung from the ceiling and shaded with cardboard. He seemed to be drying his laundry on the hot-water pipes. Not long before, Pamir commanded the kind of bombers Radzki had once so desperately sought. This London lair made Pamir seem to live as Radzki once had lived. And what Pamir was doing now—surely that was precisely what Radzki had tried once to do?

Talbott realized Steely Pamir was waiting for an answer to the unspoken question. "General," he said, "I have papers that would put Radzki's life in jeopardy."

He spoke unthinkingly as if Radzki was still alive. The effect was remarkable. If General Pamir lacked the trappings, he could still project power. His face turned to stone. He seemed resolved not to move, as if any gesture might be taken as a statement. He had become as inert as the gloved artificial hand sitting on the desk in front of him.

Fishhook broke the long silence. Leaning against the shabby white wall beside the closed door, he said, "Sally, did Jake ever suggest Radzki"—Fishhook picked his words so carefully that it became painful to listen—"Radzki perhaps didn't die?"

"N-n-no!" Sally twisted round in her chair to look up at him. "Why'd you hesitate?"

Talbott said quickly, "We got the feeling Radzki could have survived the war. I *know* his suicide in London was faked. That's all."

The gloved hand on Pamir's desk moved a fraction as he shifted the arm. "Nothing else to go by?" he asked.

"About Radzki being dead or alive?" Talbott looked bewildered. "Only our intuition. And the papers he left behind."

Pamir nodded. His eyes glittered. Talbott thought that if the Israeli had been an eagle, that is how he would have appeared, perched attentively on a crag: the frozen concentration, then a brief flicker of wings, a fluffing of feathers, before settling back again to wait.

Pamir said, "I've no wish to alarm you." Then he stopped and with his good hand picked up a paper knife. He dug the point into a blotting pad. "Well, first . . . Do you know where Jake went when he left you?"

"No," said Talbott, and recounted the way Jake had been told by Nelson to get his men out of danger.

"You know, of course, my government has to regard Jake's guards *officially* as terrorists in this country?" asked Pamir. "And that I'm representing an antiterrorist arm? So I'm *officially* Jake's enemy. Philosophically I'm also opposed to him. I don't think Israel can afford to behave as if we have no friends in the world." He let the last sentence hang in the air.

The water in the heating pipes gurgled. They could all hear a tapping at the window as the winter wind stirred the dead branches of a tree.

Sally said, "I could probably find Jake. My guess is, he'll be looking for more of Radzki's papers."

"Ah, the papers." General Pamir seemed to want to cut her short. "I can't force you to let me see them." He looked at Fishhook, as if pleading for help. "You'd better tell them, Mr. Sherman."

"Rinna Dystel's been murdered," said Fishhook.

"Oh, no!" Sally half rose from her seat. "My grandfather—?"

"Quex is okay. Rinna's body was dumped on the road outside my place, though. That was pretty horrible for him." Fishhook examined the palm of his hand as if he had become a police witness reading from his notes, determined to finish his opening statement. "She'd been injected with something after extensive bruising. She did not habitually take drugs. Her medical history shows no recent vaccinations or treatments consistent with such injections. The possibility of truth drugs had to be considered."

"Truth drugs? Why?" demanded Sally.

Pamir interrupted. "She shared with only one or two other people certain knowledge vital to Israel's security."

Fishhook plodded on. "It's thought she was in fact dying when the injections took place. They want us to assume she talked. We do *not* believe she did."

"How can you be sure?" Talbott asked.

"If she'd revealed what she knew, the repercussions would have been immediate. Spectacular! We'd all know! There'd be no reason to deliver her body to us." Fishhook summarized Rinna's sudden departure in the borrowed car and the assumption that she had met with an accident almost a hundred miles from his house. "The killers want to stampede us into doing something that will reveal what they most want to learn . . . The thing Rinna did not, nor ever would, tell them."

Sally said, "Clearly, you think this involves Radzki. So you'd better know . . ." She glanced at Talbott for approval. He nodded. "Jake's wandering around London with some of Radzki's *handwritten* notes."

Talbott was watching Steely Pamir gently rubbing the back of his gloved hand. For a second, the rubbing stopped. Then it resumed and the Israeli said with scarcely a change of tone, "You mean, he's looking? For what?"

Sally glanced at Talbott, who said, "Radzki made some kind of index to papers he'd hidden all over London. So Jake claims. He used the word *duboks*. Isn't that Moscow's usage?"

"Means hiding places." Pamir leaned forward. "What would you say was in them?"

"Death-camp details which he'd already provided the authorities. Radzki saw forms of Gestapo everywhere. Even in London, he was scared —" Talbott corrected himself. "He was *respectful* of secret power. And distrustful. So he buried copies of his reports in case others—for anti-Jewish reasons or otherwise—buried the originals. He wanted, all camp victims wanted, some record to survive, as if the documentation of hell would make hell more bearable."

General Pamir reached across his desk for an old-fashioned call button. "Power," he muttered. "Radzki certainly respected it. Maybe he buried those copies to keep himself straight . . . Radzki's own notes," he asked, turning his eyes on Talbott, "would they be in Hebrew?"

"Mostly."

Steely Pamir pressed the call button. A buzzer sounded at the door. Slowly Talbott laid the bulk of papers on Pamir's desk, but withheld the red clothbound diary. A pretty young woman in khaki blouse and skirt came into the office. Pamir said, "Our best translator. Okay?"

"Okay," said Talbott.

"Nobody else will see it," Pamir promised. "Dahlia, here, is very fast. She's cleared to the highest level."

Dahlia, untroubled by the testimonial, gave Talbott a mechanical smile and took the papers.

"By the way," said Pamir. The girl stopped. "What about the . . . er, notebook?" The girl waited for Talbott's reply.

"My mother's. Rebecca Talbott. Her diary."

"Ah!" The statement seemed to clear some obstacle in Steely Pamir's mind. He dismissed Dahlia and turned upon Sally a smile of charming apology. "Miss Ryan, perhaps you might go with Mr. Sherman? He has a message from your grandfather."

Alone with Talbott, the Israeli grimaced. "I didn't manage that very skillfully, but we don't have time for niceties." He wrenched at his necktie until it came loose, then unbuttoned the top of his shirt. He hoisted one leg onto the table and stretched back. "I've no choice, Mr. Talbott. We need your help. Nobody can give us what you can. It involves personal risk. And you can't tell the story."

"As a reporter, I always say no, right at this point! I don't want to hear anything off the record. As a reporter."

"But as the son of Rebecca?"

Talbott pulled forward his chair. "I *must* know how my mother died and why she had to die."

"We're in your hands. She would have wanted this. You'll agree when you've heard me out."

"I'll listen, but I'll reserve judgment."

General Pamir sighed. He would have to take the gamble. There was no alternative. His country's fate. Always forced into action because: *no alternative!* When your back's to the sea, and a militant multitude presses you with sacred oaths promising destruction, there's no alternative to holding fast.

He leaned forward and let the leather-clad metal hand drop like an ornament upon the desk. *"Ex pede Herculem."*

Talbott jumped. The gesture had been so abrupt. "What?"

"From the foot you may judge Hercules. The part is an index to the whole. Some part of Radzki's papers contains an index to the rest, scattered around London. But where? Someone's going to find out, soon. It had better be our side." Pamir regarded the artificial hand and began what first seemed a pointless anecdote.

"I was walking around the nose of a Spitfire," he said. "I didn't know a mechanic was in the cockpit, about to run an engine test. The starter cartridge exploded. I stuck out my arm, an instinctive reaction. The prop turned and took off my hand."

He looked up. "I don't want something like that happening now. Jake Cooke doesn't know the whole situation. He's alarmed. He sticks out his arm to defend our people. He'll lose more than just a hand. He could cost us everything."

Steely Pamir's forehead was damp. The sentences began to come out haltingly.

"Jake has fallen for the 88's version of the Hess Command. A secret Western deal with Hitler that *decimated* the Jews. One man has the real and more hair-raising version. Radzki . . . Jake thinks the Western Alliance betrayed Radzki in Operation Citadel. One man, if persuaded this is true, could change history for the worse. Radzki . . . You'll have to meet Radzki!"

"But—" Talbott's jaw dropped. "Are *you* saying he's alive?"

"He is."

"Under what name?"

Steely Pamir wiped the back of his arm across his face. "We have no reason not to believe"—he made a gesture of irritation at trapping himself in the double negatives of diplomacy—"we're still gambling he's one of us. He says he wants to come out. He mustn't."

"Come out? From where?"

But the Israeli would only say, "He will trust you. You're the only man alive can persuade him to stay in place."

"I'm not doing anything yet." Talbott's mind raced through all the possibilities. Was Radzki the prisoner in Spandau they called Hess? No! Anything else seemed even more preposterous. "Who the hell is Radzki?" he burst out.

General Pamir began playing with the paper knife again. "Rinna Dystel was our personal guardian over Quex," began the Israeli. "Oh, she helped his investigation, yes! We wanted to know all he could find out. But if he'd discovered too much, *then* she was to silence him. She was one of four who know Radzki. Another is chairman of our parliamentary committee on intelligence. Then myself. Finally your Vice President, Walter Juste, ex-CIA director, pillar of strength . . ."

Talbott listened, and some of it made a crazy sort of sense. What was it Radzki told the bomber chief? Someday he'd make all the warlords listen, because *he* would hold the power.

"Even four is too many," Pamir was saying. "The circle's starting to widen. We can't protect Radzki much longer . . . He was on his own for years. He saw firsthand how dictators work. First he was their victim. Then he saw the way to use a miraculous body of experience. Yes, *miraculous*. He felt Jehovah had assigned him to grasp the only argument to save the Jews: power. He made himself the most powerful man in the world. We know him as Yuri Gorin, Little Mother of all the Russias."

Talbott shivered. "Impossible," he said after a long silence. "The man might twist his mind to it. He can't change his face."

"A Jew who can pass Nazi inspection in youth," said Pamir, "changes shape with tribulation. His features map the realities he faces. He walks to a different tune. Where he was thin and straight with certainties, he becomes bent under the burden of experience. To survive, he lives without women and his body swells like a eunuch's. It's a law of nature that all things adapt. With Radzki, the changes are more drastic because the conditions are extreme. That theatrical skill first noted by Stalin's talent spotters is now as natural as breathing. He'd be dead otherwise."

"It's crazy!" Talbott shook his head. "A Jewish mole in the Kremlin, so secret he can't use his power? Look what's happened to Jews in Mother Russia!"

"He made trade-offs. The first priority was to reach the top. As a matter of fact . . ." Pamir shifted uncomfortably. "When he finally got there, we did wonder. Had he fallen in love with power? Would he deliver?" Pamir was suddenly tired of his own doubts. He had overcome his professional reluctance to make any kind of disclosure. Now he was over that enormous psychological hump, he wanted to bring things to a conclusion. "He's asked to see you."

"Me?"

"You put in a request for an interview, didn't you? There won't be time to go through the rigmarole of bureaucratic procedures." Pamir could see more questions forming in the American's dazed face, and he went on quickly, "You've been a pawn moved by the East Germans. Mother's fighting to keep control of the DDR, without a direct confrontation."

"So my seeing him could also be a trap."

"It could be a trap," Pamir agreed.

"You don't want him in the West?"

"He'd be just as big an embarrassment as Rudolf Hess was when *he* came over."

"Wasn't Hess invited here?"

Pamir broke into laughter. "Mr. Talbott, ask Radzki these things. He's at a conference in a place that illustrates his style. Yugoslavia. The conference supposedly dramatizes the country's return to Soviet orthodoxy. With so much at stake, no party leader will openly challenge Mother. That's his way. As powerful a confirmation that *this* is Radzki as . . . his own signature."

"Has anybody seen that signature lately?"

The smile congealed on Pamir's face. He shifted his leg back to the floor and stood up. "We don't have time to gossip, Mr. Talbott. Dammit, what *should* I call you?"

"Talbott. Just plain Talbott."

Pamir stroked his mustache. "I calculate, Talbott, if we fly out within the next couple of hours, I can have you with Radzki by tonight. Are you game?"

"You fly me?" Talbott saw in Pamir's eyes, something he recognized instantly: the fear an older pilot tries to hide; the fear that others may think his flying days are over. Looking directly at Pamir's false hand, Talbott said, "It's an honor, General."

"Good man!" The intercom buzzed. *"Ken!"* There was an answering stream of Hebraic phrases. Steely Pamir glanced over at Talbott. "It's all organized." Pamir must have already made plans. Perhaps it was a forgivable presumption, thought Talbott. Time was short. Today was . . . what? Tuesday. They'd got until Sunday. Remembrance Day.

"It won't be a luxury trip," said Pamir after the intercom had gone dead. He came round the desk. "Phantom to Rome. Helicopter to some banana boat off the Jugs' coast. Then you swim for it." He gave Talbott a challenging stare.

Talbott had faced too many such challenges to be sucked in. How many correspondents in how many wars had been lost because they were afraid to seem cowards?

"I'll have to speak with New York first."

"That's okay." Steely Pamir smiled at Talbott's evident surprise. "Quex has been briefed. Sol Farkas is in the picture. Talk to him about the Mother Application, as if the Soviet interview is in the bag. He'll know."

"You're quite the regular Santa Claus," said Talbott. "With your little sack of surprises."

"I haven't finished yet." The boyish grin vanished. "My government can't afford to wheel expensive talent like yours around the sky, not unless the stakes are *very* high. Our direct contacts with Radzki have been getting fewer. So naturally we wonder. Could Radzki have been caught and replaced by a look-alike feeding us hope? Could he be destroying Judaism while we sit waiting for him to save it?"

General Pamir broke off, sighed, stretched, and turned to gaze at a patch of blue sky visible through the barred window. "God Almighty!" he burst out. "You and I both learned to fly by the seat of our pants. We identified the enemy by the insignia he wore. Now? I don't know who the hell our friends are, nor which side of Radzki is up. Our giant intellects in their multibillion-dollar think tanks, our observers and our satellites and genius computers can't tell me. The bloody truth is, Talbott, you're the only machine or man I'd trust to make a judgment."

"It's a long time since I flew on stick, rudder and throttle," warned Talbott. "The canvas and the piano wire do wear pretty thin."

"You'll do it, though." General Pamir continued to cast a wistful eye on the same small patch of blue sky. "Seat of the pants, old boy. There's still no better way to decide which side is really up."

30

Manhattan and Long Island, New York

The day had just started in New York when Sol Farkas took the call from Talbott. The timing was bad. Sol had missed his usual gruesome breakfast in the local greasy spoon, quarreling instead with *Newsmag*'s executive producer, Tom Middleton.

"One producer dead . . . Another missing." Middleton had burst into Sol's office, necktie askew, "Now I've got a query from publicity. How do we respond to this LA *Times* gossip item? 'America's most trusted correspondent wanted by police on two continents.' *What are you doing to me, Sol?*"

Sol made no reply but pushed over a copy of the Bronfmann death report, then waited. This was the Tom Middleton who had created *Newsmag*, who worked on the run, never held meetings, and looked now as if he'd jogged all the way from the network's self-important admin center on the Avenue of the Americas. Sol held his breath as Middleton came to the end of the report.

The fiery little exec producer's face had turned red. "I want to know how the West Germans covered up the murder . . . where a poison *banned even in wartime* was obtained . . . why that sex club hasn't been closed down . . ."

"Cool it, Tom!"

The advice had the opposite effect. All the pent-up rage exploded. "Look here!" Middleton's finger stabbed at the report. *"The castor-oil plant.* What—effing—sadists—milk—the—castor—oil plant? And why? To lock up Bronfmann's mind inside his suffering body? I mean, that's what it *says,* for chrissakes!"

"Careful . . ."

"Don't tell *me* to be careful! I shelved the Massey interview, put Hess on hold . . . We *never* operate this way, Sol, and you know it! But I listened to you, and God help me! I listened to those goddam academics."

Sol had clenched his head between his hands. Now he slowly raised his bulging eyes. "Academics?" But Middleton rushed on:

" 'Detach Talbott,' you said. 'A tricky story, but *big!'* Okay, Sol, now you go face the producers. They need Talbott to cobble together existing stories in the bank. They need him for voice-overs, studio intros, stand-uppers . . . What will you tell 'em? Stick by us and they'll get their reward—a toxic umbrella up the rear end?!"

"It's the deep end you're going off," growled Sol.

"No! Someone stuck poison into my youngest and brightest. What was he, a defector, to be wasted by some Bulgarian umbrella man? What am I? Chopped liver? I've been pushed *into* the deep end by you and your sopho-moric pseudoscholars from the CIA."

Sol stopped rubbing his big ears, head still bent under the rain of words, eyes rolling up to fix the *Newsmag* boss with an astonished stare. *"What pseudoscholars?"*

"Don't tell me the bastards were bluffing. They said you'd fill me in."

"The CIA?"

"Heavily disguised as baby professors. Yes!"

It was at this point that Talbott had gotten through from London.

In Fishhook's Long Island home that morning, Quex was making a fast recovery from the surprise blow dealt him by Vice President Walter Juste, ex-director of central intelligence. Juste, having no more alternative than Steely Pamir, had disclosed Radzki's present identity. The news at first crushed the old general's professional pride. Walter Juste had withdrawn briefly to give Quex time to recover. Now, stomach churning from muddy coffee and an unthawed doughnut consumed ill-advisedly in the kitchen, the Vice President stood with shoulders bowed under a colorless raincoat, clutching an old umbrella.

Quex, looking meek, was irresistibly reminded of the CIA limerick about "the just's umbrella." His spirits were already on the rise. He understood now why his single-minded pursuit of wartime truths had alarmed so many people. Rinna Dystel's task must have been to quietly track his inquiries, looking for anything that might add to Jerusalem's store of knowledge but also nudging him away from the ultimate discovery . . . silencing him if necessary! He shied away from the implications, thinking without resentment that it must have been a growing ordeal for her. He had no doubts about the love between them. It had burgeoned so unexpectedly, indeed miraculously. But—stout girl!—she'd remained loyal to the government desperately in need of facts only Quex could turn up, a tribute to himself. He badly needed that reassurance, since it occurred to him that his own vanity led to her death.

"We've made Sol Farkas semiconscious," Walter Juste was saying. "He'll square Talbott with the network. These media types hate even the faintest suggestion of collaborating with us." He shifted position, opened his mouth, closed it again. He reminded Quex of a small-town pharmacist. His dark hair was plastered down either side of an old-fashioned middle-of-the-head parting that gave the impression of a middle-of-the-road mentality. Quex imagined him dispensing advice on how to treat a cold or stop a revolution: "On the one hand this . . . but then on the other hand . . ." Still, Walter Juste had seen more action in the foreign field than behind a desk during his intelligence career. His first job with OSS had been under General Quex Massey, who counted on the Vice President's being still a little in awe of him. Lately, though, Quex had driven Walter Juste into private paroxysms of rage by his quixotic and lawless use of the Hat Men, and that was something the general did not yet fully comprehend.

Walter Juste looked around for a place to sit, and his awkwardness prompted Quex at last to pop the question:

"Why, Walter, have you finally told me all this?"

Juste tiptoed carefully across the expensive carpet to the nearest chair. There he removed his shoes. "Neglected to wear my galoshes," he mumbled. "Mind if I prop my feet at the fire? I don't want to leave muddy footprints. Sherman's a shocking old fusspot."

"Don't worry about Fishhook Sherman. He's in London."

"Yes, I know."

Quex swallowed more humble pie. Walter Juste had even stolen his air of omniscience. Wouldn't that just put Sally in a seventh heaven!

"Why," Quex asked politely, "didn't you tell me sooner, if I was really in danger of exposing your man?"

Walter Juste noted Quex's penitential manner. The general had never been more alert, nor more manipulative, than when he became your-so-very-humble servant.

"He's not *our* man," Juste said after giving it some thought. "I'm not even sure he belongs to the Israelis."

"You dodged my question, Walter."

"We couldn't warn you. You were on your own intriguing track. And we needed to see who might make you dance to their tune."

Quex stiffened. "Nobody, *ever*, made a puppet of me!"

Walter Juste uttered a few mumbling noises. The old general stirred with renewed fire. ⅈt was bad enough to have Walter Juste steal Quex's reputation for infallibility. He had also borrowed the Artful Mumble, perfected by General Quex Massey to baffle bugs! "Out with it!" barked Quex. "Don't mince words, man!"

"We need you in London."

"Well," said Quex after a shattering silence. "That's certainly not mincing words."

"We're in deep shit!" Walter Juste flushed at his own lapse in good taste. A warm, old-fashioned courtesy was General Massey's due; and bad language for Juste was rare. "But there's no other word for it," he said apologetically. "Jake Cooke was immensely helpful when you set out to investigate the death-camp bombings, correct?"

"The *failure* to bomb the camps." Quex let that sink in before adding, "What of it?"

"This has to be handled with absolute secrecy," said Walter Juste uneasily. "You and your granddaughter are the only ones we trust who had recent dealings with the real Jake Cooke."

"The *real* one?"

Juste lowered his head. "We think this Jake is a fake. And we dare not, maybe cannot, reach your Sally to check." He heaved a great sigh and pulled himself upright. "There are documents in London, however"—he made vague motions in the air—"and other things. Would you help? You realize what it means if this should be a provocateur from the other side . . . ?"

Later, Quex sat alone. Rinna had said he would only get to London over her dead body. Now he was going, at a price that was unbearable.

Every word of Talbott's call from London was engraved on Sol's memory. The star of *Newsmag* spoke of a Sunday-night news special. Yet there were no plans to preempt for that night, and Talbott knew it. He'd suggested "reviewing all the videotapes," but that could only mean the 88's Hess Command film and the Hess interview.

"I just hope Talbott's not on the way to destroying a great career," said Tom Middleton, and walked to the windows overlooking the Hudson River. "People sense his integrity. They believe in him. What happens if he's caught up to his eyeballs in some cockamamie cloak-and-dagger stunt?"

Sol said nothing. Talbott was talent. Middleton was genius. Correspondent and exec producer were steeped in journalistic traditions. They had healthy reasons for never working with government agencies. Sol Farkas shared their professional concern. Lately, though, he'd had to face questions every newsman hopes will never come his way. If you have personal knowledge of the great harm a piece of information can cause by being publicized, do you suppress it? Do you have the right to appoint yourself a public censor? Sol did not yet know how to answer. By delaying, he'd already halfway compromised. The complexity of his own dilemma made him irritable as he listened to Middleton's tiresome maundering. He decided on a brutal interruption. "This Bronfmann report . . ."

Middleton looked round.

"Talbott always believed his mother was killed in the London Blitz because of his own recklessness. Now he knows she was killed by a needle. A needle like the one killed Bronfmann."

"Oh, Jesus!"

"So he wants revenge." Sol was remorseless now he'd started. "He wants revenge for *all* the betrayals, big and little, secret and overt . . . for the betrayal of those who died for old-fashioned values . . . for the betrayal of all the good guys who fought against evil in a war long ago *because they really believed in truth and justice.* You know what makes Talbott acceptable to the little people in this country? You want to know why they sense his integrity?" Sol gave full rein to his anger. "He stays uncontaminated by what he has to report. He keeps inside himself a pathetic schoolboy faith in the essential goodness of mankind. But now the original schoolboy in Talbott has come back with a different story and a demand for vengeance. And there's nothing you nor I can do to stop him."

31

Talbott saw the freighter first as the arrowhead to a long chalk mark across the Adriatic blue. He felt the helicopter rear back to match the ship's speed. At two thousand feet, he borrowed the pilot's binoculars and read the monogram on the funnel: HFC. "Haifa Fruit Carriers," said the pilot. They were the first words he had spoken.

Talbott had been hustled to the waiting helicopter by mechanics in the NATO corner of a Rome airport. General Peled Pamir had flown him there, talking without restraint, knowing their conversation was electronically camouflaged. By contrast, the helicopter pilot had said nothing for two hours, regarding all communication as vulnerable to Moscow's monitors; even navigation was by dead reckoning. Yet the rendezvous was faultless. He jabbed a thumb downwards to signal his intent to land on the vessel, whose registry had become decipherable: AVICADOCOR, HAIFA.

Seamen slouched at the stern, gazing up without stirring. They seemed slovenly, even hostile. One strolled to a deck hatch and jerked a lanyard. A rusty-red tarpaulin slid back, disappearing between rollers into the hold and revealing a modest platform with a yellow cross and circle. Talbott recognized the iron teeth of a helicopter bear-trap.

The helicopter drew alongside at bridge level and slid sideways. Now the details of disguise became clear. The vessel was cocooned in fake deck

structures. Painted canvas concealed the configuration of an Israeli warship: probably a converted gunboat of the Israeli Navy's Saar-2 class. Five
of the vessels, Talbott recalled, had been "liberated" from Cherbourg one
Christmas, some fifteen years before, after the French Government im-
pounded them to pacify Arab banking merchants. He felt cheered to think
the tradition of cocky independence hadn't faltered.

False sides concealed the lower superstructure. More canvas flanked a
dummy funnel. Lath-and-wire hen-coops littered what appeared to be a
freighter's boat deck. It had been impossible to fully hide the ship's central
island and missile housings, but the stage props would fool a surface observer.

The helicopter powered through the turbulent air abaft the funnel. After that, things moved fast. Firefighters in asbestos suits waddled out from
a fake deckhouse. A deck landing officer appeared from nowhere, complete
with orange skullcap and luminous wands. The helicopter waltzed in step
with the vessel until the bear-trap snapped shut, locking machine to deck.
The full blast of the rotor wash hit Talbott with the sickly-sweet smell of
the hot turbine exhaust. He suffered the familiar nausea of passing from
the motions of the air to those of the sea. Blades folded, the helicopter was
carried by elevator into the hangar below. The whole operation had taken
so little time, none but the most attentive of passing ships would have
noticed. And none were to be seen.

He was met in the wardroom by a bronzed young man in a torn and
stained reefer and peaked cap garnished with scraps of gold lace. "I'm
skipper of this tub," he said. "Aerial." He offered no further name. Talbott
knew the rules. Names were not things you asked for in Aerial's line of
work. Instead, Talbott accepted an illicit gin and tonic from his host.
"We're here," said Aerial, indicating a position on the chart. "Territorial
waters on this side belong to Italy. And here . . . Yugoslavia! We're in
between, but not for long."

Talbott tried to focus. Scuba gear filled a corner of the cabin. A faint
odor of diesel mingled with the ventilated air. The steel deck under his feet
vibrated, joining the throb of the engines to pound his head.

"You okay?"

Talbott managed a smile in response. As a young pilot, he had suffered
frequently from seasickness after a carrier landing. He forced down the
rest of the drink in a show of bravado.

"You'd better take my bunk," said Aerial, who wasn't fooled. "We cross
into Jug waters at dusk."

Talbott had spent most of Tuesday with General Peled Pamir in the
London embassy, reading the Radzki translations and going over the procedures for entering Igalo. He was stunned by the news Red Crombie
would run the mission there.

"He oversees escape committees," explained the Israeli. "Snakeheads out of China, ratlines out of Russia, travel agencies in the Balkans."

"What the hell was he doing in Berlin last week?"

"His clients go through the Eastern sector," said Pamir. "He's kind of a traffic cop."

"He was also at Quex's funeral." Talbott could not keep the sarcasm from showing. "A bit late. The only traffic there was already wrecked."

"I can't comment on that," said Steely Pamir, sounding so uncharacteristically stuffy that Talbott decided to say nothing about Crombie's curious proposition to get him out of Berlin through the Eastern sector.

Only after they were airborne did Steely Pamir loosen up. All the time in the embassy, Talbott had been digesting great chunks of Radzki's work in that atmosphere of official reserve. Perhaps Sally's presence made Pamir cautious. He had allowed Talbott no time to see her when, at dead of night, they suddenly left for the base. Once aloft, the comradeship of airmen took over. And as Pamir said, "Nothing's so secure as the inside of a Phantom with all this damned elint and counterelint gadgetry."

"Jake would find it hard to believe the Brits let you come and go this freely," observed Talbott.

"Jake?" A sigh came over the intercom. "He's not the old Jake . . . twisted, bitter now, not like the old days. Israel needs leaders who say some of the world's with us, not that all the world's against us!"

Steely Pamir's account of Radzki, during the flight, was a lot more cheerful than Jake Cooke's version. "Radzki was to conspiracy," said Pamir, "what Oppenheimer was to the atomic bomb. Why not? You're as likely to find a genius in the one as in the other!"

The warm relationship between Radzki and Steely Pamir resulted from the family connection Pamir had with World Zionism. The family lived in London, where Pamir's father had enjoyed the confidence of notables like Churchill. "As a flier," said Pamir, "I got involved in certain secret operations, as you did. In the planning stage of some, there was a need for Hebrew-speaking instructors . . ."

It seemed very odd, hearing this from a survivor who now navigated these same skies with such familiarity. Talbott saw why Steely Pamir could look to distant horizons with confidence, whereas Jake limited his vision and struggled with resentments from the past.

"I had the hell scared out of me, next time I saw Radzki," continued Steely Pamir. "I'd been demobbed from the RAF and went underground, helping Jewish survivors reach Palestine. I watched for potential recruits for 'flying clubs' we'd set up in Italy, the start of a Jewish air force. Promising kids came out of the Soviet-occupied regions. Those were incredible times! We bribed, blackmailed, bamboozled . . . We even made a fake war film in the Nevada Desert so we could acquire old Flying Fortresses, then flew 'em to a secret Mediterranean base. I tell you, nothing

Radzki did later surprised veterans of our conspiracies. But when I first found him in the guise of a Russian NKVD officer . . . Well!"

The Phantom's electronics are truly astonishing. General Pamir came through clear as a bell. Talbott continued to get a picture of Radzki different to the one Jake Cooke had conveyed.

"Radzki helped me find embryo aircrews, at the risk of blowing his cover," said Pamir. "Finally he opted for long-range plans of his own. The first big burden of guilt came when he proposed the transfer of Jews in Soviet-occupied Poland to Siberia. Moscow liked that one! Radzki pointed out Marxists couldn't turn Auschwitz into a shrine to the evils of capitalism if there were Jews around to spoil the story."

"How could you stomach him?"

"He had to strike at Jews in building a good NKVD record. He knew Polish Jews were in Stalin's gunsights, anyway. I had to believe he kept some sort of mental ledger. And we keep our own ledgers, you know."

Talbott had a sudden image of Hat Men balancing accounts.

"Radzki learned the major flaw in government by terror at Hitler's court," Pamir resumed. "A professional conspirator—that's really what he'd become by then—could exploit any country's internal security with all its built-in rigidities. Radzki developed a kind of Parkinson's Law. The higher you climb, the more boldness is your friend. Bureaucrats in secret agencies are frightened to show initiative. The Gestapo had shown Radzki how suspicions fed on jealousy; and how fear silences middle and upper management. Also, files! He kept meticulous personnel files. The mistakes of his colleagues were invaluable."

Radzki's skills put him into KGB top management after a seven-year cautious advance through provincial departments. Soviet police chiefs who had been dying to move center stage usually got their wish: they died. The famous example was Beria, whose bid for power so frightened the politburo, he was shot and the KGB formally severed from the Ministry of Internal Affairs. But Radzki's sense of divine purpose pushed aside caution. He set out to win acceptance for the KGB, and then used it as a Western politician would use a party machine, except there was no rival party machine, only rival bureaucrats scared of KGB animosity. Radzki owned the *nomenklatura*, the list of grace-and-favor jobs. He saw to it that the bulk of the population increasingly depended for jobs on himself through the KGB. The people saw him as their protector. He was the television spy hero, STIRLITZ, who had penetrated Hitler's inner circle during the Great Patriotic War. He was also the perfect civil servant.

He elected himself, in a way, to the post of Little Mother of all the Russias. There were no challengers. He controlled the key posts in the intelligence directorate of the Soviet General Staff. The grand marshals of World War II had turned into stone legends. The new military technocrats and defense scientists could not afford to handicap themselves with internal squabbles. Zealotry was left to political officers and hangers-on who derived their puny power from Radzki. There were echoes here of Hitler's court, and not by accident. Radzki saw the dictator destroy himself by wasting resources on the machinery of oppression. He had actually forecast how a future Soviet leader might unwittingly self-destruct:

"He need only follow Hitler's example by building a monstrous burden of prison camps that, together with all the ancillary services, must in time break the economy," Radzki had written in London between courier runs to Nazi Europe. "Slave labor is *not* cheap labor. Hitler's own generals are being defeated by the dirty little secret, *Endlösung,* extermination. The apparatus, the armies to round up communities, the bureaucracies with networks of police and informers, the vast industries necessary to transport, confine and exploit the slaves, none of this can be justified on pure economic and commercial grounds . . . In the clash between Hitler and Stalin, it is a question of which tyranny will be first to collapse, exhausted by the excesses of brutality at home. In the first three months of the German invasion of Russia, three million Soviet citizens *surrendered* . . . There has never been such a rout in all Russian history. The efficient Germans stretch their domestic machinery to consume the newly conquered peoples and in the end this costs Hitler more manpower and resources than he puts into the business of fighting . . . Thus the downfall of Sovietism might follow the expansion of its slave camps . . ."

Why did Radzki leave such self-incriminating writings?

Steely Pamir said, "He wanted something on record *to make him stay right side up.* As if a recording angel kept score. That's my guess and that's why I'm for continuing to gamble that in the end, somehow, he's going to justify the way he's reached the top. Though God knows what that justification could possibly be, to equal all the horrors."

The way he'd reached the top hardly bore thinking about. The way General Steely Pamir told the story, it was still difficult to fathom how the shabby refugee Talbott had known could have made the final leap to power. Some part of the puzzle was still missing.

The Phantom flight had crammed Talbott's head with more information than he knew how to handle. Stretched out on the *Avicadocor* captain's bunk, he developed a nauseating headache just trying to sort out his feelings about Radzki.

He felt the vessel heel as she changed course. Sunset had come early. The heavy beat of the diesels altered tone. He staggered onto his feet and lurched around the cabin, gathering up his gear. He had been warned to be ready to go over the side at the end of a short dash into Yugoslav waters. Topside, they would be already inflating the dinghy. He felt more than seasick, but he knew it would all be fine the moment the sea closed over his hooded head and he could sink back down into its stable, untroubled depths.

32

"You perforated Prussian prick," Yuri Gorin said conversationally, "I'll bust your balls and bung that apology for a dingdong up your fundament if you piss on me again." He stood with his back to the tinted bulletproof windows of the Tito villa at Igalo.

General Helmuth Henkell's nostrils flared. He possessed a modest talent for vituperation, but there was in Mother's choice of Russian abuse a raw vulgarity. His head jerked back as Mother suddenly roared:

"Who the fuck faked these pictures, then?"

"You know these are the Auschwitz photographs."

"And counterfeit!" The Soviet leader drew back his lips in what might have passed for a grin. "Who forged them?"

"I cannot say."

"Cannot? Will not!" Mother's voice rose, leveled off, sank to a rattle in the red cave of his open mouth. "By God, you will say, or I'll stick an orange up your arse, an apple in your gob, and serve you, picklehead and bunghole, on a platter."

"You haven't the guts," breathed Henkell. "Beyond Moscow, the masses no longer share the Kremlin's faith in your infallibility. They look for an iron fist in the kid glove. All you offer is a rusty knuckleduster."

"And you're the iron fist, eh? The perfect Aryan. Waiting in the wings to give us a shot of your sodding superman pox. You're so riddled with syph, when you piddle the stuff squirts like a sprinkler. But not in Berlin, eh? In Berlin, no doubt, you speak in the name of the good German, Marx?"

"Are you well, comrade?" Henkell ran a hand over his blond hair as if to pat in place the curls at the back of his slender neck. He could think of no way to advance the conversation without tripping another explosion. He was keenly aware that Yuri Gorin was twice his age and hounded by high blood pressure. Vanity was a deadly sin among the old men of the Kremlin. "The delegates speak of too much stress—"

"You turtle-headed fascist faker," said Mother, back to his frighteningly uninflected tone. "Answer the question."

"The pictures were obtained in America."

"Ah!" Yuri Gorin's broad shoulders filled the bottom of a window through which could be seen a rose-pink flush of snow on the topmost mountain peaks catching the last of the day's sunshine. Henkell fixed his gaze on the pinkish alpine snow floating like a delicate halo over Mother's head. "So the ingredients for your Hess Command movie come from all over. Including CIA *and* Soviet files?"

"Anyone can get CIA analyses of wartime operations," said Henkell. "To doctor the material, we first buy the services of the excellent American technicians, then turn to our superior German resources—"

"Our own archives produced the file on Operation Citadel!"

"Assembled by myself when I directed the Jewish Affairs Section for the domestic and foreign service, KGB," retorted Henkell.

Across Mother's vision raced images of General Henkell's forefathers strutting with similar arrogance across Nazi Europe and, before that, Prussian battlefields. "Numskull!" he said. "Tell me what you've done, *exactly*, unless you'd like this floor tiled with your genitals."

Henkell took a deep breath. He was about to risk everything. Outside the villa was an armed guard of *spetzotdel*, called in the West *spetsnaz*, an elite, of saboteurs and countersaboteurs, the Special Assignment Force under Soviet Red Army intelligence control. Even the Yugoslavs had been unable to interfere in the posting of the guard. The question in Henkell's mind was how far Yuri Gorin might go in making use of them here.

"I remembered a certain case from my days with Jewish Affairs," said Henkell finally. "A certain Radzki—"

Yuri Gorin became still as a rock.

"A Radzki who penetrated the top of the Nazi leadership," Henkell continued with renewed resolve. "He was many times reported dead. In London they said he'd killed himself. But he lived to be betrayed by London in a mission to save Jewish scum in Hungary. Operation Citadel."

There was no response from Mother. Nothing.

"This Radzki worked for a time with a certain Slominsky, a Jew terrorist fighting the British, also known as Jacob Cooke. A man equipped with that identity is searching for Radzki now. He is my creation."

Mother did not so much as blink an eye. The two men were locked in a profound silence. Each was only too conscious of the high standing of East German espionage, once the most prized of KGB auxiliaries and now dangerously inclined to think for itself. After Henkell had moved there from the KGB's Jewish section, the Soviet bureaucracy had given him too free a hand. The special favors shown East German operatives went back to the rather eccentric conversion of Berlin's St. Antonius' Hospital into the largest KGB apparat outside Moscow. East Germany directed the training of volunteers frantic to pursue ancient blood feuds from all over, and against whomsoever: Arabs or Irishmen, Bugis from the Sulu Sea or whirling dervishes from the new Sudan; indeed, anyone who felt he could improve his image by being machine-gunned, beheaded or blown up in some cause— just as long as this exuberance was confined to the world outside the Soviet bloc. The good work begun at the former hospital was continued under the auspices of the department of espionage, Haupt Verwaltung Aufklärung, whose title betrayed its Nazi antecedents. The department no longer found it necessary to launch tasks with Moscow's blessings. Knowing this, well aware of his value to the comrades in Berlin, and with his ace up his sleeve, Henkell stood his ground.

Finally, Mother spoke. "You heard what I told the delegates. These independent ventures are dangerous."

"And some of us believe they are not aggressive enough!" retorted Henkell. "They say you're trailing behind the revolutionary spirit of the people. They say even this Baltic crisis has caused a nervous breakdown—"

"I know what they say!" Mother felt his temper rise again. If he missed the coming military parade in Moscow, marking another anniversary of the Revolution, critics would speculate that the Baltic crisis had unnerved him. He collected himself. "One of these days," he said, "we'll outsmart ourselves. We'll deceive the other side into senseless action that will destroy all our hopes."

"Vladimir Ilyich instructs us differently," said Henkell, and then quoted his fellow German Willi Muenzenberg outlining disinformation to Lenin: "Deception is justified—"

"Another of your fornicating Germans! You propose we go back to Hitler? The Big Lie?"

"Not the same . . ."

"Not the flaming same!" rumbled Mother, anger suffusing his cheeks. "Lies! All justified if they serve the cause, no matter how foul the deeds! Not the flaming same! Our power is based on a measured presentation of information, and a stupid bastard popinjay like you comes and disarranges . . ."

The rage had him fully by the throat now. All day it had been building up, together with relief that matters must soon be resolved. Either shithead Henkell knew Mother's true identity, or he didn't. If shit-head knew, then Mother must take action immediately. Starting with shit-head? Why not? Why not anticipate? He could indulge in that one selfish moment of passion and not imperil anything, could seize this self-satisfied Naxi-Marxist and throttle him without disturbing the structure upon which he, Mother, balanced so delicately. He put a hand on each of Henkell's shoulders, lightly, as if in near-comradely affection and asked in sweetened tones again, "What's given you the guts to push the Hess deception forward?"

"It's not in my hands."

"Whoreson!" Yuri Gorin pulled Henkell towards him and knee'd the German so that he doubled up. The explosion of noise and violence invigorated the Soviet leader in a way he had not known for a long time. He spun the incapacitated German round and booted him into the open hearth. Then he caught up and swiped one of his great paws across the back of Henkell's head. Henkell twisted, clutching his crotch, buttocks heaving on the marble apron, his upper torso lost in the massive fireplace.

"Why did you fake the pictures?" Mother demanded.

Henkell's reply was a muffled groan, and then: "To sustain the disinformation."

"So Auschwitz wasn't good enough the way it was? You had to improve on it?"

"No." Henkell glanced quickly around him. The villa had been cleared. The guards could hear nothing through the soundproof walls. He was alone with a man it would delight him to kill. But if there was killing to be done, only Mother could get away with it; and so Henkell merely said, "We had to inflame Jewish extremists with evidence of betrayal."

"Citadel?"

"The ultimate treachery. Every Jew, everywhere, will conclude neither they nor Israel have friends. They'll be driven into making enemies out of their friends."

Mother thought: He wouldn't talk this way if he suspected any connection with Radzki. Henkell doesn't, after all, *know*.

"You can't stop the project." Henkell had worked his way into a squatting position. "The forces are out of control, yours and mine. Our Libyan friends want results for the billions they put out, to the 88, and indirectly to the man called Jacob Cooke."

Mother watched the other man's bloodied face while he groped under his jacket for his pistol, a P-6 with built-in silencer, standard *spetsnaz* issue. A leather ring fitted over each shoulder with an elastic band stretching across the back; the holster was sewn to the left shoulder ring. The P-6 slid out as if on ball bearings. Mother sometimes wondered how long before the evolutionary process *grew* guns out of the human anatomy: they were used more often than penises.

"If anything happens to me," said Henkell, "you can be sure there will be ideological defiance in the German Democratic Republic, and that will be worse than anything you've seen in Poland."

"Nothing will happen if you tell me how this Hess Command epic is to be displayed."

Henkell thought about this briefly. Then he said, "Action Remembrance."

"And what the hell does that mean?"

Henkell thought some more. "Our Libyan financial sponsors proposed it. The Colonel has always admired what he calls British spit-and-polish. Hates the British, loves their institutions. Gaddafi was once present at the ceremonies . . ."

The German was asserting himself again, spinning out the disclosures. There was a poker near the fireplace. Mother picked it up. Still crouching, the gun dangling from one paw and the poker from the other, he said: "The spit—" His mask broke open into a wide-mouthed grin.

". . . It's next Sunday," said Henkell hastily, and explained.

Mother considered. Then he asked, "When all's said and done, isn't this really a scheme to destroy the Jewish people?"

"Because they stand in the way of world revolution."

"Ah." Mother rocked back onto his heels. "But isn't this Jacob Cooke, this Slominsky, a revolutionary?"

"Not at all. He is my manufactured scapegoat. Everything will be laid at his door, and the joke is— Well, he's not the man they think. But he'll be seized upon as the symbol of the Jews. All those murders—"

"Bronfmann?"

"Why, yes!" Henkell was again startled by the extent of Mother's information. Where did he get it? "Also the Jewish bitch who runs the research division of Sayaret Motkal, Israeli military intelligence—"

Mother waited. He had been told General Quex Massey had been eclipsed; that Rinna survived.

"—Rinna Dystel," said Henkell.

Mother frowned. "Dystel? With American OSS during the war? Worked in Hollywood?"

"The same," said Henkell, still further surprised. He decided to spring a surprise of his own. "The Dystel woman was removed by the same team responsible for General Massey. It wasn't your ECLIPSE assassins."

Mother's pupils shrank to pinpoints.

"We worked through a prominent Englishman," said Henkell. "Very good Libyan contacts . . ."

"The spit is done with the sword," said Mother. "However, a poker does it very well too."

Henkell's face fell apart. "You're mad!"

Mother leaned back, the poker raised. Henkell drew up his knees and slid hard against one pillar of the fireplace.

"They spit boars by driving a spear halfway up, from arse to brisket," said Mother. "Then they let the boar run. Well, of course, you know all about that! Your people invented the sport. And great sport it is, eh? The wild boar with the sword sticking out of his bunghole, running until his guts burst." He stared right through Henkell, seeing Rinna Dystel . . . and the legions who had died since the beginning of his career as God's spy. "The men outside are skilled with the spit," he resumed. "Of course! You know that, too! Your specialists trained with them. Let me call in my boys and we'll see who does it best—"

"No," said Henkell. "Be reasonable."

Still churning away in Mother's mind was the name of the operation that always had seemed the final betrayal, even to him, who was so familiar with betrayal. So now he said, "Who, specifically, betrayed Citadel?"

"General Quex Massey."

"That's convenient," Mother said sarcastically. "He's dead!"

"Not at all." Henkell's voice recaptured some of its former arrogance. "Your eclipse team was fooled. I have it on 88 authority that he's even now preparing to fly to London—"

Henkell's screams went unheard by the guards outside as Mother thrust the poker into him, grunting, "Bloody liar, bloody, bloody, bloody liar . . ."

The reckless rage of Yuri Gorin quickly exhausted itself. He had known nothing like this since his service with Rudolf Hess. He felt like some celibate who for half a century nurses a secret lust and then indulges all of it in a few seconds of violent orgasm. He withdrew the poker, strangely distressed by the evidence of his own strength. The iron rod had penetrated layers of cloth. The suddenness of the blow had rammed it in like a pigsticker's sword. He put a hand on Henkell's brow. It was cold. He stood up, and felt his own warm semen slither between his legs. He was disgusted by the reflex spasm.

A terrible weariness came over him. He must be careful. He had a few hours left in which to work. He looked at his hands, torn between guilt and ecstasy.

The emergency phone purred. He picked it up. "Yes?"

He recognized the nurse's voice. She knew the ropes! He heard her say he was late for treatment. So, the American traveler was back! With news, perhaps, of a visitor? He grunted a response and padded back to the fireplace, still dizzy from his recent catharsis.

There was no point wasting time on Henkell. His pulse was elusive. Behind the bar was a place once used by lady callers. It would serve as accommodation. Nobody entered the villa without authority. Dead or alive, Henkell could be disposed of later. Right now wasn't the most appropriate time, with the alarm system on and sensitive to a sudden gunshot. You couldn't kiss off the strongest man in East Germany . . . Ah, but that was power, to be able to take one's time, maneuver bits of paper into something like a medical certificate and bland regrets. Another surge of adrenaline galvanized Mother and he dragged Henkell out of plain view.

Later, he took one of the crisp white handkerchiefs Irina had laundered for him at Sochi and mopped up the thin trail of blood, not from some fastidious aversion to leaving bloodstains around the place, but because it gave him an odd sort of satisfaction. He stuffed the handkerchief back into his trouser pocket and imagined a sensation of warm blood from a German tyrant's asshole trickling down the inside of his thigh. It felt like the end of a long wait.

Descending again to the mud baths of Igalo, Mother was granted a sudden insight into why his rage had erupted all over General Helmuth Henkell. The presence of the nurse prompted it. She was like a guard: too pretty, though, and far too clever! How had Henkell scooped up so much intelligence denied the KGB? It had to come from the neo-Nazi 88, their petrodollar financiers, and a small circle of conspirators getting closer to the secret of Radzki. Was this nurse part of the inner circle?

He felt treachery at his heels again. The name of Citadel rang in his ears. Rinna Dystel dead . . . Quex alive! Was his Yugo-red nurse walking him into a new deception?

Mother had asked to see Scott Talbott. Suppose this son of Rebecca should prove the ultimate traitor?

The professional conspirator shook himself. Why, then he would discover why all this power had been gathered so miraculously into his hands, and if he was God's spy or the Devil's.

33

Talbott lay flat on his stomach in a Subskimmer hurtling towards the Yugoslav coast. Two miles from shore, the sidewalls collapsed and the fiberglass hull sank. The coxswain switched to battery-driven underwater motors. The crew ran submerged at a depth of ten feet and a speed of five knots, sucking pure oxygen and protected against the icy water by their black neoprene suits.

Talbott thought: I'm too old for this. But he didn't feel it. He thought: it's bizarre. But it really wasn't, not in his professional world, where the outrageous was the norm. "Imagine the wildest enterprise," General Pamir had said. "Our boys always top it." Talbott had tried, and Pamir was right.

The craft slowed down. The coxswain, lying prone, consulted the guidance system, which matched a computerized map against the sea bottom over which they were traveling. An underwater searchlight sprang into life. Talbott groped for the waterproofed ditty bag holding clothes and travel papers. The Israelis had told him the Subskimmer was on trial with the British SAS special boat squadrons. The makers, Submarine Products of Northumberland, claimed it could evade radar and most sonar. Talbott hoped they were right.

The light trapped a submerged, luminescent buoy. The motors were disengaged. A yellow driver-propulsion vehicle came into view. The DPV rested in an ocean forest of holdfast kelp. Talbott purged water from his face mask and felt for the portable air tank. He checked weights and transferred from the skimmer's life-support system to the scuba regulator. The coxswain gave him time to register the position of the DPV: it was the escape vehicle, not for immediate use. The light swiveled and steadied to give Talbott direction by which to make a final check of his wrist compass. Talbott signaled farewell and flippered down the beam into the black void.

Routine took over. He settled comfortably into the familiar weightless trudge. He heard the faint vibration of spinning props as the driver reengaged motors for the long ride back. Routine steadied the nerves. As General Pamir had said: "Our generation learned in its teens to tackle the impossible with discipline . . . The breech-block movement is as follows . . . One-two-three. Just follow the sequence and you'll arrive at the prescribed result—whether it's a bullet from the muzzle or a victory in the air. You never lose that confidence in the drill, not unless it bores you to continue living." One-two-three . . . You went through the checklist religiously, and it all came right in the end.

The compass shine on his wrist intensified. Course 070 degrees, on the button. He wore no life vest. It only added to the problem of concealing equipment ashore. He was about to turn on the miner's lamp sealed into his hood when he felt shingle under his gloved hands. He finned himself upright, cautiously breaking the surface. The night sky was alive with stars. The old excitement took him by the throat. There was a three-quarter moon, perfect for poachers and pilots. He balanced himself against the surge and studied the faint shoreline. To anyone watching from the beach, his black-hooded head would be indistinguishable from ripples on the glassy surface of the bay.

"You're late."

Red Crombie's voice was like the alarm of the corncrake. Talbott, wading ashore backwards to keep his swim fins on, jumped and almost fell.

"Don't worry," said Crombie. "There's nobody within a mile except myself and the local guide."

Talbott turned awkwardly, glad to shed the flippers and scuba gear. A woman came out of the blackness between two rocks and quickly stowed everything into a canister. "We were getting worried," she said. "They told us you left the ship an hour ago." Without waiting for an answer, she dragged the bag from sight.

"She'll be your escort," said Crombie, and stuck out his hand. Talbott began hauling in the long lanyard to which he had attached the ditty bag. He knew it was stupid to feel this hostility again for Crombie, but he hadn't recovered from the Berlin encounter.

"Please change quickly." The woman was at his side again. Even in the poor light, he could see how artistically she filled an otherwise uninspired Russian swimsuit. She was waiting for him to empty the ditty bag.

He peeled off the neoprene suit. He'd pretty near lost his manhood in the cold night air. The woman unsealed the undersea bag and handed him his clothes with a small cluck of sympathy.

"Hurry, Vesna!" said Crombie.

How much more quickly could she move? Talbott again fought back his dislike of the man. Vesna had already replaced his clothes with the wet suit and was hiding it with the scuba gear.

Crombie led him to the shelter of the rocks. Vesna appeared on the beach and walked into the sea with a great deal of kicking and splashing.

"Must freeze her tits," muttered Crombie. "But it maintains her cover. At the clinic they think she's a nature freak."

"Who is she?"

Crombie explained. "Hang onto her like grim death," he added.

"If I took your advice," said Talbott, "I'd still be in East Berlin."

"Not so. I was told the West Germans were after you. Paradoxically, old man, I could nurse you through the Eastern zone, where the flap originated."

"There wasn't any flap."

"Not as things turned out. Couldn't take chances, though, could we, old man?"

Talbott turned away, unconvinced, to watch Vesna splashing out of the sea. He shivered. "She'll catch pneumonia."

"Not a major option," said Crombie. "Either she'll be gone from here tomorrow or we'll all be goners anyway." He slapped Talbott on the shoulder. "I've a piano lesson . . ."

Talbott grunted. The "piano" was a frequency-hopping combat radio. New, high-speed "chirpers" cheated an enemy's watchdog satellites. This one would relay through the *Avicadocor*, stooging around on the neutral side of the Yugoslav marine borderline. That's what the skipper had told him. He could only hope Crombie was following procedure, and not another of his private brainwaves.

Crombie's shadowy figure merged into the night. In his place materialized the far more appealing Vesna.

"Dressed?" She took Talbott's arm. "This way, then." He winced at the way the shingle crunched under their feet. On the esplanade, she told him to wait while she slipped into a wooden lean-to. She came out in hospital uniform. "Put this over your clothes," she said, and gave him a white coat. Then she led him at a leisurely pace along the empty promenade. "Don't be alarmed by the casualness," she said. "We're known as the casual Communists in this country. Nobody likes the satellite puppets, and everyone's wondering what Moscow wants from us. Except for the personal guard on Yuri Gorin's villa, security is slack. We want these bastards to see Yugoslavia's on the road to socialism by choice, not by terror."

Talbott glanced at her with respect. It was a seemingly artless speech, cleverly designed to help morale. Most welcoming committees would have plunged straight into technical details.

"You should have been a psychiatrist," he said.

"I'm very good at anything I do," Vesna replied modestly. Then she paused. "You see over there, the glow of light? Dubrovnik . . ."

A volume of *The Mediterranean Pilot* had been handed Talbott in Aerial's cabin. It recorded everything. Underwater currents, saline density, precise drawings made by naval officers to help other sailors take cross bearings on landmarks and lighthouses. The volume came from the British Admiralty's hydrographic department. There were notes on coastal communities and their strange tongues. Igalo "is at the entrance of four bays of the Gulf of Kotor, one of the most remarkable phenomena of Europe . . . Awe-inspiring gateway to the Black Mountain, Montenegro."

Kotor was a gigantic fiord bounded by precipitous limestone mountains. "A vessel with local knowledge making for the strait between . . . should cross the reef barrier along the 100-fathom line."

Talbott had soaked up the information. Now he tried to relate it to the profoundly sinister blocks of darkness, the waters like black glass. "Coastal towns Venetian in character, with Byzantine or Slav overtones . . ."

Less than a hundred miles away, over there, was the safety of the Italian coastline. It might as well be the moon. He wondered if the moon ever got high enough to shine into the gulf. "For centuries a hideout for pirates and sea raiders . . ."

He started forward again. He was not surprised that this should be the secret entrance to the Soviet bloc. It had, in times gone by, sheltered the entire British Mediterranean fleet. Every feature had been charted. There was not a submerged rock, not a spit of sand, escaped the fleet's navigators.

They struck inland to a grassy lane, parallel with the shoreline between hedgerows. Vesna quickened the pace. Her words seemed set to the tick of a stopwatch. She told him what to expect, how long he would have, and what he must do. "What you *say*," she concluded, "is naturally your own business."

They came to an ornamental garden between the Dr. Simo Milošević clinic and its private beach of dark volcanic sand. "We're going the back way," said Vesna. "If I'm detained, walk down to the basement as if you do it every day, and come out through the X-ray department." She described once more the building's layout, the turnings he would have to take. She fell silent as they approached the sentries.

"It's me," she called out in Serbo-Croat.

"Oh yes, and who's the boyfriend?" asked the officer on duty.

"Boyfriend?" Vesna showed annoyance. "This is the technician for hydromassage. You checked us out an hour ago."

"I just came on duty. You know yourself the hours of rota." The officer sounded apologetic.

"Don't worry," Vesna said graciously. "It gets dark quick. I thought you were Tolya."

She spoke in a rich, dry voice that implied forgiveness and complicity. Thank God you and I are Yugoslavs, she seemed to say. A Russian would cut off your balls for impertinence! The other guards voluntarily pushed open the plate-glass doors, grinning. Their heads came together like village gossips . . . Tito's private nurse, just a slip of a girl she was when the old man died, such a comfort to Stari, to Tito, who'd never lost his vigor right to the end . . .

Inside was a cavernous hall, all glass mirrors and chandeliers, a curious echo of art deco, populated by gravel-faced delegates summoned by loudspeaker to dinner. Vesna drew close to Talbott and talked with great intensity about nothing. How well she knew the ways of the party faithful, who followed the rules and could not imagine anyone moving in their presence with less than expedient joy and blind obedience. One-two-three. Just follow the drill. Vesna slipped slyly at an angle to the general movement of the flock until she had nudged Talbott into an open elevator. When the doors closed, she dropped the jargon and said briskly, "Allow yourself forty minutes with the Secretary-General. The whole block is cleared for his hour of thermal therapy." She checked her watch. "It began twenty minutes ago. You cannot be bugged. Say what you have to say. If he feels good about it, *he* will make the next move."

Talbott had a confused impression of doors opening to reveal white vats, rising steam, glaring lights. Then he was inside the cubicle, alone with the man he had once known as the uncle from Berlin, Samuel Radzki.

Yuri Gorin's mud bath was in the process of recirculation. The gold-flecked black sludge slurped and gurgled up from the bowels of the earth. Mother's massive head materialized out of the whirling steam. His button eyes searched Talbott's face.

Talbott met the long stare with almost physical nausea. This bearlike face, the dark-rimmed eyes, the teeth bared under a blunt snout, the shock of bristly gray hair, were these familiar simply because he'd seen them reproduced in newspapers? He'd never really accepted the possibility Yuri Gorin had once sheltered in his childhood home.

Perhaps the whole thing *was* a trap. Talbott heard the thud of the thick wooden door shut behind him.

"Son of Rebecca!"

The words fell disturbingly on Talbott's ears, a kind of recognition signal. Yuri Gorin had not moved. He might have been Mao swimming the Yangtse, only the head showing. Talbott needed all his experience of facing the high and the mighty. He remembered the warning about time limits and said, "If we're questioned, I have press credentials—"

Yuri Gorin's head rolled back. "If *you're* questioned, say what you like. It won't save you."

"It'll save the network embarrassment." Talbott grinned disarmingly. "And for your sake—"

"We should stick to the same story?" Gorin laughed in response. "Nobody questions me."

Gorin's complacency was a challenge. Talbott said, "We found your Auschwitz Index."

Gorin splashed forward, turned off a giant tap dripping mud, and stared at him, conceding nothing.

"The handwriting could destroy you."

Gorin flapped a hand like a grizzly tormented by a persistent buzz. "Who expects Yuri Gorin to write *Hebrew?*"

"Anyone wishing you harm could prove it publicly."

"Who writes the same way today as he did a million light-years away?"

"You have powerful enemies. Some of your notes are in English. Experts would point to certain idiosyncracies."

"This is what you have come to discuss?"

"A fabricated Hess Command, we *must* discuss," said Talbott. "A film that must be stopped. You know what it can do to trick Israel into self-destruction."

"I cannot stop things outside my control."

"All is under your control."

"No!" Yuri Gorin's face in the steamy light became a mask again. His eyes belonged to someone hiding behind wooden features. The real man seemed unreachable. He gestured at the huge towels piled on a square Ministry of Works chair. "There should be a robe around there. I'm not a man who stands on dignity, but I would feel more comfortable . . ." He rose out of the mud.

Talbott was surprised by the compact, almost youthful dimensions of the naked body. The chest was covered in gray hair, but the belly was tight and muscular. Talbott pulled a robe out of a shelf under the chair's seat. Gorin took the robe and hung it on a hook. He turned on the shower and revolved under it, unembarrassed. He hoisted a leg onto the side of the tub and toweled it briskly. There was a long and livid scar down the outside of one thigh. The calf was thin, the muscles underdeveloped. The ankle had a permanently swollen look. Gorin paused, looked at Talbott, and said conversationally, "That happened when I jumped, after delivering Rudolf Hess."

The revelation made Talbott's stomach turn over. Gorin was either placing his life in Talbott's hands to prove his integrity, or he'd brought Talbott here to serve some Byzantine intrigue and then meant to destroy his visitor. Just hearing Gorin utter that sentence could condemn a man.

Gorin stepped onto the wooden slats covering the cubicle's floor. He scarcely reached to Talbott's eyes. "You see things too simplistically in the West. Everything is *not* under my control."

"You've come closer than most."

"With a purpose." Gorin took down the robe and drew it over his shoulders. "I have not forgotten my sacred oath to your mother."

"You made a pledge?"

"Never again would our people be victims," Gorin declared.

"Then it's time to redeem the pledge."

"I'm beyond redemption." Gorin settled his rump on the edge of the tub and motioned Talbott to sit on the chair of towels. He had turned into nothing more than a little old man staring down at his misshapen toes. "So you finally remember Radzki?"

"With respect, I have been relearning about a man who was once called Radzki. A good man of courage is what I believe him to be. A dedicated man."

Gorin twisted his head sideways when he heard these words.

"A man," continued Talbott, "not easily fooled."

Gorin studied his feet again. "Fooled? General Quex Massey fooled me. He betrayed every Jewish agent in Operation Citadel."

"That's not true!"

"Prove it! Then we'll see about the rest."

Talbott said, "My God! The Radzki I want to remember would take any risk for his people. He hated the fraudulence of secret power. This Radzki seems to have fallen in love with it."

Gorin, as if deliberately courting disgust, blew his nose with his fingers and shook snot onto the wet floorboards. "Nobody can make judgments about power until he's got it. Then he's on top, and beyond moderation. Unless there is another to give guidance, to say when the end justifies the means."

"You won't justify anything if you run away now."

"What?"

"Isn't that why you asked for help?"

"I'm not asking for a place to hide."

"What do you want?"

Gorin hawked and spat, and scratched his chest. "Guidance. For that, I am willing to return to Moscow, and to wait. I cannot squander this power for those who betray—"

"Nobody among us betrayed you."

"That is what you must convince me is true." Gorin shifted along the edge of the tub. "But can you? You were betrayed yourself."

He looked up then, directly into Talbott's eyes, reading whatever he found there. "You fought a war, but your leaders had different objectives to yours. You thought you were saving the oppressed. Your leaders were sacrificing them."

Talbott returned the stare. "There may have been blind prejudice. Never a conspiracy."

"Jacob Slominsky fought a guerrilla war that cut across the lines of the conventional conflict, on the basis Jews must not trust anybody again who is not Jewish."

"Slominsky," Talbott retorted, "is running around London with your handwritten report at this very moment. If he learns what you've become, he'll see you as the greatest traitor of all—a Jew who afflicts his own people."

Gorin drew his head down between his shoulders. "You're a good liar, Talbott."

Talbott wondered despairingly how a leader with such supreme self-confidence could be jolted. Was he immune to human feeling? Talbott groped inside his coat and brought out Rebecca's diary. "I don't have a Bible to swear on. But I'll swear on this."

Gorin took the diary. He turned it over and over.

"Read it!" Talbott challenged. "My mother's life. I found it yesterday. In Jacob Slominsky's company, I found it. After so many years. Read it!"

Gorin held the diary between his hands and seemed suddenly to be robbed of all movement.

Talbott had never felt such absolute danger. In surrendering the diary, he had put himself in the hands of a man who had total power to shut him up for good.

"What," asked Yuri Gorin, "do you want me to do?"

Shock froze Talbott's tongue. He leaned back against the wall.

"Take your time." Gorin was studying Talbott's face as if he saw there the chaos of early dreams.

"Yes." A scheme formed, vanished. "I need to think."

Gorin lumbered to his feet and stared at the big timepiece hanging on the wall.

Talbott said, "You spoke to Rebecca of the loneliness of power." The idea taking shape in his head was hardening. "She writes in the diary that you saw how wartime leaders were cut off from unacceptable realities. Today the leaders live in possibly worse isolation. You regard each other with eyes provided by your underlings, your enmity fed by special interests." Talbott was groping. The plan sounded clumsy, coming out backwards this way. "You, yourself— Did you listen, ever, to anyone in London or Washington after the Citadel fiasco? Did you ever ask the truth of it? Or did you *want* the lies to multiply down the years to nourish your own prejudices?"

Gorin said, "You're glib, Talbott. But I'm interested. It's good I knew you when you were less glib." He reached out to press a button. "You were a *guter mensh*, a good boy. A *goldeneh kop*, a golden brain. But in those days, never a talker."

Talbott hid his disappointment. The man seemed to be closing off discussion. "Hitler's last will—" Talbott said.

"Yes?"

"—was an appeal to 'continue the crusade to purge humanity's blood of the Jewish poison.' Is that what you'll do? By your silence, endorse the last of Hitler's Big Lies? Drop us the Hess Command as Hitler's last time bomb?"

There was a knock at the door.

Gorin sank down. "Don't you understand *anything*, Talbott?"

"I understand that, under you, the Soviets carry out Hitler's last orders."

The knocking became more urgent. The door opened a crack. "Please hurry." It was Vesna, her whisper a hiss of alarm.

"We will continue at the villa." Gorin raised his voice so the nurse could hear. "Make the arrangements." Then, for Talbott's ears only, he asked softly, "Tell me, do you *still* sometimes feel afraid you might be wanting in courage?"

The question was shrewdly put. It created a different kind of bond between them. Yuri Gorin had sensed what Talbott as a boy feared, that he was at heart a coward. "Always!" Talbott said with quick spontaneity.

Gorin consulted his toes. Then he looked up, head on one side. "Me, too," he said.

Before Talbott slipped through the door, he glanced back. Gorin still held the same posture, as if he was still listening for the real answer, his mouth hanging open in anticipation. He seemed very much alone.

A clever actor? Dangerous? If Yuri Gorin was lost on his pinnacle of power, wasn't he a threat more than an asset? He was committed to ruthless measures of suppression. He seemed, though, to face imminent exposure. There must be some way to use his anxiety. With that thought, Talbott's half-formed scheme took further shape.

He had been taken by Vesna to the fourth-floor office of an Igalo doctor. She explained that all the regular doctors were "on vacation" until the conference ended. "The first step was that the leader should see you. The moment I set eyes on you, I knew he would be reassured. Now you need only wait, relax, eat, take some drink." She placed a plate of food on the doctor's desk, and brought out a bottle of plum brandy from the cupboard labeled alcohol. She read his thoughts and looked at her watch. The countdown was critical now.

"You're behind schedule," said Vesna. "We'll make it up."

"Shouldn't you . . . ?" He gestured below.

"His own private secretary collects him," Vesna said smugly. "That's why I was in so much of a hurry."

An alarm went off in Talbott's head. *"Private secretary?"*

"It doesn't mean what it says, of course." She smiled. "Kerensky. KGB. Runs the General Secretary's bodyguard. He's got a lot of blood on his hands. But don't worry. Mother keeps him on a chain. Now then! Eat! Drink!" She made him sit before food she had smuggled from the kitchens. "You need strength. Yuri Gorin is what you call a night bird. They are all the same. Tito, always talking, drinking, making love . . . Khrushchev, he was here, you know. I was too young, naturally." She swung her hips in mock flirtation. "But Brezhnev—ah, I could tell you a thing or two about Brezhnev!"

She crossed to the door. "All night talking to you, now *that* would be different!" She held up a key. "I must lock you in. To prevent intrusion, you understand?"

Talbott heard the key turn in the lock. The door between the doctor's office and the examination room was open. He could see the foot of an iron bed. He felt trapped. *Kerensky!* He shivered. Most newsmen who were informed on current Soviet affairs had heard about Kerensky and the ECLIPSE division. There were papers in Talbott's pockets . . . samples of what Radzki had left behind in London. Talbott had brought them to reinforce his credibility. They could also hang him.

He poured himself a drink and forced himself to think about the plan he'd conceived while Gorin talked. The plan depended on the Radzki he remembered. If *that* Radzki had been destroyed while being absorbed into the new personality of Yuri Gorin . . .

He shivered. Scott Talbott would be hosting his last show, a Moscow show trial.

34

Sally Ryan balanced with one foot on Steely Pamir's desk and the other on the ledge of the barred window. By stretching on tiptoe, she commanded a view of the driveway in front of the embassy under security floodlights. The Israelis had already lost one ambassador to the terrorism stalking London streets. Since then, they had changed their strategy. Instead of crouching anonymously behind concealed cameras, the Israeli mission now advertised its readiness to repay mad bombers in kind.

The door behind Sally banged open. She turned quickly and pretended to fiddle with the bare light bulb hanging from the ceiling.

"Something wrong?"

Sally smiled down at Dahlia. The translator had kept her busy all this Wednesday with copies and translations of the Radzki papers.

"My eyes must be getting very tired." Sally climbed down to the floor. "Or else that bulb suddenly dimmed."

"We switch to our own generators when it gets dark," the Israeli girl said coldly. "Sometimes the voltage drops. It's temporary."

She's catching on to me, thought Sally. She said, "These men! They're all the same. They promised to look over my notes."

Dahlia shrugged. "They treat us like robots. General Pamir wanted everything translated before Commander Nelson left with his FBI friend."

"They've gone?"

"I practically broke my neck to finish the work, and they just walked out."

Sally, concealing her excitement, bent over the papers stacked under different headings around the desk. "You know," she said casually, "I need a breather."

"I'll take you to our canteen."

"No, I mean a real breath of fresh air. Out into the streets."

Dahlia betrayed alarm. "But you mustn't!"

"Just a walk to the end of Palace Gardens? Perhaps a drink and a sandwich at the Russian Wine Cellar—"

"No, it's impossible!"

"I'm not a prisoner," Sally said gently. She offered the girl her warmest smile. "These men leave us all the dirty work, stick us into stuffy rooms, and expect us to stay bright and perky. Come on, let's take a break."

"General Pamir wouldn't like it."

"The general isn't my boss."

"But even Mr. Talbott—"

"—isn't here, is he?" Sally said.

Dahlia's face seemed to close up, like a pretty flower at sunset. She could hardly be more than twenty years old. These sabra girls, thought Sally, shouldered heavy responsibilities before most Americans were out of college. But, Israeli or American, most girls that age had a mischievous streak.

"We can nip up the street, get a couple of drinks—they do a decent shepherd's pie at the Russian Wine Cellar—and be back here before anyone figures we've gone."

"You didn't like the food I brought you?" asked Dahlia, wavering.

"Yes, of course. I just need to shake off this headache. Also . . . I need to pop into a chemist's."

"Oh!" Dahlia gave her a sisterly look of understanding. "The general's been called away," she said slowly. "I suppose we could . . ."

Twenty minutes later, outside the Soviet Russian consulate at 25, Palace Gardens, a grim little Victorian mansion that does actually face the commercial Russian Wine Cellar on Bayswater Road, the granddaughter of General Quex Massey broke away from Dahlia and vanished into the courtyard protected by high walls bearing the unpolished brass plaque of the U.S.S.R.

Sally's exit followed events which had awoken her slowly to a new danger. At first, she had been absorbed in working through the Radzki papers and scarcely noticed the passing hours. She and Talbott had been given cots on which to sleep in Pamir's office, and Sally was too exhausted to question Talbott when he said he was obliged to work. When she did come to, vastly refreshed, Dahlia greeted her with a late breakfast and a note from Peled Pamir. He wanted her to track all references in Radzki's papers to places where he had hidden parts of his so-called Auschwitz Index.

Sally had been intrigued. Later, she realized Pamir intended her to be. Then she became frightened by something she read in a note, dated by Radzki, for November 1944: "A catastrophe! Lord Moyne, chief symbol of British policy in the Middle East, has been assassinated by Jewish guerrillas following the violent Zionist path taken by Jacob Slominsky." That meant, of course, Jacob Cooke. She read on: "The Stern Gang say Moyne had to be killed because he personified British imperialism in the lands of Zion. They say he blocked every Jewish appeal for help in Nazi Europe during his time as Britain's colonial minister and later as minister-resident in Cairo running the Middle East Bureau (espionage, counter-intelligence, political string-pulling). Lord Moyne said the only Semitics were Arab, and they alone were entitled to Palestine."

Sally had to remind herself this was Radzki's interpretation. True or false, it was an insight into his state of mind in a war in which the Anglo-American Allies were fighting for good against evil. He had continued: "During Lord Moyne's office, British police murdered Abraham Stern, founder of the Stern Gang. Under Moyne's rule, the Jewish refugee ship *Struma* was turned back into German U-boat waters, where it was sunk along with eight hundred innocent souls . . . Nevertheless, Lord Moyne's assassination is a terrible blow to Jews. Killed in this manner, he becomes a bigger enemy. Churchill, ready to create an Israel, now says that after 'winning against Nazi thugs' he does not propose to deal 'with Jewish terrorists.' The assassination may satisfy those Jews thirsting for vengeance, but it also fans new flames of anti-Jewish feeling."

Sally saw an awful parallel with today in the 1944 act of violence that almost wrecked Zionist dreams. Was Jake going to repeat that mistake on a truly catastrophic scale, his fears fed by that handwritten Radzki copy of the original Hess proposals? Lord Moyne had been targeted after a few hundred refugees drowned on the *Struma*. The Hess deal seemed to commit millions to the death chambers. What exalted personage would Jake choose as a target, now he felt he had proof of such a conspiracy among Britain's rulers?

Sally, stepping into the corridor to look for Dahlia, was surprised to find Fishhook Sherman and Nelson on their way to see her.

She seized upon them for help, unprepared for opposition. "I must find Jake Cooke," she said, and they listened politely enough to her arguments. Then Fishhook began: "It's too late—"

She interrupted. "I know I can find him."

Nelson moved casually into Steely Pamir's office. If she had been less worried, she might have noticed they were shepherding her back. Fishhook guided her through the door and then blocked it.

"It's dangerous out there," said Nelson.

"London's the safest city I've ever worked in."

Nelson saw Quex's obstinacy in her face. "Londoners!" His laugh was bitter. "Nothing rattles a Londoner. Mrs. Thatcher's almost killed by a bomb, but she's still alive, right? Thugs blow up Lord Mountbatten in Ireland—well, the old boy'd had a long innings! Mrs. Thatcher's favorite cabinet minister is bombed to smithereens? The people shrug. The Queen fired at? The bullet missed, though, didn't it? There was some vulgar hysteria when dynamite tore up the Queen's cavalry horses and the Mall was strewn with limbs—Londoners love animals, and that did piss them off a bit. Chelsea old-age pensioners are torn to bits wearing their best bib and tuckers and *that* struck some as a bit unsporting. Christmas at Harrods and the shoppers bombed . . . By then, the city's conditioned itself. Like the Blitz. But don't call it safe, girl!" He tugged a newspaper from his jacket and spread it out for Sally. "Look." He pointed to the headline: TERRORIST FEAR IN CHELSEA, and read the lead paragraph: "Secret training for terrorists is said by Chelsea residents to be taking place at 85 Arab embassy properties and 120 privately owned Arab buildings in this London district alone . . . The Greater London Council admits the Libyan government so badly wanted to buy a surplus school, they out-bid all others . . ."

"What's this got to do with me?" demanded Sally.

"These are bases against Israel. You're publicly associated with Israel. You're a target."

"You're making my flesh creep!" scoffed Sally.

"It can't be long before Parson Furneval finds you're not dead," said Nelson. "He can use that knowledge to create chaos—"

"And with all your knowledge, you can't stop him!" said Sally. "So . . . let me."

"We still have the ragamuffins you call the Blitz Kids." Nelson's face brightened. "If I was a pompous old bugger, I'd never confess this. But street urchins have always been the best for dragnets. Right, Fishhook?"

"Too true."

"They're quick, nimble. Grown-ups never take 'em seriously and talk carelessly in front of them." Nelson flung out his arms. "You can pop 'em up drainpipes, hang 'em in the chandeliers, hide 'em in dog kennels—"

"Very diverting," said Sally, trying to sidle past Fishhook. "But you're not diverting me. I'll locate Jake, and I'll make him listen to sense. I was very close to him once. He respects my opinion."

Fishhook sighed and took her by the arm. "Your grandfather wants you to call him."

"To hell with it!" said Sally. "I've a job to do."

"A job your New York office wants you to drop. They're recalling you," cut in Nelson.

"They can't! That's Talbott's decision."

"But he's not here," said Fishhook, scratching the side of his nose.

It was then Sally realized things were going wrong. She hadn't seen

Talbott all day. "I won't budge from here until Talbott tells me," she said. She went back to Pamir's desk and continued to read Dahlia's translations.

"Be sensible," Fishhook pleaded. "Your grandfather feels you've been in too much danger already."

"When Grandpa Massey worries about me, it's because he's afraid I'll find out something he'd rather hide," Sally retorted.

"At least speak to him."

"No," said Sally.

Several attempts were made to put New York through to her. She told the embassy switchboard she would speak only with Talbott. She enjoyed behaving like a bitch. Fishhook and Nelson had refused to say *where* Talbott was, and she knew her only weapon now was her own stubbornness. She made one attempt to find her way out of the embassy, and was courteously but firmly shepherded back to Pamir's office by a press secretary who explained the deputy minister wanted her kept there until his return. "Then, I'm virtually a prisoner," protested Sally. When Dahlia caught her standing on the desk, she had been trying to figure a way through the tradesmen's entrance to the embassy garage.

Nobody could really stop her leaving the embassy. Dahlia presented her with the opportunity of a graceful exit. Without fuss, the embassy security branch sent two plainclothesmen to follow. The hour was late, a chill November drizzle shrouded the Soviet consulate, where four or five demonstrators spiritlessly waved placards demanding the release of a Russian dissident. "Cross here," said Sally, stepping off the curb and pointing to the wine bar opposite. Dahlia had to wait for a double-deck bus to lurch past. It obscured her view of Sally, who stood at the centerline between the two rivers of traffic, and quickly doubled back again while Dahlia continued over. The embassy tails failed to see Sally slip behind the demonstrators, and by the time they caught up with Dahlia, their quarry was gone.

35

The chief of the East German intelligence services hauled himself to the bar in Tito's old villa, stifling another yelp of pain. Helmuth Henkell reminded himself of the proper order of things. First, German grit! Then alcohol and morphine. He groped under the counter until his trembling hand found a bottle. He smashed the neck against the bartender's tap and gulped down the raw vodka.

Now to get the morphine. He forced himself to walk upright, averting his face from the humiliating poker where Yuri Gorin had thrown it in the fireplace. Mother had exceeded all limits! Even Stalin's. The time had come to get the mad bastard.

The guards outside saluted as Henkell moved stiffly down the slope to the garage. An officer asked if he should send for the regular driver. Henkell waved him aside, and said through gritted teeth, "No need."

He collapsed behind the wheel of the car. German willpower would get him through the next twenty minutes. Then he'd put Mother under some German *stress*. He retched noisily, sticking his head out through the open door, the vomit smacking the tarmac. Gorin's guards had seen enough drunkenness in their careers to find this normal. It explained the way Henkell had staggered out of the villa. When Henkell suddenly turned on the headlights, he caught two of the guards laughing.

He could scarcely breathe from the pain as he started the engine, working out each move as if he were driving a tank. Hang on! German *grit.* If Hitler had been German, we'd have licked these slit-eyed Slavs!

The vodka was taking effect by the time he reached the beach garden back of the clinic. He stopped and fell forward over the wheel.

A sentry appeared at the window. A black-ass Yugoslav *chernozhopi* this time! *Chernozhopi* was Russian for low-grade comrades in the East. It suited Henkell's contempt for the inferior races, and in his mind referred equally to most Russians. He acknowledged the man's inquiry. "Just get me Professor Dichter!"

"Dichter?"

"Otto Dichter. Deputy chief, German delegation."

"At once, General Henkell!" The sentry had been six months a guest worker in the Federal Republic and was proud of his German. "Is there anything else—?"

"Get him!" roared Henkell.

They had to interrupt the evening banquet. Otto Dichter was not too sorry. Every night was a banquet at this pestilential conference. Endless gorging. Toasts galore. Toadying to Mother. And the gross old dinosaur simply sitting there, face as empty as his head.

"I want morphine," Henkell told him. "And then I want Crombie."

Otto Dichter helped him leave the car. "That's easily done," he said. "Morphine and Crombie are both in the same place."

Red Crombie had been taken by Vesna to join Talbott in the doctor's office.

"Time's running out," said Crombie. He led Talbott into the examination room while Vesna quickly cleared away the evidence of Talbott's evening meal. "Now, look. In case things go wrong—" He caught Talbott's grimace and added quickly, "We're in good shape. You'll see Mother for the big session, soon as the pigs down there finish snuffling in the troughs. If you need to make contact, and I'm not around, here's the bag of tricks." He loosened a belt around his waist with a small pack attached. "Vesna knows the drill, but I'll run over it for you. Record your message. The machine is voice-activated. You transfer normal-speed recording to high-speed tape by punching these doodads. This one's for shore-to-ship. Tuning's automatic. An hour of tape in a burst transmission is completed in four seconds, but you can't operate until this aerial's extended." Four feet of spring steel hissed out. "Retrieve by pushing this tit." The aerial whipped and lashed back into the pack.

Heavy bangs threatened to break down the outer-office door.

"Stay here," Crombie warned.

Vesna moved swiftly behind the examination bed. Talbott stood near the inner door. It opened inwards and was still partly ajar. He heard someone in the corridor shout, "It's me, Dichter! Hurry!" There were sounds of a bolt withdrawn, and then a new voice: "I'm badly hurt!"

They heard Crombie say, "Good God, Grueber!" There was a loud thump and the injured man could be heard cursing. Words were exchanged, difficult to comprehend. The three men were talking over one another, taps were turned, cabinet doors open and shut. Instruments clattered in a dish.

Vesna hissed, "That's not *Grueber!*" She had been obliged to listen to his voice enough. She said, "It's the security boss from East Berlin. General Henkell."

But Crombie was fussing around the man. Talbott watched through the crack where the door hinged open. No question! Red Crombie was plunging a syringe into the bare arm of the man he was calling Grueber. The other paced into view: gaunt, skull-like head, flashing rimless spectacles . . . Obergruppenfuehrer Spiess from the sex club in Düsseldorf! But Red Crombie was addressing him as "Herr Dichter."

Talbott closed his eyes in almost physical pain, the scam only too clear. Spiess-Dichter and Henkell must be considered by Crombie to be turncoats: high-ranking defectors who remained in place in East Berlin. Crombie knew them by names invented for them by Henkell—but surely the American would have seen profiles of Henkell? Not necessarily. The East German apparatus was the most closely concealed of any in the Soviet bloc. No wonder Red Crombie's travel agency worked so well, if Henkell had been using it to feed his agents into America on a larger scale than the agency was getting Crombie's high-grade escapees out of the Soviet bloc!

Talbott retreated to the farthest corner of the examination room, taking Vesna with him. "Can we get out back?"

She shook her head.

They heard a body crash to the floor next door. Henkell was screaming, "A tampon! Anything!"

There were obscenities from Red Crombie. Then Henkell quietened down as more painkiller evidently took effect, and Crombie asked, "Who did this?"

"That sow-belly Gorin!"

"Ah!" Crombie sounded like a man vindicated.

Spiess-Dichter said, "You don't seem surprised."

With a loud groan, Henkell demanded attention. The question, when it came, was sharp as that of any grand inquisitor. "What do you know about Gorin?"

"No more than you," replied Crombie.

"You asked our help in Berlin with the American correspondent. It was in connection with Radzki." Henkell's voice gathered strength, fueled by professional excitement. "Is there another connection? With Mother? With Yuri Gorin?"

Talbott felt Vesna's hand squeeze his arm. She must be thinking the same thing. Red Crombie would blurt out the truth unless they took action. He was saying, still bewildered, "I don't understand—"

"I think you do," said Spiess-Dichter.

"Hey! Put away that gun!"

"Tell me, Mr. Crombie, the connection between Radzki and Mother."

Talbott thrust Vesna back and shouted, "Say nothing, Crombie! *Nothing!*" He moved to the door, still shouting, creating as much distraction as he could to give Crombie time to figure out he'd been fooled. "These men are enemies—" He expected gunfire and he was careful to approach the door with his body protecting Vesna. Instead, Spiess-Dichter burst in, gun in hand.

"Talbott!" The German's reactions were swift, disciplined, betraying no surprise. He called over his shoulder, "We've bagged the trophy."

Helmuth Henkell could be heard grunting angrily. Red Crombie appeared in the doorway, hands raised. Henkell followed him, almost erect, a weapon resembling a small, flat pistol in his hand.

Crombie said, "There's a mistake. This is Scott Talbott, one of us."

"One of *yours!* You American idiot!" Spiess-Dichter spat the words. "Not one of ours. Don't you understand yet?"

Talbott took a chance and intervened. "Who do you think they are?" he asked Red Crombie.

"That's Otto Dichter. And this is Hans Grueber, my East Berlin travel director." Red Crombie was facing Talbott head on. As he spoke these words, he winked, unseen by anyone but Talbott.

Henkell listened with the indulgent smile of a winner. The alcohol mixed with morphine had restored his color. He said, "Washington sent a fool on a fool's errand."

Talbott thought: God forgive me for thinking the same.

Henkell hooked a foot behind a steel chair, sliding it in front of Crombie. "Sit! Facing me!" He waved the pistol-like object in his hand, causing Crombie to recoil.

The man's not only a great actor, thought Talbott, watching Crombie. He's a genius at secret warfare. The whole game had been turned inside out. Crombie had fished up these two specimens with the bait of pretended trust, treating them as double agents when in fact he was not *doubling* but *tripling* them. This had been conveyed in that prodigious, swift, courageous wink. Another message was passed too. Crombie was gambling the East Germans would talk too much. Henkell's natural arrogance was inflamed by booze and drugs. Spiess-Dichter stood with his back to the wall, confidently covering them with his revolver. Crombie had become immobile, and this increased the tension in the room. Vesna understood the play. She stood almost in shadow behind the iron bed, as still as a mountain lake on a midsummer's night. They were all held by this common bond of strain. But Henkell was like a needle supported only by the surface tension of still water: the smallest ripple, and he would sink back into bullying incoherence. And Crombie would lose this unique, unforeseen opportunity to complete inquiries which, Talbott now realized, had been running parallel with those of Quex.

"Now," Henkell said finally, "tell us all you know about Yuri Gorin."

Red Crombie made no answer. He might as well have turned to stone.

The German opened his hand. "You recognize this? A surgical implantation gun." It lay in his palm for all to see. "It fires pellets. But resembles a gentleman's wallet." He opened what appeared to be a flap. "That loads it. I close the wallet. When I squeeze the bottom, a spring-released pin breaks a pellet and gas is ejected under pressure."

He smiled at Talbott. "An improvement over the umbrella. It leaves an impression of death by heart failure."

He turned back to Red Crombie, who watched him without expression. "I take this pill," said the German, swallowing it. "The antihistamine will neutralize the gas, on condition I take this other pill *after* I kill you, Mr. Crombie."

There was still no response from the American. Henkell twisted round again to address Talbott. "You could have saved Bronfmann, you see, with a pill like this." He displayed the second pill; it was the size of a shirt button, and bright orange.

"Who did the killing?" Talbott asked calmly.

"The umbrella man," offered Spiess-Dichter from his position by the wall. He drew his head down between his shoulders. His entire body seemed to shorten and swell sideways. "Come, my little darlings!" he croaked. "Dildo, fist, whip, mask? Follow your Uncle Feelie." It was an uncanny imitation.

Helmuth Henkell laughed. His eyes, dilated with drugs and vodka, shone in the light filtering from the other office. "You don't want another to die this way, Talbott?" He swayed slightly, like a drunk at an embassy party trying to maintain his social position. "What brings you here? Is it Radzki, your monster trapped in the ice of Citadel!"

He must have detected a sudden dilation of Talbott's eyes, some stiffening of posture.

"There's more we can tell you, Talbott," he said, "than you can tell us about Radzki. We have the old Nazi records. Efficiently kept by those ever-so-efficient Germans. One thing we missed, and we traced that finally to Moscow."

Spiess-Dichter made a warning noise from the back of his throat. But his colleague was talking like a drunk now, words erupting in a gout of confidence. There was humiliation to be avenged. Henkell needed to fuck others the way Mother had fucked him.

"Now, why would that particular file go into the private archives of Yuri Gorin? *Sanballats* . . . You know what that means? Traitors. That is how Jews refer to traitors." He was addressing Talbott exclusively. "*Sanballats*. After the satrap of Samaria who fought against the rebuilding of Jerusalem. Surprised? It's my business, to know about Jewry. My particular business, as a good German Marxist. And I find myself asking: Why should Comrade Gorin occupy himself with a story of wartime treachery . . . ?"

Talbott listened. The voice was obsessive, a death-bed confession almost, except Helmuth Henkell clearly did not consider himself the candidate for last rites. He was driven to give a new and totally unexpected account of Operation Citadel; a version, he said, drawn from Nazi intelligence archives in his personal possession. The performance was strange, demonic almost. It seemed designed to arouse Talbott's disgust, turn him against Radzki perhaps, make it easier to betray Radzki if there was anything to betray.

Henkell's voice rose and fell, rose and fell. Hypnotic, it would have been, if the story were less dramatic. Then the flush in Henkell's face faded and turned to a sickly gray pallor. The voice faltered. "Tell your friend Radzki," Henkell said, directing the words at Talbott, "we have the documentation he's been hunting all these years."

And if I do, thought Talbott, you'll follow me. And thus I'll lead you to Radzki. But I doubt you're even close to guessing how close Radzki really has been, all along, to you.

That was when Red Crombie flew into action. He must have felt he'd got what he wanted from Henkell; the scales were beginning to turn the other way. He was a block of ice one moment, a whirling dervish the next. Vesna seemed to be in telepathic contact. She overturned the iron bed as Crombie lunged at the weapon in Henkell's hand. The bed crashed across Spiess-Dichter's feet. Talbott sprang as Henkell squeezed the wallet-like gun in Crombie's face. Spiess-Dichter's gun blazed. A fine spray floated in the air as Henkell staggered back under Talbott's blows. There were seconds of confusion and Talbott caught a faint odor like bitter almonds. Then Vesna ran at him, clasped her hand over his mouth, and with her momentum pushed him into the outer office.

She turned as Henkell, shaky on his feet, fell through the doorway after them, his arm spilling blood. The nurse struck him hard in the stomach. He doubled up. She swung the edge of her hand up under his throat. He was still gagging as she dug her fingers into the open wound of the injured arm, squeezing until his hand jerked open and the orange button-sized pill rolled to the floor. Then she screamed to Talbott, "Run!"

"No!" Talbott fought to get past the body blocking the doorway. He could see Red Crombie inside, lying on the floor, still as death.

"Run!" Vesna screamed again. "It's too late." She caught Talbott off balance, spun him around and pushed. "We need you," she said. "Alive. Not gassed."

"That wasn't ricin," said Talbott a few minutes later. His legs were still shaking and he had lowered himself onto a bundle of dirty linen in the storeroom where Vesna had led him.

"Ricin?" Vesna's laugh bordered on hysteria. "We're behind the times here. Cyanide. That wallet ejects cyanide crystals." She crossed herself. "It was quick for Crombie, poor boy."

"And Henkell?"

"I hit him in the adam's apple to stop him swallowing the second antidote. That other one, Dichter, his first bullet smashed Henkell's arm, it flew so wild. Then he shot himself."

"Shot himself?"

She caught his glance of disbelief and said meekly, "The bed hit his feet. Later I hit . . . where it hurts most for a man. And helped him accidentally shoot himself in the face." Her eyes were round and innocent.

"I'm sorry about Crombie," muttered Talbott, feeling inadequate next to this extraordinary woman.

"Don't be. He was the catalyst. Everything that pig Henkell said was for his benefit. And I got it all."

Talbott stared at the bag strapped to Vesna's waist. "The transceiver! You taped—?"

"Yes, of course. Mother must learn the truth."

Talbott held his head in his hands. "You're a genius."

"But am I still beautiful? That is what matters in America, isn't it?" Vesna peered into the corridor. Strains from a military band floated up the stairwells. "They've finished at the trough," she said. "Mother will expect us soon." She saw him hesitate, and mistook the reason. "This entire floor is for regular medical staff," she said. "It's empty now. We're safe."

Talbott moved to the door but paused again, overcome by nausea.

"You're sick? The gas . . . ?"

"I'll be okay." Talbott pushed away from the wall. "Lead on, wonder woman. I'm in your hands."

"I wish you were," said the irrepressible Vesna, giving his face an encouraging pat.

Mother listened impassively to the dead Helmuth Henkell's loud boasts. The Soviet leader still wore the banqueting suit of tailored pinstripe, with a red Dior silk tie and jostling medals. If he felt incongruous in the mudbath cubicle, he gave no sign. Vesna sat on the edge of the tub, playing back the tape; Mother sat on the wooden chair; Talbott leaned against the wooden wall.

Mother signaled to stop the playback. "Why does he spill his guts?"

Vesna looked at Talbott. She was equally concerned for an answer. The tape had cost Red Crombie his life. He'd been the American hero she knew from Hollywood movies permitted into Yugoslavia. She'd taken it for granted there would be a happy ending. With Crombie dead, the only happy ending would be made by herself. She was the lifeline, the only traveler who knew the way. But Talbott was the only customer left who could justify it.

Talbott saw that this was a time to sound decisive. He said, with more confidence than he felt, "Henkell created the Hess Command. He saw himself the man of iron who should lead the new Marxism. He needed to impress us, the way a Castro talks endlessly to assert his unique genius."

Mother considered this. "On this tape, we hear plans to terrorize London. A curious form of self-promotion."

"Which you can stop," Talbott said quickly.

"How?"

"Go to London." The scheme had finally matured in Talbott's mind. "Go as the Soviet leader."

Mother's expression gave away nothing.

"The enemy you're really fighting," said Talbott, "means to make this coming Remembrance Day a stake to drive through the heart of Judaism. They pick a day when the world stops to pray for the millions killed in war. This year, the President of the United States will be there. The enemy's purpose is to strike when that vast audience is most vulnerable, with lies as vicious as Operation Citadel."

The mention of Citadel brought Mother's head back. Of all the matters dropped from the drug-wagging, ego-loosened, boozed-up tongue of that cow-fucking Henkell, this business of the Second World War secret mission was most strange. He had boasted that the operation was blown through an Egyptian informer working on the training base as a secretary responsible for all top-secret material. The British had acquired the Egyptian from an American military observer in Cairo. The American had vouched for him because the Egyptian was a paid informer for OSS, suspicious of British secret operations about which they were not consulted. The informer reported to his old American chief, who dispatched details in code to Washington. The code had been broken by German military intelligence some time before. Every step of Operation Citadel had been known in Berlin right to the moment it was launched. The Germans knew precisely who would parachute into their midst, where, and when. To create more mischief, and cover their foreknowledge, they leaked reports the operation was intended to fail *because the British wished to get rid of Jewish nuisances.* In fact, just before the operation was launched, a senior American officer had rushed pellmell into the desert to report it was compromised because the OSS had discovered the U.S. code was broken. The British, however, refused to listen. The long-term result was that General Henkell had been given an unparalleled source for disinformation to stir up old Jewish underground fighters.

"Is there more?" Mother asked suddenly, pointing to the recorder-transceiver.

"We heard all that was taped," said Vesna, and bent forward to demonstrate the machine was not running.

"No, no," said Mother. "This I *want* recorded. You have more cassettes?"

Vesna withdrew a blank. "One hour either side. But that is more time than our schedule allows."

"Don't tell me how much time I've got," growled Mother. He turned back to Talbott. "This plan— it is of course quite mad. However . . . if your American President invited me to London, it would disarm the critics. We are medieval still. The East German wanted to prove himself smarter than the CIA. Now I must show the politburo the White House comes to me!"

Mother's eyes danced with the swiftness of his calculations. "They wonder in Washington what side I'm really on." He pointed to the tape. "I put my life there, in your hands, Talbott, and in theirs."

He leaned forward, hands dangling between outspread knees, and was silent.

Vesna reminded him, "Talbott has only one chance at escape. At sea, before the next dawn. There is little time and three men lie dead above us."

"Arrange matters," Mother said testily. "One should seem to have shot the other. Henkell appears to have suffered heart seizure, is that not so?"

"Provided there's no immediate autopsy. Microcrystals in the body vanish within minutes. I speak," Vesna added, "as a nurse." She was still bristling from his reprimand.

"Do as a pretty nurse should, then." Mother caught her note of reproach. "Tell Secretary Kerensky your therapy with me is prolonged. It will give me more time with Talbott, but let Kerensky indulge in sexual fantasies."

Vesna blushed.

"Take pleasure, live longer, eh?" Mother prompted.

Vesna set the machine to record. "We'll all live longer," she said in a parting shot, "if I fix the dead first."

"A clever woman," said Mother after she had left. "A pity. We'll have to dispose of her later. Another operational necessity." Talbott opened his mouth to protest. Mother silenced him. "Let me show Washington why I still deserve trust. Self-incrimination's the coinage, isn't it? I trap myself on tape. They run it through their lie detectors, their verifiers. I regain their confidence by putting my head on the chopping block."

He cocked his head. "We live in the same riddle, Talbott." He wore now that oddly innocent air of those who have been isolated too long from open discussion. "You killed the boy you were, to become the man you are. I destroyed the Radzki you knew to become what I am today. Do you think our murdered selves come back?" His mouth hung open as it had before when he was lost. "It is, is it not, what the great masters of religion and psychology tell us? If they are right, does the dead self rise again, demanding revenge? Or are we little boys still, trying to act like adults, wishing secretly for the pure vision of childhood?"

Then Vesna returned. Patrol boats had made a sweep of the bay and might be back. Talbott never had a chance to learn what particular ghost haunted Mother in his solitude.

36

Sally moved warily out of the unlit grounds of the shuttered Soviet consulate and turned right, keeping to the iron railings of Kensington Gardens. She had shaken off Dahlia and the shadowing Israeli embassy officials. But once, when she turned suddenly, she had an uneasy sense of being followed still. She stopped and glimpsed a small boy near a bus stop. A voice out of the darkness said, "Need any help, miss?"

"No!" Sally jumped. "No, thank you."

"Bit lonely round here, this time of night, miss." The policeman loomed over her. "Like me to fetch a taxi?"

"I'd really rather walk," Sally said firmly.

"That's all right, then, miss." The policeman raised a finger to his helmet and moved on. Sally thought: I could use your help, dammit. You and fifty thousand other bobbies could maybe give me a fighting chance to run down Jake Cooke. She wondered if she had been seen dodging out of the Soviet consulate entryway. It had been a place to hide. But the Israelis would certainly find it odd.

At Lancaster Gate she crossed the street and plunged into the rabbit warren of quickie hotels. Three prostitutes standing under the light from the subway station shouted at her to get off their turf.

She found what she wanted: a shabby, ill-lit room in a boardinghouse kept by an old harridan who demanded payment in advance ("We normally charge by the hour, you see, dearie") and reminded Sally with a large wink that "this is a respectable place."

She sat on the stained bedsheets and spread out the notes recovered from Peled Pamir's desk. There was a street guide in Radzki's Auschwitz Index, listing *duboks* where he'd concealed copies of his reports from inside Nazi territories. The hiding places sometimes overlapped addresses she remembered Jake using in London. But where should she look first? It all seemed hopeless. She lay back against a grubby pillow and told herself there *had* to be a solution. When Jake branched out into Zionist activities conflicting with the law, he had utilized safe-houses used by wartime couriers like Radzki. Now Jake knew about the index, he would be looking in these locations for Radzki material he so badly wanted. Just why Jake was obsessed with obtaining it, Sally was still not sure. The only way she could hope to intercept Jake was to take a stab at the most promising *duboks*.

There was sharp rapping at the door. The landlady's head appeared. "Someone to see you, dearie." Her pinched voice, her toothless mouth, even the hair in curlers, expressed disapproval. Into the room came one of the Blitz Kids.

"Charlie! Why aren't you in bed?"

The old harridan caught the question, sniffed loudly, and left, slamming the door.

"We bin keepin' watch. Took turns. It was me wot seen you leave."

"Keeping watch? Who for?" She shook him by his thin shoulders.

He saw the panic in her face. "Okay, miss, okay! We're doin' it for the bloke wiv the beard."

Jake Cooke! "Where is he?" She shook him again.

"Struth!" swore Charlie, wriggling from her grasp. "No need to go on so. I don't rightly know where 'e is this minute. 'E'll be in touch tomorrer."

Sally stared at him, remembering what Nelson had said: "Street urchins are best for dragnets." This was no time to probe. Charlie's face was closed against interrogation. She asked instead, "What will you do now?"

"Sleep 'ere." The boy bundled his jacket and stretched out on the greasy linoleum. "Me orders is to guard you fer the night."

Sally was roused by the roar of early-morning traffic. She tiptoed around the sleeping boy and went down a corridor in search of the communal washroom. When she got back, the boy was gone. For a bewildered moment, she thought she must have dreamed the whole encounter. Then she moved fast, for there could be only one reason for Charlie's sudden departure. He had been waiting for daylight, to cut off and report to Jake.

The landlady was waiting when Sally came down the stairs. "That young lad left this for you." She handed Sally a note, her hooded eyes black with censure. An old man in carpet slippers and egg-stained sweater said from deep inside a huge wicker chair, "Bloody cradle snatcher. Ought to be a law . . ."

Sally stood on the sidewalk outside and scanned Charlie's note. "Just went over to see Ginger. Your bearded bloke is waiting at Hyde Park Gate . . ."

The boys were everywhere. She tapped the printed note: Charlie's grammar was better than he made out.

The address was one she had earlier pinpointed: a Victorian mansion where Jake Cooke had often stayed in other times. She crossed into Hyde Park and came out at Kensington Gore. It was difficult to believe London could be under any counterrevolutionary-warfare alert. But appearances could deceive. She had been here when a counterterror squad appeared like magic one normal business day to swarm over the Iranian embassy. Sally's office was then close by. She had watched SAS spidermen spin their lethal web around the terrorists in no time flat.

It was frightening to be numbered among terrorists herself now. Her heart pounded when she compared herself with Jake's outlaw state, armed, leading men labeled terrorists, and impassioned by his reading of those Radzki papers he'd already seen. He would fight for "Jake's Law." Long ago, in Israel, he had defined it: "If the world rejects the meaning of the Holocaust, and people are persecuted today because humanity refuses to confront the evil in its collective soul, then we have a moral right to pursue justice our own way, if only to protect our own race."

She turned into Queen's Gate, consumed by fear for Jake. He had once selected this neighborhood for his political headquarters. "A location," she had joked, "appropriate to a failed Prime Minister." Jake had not found this funny. He felt keenly his political downfall. That other underground fighter, Begin, had made it as Prime Minister instead.

She entered the short lane to Hyde Park Gate, where the very great had lived in quiet seclusion. Here was Churchill's old town house at Number 28. There, Number 18, the great Epstein had worked in his studios. Jake had seen himself as worthy of such company. Suddenly, Sally felt afraid. She pushed open the wrought-iron gate to the basement area of the house Jake once had used. The steps were slippery with the accumulation of leaves and damp. She took a last look up and down the street. She did not notice the small boy kneeling over a street drain, apparently absorbed in fishing through the grating.

Across the way, at an upper balcony, a lace curtain twitched. A large orange cat stalked along the balustrade and jumped into partly open french windows.

This was silly! What did she have to fear, between Churchill's town house and Epstein's studios? She choked off her misgivings and began down the steps. It was gloomy, almost dark, in the basement area. Thick plastic garbage bags huddled under a barred window. Each step she took made a loud, metallic, echoing *clang!* A cracked bell, tolling each argument for going back . . .

Somebody must be in residence. The bags were stuffed and bulky. They looked like three men in black raincoats. One impression followed swiftly upon the other until Sally froze on the bottom step beside a cellar door. Out of its blackness stepped a black figure. Sally had no time to scream. A large hand wrapped itself over her mouth. Another hand held her by the throat.

She was forced to gaze up, out of the basement areaway. Where the orange cat had been, a woman now stood on the distant balcony, staring directly down at her. Sally tried once more to utter some cry for help, but the pressure on her throat tightened. It was outrageous! She was being strangled slowly, in broad daylight, in the middle of a civilized city, in full view of a woman who had picked up the big orange cat and was stroking it as if nothing were happening below.

The housemaid with the orange cat withdrew from the balcony, dropped the cat, and made a phone call. "God be thanked!" she said when someone answered. "It's no longer safe here. Yes, a deliberate ambush. The men took a woman . . ."

The housemaid was speaking in Hebrew and eyeing the cat. The cat stopped licking itself and began to arch its back.

The housemaid let go the phone and grabbed a machine pistol from the sofa. A boot crashed against the door behind her. She whirled as the door burst open. The outside corridor was empty. She knew then she'd fallen for an old trick. She twisted back to the balcony. A man in the open french windows was already taking aim. Her time had run out.

Jake Cooke, at the other end of the line, heard the shot and then the silence. A smile hovered in his eyes and vanished. He replaced the phone and made his way back to the busy bar of the Sherlock Holmes, a favorite Whitehall pub.

"We've lost one *dubok*," he said, and relayed an edited version to a man guzzling beer.

"So the 88 are staking out the same *duboks?*" asked the beer drinker. He wore a red turtleneck. "Why don't we break the truce now?"

"You stick to gathering information. I'll figure the strategy." Jake nodded warningly in the direction of a man who seemed more interested in their conversation than his own pint of bitter. Turtleneck casually moved away, then elbowed through the noisy prelunch crowd to stop abruptly in front of a showcase. "My pa will want to hear about this," he said, pointing at the memorabilia. "That walking stick's really an airgun used by Colonel Sebastian Moran in the case of—" The inquisitive stranger shuffled past them.

"Your father?" asked Jake.

"Yes. He's chairman of some chapter of the Sherlock Holmes club." Turtleneck saw the stranger disappear into the washroom. "Where's the kid?"

"Outside. He's under age. Otherwise he'd be demanding his mug of lager."

Jake led the way to the street, looking dignified in his long black topcoat with fur-trimmed collar. Candlestick hovered in a bookshop doorway. As the two men drew abreast, the boy began to walk casually alongside.

"Ever hear of the state of Texas?" asked Jake.

"Yus, guv."

"Texas once had an official legation—"

"I know," said Candlestick. "Near the posh tailor in Pickering Place, up the road from St. James's Palace."

"Smart lad! Go there and wait."

"Got it, guv." The boy scooted off.

"Why'd you depend on those kids?" complained Turtleneck.

"Your father would understand." Jake was moving at a brisk pace now. "He'd know about Holmes's street arabs. Best spies in the world. Like Kipling's Kim, if you want another authority. Who paid attention to *that* kid? He could slip in and out of all camps. This Candlestick sounds a guttersnipe, but he's sharper than a London cabbie when it comes to knowing these streets."

"Why Candlestick?"

"Never wipes his nose," said Jake. "From that nose, always, hangs a tiny candle of snot." They were coming to the end of Northumberland Street. Jake stopped short. "Can you confirm Talbott's still in the embassy?"

"You know the rules!" Turtleneck reproved him. "We must not make contact with the embassy."

Jake submitted to a short lecture.

"If things get hot," said Turtleneck, astonished that an old-timer would not know the diplomatic game, "they have to disown us. We don't exist, Jake. We certainly can't make phone calls—"

"Yes, yes, yes!" Jake was satisfied. He had only wanted to make sure nobody in Turtleneck's team would discover what was really going on. None of them had worked with Jake before: not even Turtleneck. Jake motioned as if brushing cobwebs from his face. His eyes followed a busload of schoolboys. His companion was probably such a child once, obliged to run messages through British military lines in Palestine. The schoolboys hung out of the windows as the bus crawled into Trafalgar Square. It was remarkable, thought Jake, how sensitive and manipulable little boys were.

37

The patrol boats drummed out of the bay. It was their second incursion.

"I'm frightened," said Vesna, standing naked on the escape beach.

Talbott held up the trousers of a diving suit. "There's no need. In these, you'll turn into a hot-water bottle. See, the water gets trapped against your skin and warms up."

"*That* doesn't scare me. It's my future." She took the unwieldy trousers and began hopping on one leg. "Red Crombie said I'd be taken care of, but I never really believed him. At least *you* fought Mother to let me go."

"Tcha!" Talbott dismissed the scene she had witnessed. He had argued fiercely with the Soviet leader that Vesna was vital to his escape. "You're in good hands . . ."

The last remark was unfortunately timed. He was spilling babypowder over her body to ease up the skintight trousers. She lost her footing and fell against his bare body. She clung a moment, glad of his warmth, and then giggled. They were both in the mildly hysterical mood induced by danger.

"Turn!" Talbott ordered, preparing to squeeze her into the jacket.

"My tits. Don't you find them too big?"

He coaxed them into her jacket, letting the powder dribble where it

might, thinking she was indeed a handful, but not daring to say it from fear
of starting another paroxysm.

"Will the salt bleach out my hair coloring?" she asked.

"Not with this." He worked the hood over her head.

She turned to help him into Red Crombie's wet suit. "You're lucky
you're not bigger than Red," she said, and then lapsed into a somber
silence. Her mood swung round again. "If you got any bigger," she added,
rubbing powder over his torso, "You wouldn't fit at all." She began to
giggle again.

If a Yugoslav woman handed you a live grenade, Talbott reflected, she'd
still make it sexy. If this one was frightened, as she pretended, he hated to
think what panic would do to her. He zipped himself up and helped gather
the loose gear.

"America," said Vesna, "here I come."

There was no perceptible current in the bay. He swam ahead, rolling
onto his back from time to time, looking for landmarks. When the Igalo
clinic, the highest mountain peak, and the point of the headland were all in
line, Aerial had said, the cross-reference would be a lighthouse near the
other arm of the bay and an air navigation warning light on the nearer,
Dubrovnik side. Vesna was paying out line to the beach, where Talbott's
original ditty bag waited to be hauled up, complete with their belongings.
She felt a marker toggle run through her fingers and called softly to Talbott, who was already treading water. He had seen the peak above Igalo
glow pink in the first direct rays of sunlight. Now he took the toggle and
swam a slow curve, keeping the line fairly taut until he had the other
landmarks cross-referenced. Suddenly he handed back the line and doubled over to dive.

The suit, without weights, was too buoyant. He unzipped the jacket to
let in freezing-cold water, jackknifed again, forced himself almost vertical,
kicking furiously. His groping hands found nothing. He came up for air,
dived, and dived again. Still nothing.

Suddenly Vesna rose out of the water and fell sideways. He remembered
a poster advertising *Jaws!* in the clinic. Typically, the movie had arrived
several years late. If Vesna had seen it . . . every ripple on this black sea
would excite fear. He splashed over. When her head bobbed up, he took
her by the scruff of the neck, ready to stifle any scream. Instead, she bit
him. "I've got it!" she spluttered. He saw then that she was hanging on to
the buoy's auxiliary tether.

Talbott pulled himself down, following the buoy's anchor line. God, it
was cold! His hands were numb and he had difficulty locating by touch
alone the bags anchored in sequence. The small light in the hood had
failed. He had to trace the shapes of face masks inside one bag, then grope
his way along two sets of double tanks until he found the underwater
lights.

He brought up face masks and flippers, and closed his jacket again. His teeth would not stop chattering. Vesna wrapped herself around him, their wet suits holding them to the surface while she blew warm air down the neck of his jacket. The gesture gave him the strength to go back down. This time he sank easily with the weights around his waist, and turned on the underwater lights. He gulped when he saw what seemed, in that moment, more precious than a treasure trove. It was only some sixteen hours since he had first been shown the diver-propulsion vehicle sitting quietly in a forest of kelp. Now the long yellow monster seemed like a vessel lost for centuries. His mask glittered in the light as he swam the DPV's length, from the enormous eye in the blunt nose to the big, circular tail encasing four propellor blades. The designer had been right to call it a sea chariot.

He shot back to the surface, gulped air, and beckoned Vesna down. He had rehearsed her well. At his signals, she settled cross-legged on the bottom beside a twin-pack. From the tank ran the hose of a regulator. He handed her the mouthpiece. Once she was breathing, the rest was easy.

He checked her airline. He had already opened the tank valve all the way, then back half a turn. He went onto his own regulator. They were both now breathing a mixture of helium and oxygen delivered by the navy tanks, designed for prolonged underwater use.

Vesna was struggling to stay on the bottom. She'd told him she was only a hundred and ten pounds. He'd only strung six two-pound weights on her web strap. Vanity of vanities! She obviously hadn't remembered that a larger body is more buoyant. He added the necessary weights, helped her into the scuba harness, made sure the cylinders rode comfortably on her back. Then he led her slowly to the DPV chariot. When they approached the kelp, he sensed her apprehension. He swam into fuzzy green strings that rose to the surface like a magic forest, and showed her how easy it was to part them.

He made her rest beside the DPV. The rhythm of her air bubbles had signaled agitation. Now they slowed to match his own. She was completely, almost dreamily, self-possessed.

He hauled on the rope to bring the buoy down within reach, freed the attached beach line and gave it to Vesna so that she could pull in the ditty bag. He made a visual check of the chariot. Unwanted gear would be stowed in capsules by the button marked DESTRUCT. Their discarded clothes would be first to go. He hadn't told Vesna, but she would guess why it was necessary to strip to the buff. If their corpses fell into hostile hands, there would be nothing to identify them.

He hesitated over the radio buoy. Surfaced, it would emit a coded pulse for the mother ship. Even a brief transmission might be detected. Then everything would be lost. He decided to have faith in Aerial, whose Subskimmers were to meet the DPV three miles out.

Vesna swam over with the neatly coiled line and the main storage bag. He showed her how to snap open the stowage capsules. There must be no litter to betray the manner of their exit. He led Vesna to the hull-wide compartment. Unlike others, flooded when underway, this was crammed with waterproof electronics, including the signal station, with its hair-thin fiber-optic cable.

Talbott drifted astern and tested the starter buttons. He looked at Vesna's face, framed by her mask. Suddenly her eyes widened and the bubbles from her regulator quickened.

She had picked up the pulsations, faint at first. Talbott froze. The pulsations mingled with the soft beat of the air bubbling through his own regulator. He stopped breathing. The sounds came from beyond their own small world of the yellow chariot and they were increasing in strength.

So the patrols out to sea had been a trick. The surface diesels made a sullen thumping sound that came from all directions. Talbott returned quickly to Vesna's side. She was already gripping the big handholds. He showed her how to flatten her body into the recess. He swam to the anchored underwater lights and turned the time switch to give him a measured thirty seconds more of illumination. He rejoined Vesna, started up the battery systems again, and switched on the propulsion motors. There was a sudden turbulence astern as the props began to spin and the DPV jerked forward, bumping along the bottom and then rising abruptly as Talbott overcontrolled the elevators. He corrected quickly, fingers tingling at the prospect of the craft bolting clean out of the water.

The thud of the patrol boats obscured the faint whir of the DPV's electric motors. Talbott had been warned against the Yugoslav coastal vessels. The first underwater stun-grenade clouted his eardrums and almost threw him off balance.

Vesna, hugging the hull, raised her head. One of her legs drifted out, creating a lopsided drag. The DPV was beyond the range of the anchored lights, and Talbott navigated by the vehicle's forward beam and two downthrusting lights. He knew from Aerial's briefing that the bottom would soon fall away. He could lose the hunters by diving deeper. But Vesna was inexperienced. The higher speed was already giving her trouble. She might be better off to let go now and swim to shore unseen . . .

Come off it! Talbott admonished himself. She'd be caught.

Still, she was an obstacle.

A patch of eelgrass appeared, under a rock formation reaching to the surface. Two giant barriers of rock formed a canopy that must blind vertical sonar or rip open a speeding boat's hull. There was a gap, just wide enough if Vesna clung tight to the DPV's hull. Even as he watched, one of her legs wavered and a flipper was torn away. He reached to grab it, and upset the vehicle's delicate balance so that it nosed abruptly upward again.

Another grenade thumped astern. Talbott wrestled the DPV down so violently that it was still twisting as they entered the gap. A chunk of coral banged against Vesna's air tanks. A rush of water shifted her face mask.

An operational necessity. The evil phrase flashed through Talbott's mind. Vesna, drowned and caught under the rock overhang, would cease to be a liability. Talbott need do nothing. And a Soviet leader's confessional tape, together with a cause more important than Vesna, would be saved.

A lot more lives were at stake than this Citizen Levi, thought Mother, hunched over his paperwork.

"So, then, in this matter of Levi?" Secretary Kerensky cleared his throat.

"Yes, I heard!" Mother glowered at the dawn breaking outside Tito's old villa. Benjami Levi, Jewish activist for human rights, seized upon a snowy Moscow street four years ago . . . Would it really hurt to let him go? "Very well, read me the telegram." There was still time before the helicopter ride to Titograd to board a politburo jet.

"It's signed by a group of American scientists . . . 'Since the Soviet Motherland soon marks the Bolshevik Revolution anniversary with a parade of power that assures the world of Soviet strength . . . when all the world sees how powerful is the U.S.S.R., cannot physicist Levi be pardoned?' "

Mother remembered another appeal: *When you command such power, Bomber Harris, will you not listen to a poor Jew?*

Kerensky read on: " 'Motherland is neither a geographical nor a national concept. Motherland is freedom. The Great Soviet Mother—' "

"Et cetera, et cetera et cetera!" exploded Mother. "A pox on all the scurvy bastards." He puffed angrily on a Yugoslav cigarette. The naïve, bootlicking fools! Didn't they know the man who originally wrote those last sentences was the notorious Yugoslav dissident Mihajlov? They had quoted an enemy of the Kremlin and thus made it impossible to reinstate physicist Levi! There was one thing Mother could *not* do before winning the Soviet Defense Council's essential approval for the London journey. He must not seem to placate Americans! He ground out the cigarette as if it were Levi's life he was extinguishing.

"Give me a *papirosa!*" he ordered the secretary. "For the love of God." He took from the proffered tin box a thin cardboard tube half filled with Caucasian tobacco, pinched it between thumb and forefinger, and lit up with a sigh. Once upon a time he had choked on harsh decisions the way he had choked on the alien Russian cigarettes. Now, inhaling the pungent fumes, he drew satisfaction from the way he'd learned to overcome scruples.

An explosion shattered the silence outside. The reverberations had scarcely died away in the mountains before there followed another.

Mother gave no sign of hearing. Instead, he asked for information he must have been given a dozen times already. "What time do we arrive in Moscow?" He nodded when Kerensky told him, and continued smoking placidly.

Tonight he would face the Soviet Defense Council. By then, he must have the invitation from Washington. The council could hardly refuse. Remembrance Day in London would come the day after the biggest display of Soviet military power ever to mark the anniversary of revolution. There would be no invitation if Talbott failed to deliver Mother's message. And somewhere out in the bay, Talbott was evidently being hunted to death.

Another explosion shook the windows. Mother took the telegram from Kerensky, read it, and said, "Destroy this. Do not even acknowledge receipt. Then arrange for the case of Citizen Levi to be sent to me for review."

Perhaps, thought Mother, I have listened to the wrong voice. Perhaps I should have been saving my people one by one. Then he pushed all doubt from his mind.

Killing Vesna was the obvious solution.

Talbott clung to the roots of the giant kelp and thought how nobody on this earth could argue such a decision.

If Mother's message had been transmitted already, then there would have been an argument for saving the Yugoslav woman. But Mother's tape was still coiled virginally inside the burst-transceiver, locked to the yellow hull of the DPV lying silent here on the seabed.

Talbott peered up through the kelp's palm-tree stalks rising majestically to the rock ledges on the surface. The kelp branched and forked, a forest of whiplike vines and ball-shaped bladders. A drowned body would rot away here unseen.

The kelp joined the rocky overhang to make a canopy. This outfoxed the sonar detectors of the patrol boats hunting back and forth across the bay. Their pulsations died into the murmur of a regulator as they slowly retreated to look elsewhere.

Killing Vesna wasn't easy.

Her body had twisted belly up, like a fish with a bloated air bladder, while he was still probing for shelter with the DPV under full power. He had only to pour on more speed, sideslip, and she would have been snatched from the chariot as it plunged into sanctuary.

She must have known she was in the way. He was shocked when she actually tried to kick free of the submersible. He saw her deliberately spit the air regulator out of her mouth.

He had to grab her before she could swirl by. He punched her, then jammed the regulator back between her teeth. He was straddling the idling DPV's tail cone by then. He had thrown the gears into neutral without conscious thought.

No, it wasn't easy to kill Vesna. It was impossible.

Without her, he might have reached the rendezvous by now. He checked the time. The twin-packs held extra air, but the journey would be arduous.

They were heading into strong sea currents. No chance of floating up on friendlier shores.

He looked at Vesna beside him. She was shifting position. She turned and gave him the thumbs-up. Her mouth was bleeding. Was she really cured of this urge to sacrifice herself? He mimed his need of her, a difficult thing to do. He had to make the message physical and intimate. She blew him a kiss.

Together they withdrew the DPV from the ocean's forest. The lights were all ablaze. After Vesna's attempt at heroic self-sacrifice, he'd thrown caution aside. He knew their chances were good. Their semi-closed-circuit tanks produced fewer bubbles than normal, and these would blend on the surface with the creaming waves. There was little likelihood they would be detected.

The props kicked back a surge of vegetable matter as he brought the chariot up to steering speed. They were now an hour behind schedule. He must soon radio the mother ship. If Aerial abandoned the mission, nothing lay ahead but open water and the faint chance of being picked up by some vessel heading into the safety of the Ionian Sea.

He came to rest again when he judged they were beyond the northern headland. The automated signal disks were color-keyed. He selected green for *Go!* It whirled along a plastic tube into the base of the radio buoy. The black-painted buoy wobbled out of sight and the fine fiber-optic umbilical stopped threading through the storage spinner. A red light blinked. The burst-transmission had started. And ended. The light flashed again. If Talbott took no further action, the *Go!* signal would repeat itself at short intervals. He let thirty seconds tick by. It seemed an eternity of self-advertisement. He recalled the buoy; and the sinister black ball reappeared with startling alacrity, nuzzling its way back into its berth like the intelligent little robot it really was.

Commander Aerial Trumper had just directed the skimmers back aboard the *Avocadocor* when the watchman ran up from the radio shack with Talbott's signal. "Belay that last pipe," said Aerial, reversing his orders. He was a young man with an old salt's love of the sea. His father, a Russian-born Jew, had skippered the hulks loaded with refugees from the newly liberated death camps after the Nazi holocaust. Later, as an admiral in the new Israeli Navy, his father had paid a courtesy call on the Royal Navy. Crusty British Navy lordships had reminisced about the old days. "My biggest headache, as a destroyer captain," harrumphed one old codger, "was a Jewish escape committee whose chairman ran our blockade. We could never catch the blighter. Must have been a remarkably good seaman." The headache had been Aerial's father, who owned up amid applause and another round of port. The old codger had nudged the Jewish admiral and said, "Hope you'll have something better than leaky old tubs if you get into a real war, eh!" Aerial's father merely smiled, sipped his port, and thought to himself that Israel had never stopped being in a real war.

The skimmers bobbed alongside again. There were two, each with a skeleton, two-man crew. Lightly loaded, with new 100-horsepower outboards, they had a surface range of forty sea miles at 35 knots. If caught, their crews carried inside their wet suits the necessary remote controls to blow them up. Nobody else, Aerial reflected proudly, took these risks.

He knew the danger of a diplomatic incident, high-level protests, adverse publicity. He also knew the Kyrya was past caring. Fear of causing a diplomatic disturbance had never saved anybody's life at Auschwitz.

Aerial's instructions had been to dispatch all signals directly into the special Washington net. Already that brief *Go!* message would have landed on the desk of an American so highly placed, nobody dared refer to him as a single person at all. Instead, the code name was in the plural, TITFERS. Aerial knew it was somehow connected with Tito's favorite radio broadcast from London, but he had no desire to find out more. It was enough that he was playing a role in something of the utmost importance to his own country's survival. His old man had told him that, sucking his pipe contentedly in a cluttered, windowless cabin in the Kyrya.

Another hour passed. Talbott eased the DPV chariot close to the sea's surface and raised his head. Waves rose up, limiting his vision. He searched the sky overhead, his mask pushed up. He could see no aircraft.

He decided to bring the DPV all the way up. A brisk winter wind froze the exposed part of his face. Vesna bobbed up beside him and shivered. "It's warmer under water," she said, sounding surprised. "And I'm getting seasick."

The problem was air and batteries. Both were running dangerously low. Here on the surface, they could breathe naturally and conserve juice. Talbott yanked off a glove and groped inside the emergency compartment until he found two flares. He got himself into a half-standing position, unable to slip easily out of the air-tank harness. He fired off one flare. The DPV danced violently. Then a cresting wave threw him backwards into the sea.

Scuba gear, underwater, weighs nothing and becomes almost part of the diver's anatomy. For someone swimming on the surface, though, with half-empty tanks pitching and rolling on his back, octopus regulator floating free, weights bunched up around his waist, and no snorkel or life vest, the gear becomes a deadly menace. The diver's range of vision is close to nil. If he gets downwind of the dive boat or caught in an adverse current, he has little chance of regaining the boat. He needs a partner.

Talbott needed one badly now. The emergency happened so fast, he lost precious seconds before he reacted. Then it was too late. He was drifting rapidly away from the DPV. Vesna was first to register the approach of disaster. She started the motors and brought the craft round until, broadside to the wind, it stubbornly swung there in a narrow arc. A diver-propulsion-vehicle is not designed for surface maneuvers in heavy weather.

Vesna lost sight of Talbott. She pulled her mask down, sucked on the air regulator, knelt precariously on the sternboard, and glimpsed his head in the curl of an extra high wave. Then she submerged. If she had learned anything this morning, it was that navigation under the surface was undisturbed by wind and waves.

Talbott had one last, fleeting vision of Vesna going down. Then he was alone. He went back onto his air tanks and allowed his body to sink into a vertical position. At least he conserved energy this way. But he seemed to have lost all muscle power. He let his limbs go slack and brought his rate of breathing down below the panic level. His air gauge read in the red, danger zone. He might have another twenty minutes, although it indicated empty.

The odds on Vesna finding him were laughable.

The leader of the skimmers saw the flare a mile inside Yugoslav waters and dead ahead. It was about where he would expect to find his customer, provided the customer stuck pretty close to the designated course, speed and range.

He shot across the invisible boundary at full speed. Yugoslavs were less guarded than most Communist countries about territorial limits, but Aerial had warned him that, since dawn, coastal patrols had filled the ether with alarm signals. On his starboard flank, he saw the other skimmer throw back spray as it matched his own speed.

The skimmer leader, a chief petty officer, reached Vesna within two minutes. She had resurfaced after a fruitless attempt to navigate in Talbott's direction. At first, the CPO thought she was frightened for herself. Then he saw she was alone, and trying frantically to tell him to search the area. The second boat picked up the customer another three minutes later.

The customer was in bad shape. He had obviously wasted too much energy trying to swim. Inexperience, thought the CPO. And age. The customer's hair was as gray as his face. Must be at least twice as old as their oldest coxswain, who was twenty-three.

They sank the DPV after the woman removed a watertight bag. The CPO figured she must be some political refugee, hoping to sell the family jewels, from the way she nursed the bag.

Back in neutral waters, the CPO slowed down and checked on the customer, who was transferred to his boat. A few snorts of brandy revived the customer, who shook the CPO by the hand, but only after hugging the woman.

"Anything we should do to improve the service?" the CPO asked with a formality that seemed bizarre. He did not explain a standing order that the question be asked immediately, before a customer had the chance to die from injuries or exposure.

Talbott managed a grin. "If I'd had a snorkel, I could have floated out there indefinitely."

The CPO stared into the purple-ringed and bloodshot eyes, and judged Talbott might have floated but he wouldn't have been alive, with or without the breathing tube. Still, he liked the goy's chutzpah. "Anything else?" he asked before revving up the motor.

"Yes," said Talbott, summoning up a last reserve of energy to point his chin at Vesna. "Build one of those into every chariot."

38

London, England: Thursday, late evening

"Henkell's dead!"

"Then, I've nothing more to lose."

Able to listen but unable to speak, Sally lay naked on her back, marble against bare skin. She smelled leather and men's sweat, heard snatches of meaningless male talk.

"Henkell bullied the Russians with the threat that if he died, the entire archive on Hess in Spandau would automatically come out."

Jake! It couldn't be. Sally strained to see, but there were only lights lost in mist.

She must have passed out again. A rough hand stroked her forehead. She stared up into the seamed face of the old convict at Grandpa Massey's graveside.

Non sunt multiplicanda entia praeter necessitatem . . . Don't complicate things to the point of fantasy. Good advice. Who'd given it?

Not this ugly old man. He hadn't spoken. Yet she heard the echoing Latin tag. A schoolboy joke? Yes, of course. Between General Massey and this . . . this Hat Man.

Where the hell was Talbott?

"Earth to earth . . . ashes to ashes." The voice was in her head. A real

voice said, "Don't hold the Cenotaph in reserve. Do a Guy Fawkes on it."
Another said, "When Big Ben strikes eleven . . . ?"

Eleven. The eleventh hour.

Hadn't she broken out of the Israeli embassy at the eleventh hour? She
felt herself slipping back into a coma. With all her willpower, she fought
for the light.

"You're quite safe," said the old man. "I'm beyond sensual needs. The
Libyan only likes little boys."

He was talking to her, this wrinkled prune. Tiny black eyes like currants
examined her with prurient curiosity.

She felt the wet marble against the palms of her hands and her naked
back.

"No more pain?" asked the face wobbling above her.

She turned her head aside. Women wearing togas stood on pedestals,
holding torches aloft. They were very small ladies. They wore wreaths
around their heads. The torches burned with flames of electricity. The mist
was steam, flooding through the high-ceilinged cavern. She got the Greek
women into focus and they dwindled to statuettes.

"Throat dry?" asked the old man. "Here, drink this." He put a hand
under her head and raised it to the glass. She closed her mouth.

"Don't trust me, eh?" He put the glass to one side and spoke to the man
she had seen walk past, a thick towel around his waist. Something was
ripped from her belly and she covered herself. Hot towels. She'd been lying
under hot towels. She lay still as they were replaced, one by one.

"There now," said the gravelly voice. "You're perfectly respectable and
deliciously intact." He reminded her of the palace parson, Marcus
Furneval, joking with Quex at the funeral feast.

He *was* Marcus Furneval.

"Where's Talbott?" asked Furneval.

"You've asked me that," said Sally. "I told you. I don't know."

This time when Furneval struck her, she was ready. "You'll hear the
questions whether you're conscious or unconscious, drugged or stone-cold
sober," he said. "You'll hear them repeated until you give honest answers."

She watched his face come down to meet hers. She could smell his
breath. His ill-fitting dentures clicked away at her. She tensed her stomach
muscles, drew up her right arm, and slammed the palm of her hand under
his chin.

He should have lost balance. Instead, he laughed. "Come on!" he jeered.
"Hit me here, on the *point* of my chinny-chin-chin!"

What she did instead was hook back a leg and lash out, her foot sinking
into his soft, ecclesiastical stomach.

"Slapped across the belly," gurgled the parson, "with the tail end of a
wet kipper!" He bobbed back. "You'll have to do better than that, dearie."

In her grandfather's house, he had appeared as a verbose old friend.
Then, at the No-Man's-Land Tuckshop, he'd turned into Black Mac, per-

haps the killer of Talbott's mother. On each occasion, she'd seen him as smaller, grayer. Now he wore an old track suit, carried the aroma of the boxing ring, and seemed more . . . primitive.

"She's full of fight!" he shouted, flapping an arm at a man naked except for a towel. "Needs a sparring partner."

The man was dark-skinned and covered in tattoo marks.

"His name's Sami Esmail," said Furneval. "Holy warrior. Don't worry, he won't put you in the family way. He keeps to good, healthy buggery. Sami the sodomite . . ."

The tattooed Libyan held his hands up in front of Sally. His fingernails were scarred and broken.

"Where," he asked in good German, "are the rest of the Radzki papers? The ones Radzki wrote himself?"

Dear God! Sally closed her eyes in sudden fear. What had she said, lying here drugged? How long was it since she'd run out of the embassy? Had she carried anything that would give them a clue, something of Radzki's, meaning to show it to Jake?

"Jake Cooke works with us," said Furneval. "Help us, you help Jake."

"If you won't, you'll only get hurt," the tattooed Libyan warned her.

"You'll never get out of here," said Furneval.

Sally opened her eyes. "Like Rebecca? Buried alive?"

The Libyan hit her with a thin rod across the bottoms of her bare feet. She pulled her knees up and he whipped her across her shins.

"That's enough," said Furneval. "For now."

Sally tried to sit up. The Libyan came round behind her and pushed her back. She twisted, trying to get off the slab, not caring that the towels fell and exposed her nude body. But the Libyan had her pinned by the shoulders.

"If it hadn't been for Talbott's mother," said Furneval, "you wouldn't be in this mess now. Rebecca!" He turned his head and spat on the floor. When he looked back, his tone had changed. "We've little time, my dear. Ask me questions, I'll answer. You'll have to give answers too, though. That's the way the game is played. The other kind of game won't be nearly as much fun." He gave her one of his ghastly, pink-gum smiles and then, without warning, jabbed her hard with his bunched-up fist: a short, powerful blow under one breast, taking her breath away. "I've had a good, long innings," he said. "The game's ending for me. It makes no difference if you choose the soft or the hard option."

Sally jerked her head forward and spat in Furneval's face. The Libyan grabbed her by the hair. Furneval scraped her exposed belly with one hand, and slapped her face. She curled up, screeching like a wildcat, nails blindly raking. The sulfurous air made her flesh slippery. She became all teeth and nails, a freshly boated shark, knotting up and then slithering and twisting over the moist marble. Sweat in her eyes redoubled her fury. She felt her nails dig into something soft. At the foot of the slab, she dimly perceived Furneval standing square, crotch vulnerable. The Libyan was somehow behind her head. Her fingers were now tangled in his black, curly hair. With her grip on the Libyan for leverage, she shot both legs forward with toes stiff and pointed. Furneval roared with pain. Still hanging to the Libyan's hair, she twisted her body until she was almost kneeling. She heaved back and took the Libyan by surprise, her thumbs digging for his eyes.

She slipped like an eel to the stone floor. It must have been washed for centuries with successive clouds of steam. Fluted columns vanished into the misty upper levels of the cavernous hall. She saw a pool filled with opaque, steaming water. Stone steps descended. At each corner stood imitation Greek statues of naked boys. She ran for the safety of the pool. Men came from behind Victorian drapes. She slid into the pool, going feet first, her body inelegantly arched so that she found herself staring up into clouds of steam parting with the sudden inrush of air. Across the fluted ceiling ran thermo-wrapped pipes, incongruous and irrelevant. Yet she thought she saw a face there.

The icy chill of the water shocked her into full clarity of mind. She saw a metal plate in a plinth at the pool's edge, and a faded inscription: *Royal & Ancient Ironmongers Turkish Bath Club: Private Members Only.* Men were wading through the water around her. Their laughter rang in her ears as she dived under, breathing in through her open mouth the frigid water, determined to drown herself.

39

President Donovan, as luck would have it, was only a hop, skip and jump by chopper from the White House when the Mother report arrived. The President was talking to students at Georgetown University about the Baltic crisis, because he believed if the young had to fight wars, they should at least know *how* they got into them. Donovan figured if he joined in a student debate, what he said would spread like wildfire through the campuses of the nation, carrying more weight than anything the media chose to tell.

The Mother report had reached Jerusalem from Talbott late Thursday night. Because of the time difference, it landed in the lap of Vice President Walter Juste toward evening in Washington. Donovan was winding up with an exchange of friendly banter before returning to Marine One, the White House helicopter.

He had crossed the green turf of the Jesuit priests' cemetery when Walter Juste caught up. "Okay if I ride back with you?" asked the little man with the umbrella.

Donovan gripped his Vice President's arm in warm affirmation. When Walter made a sudden and informal move like this, the President had no doubt there were very confidential matters demanding immediate discussion.

Students crowded the slopes by the playing fields. A girl asked why the President would not be meeting the antinuclear marchers this weekend. Donovan gave her a big smile. "Reckon I do more good back at the ranch figuring ways to get us all, Russians and ourselves, out of the mess we're in."

There was a roar of approval, for the President had already presented his arguments persuasively. Nevertheless, he paused. "When the Spanish armada charged into the English Channel," he called out, "Drake got the news and went back to his game of bowls. He still licked the armada!" He gave the familiar stiff-armed wave and hunched forward to run to the waiting helicopter, its blades already turning because that was the way this President liked it, the wind blowing in his hair, seeing himself as a mixture of cowboy and fighter pilot. He knew the students would see him this way too, even those critical of his hard-nosed view about the Soviets in the Baltic Sea. He was still feeling pleased with himself when he settled into his seat.

"That was a bad analogy," said the Vice President. "The Channel was England's backyard and the Spaniards were trespassing. We did the trespassing in the Baltic." He clutched his umbrella as if he meant to choke it.

"Sometimes, Walter, I wonder whose side you're on!" The President craned forward as the machine began to rise. "Okay, you bumped everyone else off this wagon, so it must be serious. What's on your mind?" He peered through a window and waved to the crowd slipping away below.

Walter Juste decided to lead up to it gradually. The President hated to mess in clandestine affairs, complaining that the good old need-to-know rules were broken too frequently.

"I dislike melodrama no less than you," Juste began.

"Hell, this is about the only place we can safely talk," the President said cheerily. "Take Liz, now. She keeps a tight rein on these things."

Juste winced at the President's fond way of referring to Elizabeth, Queen of England. Nevertheless, it gave him an opening. He said, "I'm not sure we can trust her security people while you're in London."

For a while, he thought the President had failed to hear him. It had been one of those warm, sunny November days that sometimes come as a gift to the nation's capital. All, the President evidently felt, was right with the world. The helicopter hovered theatrically on a level with the sports field built on top of the Yates Field House. Hundreds of students waved. "Our greatest natural resource!" exclaimed the President. It was something he was fond of saying in times of crisis.

Marine One dipped away to pick up the Potomac River. The pilot knew his job. A stagy departure, then a quick dash to the next appointment. Walter Juste said, "Could we take extra time? Fifteen minutes of sight-seeing would do." He gestured at the city spread out below. Washington, caught between dusk and dark, glowed. A fiery sky ended the day, dramatized the set. Buildings soared from necklaces of artificial light. This was guess. In Cockspur Street, the boy let him catch up. "Your girl's a prisoner in them Turkish baths, through the yard there. Charlie's watching out for 'er."

The meeting between the real Jake and Sally took place in a cubicle behind a notice: "Open Daily Since 1798—Private Members Only." Above was the insignia of the Ironmongers Turkish Bath Club.

Sally had no doubt that this was Jake Cooke, otherwise Jacob Slominsky. He was naked to the waist. The first thing she saw was the old chest scar. It was four years since she had last seen that livid mark.

He was lying on a cot when she entered, and sprang to his feet with an expression of stunned disbelief. Then he saw Sami Esmail, dragging himself along the floor outside. Sally held the ring of keys Sami had given her to unlock the door.

"Where's Kraaft?" He saw the blank look on her face and added impatiently, "The look-alike. Did he get away?"

Sally shook her head. It was obvious this Jake's mind was several moves ahead of hers. And that, like the scar, was proof of his identity. "I don't know," she said. "I've only just discovered there are two of you."

Jake slowed down then. But only enough to take in the facts about her own imprisonment. Enough to throw one of his blankets over her.

He dressed while he talked. Each sentence was a small masterpiece of economy. And that, too, was the real Jake.

"You mean," she interrupted at one point, "I've been fooled from the beginning by this other Jake—this . . . Kraaft?"

"Like everyone else."

"So the men with him—in the wasteland—they thought he was you?"

"Apparently." Jake bundled up his belongings. "That's why I have to move fast." He stopped in the doorway, frowning down at Sami Esmail. "We'll need him for evidence if we can keep him alive. Stay here and watch him."

She wondered how she could possibly have mistaken anyone for the real Jake. His body and his mind moved like greased lightning. She had never seen the bogus Jake in broad daylight, but the mannerisms and features were uncannily like the genuine article. He'd certainly learned all Jake's habits of speech. The difference was in the speed of his mind. Jake absorbed all she could tell him and then spat out answers. He had been in the 88's hands for several weeks. He had been held in many different hideouts. He had learned about each in the way he had learned the layout of the Ironmongers, by squirreling scraps of conversation and keeping his eyes open. He now returned with a porter's uniform for Sally and a bath chair for Sami Esmail.

At this hour the club was deserted. Where Jake and Sally had been imprisoned was an exclusive section behind steel doors. The old club had fallen on hard times with the sudden climb in London property taxes and the President's favorite moment, when the footlights took over and the audience was plunged into darkness. "Of course," he said, and spoke over the intercom to the pilot.

"That little lady," said the President, turning back to Juste, "flew down to the South Atlantic, had to refuel four times in midair, and not a word leaked out. I can't even go to the bathroom without the whole world knowing."

"What little lady?" asked Juste, momentarily baffled.

"Liz," said the President. "In the Falklands."

"You're thinking of Maggie," Juste corrected him, not without a trace of malicious satisfaction.

"Liz. Maggie Thatcher. They'll all be there Sunday," said Donovan. He fixed his bright blue eyes on the Vice President and folded his hands in his lap, a signal that the joking was over.

"That's the trouble!" Juste picked up his cue. "Mr. President, we have a security problem. We've got something much bigger, too." Walter Juste, in his years directing central intelligence, had mastered the art of condensing facts. He spoke quietly, without interruption. The pilot, supposing that the President wanted to enjoy the spectacle and the brief respite, made a wide sweep around the city. Inside the cabin, Juste completed his summary of the situation.

"Never did figure why they all called him Mother," said the President. His younger critics would have thought the remark typical of an airhead. The Vice President heard it as a line of dialog thrown into the script while the plot turned another corner. Accordingly, his response was not carefully considered. He said, "Russians have this mystical reverence for the Rodina, the Great Soviet Motherland. When Yuri Gorin became KGB chief, he quietly campaigned to have himself known as Mother. It made the KGB palatable, even to the West. Identified him with Mother Russia. What was good for Mother was good for Mother Russia . . ."

"He's a pretty damn quick fella," President Donovan interrupted sharply. "Pretty damn clever. He faces exposure, you say, but could turn all this into triumph. All he needs is me? A summit in London on a day dedicated to remembering when Americans and Russians were allies? Do I have it right?"

"Not exactly, but I'll see you have the accurate details."

"Don't baffle me with all that intellectual bullshit, Walter. How'd you know this isn't a trick? Seeing he's so damned smart?"

Walter Juste shifted uncomfortably, his tummy rumbling. The President had a nasty, streetwise way of going to the heart of things. It gave indigestion to advisers whose years of scholarship had to yield to Donovan's savvy. "We are not forgetting to plan for that contingency," said Walter Juste, and realized how fatuous he must sound.

"I suppose you know, Walter, a favorite Russian cuss is *'fuck your mother'?*"

"Yes, so I've heard."

"Suppose there are people manipulating this man? And suppose that's what they're saying, to us? 'Fuck your Mother . . . fuck your mole in the Kremlin.' " The President brooded. "How long have you known Mother was a mole?"

Walter Juste shuddered at the persistent directness of the man. "A . . . ah, *very* long time," he said at last. "It would not be inaccurate to say since the birth of Israel. That is, I wouldn't say we were sure . . ."

"Okay." President Donovan felt no urge to pry further. He recognized when double negatives semaphored a bureaucratic cover-up. Never mind. Walter Juste was being as honest as he could. Donovan was itching for action. If the presidency had been turned into show biz, as his critics claimed, then now was when the show must go on. It was obvious from Walter's earlier briefing that the CIA never expected these developments when it began to pry into what led General Quex Massey to start *his* investigations . . . Donovan shied away from that line of profitless speculation. He said, "I cannot invite Mother to meet me in London without the Brits' prior knowledge."

"The proposal would come from their Prime Minister."

"See here, Walter, the *initiative* should be seen as coming from me."

Walter Juste understood perfectly. "If it works, you'll be everyone's hero. But if it goes wrong, you're a cooked goose."

"Take out the politics, then. If the centerpiece at this Cenotaph shindig is to be Liz, then for God's sake get her to invite the Soviets on our joint behalf."

"The Queen of England?"

"Why not? You tell me there's talk of ancient scandals. She can nip that in the bud!"

"There's a former king involved."

"Her uncle. Didn't he give up the throne for that woman from Baltimore? So, Liz and I join hands! A big show of unity! Let bygones be bygones. Those Russkies will get the message."

Walter Juste's silence conveyed disapproval.

"My God," said the President, "your agency habits make you so damned obtuse. Think with your heart, Walter, not your head! The naval confrontation gets worse. Some pond nobody ever thought much about is suddenly on everyone's lips. The Baltic. It could be our Sarajevo . . . Two world wars cut down the flower of our youth, Walter. That's what we'll be remembering, come Sunday. So . . . . ?"

Walter Juste stroked his chin with the hook of his umbrella. "So the monarch in a country where we gather will issue a call to remember wartime comradeship in a new search for peace?"

"Put some Shakespeare into it, Walter, and you pretty well get the idea," said the President, taking charge in the way Walter Juste had figured he would.

London, England: Friday morning

The Queen and her Prime Minister held an impromptu conference. The Foreign Secretary thought the Washington suggestion outrageous, and fumed: "We can't have the American President decide suddenly to hold a summit here."

The two women who ruled Britain had different ideas.

The Queen said, "We bear the babies who grow up to fight these wars," looking across at the lady from Number 10.

The Prime Minister took her cue: "It's an original approach to the crisis, and about time, too."

"Mmm," said the Queen. "The Soviet leader's presence would give fresh significance to what has become far too routine an occasion."

"But we're being treated like a damned movie set, begging your pardon, ma'am." The Foreign Secretary turned to the SAS counterterror expert for support.

Grimweather said, "The terrorist alert heightens the drama and increases the risks."

"If terrorism is allowed to undermine national traditions," said the Queen, "then we need President Donovan to remind us that we shall lose everything we stand for."

"Yuri Gorin's presence would discourage radical terrorists," Grimweather ventured. "But—" He gave a discreet cough.

"You wonder how we can stand shoulder to shoulder with a creature like Gorin?" demanded the Queen.

Grimweather and the Foreign Secretary nodded in unison.

"Murderers kill for many reasons," said the Queen. "This one killed for power and position. When a man reaches that point of power, nobody refuses to meet him and nobody deplores the way he got there. We seem to remember an uncle who found no difficulty meeting with Hitler."

Everyone looked uncomfortable except the Queen. She added, "There is said to be an attempt to blame this uncle for the Holocaust. Is that true?" She fixed her periwinkle-blue eyes on Grimweather.

"Your Majesty will have seen the neo-Nazi demands," he began.

"Yes," said the Queen, very crisp. "We shall resist all attempts at intimidation."

"You must not put yourself in danger," said the Prime Minister.

"On the contrary." The Queen saw how they froze. "The monarchy is under attack. Therefore the monarch takes first place on the battlefield. This is no ordinary challenge. This is cowardly warfare. It can only be answered by mobilizing the values, and the symbols of those values, upon which our freedoms depend. It is said that royalty has outlived its time. That Remembrance Sunday is idle ceremony. We shall observe this day in the manner required by our traditions, with the monarch laying the first wreath to honor the dead."

The Prime Minister and the Foreign Secretary exchanged startled looks. Grimweather stood with hands clasped behind him, and thought of the terrible fury of Boadicea, Britain's greatest warrior queen, who had burned down London rather than bend to Roman conquerors. *There* began the traditions of which this Queen now spoke. Almost two thousand years of stubborn, sometimes eccentric, always unexpected resistance to bullies had become the hallmark of these islands' proud independence. Everything else, thought Grimweather, fails: we oppose the technology of overkill with more technology, while we are quite unable to invent a machine to combat terrorism nearly so well as family loyalty.

The others were silent too. Perhaps similar thoughts ran through their minds. There are set procedures for so much that is ceremonious in the United Kingdom. They have been rehearsed over and over again, and this is what makes them flexible. When a king leads troops into battle across the Channel, or when a Churchill grasps the leadership to fight off a fascist invasion, the procedures are swiftly adjusted. The British establishment has a sufficient sense of history to slice with immense self-confidence through the red tape. Procedure permits informal exchanges between men and women who know each other well. Agreements are hammered out in moments. The paperwork is left for later. The Queen was quite properly recalling the core of Remembrance Sunday; the ritual; the focus on ancient tradition and family ties; the clannishness of an island people for whom the royal family embodies the spirit of a large and boisterous family with all its follies and all its grandeur. Neither tyrant nor totalitarian has broken this family feeling, which extends, against all reason, to former colonies and territories overseas. The monarch stands above politics, and thus holds together that odd assortment of peoples around the globe who celebrate family events in the monarch's life though their leaders range from Moslem Malays to black African revolutionaries and one-time headhunters of Borneo. It is essential to this curious unity, though, that leadership comes from a monarch free from political ties and not from an elected Prime Minister.

The Prime Minister recognized when it was best to graciously surrender. "I shall gladly take a back seat," she said, and everyone knew what she meant. It would be good to get out of the firing line, though it went against her nature.

"If I am to invite the Soviet leader, then I expect him to be fitted correctly into the Order of Procession," said the Queen, closing all possibility of argument. Her memory in such matters was infallible. She quoted from standing Home Office orders: "The Queen lays the first wreath in the center of the top step on the north side of the Cenotaph. The Duke of Edinburgh lays a wreath to the right of Her Majesty's . . ." She ran through the names of her immediate family. "Then," she said, "we come to our Prime Minister and at that point must consider where to inject our visitors who are not part of the Commonwealth." She listed the high commissioners from Sri Lanka and Canada, from Australia and Sierra Leone, from Zambia, Swaziland and Tonga: thirty-five countries in all, she remembered each representative's name as the head of a family recalls sisters and cousins. "We should ask how they feel about placing the Presidents of the United States, the Soviet Union and France ahead . . ."

The Foreign Secretary said, "A question of protocol—" but was interrupted by the principal private secretary, whose post is of huge importance, for the task of the PPS is to keep the monarch fully informed and to explain the implications of any action the monarch may contemplate. Therefore, when the PPS spoke, the Foreign Secretary stepped back.

"Ma'am," said the PPS. "Fleet Street will make a carnival of this come Monday. If we live to see Monday. The headlines will read, The Queen Takes Charge, and so on."

"Then see to it the BBC offers an explanation at the time."

"Ma'am." The PPS lowered his gray head in mute assent. The history of private secretaries shows that they attend to the ritual side of their duties with relish, while not hesitating to challenge a wrongheaded monarch. By that simple word and gesture, the PPS signified approval. The Prime Minister pursed her lips. That nod had truly retired her. At least, she told herself, for now. For she had a keen memory, too—for parliamentary rights.

"The BBC," said the Queen, continuing a trend of thought, "must not cave in to threats."

"It won't be a simple question of ignoring threats," said Grimweather quickly. "Not if terrorists break into Whitehall. Every broadcast network in the world is involved."

"You agree we must not give way to blackmail?"

"Indeed, ma'am."

"Even if an attempt is made to prove this uncle a traitor."

They watched the Queen with more than mere respect.

"Television," she said, "has been the exclusive weapon of terrorism for too long. By the manner in which we conduct ourselves, let us turn it into a two-edged sword." She flashed Grimweather a smile of dismissal. He had already reached the door when she called out, "Let us hope we have not spoiled your weekend, Mr. Grimweather."

He came to attention and dropped his head in a curt bow. "By y'r leave, ma'am . . . I fear it will in any case prove a long one."

Part IV
The Long Weekend

40

Scott Talbott flew again in the Phantom piloted by General Peled Pamir. There had been delays. The helicopter had arrived too late to lift him off the *Avocadocor* before nightfall the previous day. The transfer at Rome had not been smooth. Now Steely Pamir was making clear his discomfort over Talbott's unexpected initiative. Many Jews would be alarmed by Yuri Gorin's sudden presence in London.

Talbott felt irritation. His pilot sensed it. "Well, what's done is done," said Pamir. "I'll pipe down."

There was a long silence. Talbott, secure in the body-molded seat's webbed embrace, thought about the insecurity of a people. Even people as tough as Steely Pamir. The joining of hands between a Soviet dictator and Western leaders must revive ancient fears among those who had been excluded for centuries from the making of history while others settled their fate.

"I know this Masada complex of Jake Cooke's kind," Pamir said finally. "The Jews at Masada helped each other die, rather than yield to the Romans. It happened two thousand years ago. For men like Jake, it could be yesterday. They forget the Masada heroes provoked the decisive Roman assault that drove our people into permanent exile. It could happen again. Suppose Yuri Gorin's planning that—"

"You weren't there to listen to his story."

"You confirmed what I wanted to know: he *is* Radzki, he professes to hold true to Radzki's faith. Everything hangs together except"—Steely Pamir thought for a second—"Radzki must have had power over Stalin somewhere down the line."

"Why?" Talbott asked carefully, for he had felt such misgivings.

"Once Radzki started out, one step logically followed the other. But there's still a missing link. A gap. Between Rudolf Hess coming to trial as a war criminal and Radzki's transformation into a full-fledged officer in Stalin's secret police at home."

"A missing link?" That was precisely how Talbott had thought of it.

"The Soviets want to wipe Israel off the map," said Steely Pamir. He broke off to deal with ground control. "Don't forget," he resumed, "Radzki impressed Stalin because he knew better than anybody how to help the Jewish race destroy itself."

"Israel would destroy itself if it blindly attacks a London summit," Talbott said. "People will ask: 'What's wrong with a super summit? It's no more whimsical than launching nuclear missiles in a moment of distrust. If a madman can push to annihilate life on earth, surely we can tolerate an act of imagination to save life?' "

Steely Pamir sighed. "I'm the one who lectures men like Jake to stop being paranoid. Yet this thing makes me paranoid too." Then he stopped talking as he prepared for landing.

Talbott wished he could convey his own sense of Yuri Gorin. Mother didn't just talk about a divine spirit guiding his actions. He became Radzki. It had started with his account of the final months of Auschwitz.

It is 1944 and the tide has turned for the Soviet armies. The Western Allies have launched their June invasion across the English Channel. The massacre of the Jews takes up a large part of fascist resources. Radzki, the only agent to survive Operation Citadel's final chapter, has learned that Rebecca's sister Frieda is in Auschwitz. He knows, from his last visit to London, that Polish airmen have volunteered to drop arms. FRANTIC is the code name given to several operational missions that will carry U.S. bombers over the death camps. Knowing this, Radzki wants to reach Frieda. He takes the place of a Polish worker at one of the general labor camps in the Auschwitz complex. Switching identities, even inside a camp, is routine for Radzki after four years of underground activity. As easy as slipping into someone else's topcoat, as they used to say. He discovers Frieda has fallen sick. She is either marked for "selection" or has been already selected for execution as "a useless mouth." He knows, through the clandestine radio contacts necessary for coordinating supply drops, that the Allied flights are set for certain days.

On August 20, 1944, a FRANTIC mission bombs the German synthetic oil and rubber plant that draws its slave labor from Auschwitz III. "I am in that camp, helping organize a breakout," Radzki, as Yuri Gorin, recalled for Talbott. "There are 127 Flying Fortresses of the 15th United States Air Force, flying all the way from southern Italy with a fighter escort of one hundred Mustangs, as I now know. They hit the factories and leave untouched the camp where thirty thousand Jews pray for an end to the horror. One bomb could do it. The gas chambers of Birkenau are only five miles away. Two days later, I learn that poor Frieda is to be gassed that afternoon. That afternoon, 261 Flying Fortresses bomb the oil refineries at Blechhammer and Bohumin. We see them high up in a clear blue sky. Can you imagine? That is a very large number of bombers, all crowded together, streaking white contrails across the blue.

"Is it possible to know, if you are not there, the agony? I can do nothing to stop the march to gas chambers of Frieda and her companions. She looks up. She must see. She must wonder about Allied explanations coming through the underground that the air-force commanders cannot stop the death machinery with bombs because the camps are out of range. That's my personal nightmare," said Radzki, speaking as Gorin. "That young girl, being led naked to the gassing, and looking up to see that great armada sailing past, and in her last moments on this earth learning the truth: that she is of no importance to humanity or to God."

Later, Yuri Gorin had said, "If I go to London, I must kill the lies that are added to such nightmares. I cannot always control these lies, though. Keep that in mind, Talbott!"

Talbott had it in mind now, while London wheeled under their wings. He could see why General Pamir was worried, even as he admired the professional way the Israeli greased the Phantom onto the RAF runway.

London: Early Saturday morning

Sally stared up into the curved recesses of a stone ceiling. She had a phantasmagoric sense of being adrift in the Paris morgues of another century, lost in a novel by Émile Zola. She was naked on her back under steam-shrouded lights. When her flesh made contact with the wet marble, she felt corpselike, as if the blood had been already drained out of her. Faint lines of pointed arches hovered in the far corners of the vaulted chamber. She could not move to look more closely, because a restraint of some sort bit into her forehead. She could not dispel the illusion of mortuary slabs in the Paris catacombs.

The tattooed Libyan loomed over her. "It must have been this way in the gassing chambers your grandfather refused to bomb," he said in pedantic German. He had dropped his pose of ignorance. He leaned his buttocks against the edge of the slab, close by her head. "Prussian cyanide, wasn't it?"

She made no attempt to reply.

"Cyanide," said the Libyan. "Salt of prussic acid, released by the body juices, kills by paralyzing the nervous arrangements of heart and respiration." He sounded as if he read from a manual of instruction. "Zyklon gas was the derivative. Eighty bitter almonds contain sixty milligrams of prussic acid . . . Whoever coined the term must have had the gift of prophesy. It is of *Prussian* origin."

Sally turned her eyes away. She had been wheeled into these catacombs after her attempt to escape. If Parson Furneval now thought he could conjure up nightmares through Sami Esmail, he was wrong.

"The camp doctors were able to substantiate," said Sami, "that the brain cavity is the best place to find the telltale bitter-almond smell."

She shut him out mentally. A drop of hot water stung her face. She squinted up at the high, vaulted roof, where pipes snaked through the gloom. She thought again of Zola's underground mortuaries, where pipes dripped so heavily they washed blood away from the slabs. Then she realized it had been Sami Esmail who made her think about Zola. The erudite, sick bastard! Now she couldn't shut his voice out of her ears. He'd seen her look up into the ceiling. He was back on *that* track again. "People of Paris," he said, "would come all night long to view the unclaimed corpses, standing on overhead walkways. They were hypnotized by the panorama of random death. Male necrophiliacs loved the spectacle. They thought they saw between the stiffening limbs, those bearded little passageways where they could spend their way into the life eternal."

She had several obscenities on the tip of her tongue. Before she could spit any at him, Sami said, "I did my Ph.D. in French literature."

She was ready with a retort when she saw a bulge in the central pipe far above her head. The bulge had not been there before. It oozed along like a piglet being slowly digested by a black python. Then Sami's head got in the way, and she concentrated on holding her temper, feeling the hope surge through her body.

"Your ear." His hand closed over one side of her head. "Talbott will certainly recognize your ear." He loosened the head strap. She craned forward and saw a large kitchen knife in his other hand. He smiled down at her, and released more straps. She thought: He can't really mean this; nobody knows where Talbott is, and there isn't time.

It was the palace parson, Furneval, who'd said there wasn't time. But how long ago was that? Had she unwittingly given them enough already to go on? The past hours were a blur. She remembered the struggle in the bathing pool, then being strapped to a trolley and wheeled here through subterranean corridors. Sami had worked on her, forcing castor oil down her throat and enjoying her later humiliation. Sometimes Furneval appeared and repeated the same questions. Then Sami took over again. He had an uncanny sense of her changing mental state. When she became mentally nauseated, he resumed the verbal bullying. "Your grandfather gave the camp guards all the time in the world to perfect their techniques," he had said. "We learned from them." Or "German shepherd dogs can be trained to rape, did you know?" She remembered a big Alsatian straining at a leash somewhere in one corner.

Yet she sensed she had won an ascendancy over the Libyan. He made two other men handle her transfer from the trolley to the slab, as if he feared physical contact with the dead. She had heard Africans say that some had a superstitious dread of such contact. He must think of her as dead already.

She concentrated on what looked like a pale moon hanging among the black pipes coiling overhead. The main pipe was thick enough to be one of Zola's morgue walkways. The steam from the marble baths parted, then closed again. The moon grew, then shrank, advancing with the snail-like progress of the bulge in the pipeline. The moon had a rabbit in it, or else eyes and a mouth. She had an insane need to cover herself, to shout up to that face, to deny she was a Paris suicide waiting to be identified.

Close beside her, a voice she knew said to the Libyan, "You don't mind being alone with her?"

She rolled her eyes sideways and glimpsed a beard, a thin ascetic face which chose that moment to turn away. Jake Cooke! She strained against the leather straps and heard that familiar guttural accent telling Sami Esmail, "Well, enjoy yourself."

She tried to cry out, but no words came. She must be going mad! It could not possibly be Jake. Something he had once said to her echoed in her head: "The whole world's become a death camp."

The face hanging high above her had been reduced to a quarter moon behind scudding clouds, and her vision dimmed.

41

Talbott knew something was wrong by the way Dahlia's eyes kept darting in his direction. General Pamir's secretary had been taking notes all night long while Talbott went over the meetings with Mother, again and again.

"Why are you so sure," Steely Pamir asked for the hundredth time, "Mother thinks like the old Radzki?"

"He sees the whole world as one big concentration camp," replied Talbott. "He says mankind has to wake up to the fact we're all inmates. I can't explain it any better."

"God abandoned *the Jews*. That's the line Jake Cooke takes." Pamir shook his head in disapproval. "That the world's a death camp for Jews, if we don't act."

"Mother totally disagrees," Talbott almost shouted. "For the Holocaust to make sense, he says, the Jews must save humanity from itself. God abandoned all humanity, not just the Jews!"

"You believe this?"

"He does. The conviction gives him strength. It made him see me as a divine instrument, someone who came at the right moment with the answer. Who showed him how to employ all that power."

General Pamir gave a great sigh. "Get everything typed up," he told Dahlia.

She stood, and hesitated.

"Yes?" Pamir looked up at her.

"The boy . . ."

The general sighed. "A kid from the slums wants to see you, Talbott." He shifted in his chair under Dahlia's stare. "Have we anything else to discuss?"

"Not me," said Talbott. "I've done what I could. It's up to others now."

General Pamir glanced again at Dahlia. "You can go."

"Tell him now," she said.

Talbott recognized the unmistakable voice of an Israeli sabra correcting the commanding officer. He was certain something had gone seriously wrong now, and that it involved Sally. He said, "I'd better see my producer, if we've finished with all this."

"She's vanished," General Pamir said bluntly.

"But she was here. Safe."

Dahlia said, "It's my fault." She gave a brief, unemotional account of what had happened.

"I couldn't tell you sooner," said Pamir. "There was nothing you could do, and we'd got other priorities."

"You mean, the priority to have me waste several hours going over the Gorin case once again?" Talbott was on his feet, red with fury.

"Nothing can be as important."

Talbott stared down at the other man, then shook his head dumbly and moved to the door.

"You'd better see the boy," said Dahlia. "I think he knows where she might be."

"You *think?*" Talbott whirled on her.

"He won't talk to anyone but you."

"Where is he?"

"This way," said Dahlia sympathetically.

Charlie, the cocky little leader of the Blitz Kids, clung to the moist and slippery pipe in the maze of service conduits running through the centuries-old Turkish baths. Once, the building had been an abbey built over one of London's many underground rivers, the Neckinger. Next door was the Thomas à Becket pub, and beyond that was a gymnasium where a convent once stood. Nuns were said to have been buried alive in the cellar walls. Their ghosts had been on Charlie's mind when he wriggled through a street grating and wormed his way along the uncovered pipes. Then, frightened and flushed with shame, he found himself staring, for the first time in his life, at a woman naked.

There was a further shock. He had no sooner realized it was Sally down there than "the bloke wiv the beard" had appeared, the one they called Jake Cooke. Instead of freeing Sally, he was talking and laughing with the loinclothed guard.

Charlie blinked. He saw it all. Jake Cooke had used the Blitz Kids to trap the American girl. But why?

The boys had continued to do as Jake asked because, he said, it would save the girl and Talbott. Their streetwise caution, though, led one to trail Sally to Hyde Park Gate, where he had seen her bundled out of the basement areaway into a commercial minivan. Another of Charlie's ragamuffin "digzees" in his network of lookouts had already followed Jake from the Sherlock Holmes pub in Whitehall to the Turkish baths. When Charlie heard about Sally, he had come straight to the baths to tell Jake. But the porters denied knowledge of anyone answering Jake's description and scornfully dismissed the boy. All except one, who recognized a fellow victim of the modern age, and told Charlie: "Listen, mate, even if yore pal come 'ere, we'd never know it. Not wiv them sheikhs greasing palms wiv petrodollars and turning 'arf the place into a bleedin' private brothel." That was when Charlie had decided to break in.

Now it appeared to Charlie that the loinclothed man was going to assault Sally. The boy groped backwards with the wild idea that if he got above the man, he could drop directly upon him. The bottoms of Charlie's boots were metal-tipped for longer wear. The boy imagined driving those metal studs into the man's skull. But then one foot slipped and the metal struck another pipe with a loud, echoing clunk.

Sami Esmail's head jerked back. The face he saw in the arched ceiling had to be that of Talbott. Talbott had been his quarry through Frankfurt, Düsseldorf and Berlin. Talbott was never far from his mind. Talbott and the girl. He crouched, passing the long-bladed knife from hand to hand, stalking the figure above as it began to retreat. He had been told never to kill Talbott; but now he had the excuse for which he lusted. He saw a leg fall through a gap where the main overhead pipe separated, and then the chalky smudge of a face between the wisps of steam. He flung the knife. It turned over in the air and the heavy steel handle caught Charlie across his throat so that he was shocked into losing balance and fluttered noiselessly to the stone floor. The thud when his body struck sounded all the more sickening.

The still form lay at a distance, in shadow. Sami turned from it and laughed. "Your lover fell into his own trap."

He let Sally sit up. He was drunk with laughter, and trembled with the excitement. He forced her to the slippery floor, pulling her head back by the hair so that she had to roll her eyes downward to study the shapeless form. Even from that far away, it did not look to her like Talbott.

She was gripped by both wrists from behind. She could guess what Sami Esmail wanted besides her despair at the sight of her lover dead. He needed violently to humiliate her. His chest against her back was hairy and wet with sweat. She remembered Parson Furneval's sneer: Sami the sodomite.

She pretended to wail in grief, tossing her head from side to side. One hand let go her wrist to grab hold of her hair again. She jerked forward, as if to reach the inert body. One of the Blitz Kids! Blind fury gave her strength. She twisted so swiftly that she broke Sami Esmail's slippery grip. Facing him, she brought her knee into his groin. His breath was expelled in a shriek of pain. The effluvium from his lungs almost smothered her with a stench of spiced food and rotting teeth. He was caught in the one brief second when his weight and limbs were awkwardly distributed. Sami Esmail, like so many overconfident masters of unarmed combat, was unused to amateurs who spring cunning surprises not in the book. His feet shot out on the slippery flagstones. Sally heard a crunch like a walnut squeezed between nutcrackers. It was the sound of a vertebra cracking. She toppled on top of him. He was screaming in agony, his arms closing convulsively around her. She thought he would crush her in his paroxysms of pain. He held her down on him. Her arms were squeezed between their bellies, but her hands were free between her thighs. She groped his crotch and her fingers found his wet testicles. She wrenched and twisted until he was gasping for breath again, arms flung wide. She dived away and reached for the abandoned knife. She stood, and finally saw it was Charlie lying dead nearby. She would have driven the knife, then, into the Libyan. But he was lying helpless, yellow with pain and fear. She told him to get up, but he could only thresh about. Bubbles formed around his mouth. He clawed impotently at the floor. When she raised the knife, he made a spasmodic effort to protect his genitals.

"Can you get me out of here?" she whispered.

His answer was a low-pitched groan. She put the flat of the knife across his stretched throat. With her free hand, she grasped his testicles again. She thought of Charlie and twisted her hand savagely. Sami shrieked, his mouth filling with vomit so that the scream drowned in his throat.

She had never seen a man reduced suddenly to such absolute submission. She thought: He's more at home with women hidden in tentlike garments. If he bothers to screw, he mounts like an animal and finishes in split seconds. He'd much rather play with boys, thought Sally. She glanced again at Charlie's small, lifeless body.

Rage had turned her eyes to icy blue. The effect on Sami Esmail was electric. "Speak—" he gasped, and twisted his head to void his throat. "I want . . . speak."

She shifted the knife from his neck to his groin.

"The prisoner. One of yours." The face wrinkled with fresh pain. "Please," he begged. "A doctor."

"What prisoner?"

"Your friend. Jake Cooke."

She had forgotten her delirious impression that Jake had been here. But —? "You mean *your* friend?"

"No." Sami Esmail's eyes pleaded for her to trust what he was saying. "There are two Jake Cookes. Only one is real."

It was one of those crisp November mornings in London when the early-Saturday silence descends with the breaking light upon those royal parks stretching from Kensington Palace and the Round Pond to Birdcage Walk and Whitehall. A flight of Canada geese circled the embassies at the western side of the first great park of Kensington. Great oaks buried their heads in the layers of mist and scattered golden leaves over the still-green grass. Once, there were huge elms, disposed like the guardsmen at the Battle of Blenheim. At any moment, it seemed, an ancient king would ride out of the pearly gray with a retinue of horsemen.

But the figure riding towards Talbott was diminutive and mounted astride a bicycle.

"Oi!" shouted the rider. "Wait fer me, mate!"

Talbott came to a stop.

The bicyclist turned into a small boy, and the boy became recognizable as Ginger. "I tried to get yer over in that place." He pointed with his chin in the direction of the embassy. "They wanted me to stay inside. I wasn't 'avin' any of that. I know about them diplomats."

"They told me you'd wait in the park."

The boy looked past Talbott. "None of them wiv yer?"

"I'm as suspicious as you are, when it comes to diplomats." Talbott turned slowly round. There was not a soul to be seen. "Now then, where is she?"

"I can't tell anyone but you."

"Yes, yes. I won't pass it on."

"Follow me, then." Before Talbott could stop him, the boy had remounted the bicycle and was pedaling towards the Albert Memorial, palpable as smoke in the bare treetops, its gilded harshness softened by a timid ray of sunlight piercing the rising mist. By the time Talbott stood under the somber gaze of Albert's statue, Ginger was nowhere in sight. Talbott began to circle the alarming shrine, dedicated in blue mosaic letters on glittering gold to "Albert, Prince Consort." Queen Victoria had erected it to the German princeling whose death plunged her into dreadful grief. As a boy, Talbott had wondered if a man and woman could really love each other with such intensity. Now he knew.

Albert with his Gothic umbrella and magisterial pose stood high above the marble groupings of his empress wife's colonies: America, Asia, Africa and Europe. Talbott wished for some of that imperial certainty as he trod softly from one corner of the huge memorial to another. Then came the squeak of a bicycle. On it was Ginger, holding another by the handlebars. "Quickest way there is," said the boy as Talbott caught the spare cycle by the saddle.

Ginger led him through cobbled alleys and across turfed spaces, wobbling dangerously between traffic when it proved impossible to avoid the roads. Where Ginger had stolen the bicycles, Talbott would rather not

was glad to oblige wealthy foreigners without asking too many questions. The 88 had bought into Ironmongers through Mideast and tax-haven banks, the way buildings later occupied by Libyan peoples bureaus and guerrilla training schools were purchased. Sally dredged up a moment in her drugged sleep when Parson Furneval had said he was leaving the premises to Sami "until we're back."

"He won't be back," said Jake when she told him this. "Not until he's ready to spring me on an unsuspecting public."

"He told Sami to have me broken in . . ."

Jake turned such a glare on Sami that the man readily explained the process of opening the steel doors. Sami had no problem remembering the combinations: he was desperate for medical attention. It confirmed Jake's belief that Furneval and the others would not be back until whatever action they planned had reached its climax. Sami was terrified of being left inside their sanctuary.

They pushed through more swing doors to where members had repaired after a night on the town to steam alcohol out of their systems and sleep off their hangovers. The emphasis was on quietness. The corridors were still padded. The old-fashioned elevator worked by pulling a rope, and rose in majestic silence. A venerable hall porter stirred in his worn cane chair and said, "Cor's truth, bit early ain't it for a bloody constitutional?" and fell asleep again.

They pushed the patient through the big main doors into the street outside and stood blinking in the welcome daylight.

The real Jake Cooke said, "Keep in contact through the Israeli embassy." He was squinting at something, with his back to her. She reached out automatically to turn down the collar of his jacket. He looked like a prosperous banker, as if the 88 had preserved special clothes for a special role. There was a shrill cry from down the street. He said, "Your friends are here."

Sally turned to where he pointed. When she swung back, he was gone.

Talbott was making a further survey of Ironmongers. He found it hard to tell, in the jumble of buildings which included betting shops, a pub, a pawnbroker and a laundry, just where the baths began and ended. Ginger had shown him where the Blitz Kids' leader had wriggled through a street grating. But that had happened hours ago. There was no trace of the boy.

Then came a startling yell from Ginger. "There's your girlfriend!"

Talbott saw Sally peering in his direction. A bearded figure turned abruptly away from her and withdrew into a narrow walkway. Sally appeared to be pushing a wheelchair. Talbott began to run, Ginger flying at his heels.

Traffic had started to cough and wheeze where Queen Victoria Street sloped past Blackfriars to the river. Above the rattle of a milk van, they shouted explanations. A ship hooted on the river. A truck-and-trailer rig stopped in the middle of a crossing and the street began to fill with the indignant honking of stalled vehicles.

"I thought I saw Jake with you?" said Talbott.

Sally glanced warningly at Ginger, who had become all ears. To change the subject, she said, "That poor boy's dead."

"Charlie?" demanded Ginger.

She turned to face the youngster, angry with herself for blurting out the news. "He saved my life," she said helplessly.

"Was it 'im killed Charlie?" The boy planted himself square in front of Sami Esmail, squirming in the wicker bath chair.

"We must get somewhere safe!" Sally called out.

"Why don't 'e speak?" Ginger studied the bath chair, perched at the edge of the curb. Water gushed along the gutter from a burst main.

"Shock," said Sally. "I think I broke his back."

Ginger shot her a look of renewed respect. His face was wet with tears. He said to Sami Esmail, "If I called the cops, I'd be doing you a favor. But I can't."

"He's right," Sally told Talbott. She raised her voice above the thunder of a STOL aircraft climbing too slowly from the river. "Parson Furneval told me . . ." Her words were drowned by the noise overhead. "Can we get to the embassy? It's dangerous here!"

"And dangerous there," said Talbott, remembering General Steely Pamir's last words: *Godspeed in finding your girl. Then get on with your job and we'll get on with ours. If there's the slightest suspicion we worked together, you'll lose your credibility, and I, my diplomatic status.*

Sally said, "Then, nowhere's safe."

"Safe enough for me," said Ginger savagely. " 'Cos I'm just a kid, see. Nobody takes notice of kids except sodding geezers like 'im."

"If you know somewhere, tell us," demanded Sally in growing desperation. She still expected Parson Furneval to come swinging out of the traffic with his friendly thugs, no matter what Jake said.

Ginger put two fingers in his mouth. Traffic had come unstuck again, and a taxicab seemed to rear back like a black bull at the boy's piercing whistle.

"Paddington 'Ospital, tell 'im," Ginger instructed Talbott. "Say it's an emergency." He seemed to make no move, yet suddenly the bath chair toppled and Sami Esmail went sprawling in the road. "It's an emergency now," Ginger added.

The driver was not exactly thrilled to have his taxi turned into an ambulance. It was either that, though, or listen to Ginger wail about his injured uncle and how Ginger would report this as an accident because Ginger had *seen* the taxi clip the bath chair . . . "Orl right! *Orl right!!*" the cabbie screamed. "Wot you mean is St. Mary's 'Ospital!" The two of them kept up a cross fire that allowed Talbott and Sally to sink back, with Sami

Esmail squashed in the leather upholstery between them, rolling his eyes in mute appeal.

They walked from Paddington, just Sally and Talbott. It would be safer, said Ginger, to take cover in the crowds gathering for this Remembrance weekend, and proceed on foot to the safe address he had given them. He was fitting rapidly into the generalship vacated by Charlie. When last seen, he was clutching a wad of five-pound notes Talbott had given him and coaxing hospital orderlies to move the injured Sami Esmail, but not too rapidly.

Sally would never forget standing where Jermyn Street opens into Babmaes Street, named after the pimp who supplied King Charles II with whores. It was there Talbott disclosed the identity of Radzki and the plan to bring him, as Yuri Gorin, to London for the next day's ceremonies. It was there Sally revealed there were two Jake Cookes.

By the time they digested all the implications, they had reached the oldest of London's elegant squares: St. James's. Talbott suddenly seized Sally. "She shall have all that's fine and fair," he recited. "And ride in a coach to take the air. And have a house in St. James's Square." Then he kissed her.

She was delighted and alarmed. "Are you crazy?"

"No. Look across the square."

Sally saw two police officers watching them with tolerant grins. Nearby was a newspaper billboard: NEW HESS SCANDAL! DID WE PAY HITLER WITH JEWISH LIVES? WHY WAS NAZI INVASION CAN-CELLED? SOVIET BOSS ARRIVES TOMORROW WITH TOUGH QUESTIONS!

"Kiss me again!" Sally demanded. "Those cops may not be sure I'm a woman." She took off the borrowed porter's cap, shook out her hair, loosened the top brass button of the uniform tunic, and moved Talbott's hand inside to cup one of her breasts, loose in the man's undervest Jake had found her. She didn't care about tomorrow's new disclosures. Her face shone in the early-morning sunshine. She felt his body throbbing against hers. They needed one another more than the world needed them, she decided. Kraaft was loose, free to pose as Jake Cooke, groomed for the part of a martyred Jewish warrior willing to put all humanity at risk. A Soviet leader was coming who might become one of Kraaft's victims. And there was no counteraction that she or Talbott could take during these next few precious minutes.

"Next thing you know, they'll be doing it swinging from the lampposts," said one of the officers. Then they moved off. They had been told to keep a look out for two Americans posing as news correspondents. Nobody had said anything about a man and a woman in love.

42

Secretary Kerensky was still pinching himself as Mother's limousine reached the tarmac strip cutting across the triangular compound at the heart of the citadel of churches, palaces and barracks known as the Kremlin. The urgent invitation for Mother to join Western leaders in London had finally arrived on the very eve of the Soviet Union's biggest exhibition of military muscle. Mother had insisted on the display taking place on Saturday, arguing that the Soviet economy could no longer stand the loss of a working day and the accompanying drinking bouts and absenteeism. Mother's victory over tribal rites was further proof of his unprecedented power.

Kerensky had always thought he understood how Mother acquired that power. Now, in the early light, he wondered if there could be some more metaphysical explanation. How else account for Mother's masterful handling of events last night?

There had been a banquet to celebrate the Bolshevik Revolution. It took place under a giant fresco of the Last Supper, in the Kremlin.

The banquet was held in the Granovitovaya Palata, or "faceted palace." The huge Christ and the greatly enlarged Apostles had gazed down from ancient walls upon the thirteen politburo members, one on one, you might say. Around them spread the party leaders of the non-Russian republics of the U.S.S.R. and the elite of the Warsaw Pact nations. Among the guests were Soviet defense councilors, very conscious of what they would be showing off on the morrow: numerically, the world's biggest war machine. Yet the banqueting hall was chiefly notable for what President Richard Nixon, when he was feted there, described as its overwhelming religiosity, with its walls and ceilings covered in icons by Andrei Rublyev: a peculiar setting, thought Nixon when he sat in this same red-hued chamber under massive and ornate chandeliers, for a dinner given by the antireligious Communist leaders of the Soviet Union.

The old generals and admirals had filled their glasses with vodka and plastered slabs of black bread with Beluga caviar when, taking everyone by surprise, Mother stood up and launched into an unprecedented nine-minute speech. The army and navy brass, and their political chiefs, were left holding their laden hands aloft, slowly lowering them as it became clear the leader was not addressing them exclusively.

He stood under the huge Christ and surprised them all with the announcement that the United States, remembering the Soviet Union's magnificent role in winning the Great Patriotic War against fascism, had called upon the Soviet people to join hands with its former allies in marking the defeat of fascism. Somehow, and Kerensky could not properly remember just how Mother had said these things, the fact that the queen-empress of history's last and largest empire endorsed and relayed the invitation made the tribute seem all the more flattering.

All Kerensky could clearly recall was Mother spouting the usual pious hopes about peace. His listeners accepted this as the obligatory repetition of party propaganda. They soon woke up, however, to the fact that Mother actually meant what he was saying. Since all the phrases were part of the orthodox liturgy, it was impossible for anyone to later object. Kerensky was quite unable to explain in practical terms the torrents of emotion that flowed between Mother and his hard-boiled and yet curiously revitalized audience. It was as if party hacks had actually yearned for someone to put meaning back into the tired old clichés.

Kerensky had come round this morning with a sense, no doubt shared with others, of disbelief. Still, the picture of last night was vivid in his memory. The Last Supper mural had been really *seen* for the first time in Soviet history as a religious work, unless you counted the times President Nixon joked with Brezhnev about it.

Nobody at the top fought the decision to go to London. It would be like doubting that the West acknowledged Soviet moral supremacy. The Queen, while belonging to the garbage heap of history, nevertheless spoke for ex-colonies and dominions around the globe. The White House and Whitehall had been forced by Mother to concede Soviet greatness.

What really impressed Nick Kerensky was that he'd experienced a kind of rediscovery of inherited religious faith, as if the party-godhead spoke with the omnipotence of God Himself.

Near the Kremlin Theater, the limousine stopped to let off Kerensky. He went first to the Council of Ministers building, cleared up some paper-work in his office there, then marched over to the other office in the secret building at the far end of the Arsenal. He passed through the museum of antique weaponry, mounted stairs to the third floor and entered his own annex with a view of the Alexandrovsky Gardens, outside the Kremlin's wall. Beyond the gardens, the city was astir. Soon the people would flood through Red Square, some goose-stepping in uniform, some riding tanks and hauling missiles, some waving the tools of their civilian trade, all rein-forcing Mother's statement that in London he would be dealing from a position of enormous, united strength.

The secretary took from a steel safe an envelope crammed with Ameri-can documents. Mother had requested the material after first discovering the Hess Command project. The documents gave details of satellites in a global television network covering more than one hundred countries. Mother's handwritten notes simplified some of the jargon: *Z, let us say, is a satellite 22,300 miles above the Indian Ocean, moving at precisely the speed of the Earth's rotation. It can relay, live, to Earth dwellers in 40 percent of the planet and reach the rest through relays via two other satellites . . . A single broadcast van is all that is necessary to transmit to Z . . .*

Remembering Mother's eloquence from the night before, Kerensky won-dered if the old man had some wild notion to capture the satellite network and expand his audience beyond the dimensions of the Last Supper.

Inside the original study used by Lenin, preserved just as it was when he had left it for the last time, Yuri Gorin stood with one hand resting on a bronze statue of a monkey examining a man's skull.

Gorin turned at the timid knock at the door.

"Back so soon, Kerensky?" He followed the secretary's gaze, and gave the monkey a pat. "Vladimir Ilyich said this depicts what will happen when man destroys himself in the final war. 'Someday,' said Lenin, 'an ape will pick up a human skull and wonder where it came from.' "

Kerensky had heard this so many times before, he might have been forgiven for ignoring the remark. Instead, it caused him to give a small start. Recovering, he said, "The Aeroflot charter to London. We delayed, comrade, with some story about mechanical trouble."

"I remember."

"It is now twelve hours behind schedule. Our trade delegation . . . ?"

"Tell them the mission is postponed. You will take your ECLIPSE team in their place. The documentation has been prepared by Petrov in the thirteenth section. Twelve men from the ministry, same names, different tasks."

Kerensky tried to hide his shock and moved into the oval chamber.

"Shut the door," said Mother. "Have the British embassy informed that the trade mission is leaving after unavoidable delays. You can put away your notebook, Kerensky, and listen carefully." Mother continued to talk for another fifteen minutes, restlessly moving around the study, from the portrait of Karl Marx to the old wooden desk Lenin had used, then running his hands over dowdy brown wallpaper, unchanged in sixty years. When he had finished, he came to a complete stop and turned once again into a block of stone.

Kerensky knew when to leave. He felt elated, despite the large hole in the pit of his stomach. He'd complained so much about the lack of action since his transfer to Mother's personal secretariat. He hated the routine desk work. He was tied to Mother's apron strings in his role of court spy. This was in the ancient czarist tradition. It made him no friends. He had intrigued to be returned to active service. Now he'd got his wish with a vengeance.

The curious thing was, Mother must have known the invitation to London was in the works. Otherwise, why had he called earlier for those technical papers on satellite systems and the formation of a small hand-picked ECLIPSE team noted for their toughness, their diplomatic elegance and mastery of English, their expensive suntans?

There was nothing anyone could do now to oppose the old man. Kerensky smiled to himself, and his heart beat faster. He had a pretty good grip on English himself, after his years in America. Nobody would dare stop Mother, he told himself, because nothing in the program contradicted party dogma. "My career stands or falls with him," he thought. "And I'm on the side of Motherhood. Motherhood with a gun!"

Long Island, New York: Saturday morning

Quex watched the Soviet leaders on a TV newscast. With him sat Walter Juste and the chief Israeli defense liaison officer.

The voice of the correspondent in Moscow came over the scenes in Red Square: "Yuri Gorin's appearance on the Kremlin wall ends speculation about the Soviet leader's political as well as physical health . . ."

"I suppose Mother wouldn't be putting one over on us," said Walter Juste, studying the new rocket launchers grinding past the cameras.

Another news item appeared, this time from London: ". . . unprecedented security measures . . . in response to new neo-Nazi threats, counterterrorist alert upgraded from BLACK ALPHA, the code name for the normal state of readiness, to BIKINI BLACK AMBER, the code for the highest stage of emergency."

Sol Farkas turned off the TV set. The network executive sensed Quex's impatience.

Walter Juste grumbled, "What's the purpose of code names if the networks broadcast them, Mr. Farkas?"

"At least the public knows the danger," Sol retorted. "Or don't the democratic rules apply when lives are at stake?"

"Danger or no danger, I have to get to London," said Quex.

Walter Juste jumped in hastily. "To get a good look at Yuri Gorin," he explained to the Israeli.

"Didn't Talbott do that?" The Israeli look surprised. He was a veteran of intelligence, recently admitted to the widening circle of those aware of Gorin's origins.

Walter Juste stroked the central parting of his silver hair and said uncomfortably, "Talbott should have been debriefed by at least three experts. Quex will make up for the oversight." He could not say Quex also had another mission.

"If General Massey goes," said the Israeli, "the whole world's liable to discover Israel helped a famous American fake his own death."

"We've anticipated that," Juste said. "He'll travel with the President. A few at the top in London will be told. Later, our government will issue a statement taking responsibility for actions required to deal with the terrorist threat against the general."

The Israeli was not satisfied. "Why court trouble? Talbott's demonstrated his reliability. He's worth any ten other experts. Don't waste an asset like Talbott."

The others maintained an uneasy silence until Sol Farkas finally said, "Talbott? We've lost all contact with Talbott."

43

Talbott was looking out on a kitchen garden at the back of the Overseas Empire Club, between St. James's Street and Green Park, with Buckingham Palace barely visible through the black trunks of the oak trees marching on to Hyde Park. Two small boys had been waiting to bring Sally and Talbott into the storeroom of the club, whose decay was measured by the bric-a-brac of folded Victorian drapes, broken cane chairs and the discarded head of a Bengal tiger drooling sawdust from the top of an old washstand.

The leader of the new boys was called Bloggs, but he deferred to Ginger, who looked dangerously grim.

"You'll be safe in this place," yelled Bloggs. He was wearing transistor headphones and the inevitable expression of the half demented. "It's in the special zone."

Talbott asked, "What zone?" Then he shouted the question. Finally he jerked the headphones from the boy's head. *"What zone?"*

"Eh?" Bloggs returned to earth. "Sorry." He fiddled with the Walkman while Talbott speculated on how such a ragamuffin had acquired it. "Me dad works as part-time porter in this club," said Bloggs. "It's in the zone where cops can arrest anyone wivout a warrant under the emergency. So the club's bin shut." Bloggs had been listening to the newscasts. "Roadblocks are going up, wiv trucks full of concrete. They've declared a BI-KINI BLACK AMBER alert to protect the Queen. She don't want mad bombers telling 'er wot to do."

"Did you say 'mad bombers'?" asked Sally.

"Yus, miss. That bearded bloke you call Jake, 'e told one of 'is mates and we 'eard 'im."

Sally looked over at Talbott and gave a small nod of confirmation. Parson Furneval had used the same phrase to the Libyan when she was still their prisoner.

Talbott was half sitting on a ledge by the dirty windows. He said to Bloggs, "Bring us up to date."

Then the full story came out. The boy Candlestick had been sent to premises close by the club where, long ago, Texas once had its own lega-tion. After what had happened to Sally at the other rendezvous, Candle-stick approached this one cautiously. His instructions from Jake Cooke were to make the adjoining Blue Ball Yard the point of contact if the Blitz Kids found Talbott. But Candlestick needed no more than a single circuit of the premises to convince himself they were, as he put it, "booby-trapped." He had used his own initiative to work out with Bloggs and Ginger the alternative plan. On the way, he had seized an opportunity to "nick" (steal) the Walkman so Bloggs could keep them all abreast of the news.

"Jake—your bloke with the beard," said Talbott, "is *dangerous.*"

"You tell the other kids," added Sally. "You understand? He's not what he pretends to be. His real name is Kraaft. If you run into someone else who looks like him"—she glanced helplessly at Talbott—"check with us."

The boys seemed to agree too readily. Talbott said, "You *must* believe us."

"We do," Bloggs intervened. "You and the lady's both up Queer Street. But we'll stick by you. Gingie says you dun a lot for us, 'specially you, mister. You and Gingie's uncle."

"Uncle?"

"My other name's Boardman," said Ginger.

"Good God! Related to Jimmy Boardman?"

"Give the gent a coconut!" said Bloggs.

Sally hid a smile. The boys must have been eavesdropping when Talbott had told her about his former school friend, killed on the Murmansk run.

"Where's Kraaft now?" asked Talbott. "Does any one of you know?"

"Hashtray," said Bloggs mysteriously. " 'Umidor." He stood in the pas-sageway between the stacks of old furniture and peered anxiously to where Ginger was already moving away.

"Doesn't make sense," said Talbott. "Why would the man talk in rid-dles?"

"Afraid of being overheard?" suggested Sally.

"Hashtray," muttered Talbott. "Tray of mashed potatoes? A restaurant? 'Umidor sounds Arabic." He looked round for Ginger.

"Gingie's gorn," said one of the other boys lingering in the doorway. " 'E said 'e's in a 'urry."

Talbott had no time to puzzle this out. He said to Bloggs: "This might be very important."

"I don't know no hunderground restaurants called 'Umidor," Bloggs said stubbornly.

"Hunderground?" echoed Sally.

"Thermidor!" said Talbott. "That's more probably it. Like lobster thermidor. It must be a restaurant."

"But Candlestick said a Hunderground 'Umidor, cum to think about it," said Bloggs. "And the word is 'Umidor, not thermidor."

Sally began to giggle. She recovered under Bloggs's suddenly baleful eye and asked him, "Don't you mean *humidor* and *ashtray?*"

"That's wot I said, miss. 'Umidor and hashtray."

"O my Lor'!" she said. She could not hold back her laughter. Afraid of further offending Bloggs, she included Talbott. "You cockneys! Sometimes I swear you speak a foreign language."

"It's pure English," Talbott cut in, equally anxious to keep Bloggs's goodwill. "The oldest and purest! Right, Bloggs?"

"Not 'arf!" said Bloggs.

"Only . . . why would Candlestick think those words important enough to pass along to you?"

" 'E whispered them to me like 'e wuz afraid. Then this bloke wiv the beard made 'im cum away." Bloggs suddenly saw that he had been telling his story the wrong way round. "See, I don't fink Candlestick wanted this bloke to know we're wiv you. You're supposed to stay here until we get fings worked out, like which to trust."

"And have you?" asked Talbott.

"Now we 'ave. Mind you, we always trusted Nelson of the Yard."

"Can you get Nelson?"

"That's me next orders," said Bloggs.

Bloggs dodged into the park, trailed by his aides. The trees were already lost in the early twilight.

"Suppose they run into the real Jake?" said Talbott.

"They won't." Sally described Jake's sudden disappearance outside Ironmongers. She had been waiting for the opportunity to recount the preceding events, the strange snatches of overheard conversation, and the clear proof of Parson Furneval's perfidy and hidden influence somewhere in the dark recesses of British security.

"You're sure you heard the name Henkell?" asked Talbott.

"Several times. I remembered it because there was some joking about bombers and the Heinkel bomber planes raiding London in the Blitz."

What was the connection between Henkell and new information on Hess that would embarrass the Soviets? Talbott rubbed his face. Every answer led to new questions. He let Sally finish and then he demanded: "How can you be sure this one's the real Jake?"

Sally looked away. "He's got a big chest scar, for one thing. Runs diagonally from left shoulder to the bottom of the right rib cage, then zigzags less obviously to the groin."

"Ah."

"Do you realize," Sally asked, trying to get past the sudden, awkward silence, "we never saw Jake's look-alike by daylight?"

"He gave off the right emotions."

"Do you think he had all the facts?"

"Inside out," muttered Talbott. "He's like the man Stalin trained to kill Trotsky. By the time the assassin wormed his way into Trotsky's circle, he'd become the disciple he pretended to be."

Sally shivered. "It's awfully dark out there. I feel as if it's always been dark."

A small security van crept along the pathway between the club's kitchen gardens and the open park. Talbott automatically moved back from the windows. "I suppose the one person we could still trust is your grandfather."

Sally told him about the attempts at the Israeli embassy to make her speak with Quex. "Then Fishhook claimed the office wanted me back in New York."

"Christ! Those kids are right. 'Don't trust nobody.' "

"So the other side wins, after all! *Distrust.* That's what Parson Furneval talked about mostly. How to divide Israel, and divide the West, through distrust." Sally watched the melancholy light in the park deepen to black. "My God, the old beetle crusher really thought I was a corpse already." She hugged herself. "He said he'd learned something about secret power. All you needed was your own center of power and a passive bureaucracy, divided into watertight compartments, accustomed to taking orders from the top without question."

It occurred to Talbott that Mother had said somewhat the same thing. The formula translated into any language. He longed for some good plain English. Sally could have died! That was a simple, straightforward statement that any amount of political analysis couldn't muck up. He took her in his arms.

She was still snagged in a passion of delayed rage. "The bastard told me how he wangled things as a palace insider . . . He *never* gets to advise the royals . . . He uses that royal chaplain title . . . It's honorary. There've been dozens. 'They're such bloody snobs,' Furneval said. 'All I did was write myself a memo on palace stationery, then nip over to Whitehall and sign my own authorization. Nobody questions the royal pleasure.' "

"The Queen's pleasure!" Talbott tightened his hold on Sally. "Did the parson talk about you being detained at the Queen's pleasure?"

"Held at the Queen's pleasure? Yes, he said he could do that. Lying bastard!"

"He wasn't lying. It's an ancient formula. Maybe he can . . ." Talbott suddenly laughed softly, feeling her indignation expire.

"Hold me for *your* pleasure," said Sally, reaching to kiss him. "We've nothing else we can do. I've incited a Bolshie cleric. You've got a price on your head. We can't call New York, because the office obviously leaks like a sieve." She had her porter's jacket open. The borrowed trousers were loose at the waist. She kissed his mouth, his neck, inside his shirt. She was naked under the uniform. His hands slid down to her hips and he knelt with his head against her thighs. She wriggled out of the trousers and his mouth brushed inside her legs, over her belly. Then he was standing again, watching her face pale in the light from outside. All constraint vanished. There was a sweet inevitability in the way they slowly finished undressing one another, in the way they sank whispering together to the floor. She drew him down upon her, raised her legs to embrace him, crossed her ankles against his firm back and soon had locked herself to his rhythm, compelling him into her. From this first moment of physical love came a strange and magical union. "Words," she said softly. "I need words." And the words he had never been able to speak before, he now could speak to her. She felt his armor dissolve in the friction of words and bodies, felt the old fears explode in spurts of such relief that she thought a spear of fire plunged out of his own carapace of ice, piercing the scutum that once threatened to thicken between them. For a long time after, their bodies still trembled with renewed eruptions. "The colors!" she cried out. "Oh, my darling! Don't you see? Such light! Such incredible colors!"

They fashioned a bed from old drapes and cushions. There they made love again. They drifted into a sleep so deep, it was as if they never had slept before. They awoke together, suddenly aware of how close they had come to losing each other. They were filled with a fresh and magical energy. They made love, talked, slept, made love. Talbott said, "Rebecca wrote in her diary about a man who wanted to love the whole human race when all she wanted was to have him love a single human being." Sally stirred, laughed, dozed. She said, "You should have heeded your mother sooner." They seemed to laugh a lot, quietly, in total certainty about each other.

And then Sally abruptly raised her head from his chest. "Where is the diary now?"

"With Yuri Gorin."

He heard her gasp.

"Don't worry," said Talbott. "If he's the Radzki my mother loved, he'll bring it with him."

She listened to Big Ben boom the hours like a countdown to that critical two minutes of silence for dead warriors. She snuggled against the man who had always put the camera between himself and others; who'd cut himself off, the way he had locked shut the hood of a fighter cockpit against ugly home truths. He had left himself so little time to know and love just one person.

She must have drifted off. Suddenly Talbott was gripping her arm. She saw a tall figure. It was a man, silhouetted against the light slanting up from a distant corridor so that his fedora seemed out of proportion. The lines from Ibsen entered her head: ". . . there's a hat—black, huge . . . You put it on, and then no one on earth can see you!"

She stood up, more angry than apprehensive.

She felt Talbott touch her, warning her. But it was too late. The tall figure turned sideways to the lighted doorway. He hissed her name.

"Fishhook!"

"Thank God! Where are you, Sally?" His head moved blindly in her direction. "Is Talbott there?"

She ignored the second question, covered herself, and rushed to greet the former FBI man. "I was so worried."

"Not as worried as we've been. After you ran from the embassy—" He began to talk. He talked too much. It didn't seem like Fishhook to be so talkative. Then he said, "I suppose Talbott's hot on the story?"

She volunteered nothing, though it went against years of trust and affection. Fishhook had watched over Grandpa Massey with a loyalty that expected no reward. But it was just this loyalty to Quex that worried her.

He was searching for a light switch. "You shouldn't be here in darkness."

She caught his arm. "A light's dangerous. And close that door! How did you find me?"

"The Blitz Kids." Fishhook chuckled. Again Sally had to resist confiding to him. Dear harmless Fishhook, who never spoke much but always made her feel safe. The corridor light vanished as he closed the door and leaned against the wall. "The kids reported to Nelson!"

Furniture scraped. Talbott disentangled himself from the junk pile and said, "Well, welcome to the bosom of Nelson's family."

Fishhook betrayed no surprise. "I kind of sensed you'd be around," he said. "You were right to distrust us. We tried every trick in the book to get Sally out of danger. We were hampered by the fact she's in a free country! That's why we tried the office recall. The Agency had finally gotten round to telling us. Your Jake Cooke's a fraud. We couldn't say anything while you were in the embassy, Sally, without tipping off the Israelis—"

"*What?*"

"Top-level order. Trust nobody."

"Not even trust your own common sense?" demanded Sally.

"That went out the window with mutual aid between departments,"

Fishhook said bitterly. "You can snarl up any bureaucracy with petty jealousies. When you stir up mutual suspicion within the institutions of intelligence, you get a gridlock."

"So Parson Furneval told me. He said all you had to know was where the central switchboard was, and then even a chimpanzee could create chaos."

"The Rev's a good deal better at it than a chimpanzee," said Fishhook, and stopped. "The parson! Where did you find the parson?"

"I think you'd better tell me your parson story first," suggested Sally.

Fishhook had been on a fishing expedition. "Get the Boffin before he's bumped off," Nelson had advised him.

The Boffin was a back-room expert on the Nazi years. He lived in an alcoholic haze in a run-down cottage some forty miles northwest of London, near Bletchley. He knew more about the breaking of Deputy Fuehrer Hess than was good for his health.

Fishhook arrives after dark, parks his rented car in a lane, hotfoots it through fields to the cottage. A young woman astride a bicycle plants herself in front of him. "There's no point you seeing him," she says. "He's sick. Sick in the head."

Fishhook can already see a yellow light shining from the cottage. He steps around the woman, who adds, "My orders are to stop you."

Fishhook gets his dander up at this and charges along the footpath, calling the Boffin by name.

"Heyho!" croaks a head in the window. "The Redcoats are coming!"

Fishhook gives an answering whoop. This schoolboyish routine originated during the war when his English colleague analyzed ULTRA intelligence and Fishhook relayed certain segments. Their pranks relieved the tension. Now the Boffin shouts to the woman, "Dammit, you silly bitch, unbolt this door!"

Fishhook sees the door is locked on the outside. There are bars over the windows. He stands in absolute fury. With Fishhook, silent rage is like a thunderclap.

The woman nervously slips the bolts. "If things turn ugly," she says, "it will be on your own head." And away she goes.

The Boffin ushers Fishhook into a patched apology for an armchair in front of a sad little coal fire. There are books stacked all around, files and folders spilling their contents over the tatty carpet.

"Heard you'd be coming. Got a call," says the Boffin. "That's how they knew. They read my mail, tap my phone. But they give me unlimited booze and fags." A cigarette hangs from his thick lower lip. He shuffles to a bookshelf crowded with bottles and dirty glasses. He blows the dust out of one glass and hands it to Fishhook together with a bottle of scotch. "Your favorite tipple," he says, slumping into another decrepit chair on the other side of the smoking fire.

So far, Fishhook sees no evidence to support an insanity plea. The Boffin is sloshing back brandy. He's half-seas over, but then he always was. He functions best that way. So Fishhook comes straight to the point. "An American TV producer named Bronfmann was killed recently—"

Before he gets any further, the Boffin starts clucking. "Dear oh dear oh dear! I'm most awfully sorry. I quite liked Bronfmann."

"You saw him?" Fishhook almost shot out of his chair. "I'm surprised he got through that woman's guard."

"She brought him to me!" The Boffin begins searching around his tiny island of papers. Then he gets up and gives the fire a savage poke. Fishhook knows this is the time to stay silent. Let the Boffin ramble along his own path. "Funny thing, old boy," says the Boffin, "is that I'm supposed to be loony. Yet they send me this Bronfmann—a mere lad—to sit at my feet and listen."

The Boffin flops down again, lights another cigarette, tosses back more brandy. "Maybe I'm nutty as a fruitcake, but they still need what I've got up here." He taps the side of his head. "That silly bitch, she's my keeper. We get pissed at the Dunscombe Arms some nights when she takes me out on the leash. The locals grin and nudge. Can't beat the local English yokel when it comes to a dirty mind. They think I'm having it off with my secretary." He puffs away, tosses back another slug. "In a way, I suppose she is. My secretary, I mean. See, nobody digs up dirt the way I can. They send me old reports, mostly out of the Soviet bloc. I go through this stuff like a regular little termite. Munch, munch! Scribble, scribble! Then they take away my notes, just like Hess."

Fishhook lets him prattle on. You can never rush the Boffin. His mind works in mysterious ways.

"What Bronfmann wanted was—I think he said 'background'—concerning the flirtation between the Duke of Windsor and the Nazis. Told him it was that woman from Baltimore. She was at the bottom of it—that Mrs. Simpson. She'd snaffled the King of England only to see him forced to abdicate because he'd married beneath him. She shared his exile in Paris and dreamed of ending it with a vengeance—as Queen. She saw Hitler as her ally. All Hitler feared was the Brits, and after France fell, he could call off the invasion if he'd got a popular King to put back on the throne of England. The ex-King and Mrs. Simpson escaped from Paris for neutral Lisbon, where negotiations could take place . . . *But!* They were only fools, not traitors. So some say."

The Boffin leans forward and his voice is little more than a whisper. "And so our government becomes party to what some have called a foolish and wicked conspiracy. But you tell me if it really was something nasty in the Gothic line."

Fishhook has to strain to hear the rest. The wind howls in the chimney.

There is a dusty smell from the nearby brickfields. The brick dust tickles his throat and the Boffin is convulsed by bursts of coughing. But he concludes his disclosures. Fishhook can hardly believe what he hears.

"So there you are. That's how Hitler was kept on the hook," says the Boffin, his voice suddenly clear again. "All through the danger period, from the Battle of Britain right up until Hess flies over here and Hitler turns round and attacks Russia. All those months when he could have invaded Britain, he didn't.

"All the documents are still to come. London's waiting. I go through the stuff. When it's all put together, they'll destroy it."

Fishhook asks, "Where would you be getting more documentation?"

"Soviets. For a long time we knew they'd grabbed a lot of Nazi intelligence archives . . . German and Russian secret services intertwined even after the war broke out. Moscow and Berlin mechanically exchanged intelligence for nearly two more years! That's when Szmuel Radzki got his start."

Fishhook almost crushes his whisky glass.

"It's what I told Bronfmann," says the Boffin, his face a picture of innocence, his thick lower lip dribbling slightly.

Then the front door of the cottage bursts open. The woman with the bicycle has returned with some imposing young men dressed as medical orderlies. The Boffin rises and says with great dignity, "You don't have to behave like gorillas, you chaps. I'll come quietly."

Fishhook makes menacing gestures and the Boffin says quickly, "Please, old friend, don't waste energy. These young gentlemen feed me my pills. I'm still on license from the local loony bin. They pop me back inside if old friends get too—ah, friendly."

They are all waiting for Fishhook to leave. He feels compelled to chance his one and only question. "Who sent Bronfmann to you?"

"Marcus Furneval," says the Boffin with infuriating serenity. "He's the Big Bwana who runs this nuthouse."

Fishhook Sherman tried to sense the significance of the long silence which followed.

Talbott opened a window to let in the cold night air. The soft murmur of London traffic sounded so safe, so *normal.*

Finally Sally said, "Your Boffin, then, put the notion into Bronfmann's head to go to the Soviet embassy."

"And the parson panicked," put in Talbott. "Furneval's run the Hess deception from the start. Not for Russia. For the East Germans, the new zealots of Marxism."

"Did *he* have Bronfmann killed?" asked Fishhook.

"Can't have been planned that way," said Talbott. "Bronfmann was grabbed for what he might have found out. He was killed to give the new Marxists and the old Nazis a grip on me."

Fishhook froze by the window, counting four solemn notes from Big Ben. It sounded like Marx-ists! Naz-is! He'd always said they were opposite sides of the same coin. The old FBI way would be to clamp the manacles on comrade-fuehrer Furneval. Instead, the softheaded forces of law and order were letting Furneval orchestrate security for tomorrow— No! Today . . .

Seven hours to go. Fishhook bent his big frame, braced his arms, leaned out.

A bleached pumpkin bobbed among the frosted winter cabbages. It squeaked, "Mr. Sherman!" The round blob became a boy's face. "You'd better come out," said the boy. "We've found the way in."

" 'Out'?" Talbott appeared at Fishhook's side. " 'In'?"

Fishhook straightened. "He means the way in to the Churchill war rooms."

"The war rooms?" echoed Sally. "They run under the Cenotaph, don't they! Of course . . . Humidor-ashtray! Wait a minute!" she cautioned Fishhook, who was clearing his throat to add something. "Churchill put it in the secret underground war rooms."

"Put what?" Talbott almost screamed.

"A gift from the Zionists." She quoted slowly from Churchill's memoirs. *"The Hebrews showed their gratitude by carving me such a fine humidor-ashtray."*

44

London: Sunday, Remembrance Day, dawn

There is no easy way into the Churchill war rooms, one of the best-kept secrets of World War II. For forty-five years after the Battle of Britain, only a privileged few could descend to the eleven miles of tunneling. Another twenty-three miles of subterranean passages remain closed to the public even today. Scarcely anyone, lacking certain security passes, penetrates beyond the central complex. This stretches beneath Whitehall between King Charles Street, No. 10 Downing Street, and out towards Buckingham Palace.

Some of the support beams come from Admiral Lord Nelson's last ship. Parts of the labyrinth date back two hundred years, to when Samuel Pepys was secretary to the Admiralty. During bad nights of bombing, Churchill would escape his guardians and come up to contemplate Admiral Nelson on his column, triumphant above the havoc.

Today, nothing below has changed much. In the map room, Churchill's flags and notes still cover walls and desks. There is the telephone cubicle where Churchill would make his calls to President Roosevelt: the booth was disguised as a toilet, and whenever Churchill sat inside, he slid the bolt to ENGAGED. Five hundred men and women once worked in the tunnels per shift and knew little about one another's existence.

There are stories today about missing persons. A platoon of Queen's

Guards is still said to have been swallowed up in a further network of tunnels extending under the Thames to Waterloo. Ghosts are reported. It is unsettling to come across names on the original blotting pads, marking the places where the war cabinet sat: Mr. Churchill, Mr. Eden, Lord Ismay, Mr. Attlee . . . Pages are still pasted on the walls, hastily torn out of school geography books in the emergency of 1940, when no large-scale maps of Europe seemed to be handy. The aura of the great man hovers in the monastic cell where Churchill slept. The bedroom holds very little except his public-works iron cot and the Hebrews' humidor-ashtray.

Nelson of the Yard knew the war rooms only too well. Sealed within that subterranean world is what is called the Yellow Submarine, although its true name is seldom spoken: the Data Center. This is limited to three layers of modernized passageways where certain intelligence data are absorbed, digested, and fed into the compressed and highly miniaturized files of computer technology. It is all very sophisticated and, Nelson suspected, would have driven Churchill up a tree. The center is buried under the Foreign Office. As far as Nelson was concerned, that was where it could remain. He belonged to the old school, like Churchill, who, being asked where some item of information could be found, would point to a ceiling-high stack of papers and say, "Two feet and some four inches up from the bottom."

Nelson was in his real element now, his peaked cap down over his eyes and his raincoat collar up, leaning between busts of Admirals Jellicoe and Beatty, against the south wall of Trafalgar Square. A false dawn smudged the sky when he saw Sally, Talbott and the lanky figure of Fishhook loping behind two small boys.

"I've had an old entrance opened," Nelson said without preliminaries. "This way." The odd little procession darted under the massive Admiralty Arch, where more statuary repeated the theme of naval power and glory. "We've learned more," he told Talbott, "about your imposter, Kraaft. He fooled the real Jake's followers, too. He's the product of the 88 all right. He's also figured out parts of the Auschwitz Index."

"How'd you know all this?" asked Talbott.

"General Pamir. His contacts and the Radzki material completed the picture. The 88 planned to use the old underground war rooms ever since they learned how Radzki briefed pilots down there for the raid on Spandau."

Suddenly Talbott understood his confused reaction to the photograph of Radzki shown him at the No-Man's-Land Tuckshop. It must have been taken on the eve of Radzki's last mission for the West. And Talbott had been there, in circumstances so strange he'd never come face to face with the courier-agent. He stopped dead in his tracks. Nelson had to give him a tug. "No time for meditation," Nelson grunted. "You can have your post-mortem after the action!"

A tarpaulin billowed in a chill wind blowing up from the Thames. Guy lines creaked and twanged; support poles swayed. The contraption had been improvised to look like a road crew's tent, but it inflated and sighed with the black menace of a roped monster. Nelson lifted a flap. "Through there's an old tunnel." He shone a lamp on a patch of wall with an inset steel door.

Ginger appeared at Talbott's elbow. "That bloke wiv the beard you called Jake," he said. " 'E took 'is men into them tunnels."

"Kraaft," Sally corrected him mechanically. "Remember what I told you? His real name's Kraaft."

Nelson said, "And the real Jake's your responsibility, miss." He tugged papers from his pocket. "These are phony credentials for you and Talbott. It's dangerous but I've no choice. You'll search aboveground for Jake, and me and Fishhook are going down there."

Talbott crouched beside the tarpaulin with Nelson's shaded flashlight. With half an ear, he heard Nelson say, "Start looking by the Cenotaph. He'll be there, either above or below."

By then Talbott was lost in helpless anger. He was holding a two-page outline stamped REMEMBRANCE DAY with the crest of the Home Office, Queen Anne's Gate. At the bottom, he read:

"11:02 A.M. The firing of a gun marks the end of the Silence. The Last Post is sounded by buglers of the Royal Marines . . ."

Every second of the ceremony was laid out! A guide for bomb throwers. Drawn up like a military operation. Like the Charge of the Light Brigade, gallant but suicidally out of date. Nothing would reverse these orders now except a declaration of war.

He read from the top of the Order of Procession and his blood ran cold. **"LEAVE THE FORMER HOME OFFICE FRONT DOOR AT 10:55 A.M.,"** it declared.

"The letter 'W' indicates bearer of Wreath to Cenotaph . . . Leave the Whitehall building 10:59 A.M. in the order shown:

"HM The Queen . . ."

In utter disbelief, Talbott read on. Even the United Nations, on the most solemn occasions, never assembled its political stars under open skies. Here, apparently inserted at the last moment, were leaders of the old Grand Alliance against the great dictators. Here were admirals and generals, dukes and princes. The Chief Rabbi and leaders of Christian faiths . . .

And the Queen.

Talbott thought of Bomber Harris and his Target Information lists. He glanced through the names of Commonwealth countries and imagined the market for terrorist weapons among the malcontents that dwelled there, and the targets their representatives would make.

And . . . the Queen.

He saw the precise instructions for the royals: "Then the Queen lays a wreath . . . The Duke of Edinburgh . . . The Prince of Wales lays a wreath on the left of her Majesty's . . . The Duke of Kent on the right . . ." Here were all the glamour names: Princess Diana, the Queen Mother, Prince Andrew, Michael of Kent . . .

The Leader of the Loyal Opposition.

"Prayer will be offered by the Bishop of London: 'O God our help in ages past' will be sung, accompanied by the Massed Bands of the Guards Division . . . Trumpeters of the Royal Air Force . . ."

Talbott felt Nelson studying his reactions.

"It reads like an operational briefing for terrorists," said Talbott. "You'd think Furneval wrote it!"

Nelson heaved up a grim chuckle. "It's done every year! You can't make the Queen change *that* routine out of a fear of bombers. She'd say it was surrender." Nelson handed over another sheaf of paper. "All this bumf goes into general circulation too."

Talbott read: SPECIAL BRITISH ARMY DISTRICT ORDER. There were seventy-eight sections, naming military, security and special units, each one's location, and where and how each would proceed. It began: "Watches will be synchronized with Post Office time (dial 123) not later than 0900 hours."

"If I were you, and Scotland Yard," said Talbott, "the first thing I'd do is make sure the enemy hasn't sabotaged the Post Office."

This time Nelson's chuckle was genuine. "Don't think I didn't."

There was no need to synchronize watches for Sally and Talbott. The buzz of humanity, the rattle of drums, the screech of gears as big sightseeing charabancs squeezed into parking lanes, the flash of cavalry swords, jingle of spurs and hooting of riverboats, made Big Ben's voice more insistent. The hour of nine struck when Talbott decided to risk moving with the crowds. As Nelson said, two Americans wanted for questioning were unlikely to stop traffic now. Londoners were turning out as never before. Rumors of terrorist action sharpened their appetite for drama.

Talbott had already made one quick survey of the Cenotaph, leaving Sally in Trafalgar Square. By daybreak, the uniformed and auxiliary police were stuck in a thick treacle of pedestrians. Few sightseers knew that under their feet was a township once servicing the Churchill war rooms, or that the Cenotaph was only the dazzling white tip of an iceberg. Those who remembered the underground war rooms did not always know that only a small part of the township was open to a limited public, and now remained closed.

He fought his way back to Sally, trapped between the four famous Landseer lions which crouch beneath the bas-reliefs cast from guns captured by Admiral Lord Nelson. Near a statue of King George IV, improbably barefoot and riding his horse bareback in a toga, Talbott answered Sally's question "Why did the Hebrews show Churchill their gratitude?"

It is the last days of Hitler. Churchill and Roosevelt consider who should run postwar Germany. There must be some good Germans left? Yes, locked in Spandau. "Then, get them out!" Churchill orders.

The project is so secret, Radzki briefs the specially selected pilots in the place known only to Churchill and his staff.

Talbott remembers arriving at the Citadel, the Royal Navy's bombproof headquarters, and going down fortress steps, through dummy portals, to a deep chamber smelling of damp earth. The light there falls on scale models of the jail and Berlin. The speaker is in darkness, unrecognized by Talbott, who thinks Radzki's dead.

In truth, Radzki is now risking his life again to help bomb Spandau. For the release, not of Jews, but of Germans.

As it turns out, the operation is scrubbed. The bombing of Spandau is made unnecessary by the fall of Berlin.

And Radzki is left to reflect on the irony.

He is grateful to Churchill, though. Churchill, near the end of the war, agrees to arm the Jews and even give them their own flag. Churchill also rounds upon his bomber chief for razing German cities "simply for the sake of increasing the terror, though under other pretexts."

So Radzki is grateful. He could not stop Bomber Harris from terror-bombing; he could not persuade him to bomb for humanity's sake the machinery for mass murder. But Harris did get his knuckles rapped when it was all over.

And Radzki is grateful.

"Kraaft knows all this," Sally told Talbott. "He was heard talking about 'humidor-ashtray.' The code words must have been adopted by the real Jake Cooke. But it was Kraaft and Furneval who spoke of 'doing a Guy Fawkes' on the Cenotaph. So the 88 and their Libyans must be in the underground tunnels."

And above them, thought Talbott, Yuri Gorin will stand, the Radzki they're hunting.

The Cenotaph and the processional way became briefly visible to Talbott as police lines forced apart the growing crowds. The uniformed police wore traditional bobbies' helmets. Behind crouched riot police with space-age visors, neck armor and shields. He saw the symbols of the past vanishing under the exigencies of modern street warfare. Whitehall, arena for state ceremonial, would in the next few hours present an ancient spectacle born out of the great institutions evolved in the chaos of democracy. Those institutions had survived the worst that dictators could throw at them. Now a handful of fanatics were forcing change. Between Londoners and their cherished emblems intervened police who were heavily armed for the first time in history; between cockney kids on an outing and the Household Cavalry stood cameras ready to shoot scenes of riot to satellites in space. "And if there's a massacre," he said, "the Jews will be blamed on television . . . but they'll have the consolation of knowing it was in the greatest pomp and circumstance."

New York City: Sunday, 4 A.M.

"Mr. Sol Farkas?" asked the London operator. "I have a collect call from a Mr. Jake Cooke. Will you accept?"

The network vice president tried to gather his wits. "Yes, I'll accept."

During the long pause that followed, Sol rubbed his face, twisted in his chair, and stared down at the lights reflected in the Hudson River beneath his office. He was keeping a self-assigned night watch and had fallen asleep over his desk.

"They call me the killer of Deir Yassin," said a voice that sounded at first familiar.

"They call me the killer of Deir Yassin," the man had said who came to see Sol Farkas in great secrecy on the day Talbott left for Düsseldorf. Such a long time ago, it seemed now. "You knew the truth. Why didn't you speak up?"

Sol had never spoken up for a very good reason. He had been at Deir Yassin during the struggle for a Jewish national home. He was also an American with no wish to lose his citizenship, for he was still technically in the U.S. Army Reserve after serving in the American OSS intelligence war against Hitler. He had sensed no conflict in lending his skills to the Jewish underground fighting to create Israel. It seemed in keeping with the moral aims of the world war just ended and a logical transition from his last wartime assignment. Sol had been the last-minute replacement in a team of Jewish agents to be parachuted into East Europe . . . Operation Citadel. He was pulled from the mission suddenly by a senior American officer who gave no explanation.

Sol was told later by Menachem Begin, who would eventually become Prime Minister of Israel, that it was never intended to have anyone return from Citadel. All the other agents were said to have been labeled "troublemakers" by Lord Moyne, and the story condemned him to death. It was the key to Sol's rejection of the lovely belief in an Israel designed only to be the repository of spiritual values, an Israel eschewing all militarism in any form. He decided Israel could be born only out of violence and must be preserved through military vigilance.

In 1948, three years after the death camps were overrun by Allied armies, he was defending Jerusalem against marauders. A night attack in April was launched against the suburbs by Arab guerrillas using Deir Yassin as a base. The New York *Times* reported "these peaceful villagers" had been "massacred by terrorists." The terrorists were said to be Irgun or Stern Gang. Sol saw things differently. His unit had been ambushed by

Arabs. The rescue was led by Jacob Slominsky. The distorted stories bandied abroad, the public outcry against Jewish self-defense, made Sol understand the peculiar burden placed upon the Jews; they must earn non-Jewish respect by suffering, not by striking back.

Sol had seen no sense risking his American birthright by raising a stink. If he went to the newspapers with his own account as a participant, they would issue no corrections. But he *would* catch the attention of authorities in Washington! Deir Yassin was a one-day sensation. His would be a belated, solitary voice, endangering only himself.

Sol said as much to his unexpected visitor all those years later. The man had listened politely, and Sol began to see how lame his excuses must sound to tough old veterans of the Menachem Begin school. Sol therefore added self-righteously that he had once again returned to believing Jews survived the centuries of persecution in order to lead humanity in the ways of the Lord.

His visitor merely observed dryly that this high-minded philosophy permitted Hitler to very nearly wipe out the Jewish people. He showed Sol what appeared to be highly classified Israeli intelligence documents. These traced negotiations between the Nazis and the British, after which Hitler turned his armies against Russia instead of across the English Channel. The visitor talked about Hess, and so on. The thing that got Sol most of all was the report on Operation Citadel.

The caller from London spoke in the same dry manner Sol remembered.

"Where's Talbott?" Sol demanded as soon as his mind began to work again. "What's happening there? Are the 88 going ahead?"

Jake Cooke tried to dam the flow of questions. "Just listen if you want to stop a catastrophe a million times worse than Deir Yassin!"

"No, you listen!" Sol's eyes were bulging now. "Every other network's packed London. I've got two crews stuck at Heathrow, delayed by security. My best man's vanished. I've a story I can't use—"

"Shutup!" cut in Jake. "You'll get Talbott and the biggest story of his life, provided you do as you're told! I can't talk long. This is what you do."

Afterwards, Sol moved down to the control center. Some reporters on the graveyard shift had drifted in to watch the banked monitors. Sol in his old gray rolltop sweater and faded jeans looked more like the building janitor than the vice president of news and public affairs. The newsmen admired Sol's nose for trouble. He had moved in before on big, fast-breaking stories. His confident presence was welcome reassurance for the producer of any news special.

"Any call from England, I'll take on this phone," Sol told the night news editor. "The switchboard's already alerted. Any call out I make gets priority. Understood?"

"Sure thing," the night editor said loyally. Then they both looked up as image and sound came over the test feed from London. The noise and confusion made Sol's heart thump, but his seamed face showed nothing. In the cold blue light from the TV monitors, he seemed to be carved from granite.

The old war-horse smells the battle from afar, the night editor told himself comfortably. He would have felt less confident if he had known what was going on inside Sol's head.

45

The Cenotaph: Midmorning

A woman in the crowd plucked Talbott's arm. "Get over to the remotes." She pointed to a dish antenna rising like a white daisy against the sooty-walled Treasury. "Jake's orders!" She was gone before he could catch her arm. He freed Sally from a mob of grannies, small children and what seemed a spearhead of suddenly mobilized perambulators. He steered by the dish, forcing a passage, waving the forged press passes to break through security around the BBC's outside-broadcast vans. The passes were made out to Baron von Bülow and wife, of the Vienna News Center. The crisis had drawn too many newsmen for the police to check each one. Nelson had imprinted the false names on official ID cards. Talbott gave him full marks for imagination, and hoped their luck would hold. His face, familiar when seen on the screen, seldom drew attention in the street; and since Bronfmann's death, Talbott had been so little exposed that recognition was unlikely. People seldom associate a professional image with one randomly encountered far from its habitat. But Talbott was now back in that environment.

The remotes were drawn up like a circle of wagons. Each remote beamed directly to a satellite. The BBC had pooled resources with commercial rivals to help meet overseas demand for live coverage. Two American networks had flown in entire satellite ground stations. Talbott looked

in vain for his own network logo, then paused to watch a stand-upper delivered by one BBC man he had last seen in Egypt.

"The Sovereign's exclusive rights include the right to *warn*," the reporter told several million viewers. "The Queen may well have decided to exercise this right, with the world in one of the worst crises since the Second World War. Her Majesty's possibly unique invitation to Soviet leader Yuri Gorin met with an astonishing response, offering a first glimmer of hope. Gorin arrived a short time ago at Heathrow Airport, within minutes of the President of the United States . . ."

On the monitor, the BBC's man faded into close-ups of the American President shaking hands with the Soviet leader.

". . . unique gesture of goodwill on the part of President Donovan, who waited at the airport for Gorin," continued the BBC commentary. "The Queen, for her part, seems to have taken a lead to break the deadlock. This is rare, given the complicated metaphysics of Britain's limited monarchy. We go now to Lord Cromer, an authority . . ."

Talbott and Sally broke away. The fairground atmosphere intensified with the striking of the tenth hour from Big Ben. Reporters barked into temporary phones hooked under wooden benches.

"Scotty!"

The network's London bureau chief shouldered his way through. "Sol Farkas is having a fit! This way. We're holding an open circuit . . ." They had set up near the St. James's Park end of Downing Street. "We're expecting trouble—" The bureau chief grinned suddenly. "Nothing like the trouble I hear *you're* in." He swept Talbott into the mobile studio.

As if nothing had happened since Talbott had last spoken with him in Berlin, Sol Farkas came booming through: "You'll anchor the show when we go live. We'll clear tonight for a special. Focus on Jake Cooke—"

Talbott tried to interrupt. The circuit began to break up each time he spoke. Normally, it was clear as a bell between London and New York. Finally he cursed whoever was interfering, suspecting it was Sol himself, avoiding backchat. "You'll look pretty stupid," he finally yelled, "if I get arrested on air!"

The answer came through without interference. "If you do, it'll be dynamite! But you won't. They've all got bigger fish to fry!"

"We've lost Jake Cooke," said Talbott, dropping his voice.

"I just spoke with him." Sol, too, was suddenly cautious. "Go to the yardman with the blind eye." He cut the connection.

Talbott was angry with frustration when he rejoined Sally. Some of the technicians watched him with open curiosity.

"What the hell's Sol mean?" he asked Sally when they were away from the unit.

"The yard? Scotland Yard. So the yardman is . . . Nelson? The man who turned a blind eye was Admiral Nelson, whose statue we were under. So *our* man's in Trafalgar Square, waiting."

"What if he's Kraaft?" demanded Talbott. "Not Jake?"

"Sol just spoke to him," Sally said reasonably. "Sol wouldn't get it wrong."

The news vendor stomped his feet, blew through his fingers, and once in a while shouted, "Read orl abaht it! More Hess revelations!" He stood in the sunken square beside an empty billboard. He had no newspapers to sell, but the passing crowds were in too great a hurry to notice. He had his eyes fixed on a man leaning over the street railings above the Landseer lion to the right. The man suddenly straightened up and very slowly took off his bright blue parka.

Talbott was in the square.

The news vendor flapped his arms in a show of keeping warm. He wore a woolen Balaclava helmet. A war-surplus army greatcoat cloaked him from neck to knees. In the old days of the Jewish underground, he had been called a master of disguise. Suddenly, without appearing to direct the words to anyone in particular, he said, "Little Idiot! Shalom!"

These words had a startling effect on Sally. She said, appearing to address the wall, "Talbott, this is the real Jake. I guarantee it."

"Better you call me Jacob," said the news vendor.

"I should have known the difference," said Talbott.

"Never mind. Kraaft has all the resources of the state to perfect his illusions," said Jacob.

"What will he do now?"

"He's already taken charge of the 88's local forces. They'll shove the Hess Command down the world's throat."

"Can we stop them, Jacob?"

"*We*, Mr. Talbott? Your best hope is to pretend to cooperate."

"So your Israelis still think Kraaft's for real?"

"No." Jacob was silent for a moment, as if mulling over how much to tell. "No, my men know what to do. *If* I give the order. I'm not sure we should." He paused dramatically. "I've just learned . . . *Mother is Radzki!*"

"Yes," Talbott responded impatiently.

"Radzki's a Jewish traitor."

"Radzki's *with* you!" Talbott said urgently.

"So they tried to convince me." Again Jacob hesitated. "At our embassy. I don't necessarily trust embassies."

Sally leaned back against the granite wall and closed her eyes in near despair. The real Jacob had been found. A terrible danger should be ended. Instead, Jacob was seizing on the one devastating truth hidden from him until now. He misread its meaning. Who could have enlightened him at this, the worst possible moment? General Steely Pamir? It seemed unlikely. The Israeli counterterror expert knew Jacob's philosophy of terror against terror too well. Pamir would be frightened of Jacob's going off half-

cocked, a grenade on a short fuse. The Kyrya in Tel-Aviv? Jacob would
have no trouble reaching his own sources there without using Pamir's
embassy or other resources. Jacob had shown her the tricks of the trade,
years before, perfected from the inspirations of Haifa's air-force technical
students. Public phones were designed for making free and untraceable
calls overseas, if you had a bit of plastic and a match folder.

Somehow, Jacob had been brought up to date. By someone who shared
his belief that all rules can be broken to keep faith with that extra commandment added to the 613 Jewish biblical precepts: *Don't give Hitler a
posthumous victory.* What he didn't understand was that Radzki had broken more rules, taken greater risks, than anyone—in order to keep the
commandment!

Sally threw caution aside. "Talbott just *talked* with Radzki!"

"I've just flown to the moon," said Jacob.

"Didn't General Pamir tell you?" she pleaded.

"If he knew, he wouldn't."

She saw an opening. "You know about Talbott's mother, Rebecca. She
kept a diary. Talbott's entrusted that diary to Radzki. *There's* your proof."

"And all I do is walk up to the Soviet President and ask to see it?"
Jacob lifted his right hand as if reaching for the sky. "You must think I'm
God's fool."

Talbott stretched to see whom Jacob was signaling. Sally had already
spotted a man. He was a screever, a pavement artist, removing a sign tied
to the railings on the porch of the National Gallery, opposite. He was far
across the square but placed high above the crowds and easily seen.

When they swung back to face Jacob, he was gone.

"Quick!" Talbott began to fight through the mass of people. Strong
hands grasped him. Cold steel brushed his cheek. He swiveled round. A
young man raised a pistol, so close it was likely to escape general notice.
Another man hemmed in Sally. The crowd, good-natured and almost fes-
tive, might as well be a million miles away behind the sudden barrier of
four dangerous men who had Talbott and Sally boxed in. "Stick with us,"
said the first. "It's time to get below."

There seemed no way to stop the mechanism. It was like the timer on a
bomb. The crowds ticked away the seconds. The four men used the flow of
the crowd as boatmen use a river's current. The general noise was deafen-
ing enough to cover a quick exchange between Talbott and Sally.

"You *sure* that was the real Jacob?" asked Talbott.

"Absolutely. You didn't hear what he called me?"

"What?"

"He used a term nobody else would know," she shouted. *"Little idiot.* It
means something else in Hebrew—"

Then their escorts pulled them apart.

The sun broke through the wintry blanket of cloud as if to herald the
circus. Cavalry horses clopped through the narrow lane still left open from

the Mall. Big police horses backed into the crowd. Helmets glittered. Banners bobbed above the people's heads. Talbott thought he glimpsed the big black busbies of Scots guardsmen nodding along a parapet of the Citadel. He was sure he heard the skirl of bagpipes.

Suddenly they were standing in front of the same public-works shelter. The first man opened the flap as unconcernedly as a pickpocket lifts the flap of a pocket, with the same contempt based on the same sure knowledge of the general obliviousness of huge crowds.

Sally went in first. Talbott followed, down the old wartime steps through three levels, down to a dark tunnel. Above, the circus was coming. Are we the clowns? he wondered. He felt Sally's hand reach for his. Then they were separated again, to move in single file through narrow doorways and low-ceilinged tunnels. Ducts belched air from the bulbous vents. There was a chamber lit by a few naked bulbs. Its walls were of compacted earth. Old air-raid warnings were still suspended from pneumatic message tubes. A poison-gas alarm dangled from a beam. More men joined them: some slid along narrow benches, sitting before a small, backlit stage. Others sidled through to another exit tunnel. Talbott and Sally were made to perch on a bench at the back of the cramped chamber.

Somebody was speaking. Talbott thought he heard, or perhaps he remembered: "In the morning, everywhere, the solemn two-minute silence . . . It fell like an enchantment: indoors and out, no one spoke, nothing moved: the cars and buses and drays in the streets halted, the carts in the lanes, the cowman in the stall stood still." The words were written by Richard Hughes, playwright, novelist. Was someone reading them or were they another echo from the past? "Nothing moved . . . Nothing moved . . ."

The Soviet leader stood below the great white stele of the Cenotaph. This is *our* memorial too, he thought. He removed his fur hat with the first booming note from Big Ben. "On the first stroke," he had read in the Queen's guide, "the Two Minutes Silence will commence."

The Queen had "graciously invited" him to share the small square of macadam where normally she stood in isolation. He reflected that he could have used some of that graciousness forty years ago. He held in his mind's eye the position of each ECLIPSE operative. They were easily identifiable by their suntanned faces among the granite-faced members of the Soviet military team, resplendent in dress uniform. The British, rather primly he thought, had admitted them into the ranks of princes, prime ministers and plenipotentiaries behind Queen Elizabeth. The American President was removed from Yuri Gorin by a distance of several paces to the rear. Gorin could not turn to see President Donovan. Nor could he see beyond the first rank of dignitaries, or he would have been shocked by the presence of Quex, the man supposedly eclipsed. But Gorin did not need eyes in the

back of his head to sense the tension. These British expected something untoward.

Yet, thought Gorin, they behave as if a power greater than themselves leads them, a power they mistake for tradition. They had walked out, the Queen with Gorin at her side, and behind them the members of the family. To Gorin, told they were placed in order of line of succession, they seemed a banal lot until he recognized the Princess Michael of Kent, whose father had been a member of Hitler's SS. It struck him then that the Queen was not one to yield to blackmail. She had ensured that her family closed ranks about a young woman who had been the target of attacks unconnected with her personal morality.

Yuri Gorin dragged his attention away from such historical anachronisms. He saw his duty clear. His own past fitted at last into a symmetrical whole. All his operational necessities had brought him to this moment. Two minutes! A meager ration of hope in a century of despair.

The Queen, such a tiny figure in black, stood alone at a chalk mark in the roadway. Gorin remembered another mark casually drawn to inform an earlier monarch where to kneel before the ax. If this queen died here, a multitude would bear witness. He had assessed the television cameras peering from buildings and roving above the processional way.

Up Whitehall now throbbed the long boom of Big Ben striking the eleventh hour. Looking down on crowds so densely packed they resembled fields of corn, Sky-Roamer cameras showed what seemed a giant scythe reaping the harvest of heads bent in prayer. The heart of the kingdom stopped. The scythe would move with the sun across nations drawn together by the common law and language of America and the British Commonwealth, across Africa and India, across Asia and Australia . . . Its shadow would darken the United States, where men had a different way of showing support of the same values.

In the whole history of the world, thought Gorin with a slight shiver, there had never been such a ceremony, fertilized by a century of wars. He realized he'd never shaken off a sense of London as a center of power whose ancient rituals put civility above military pretension. This two-minute silence had grown in significance, helped by the technology that enabled satellites to spin a web of dreams for the fireside screens below. Yet the simple poppy remained the essential symbol. The red poppies were scattered along old campaign trails, representing the lifeblood of the young sacrificed in successive generations of conflict. Old soldiers had worn the poppies each year since the first great war of the century. Today they bloomed again in hamlets as remote as those of retired Gurkhas in Nepal; in the lapels of prime ministers and presidents; beneath war memorials from Tasmania to Trinidad. Along Fifth Avenue, and before the Washington Monument, the survivors of war paraded and wore their poppies as if sprinkled with the blood of the dead.

During the silence in London, the commentator's voice was no longer heard. Television screens unveiled a Britain felled by an unnatural calm. Two minutes, thought Yuri Gorin, must equal one half-millionth of a year. Such calculations he made to stay awake during the long speeches of party colleagues. Well, let's see . . . How many seconds in a year? The fraction of time was even more startling. A tiny moment of extreme vulnerability. A kingdom bared its neck to the axman in the manner of a doomed monarch. It was ludicrous and yet magnificent. As if knights in battle were to dismount, set aside their shields, and mumble prayers, trusting only in God. Ah, but hadn't God brought him here, to this place and time?

A Sky-Roamer near the Palace of Westminster, the Houses of Parliament, zoomed in for a closer look as a sudden motion passed over the crowd like a breeze on water. Another camera picked up the strange movement around the chief of the British defense staff, standing near the plump high commissioner for Fiji.

Little ripples of activity stirred elsewhere. A score of cameras fed differently angled pictures into the mobile studios where directors and producers scanned the monitors in puzzlement. They saw men cast off their winter clothing, expose guns and thrust forward in a disciplined pattern. It was like a ballet: a beautiful spectacle if you sat watching the monitors in a remote unit, detached from the reality. Each gunman, seen from above, moved in the same relationship at the same distance from the other gunmen, though separated by close-packed spectators. The gunmen pulled colored stockings down over their heads. Seen through the sky-cams, they became colored counters. "Like someone's playing tiddledywinks," said an awed cockney cameraman, reading off the colors: "Red, yellow, blue, green . . ." There seemed to be four gunmen for each color. Each group converged upon the Cenotaph. The eruption had relatively little distance to cover. The encirclement was completed within seconds. The sullen boom of a cannon marked the end of the silence. The notables around the Queen raised their heads, listened to the sad call of the Last Post buglers; and with varying degrees of slow awakening, saw they had been taken hostage.

Talbott and Sally watched the dreamlike sequence on a giant screen in the old wartime briefing theater belowground. A pool television commentator resumed his prepared text after the long and eerie silence: "When all the wreaths have been laid," he said in a reverential tone, and broke off.

"Oh, my God!" His voice lost its detachment. "We're under attack. Men are breaking into the studio here in the Treasury. I repeat, we are being attacked—"

The Cenotaph scenes dissolved to the commentator himself. Millions saw the plump, familiar face thrust aside. A bearded stranger appeared. "Your careful attention, please! Do not terminate transmission! Do *not* terminate! Any interference with this broadcast will have fatal results. We require only your cooperation. We ask confirmation within the hour from every network that live transmission is continuing. If this is not done, we will begin killing leaders and representatives of fifty countries here assembled. Pay attention! Their lives are in your hands!"

Talbott jerked forward. He had seen the face before. One of the guards tapped him on the shoulder and indicated another exit. Sally was on her feet. The man on the screen said, "All warnings are issued by order of the Israeli Government and TCT terror-counter-terror organizations under command of Jewish guards."

The guard at Talbott's side stopped on his way to the exit and glanced back quizzically at his comrade. Another guard in the tunnel mouth was beckoning with a flashlight and shouting in another language. Talbott's guard shrugged and hastened forward his charges. Sally said, "That's the man who killed Bronfmann!" just as the face on the screen vanished.

Quex sat in the wheelchair among the dignitaries behind the Queen. They were all frozen into place: all except Yuri Gorin, who moved to a position where he could most protect the Queen from the guns trained upon her.

The guns were trained on Quex, too. And on a frail-looking bishop. Quex had read somewhere that the bishop's job was to bless the dead . . . "allowing us never to forget it is the bishop who anointed the Monarch and before whom the Monarch knelt while the Holy Spirit was invoked . . ." Quex wasn't sure if it was bishop or archbishop. He was not in any other way confused, though. His mind flamed brighter than ever—as it should, he told himself cheerfully, when the body's about to give up the ghost. Events past and present were telescoping. Some faces around him belonged to a different era. He wished Rinna could be beside him to savor all this. It beat any of her prewar Hollywood stage sets.

"There is a totally binding, top-secret decision on Her Majesty's part that no terrorists will make use of her," Quex had been informed by the Queen's principal private secretary, the PPS. "Naturally, since we have put London under full CRW alert, we offer all our guests the option of staying away."

To their credit, nobody ducked out. It would have been difficult for the men, in the face of one woman's grim resolve. "The Queen's advisers," the PPS had added, "consider that with political leaders present from all parts of the political spectrum, no terrorist will dare act."

The advisers had guessed wrong, thought Quex. The gunmen had halted within fifty feet on all sides, leaving between themselves and onlookers a gap so narrow that a counteraction would endanger civilian lives. A television monitor had been placed where the Queen's wreath was to have been laid, on the top step of the Cenotaph. Pictures appeared briefly on a large projection screen of Yuri Gorin in close-up.

Studying that image at close quarters, Quex thought: "Mother is Radzki, no question." He'd assured President Donovan of this earlier. Now identification was doubly assured, Quex's small task seemed done. Yet here he was with the very odd sense that his job wasn't really done yet at all.

Yuri Gorin checked again his position in relation to the Queen of England.

She had been ridiculed as stuffy. He saw a reason for that so-called stuffiness now.

She was said never to show emotion. What he saw in her small, set face was iron control.

"We cultivate stuffiness," she had once said. "It goes with the job. We Are."

That, thought Mother, is true power. It doesn't need knobkerries or nuclear warheads to reinforce it. The monarchy, she'd said, rested on "respect for the homespun dignity of man." You couldn't yield to terrorism if you stood for homespun dignity.

Once, asked what she would do if her people demanded an end to the monarchy, the Queen had said with a sudden grin, "We'll go quietly." Once, during the transfer of power to a former colony, as the lights went out at midnight so that the union jack could be replaced in darkness by the flag of the new republic, she'd asked the black President in a stage whisper, "Are you sure you won't change your mind?"

What she won't do now, thought the Little Mother of all the Russias, is go quietly at the point of a gun, or change her mind under physical threat. It will take the political scandal of alleged Nazi collaboration to undermine her. And I can help her survive it.

The monitor's large screen had been turned up full volume. Someone had rewound the videotape of earlier coverage. Viewers were transported back to the segments preceding the sudden hostage-taking. Again they heard reports from John O'Groats to Land's End . . . "In even the smallest hamlet of these islands there's full awareness of the unique importance of this year's remembrance," said the unseen announcer.

Almost imperceptibly, his voice changed. An old news-tape from a different occasion began to run. "When the Queen rides horseback, as she does here, at the head of the Household Cavalry, we feel the power of ancient traditions at this heart of state ceremonial . . ."

The coverage was being eased away from the present nightmare. A muscle in the Queen's face twitched.

"The Queen is last of a long line," continued the library-footage commentary, "embodying the spirit of a people fearsomely intransigent. Nothing and nobody has ever broken this small and stubborn figure . . ." The Queen was seen bringing her horse, the mare "Burmese," back under control after a pistol had been fired from the crowd as she rode down the Mall a few years earlier. Then the screen went to black.

The bearded man reappeared. He held a gun to the head of a wriggling boy and said, "The Jewish executive council has warned there must be *no* interference in live coverage . . ."

Other hands appeared in the picture. The boy was not giving up without a fight. His arms were pinioned. His spindly legs still struck out. The legs were bare between his torn shorts and the socks around his ankles and clumsy boots. One boot found a target. Millions heard the deep grunt of an unseen assailant's pain.

"For each breach of rules," said the bearded man, sounding breathless, "a hostage dies." The gun exploded.

Yuri Gorin hunched his head down and glanced sideways at the Queen. She had given a small start. A host of other witnesses must have jumped out of their skins. Here was the real test for the monarch.

"Responsibility for each execution rests here," said the voice over a sudden shot of the Queen with her family behind her. Direction was clearly in the hands of the 88 now. They've got, thought Yuri Gorin, their own technicians in there. He wondered where *there* was: an improvised studio inside a government building? That was suggested by the wide-angle shot of the dying boy. "Remain tuned," continued the voice. "See the facts of the war against the Jews. Fully documented with previously secret film." It was the voice now of a carnival barker. The boy with his head in a pool of blood dissolved into the white and austere Cenotaph flanked by faintly stirring flags under a cold sky. The pale and empty sepulcher startled open the mind with its reminder of the loss and courage and vanity of bloody wars rooted in quarrels long forgotten. Microphones caught the low moan of horror sweeping like a wind down Whitehall.

Talbott lurched blindly up a flight of tunnel steps and almost fell through a suddenly opened door to find himself squinting against the glare of television lights. He heard Sally cry out, "Oh, God!" A boy was sprawled on the floor. Masked gunmen stopped him from running forward.

The boy, he thought, is Candlestick. That man stroking a greasy beard is Uncle Feelie, doorman at the Düsseldorf sex club. The woman beside him at the desk is the grotesque Madame Obedience we saw parody the sex act; now she mimics a furry-pearly lady-in-waiting. The dead boy seems like the doll those 88 maniacs decapitated on the dance floor. But this is a government office, overlooking the Cenotaph. And all this horror is a continuation of the 88's neo-Nazi production flying false, Jewish colors.

What had happened in the underground tunnels? In the total blackness of the lower labyrinth, there had been sharp exclamations, a scuffle, and finally guns prodding him up into this venerable office of the Treasury Chambers. A *Newsmag* segment had once revealed how the Churchill war rooms were reached through the Treasury, fountainhead of sterling, the vital essence of the kingdom. The Sovereign's head of government was, historically, First Lord of the Treasury; the title of Prime Minister came later. A king, long dead, had said, "Without the money, there is no power. Without power, there is nothing."

Power came out of the gun, thought Talbott. Now it also comes out of the camera. There were three big studio cameras under the blazing television lights. They seemed sacrilegious in this chapel dedicated to the power of money. The television crews were white to the gills. A lighting man was throwing up. Two more Blitz Kids cowered in a corner. In the square outside, visible to Talbott through the long windows, regal power had been checkmated. American, French and Soviet leaders stood within a ring of guns.

A lofty vestibule led into the street. Through the open doors, Talbott saw stockinged heads move with deliberation between two knots of officials under guard.

Talbott heard the words ". . . PPS, private principal secretary." The order of the words was wrong, and the PPS looked pained: he was a ruddy, gray-haired man in tight-fitting black suit, the leading court figure "shaping the whisper to the Throne": a channel to the Queen, tireless in his devotion, meticulous in preserving neutrality when dealing with politicians, watchful of royal security . . . and undoubtedly, Talbott suddenly realized, acquainted with the palace parson, Marcus Furneval.

Madame O and Uncle Feelie stood aside, squalid faces wreathed in toothy smiles. A spotlight blazed down on Jake Cooke seated at the desk before a microphone.

But it couldn't be Jake! Talbott looked around for Sally's confirmation. She was nowhere to be seen. He stared back at the figure receiving the PPS. It resembled Jake. But it was Kraaft!

The PPS gestured at the armed men and demanded, "Are these your thugs?"

"They are!" rasped Kraaft. He gave a signal. "Including these."

The knot of men in the doorway parted and four dark-skinned men walked through.

"Walking arsenals," warned Kraaft. "Those belts are plastic explosives."

Grenades dangled from their belts. Their fists glinted with knives and knuckledusters. Each man resembled Sami Esmail, who had terrorized Sally. Each looked fanatical enough to blow himself up for the sake of Marx or a mad mullah.

Talbott saw a red light blink. Kraaft drew himself up and said into camera, "I am Jake Cooke, whose nom de guerre was Jacob Slominsky, leader of the Israeli terror-against-terror organization."

"Lies!" shouted Talbott. He reeled from a punch in the kidneys. A large hand, tough as leather, closed over his mouth.

Kraaft continued smoothly: "We have arranged for the Queen to view the Hess Command in more comfortable circumstances . . . How is that for sound levels?"

"The Queen will not be moved," said the PPS. A voice from among the television crew called out, "That's good for sound."

"We make decisions about who moves where," said Kraaft.

"Furthermore," said the PPS, "get your thugs out of here."

"What does PPS stand for, exactly?" sneered Kraaft, looking over at Uncle Feelie. "Pipsqueak?"

"Next to the Queen, the most important nonelected officer in the kingdom!" the PPS himself replied. "On these occasions, I speak for the Queen." He stood with his hands clasped behind his back, legs braced. He said, "Don't threaten us. Get these thugs out of here or the whole lot goes sky-high!"

Kraaft spread his hands. "All will be killed—"

"Including your broadcast," the PPS said softly. "Think about it. The months of preparation, careful organization . . . blown apart. No Hess Command. No plea for justice."

Kraaft said something in Arabic. Uncle Feelie heaved his great bulk into motion, came to a stop in front of the PPS, and swung at him with a wooden bar and chain. The Englishman was some seventy years old. The Queen had recently knighted him. He was fingering the blood-red poppy in his jacket lapel when the blow cut open the side of his face. The Englishman remained rigidly at attention, but his eyes strayed to where he could see the Cenotaph stained with poppies, the crimson tears shed for those who had died for an ideal. The PPS loved those things binding his Queen to the people, making her their slave, embracing her in iron duty. The essence of this was the poppy of Flanders. That battlefield's dead had been plowed into the soil long ago, but crippled ex-servicemen had ever since fashioned artificial poppies just for this annual day of rededication to ideals the PPS esteemed above all things. He said, "I don't think that sort of behavior will help, not in this country." He turned to the scene outside. "Unless every man jack of your walking bombs is moved to a safe distance, the Queen herself will give the signal." He pointed. On a far rooftop, figures swarmed like black ants. "Special Air Service," said the PPS. "Everywhere."

"If they take action," said Kraaft, "your Queen's *kaput!*"

"All will be *kaput!*" replied the Queen's chief secretary.

Tiring of the game, Kraaft said, "I want the American, Talbott." He had caught a signal from the doorway. "Scott Talbott," he announced, "will introduce the Hess Command."

Talbott braced for another kidney punch. Instead, a spotlight framed Sally trapped in the muscular arms of Madame O. Talbott did not underestimate the woman's versatility in perversion and murder. He let himself be propelled forward.

Kraaft slid his chair sideways. Another was placed in front of the microphone. He said, "Viewers, a reporter trusted for his integrity—Scott Talbott!"

Talbott found himself sitting down. On a monitor by the desk, the scene
had switched to Australia; to tapes, now several hours old, of ceremonies at
the Cenotaph in Canberra, where the time difference dictated an earlier
remembrance. Kraaft brought his face uncomfortably close and hissed:
"Improvise. Expand. Say anything you like within limits obvious to you."

46

"What the hell have I done?" muttered Sol Farkas, staring at the image of the man he believed was Jake Cooke. The producer at his side heard only the heavy volume of sound from the monitors in the control booth at the East Fifty-second Street news center. Outside mikes in London poured a confusion of noise into the feed, from which the engineers tried to isolate the terrorist leader's words.

In Rockefeller Plaza and along the Avenue of the Americas, other networks swung into action. Everyone had expected and planned for trouble; nobody had quite anticipated this. Frantic calls went out to the Hamptons, to Connecticut and New Hampshire, rousting out executives who had gone to bed in the reasonable expectation of a lazy Sunday sleep-in.

Calm BBC voices cut into the cacophony to record each linkup with a new foreign network. Sol was astonished by the speed with which the Soviet and China blocs plugged in. The BBC was taking no chance on another child's execution, and broadcast the service messages from each foreign capital as evidence of their authenticity. The broadcasters called in from Paris, New York, Rome, Karachi, Bangkok, Singapore, Tokyo, Cairo . . .

The recital emphasized that Israel was alone, and Sol's face glistened with nervous perspiration. Was this why the Communist nations collaborated? He had not been convinced they would care much about the safety of Soviet leader Yuri Gorin, weighed against the political implications of submitting to terrorist threats.

Sol could account easily enough for the mechanics of what was happening. The broadcast vans transmitted straight up to one space satellite, which relayed to two more satellites orbiting off Brazil and off Samoa. There was a well-established procedure for joining the system through Intelsat, in which 109 countries shared ownership. Its satellites responded to 300 earth stations around the globe. Overall direction resided with a spacecraft control center in Washington, D.C., from where instructions went out through the 42-foot sugar-scoop and the 54-foot dish antennae at Andover, Maine.

These were technicalities known to the Communist networks, whose controllers unabashedly milked Western space transmissions. In reverse, the terrorists need only exercise close ground management of the improvised studio in the Treasury to dictate what appeared on millions of television sets. And nobody, least of all the Washington center, dared risk universal condemnation by interfering and provoking a massacre.

"All-India Radio reporting from New Delhi," said an Anglo-Indian accent over pictures of the terrorist leader on the primary screen in front of Sol. "It is now coming up to 1800 hours and all AIR radio and television programming has been interrupted to carry this live broadcast from London . . ." A broad Kiwi voice intruded: "Soon be Monday morning here in New Zealand, London! But everybody's up and tuned in . . ." Kraaft stared into the camera, listening to the weave of voices. "Hullo London! Jamaica calling London. The time it is here now past seven Sunday morning and all Jamaicans pray for the safety of our high commissioner. Nobody is going to church. All will be at radio and television sets until the crisis is over. This is Jamaica Broadcasting Corporation calling London."

Sol stared back at Kraaft's image and rubbed his boxer's ears as if to dispel a bad dream. This man on the screen had come to him representing the most secret of Israel's military intelligence agencies. He had shown Sol material that at first Sol thought was intended to prove the man's credentials. Then he had discovered the material was much more personally convincing than that. It was the file on Sol Farkas at Deir Yassin.

Sol saw "Jake Cooke" dissolve to a panoramic view of Whitehall. Presumably, while the technical problems had been solved, the human problem of making Scott Talbott perform still presented difficulties. Talbott had been introduced by "Jake" and then there'd been fill-ins, the dramatic voices from overseas, and now the cutaway showing the standoff between terrorists and hostages at the Cenotaph. You could see the wide central path down the middle of Whitehall. Along it, by now, there should have been parading the massed bands, the blind veterans, the soldiers in ceremonial uniform, the remnants of the civilian organizations that once fought the London Blitz . . . Instead, the crowds were motionless as if the two-minute silence had left them dumb. Around the hostages there was a wide expanse of roadway across which it seemed impossible for anyone to cross undetected by the gunmen.

Gunmen, thought Sol. Gunmen that the world would blame on Israel. The dreadful accusations would be resurrected, ancient and modern, true and false: the God-killers who murdered children and blew up the King David Hotel; who crucified Christ and hanged British sergeants from Jerusalem lampposts. The invaders of Lebanon. The killers of Deir Yassin.

"Everything okay?"

Tom Middleton was watching Sol with a puzzled frown.

"Sure, everything's just great!" said Sol. "The guys know their jobs."

"I'm Scott Talbott of. . . ." Talbott's face suddenly filled the primary screen. ". . . a makeshift studio guarded by gunmen . . . wrongly described as Jewish terrorists."

Sol lifted his head. Talbott looked pale, drawn, ill. His voice sounded to Sol strained and unnatural. *Listen to his words, though!* His words were two-edged. Jesus, be careful! That opening sentence was a not-very-subtle warning to the security agencies that the gunmen were not the Jews they claimed to be.

"However offensive," Talbott went on, "these scenes go back to the deepest and most haunting fears of the Jewish people. They built a dream in Israel and they fear the dream will vanish . . . To those who are not Jewish, it might seem the long Jewish memory makes for a Jewish neurosis. What you are about to see, however, is the reality behind the nightmares and *also a nightmare vision of reality—*"

The closeup of Talbott abruptly changed to the scene outside. Police vans crawled along the fringes of the crowd, apparently amplifying the audio part of the broadcast on terrorist orders.

Middleton said, "He can't be justifying the terrorists?"

"He hasn't finished yet!" Sol snarled back.

47

Talbott made the cameras blink. He conveyed something closer to the truth than the 88 wanted the world to learn. The second time the red light blinked off, Talbott knew the 88's crews had switched to the scene outside, cutting him off. A spotlight was again directed at Sally in Madame O's embrace.

Sally's white face against the rouged horror of Madame O transported Talbott back to the Blitz. Oh, how cunningly Parson Marcus Furneval had briefed the 88 on Talbott's obsessive fear of precipitating calamity. The 88 could now measure Talbott's state of mind. They could tell when the walls began to close around him and he felt his mother's grasping hand, saw Black Mac's shadow. Detecting these moments of nausea, the terrorists switched their television coverage to the streets. They were quick learners. They were teaching Talbott he could make the camera blink, but on their terms.

Yet they needed him for credibility. They cut him off, but they had to keep coming back to him. He would have to play along, stutter and fumble his way through an ambivalent introduction. During this long delaying action, his mind ran along two tracks. On one, he formulated a commentary that wasn't as supportive as the 88 might think. On the other track, he worked out a plan of his own.

What had drawn millions to the symbolism of Veterans Day in America, and to this same day of remembrance here? It was the simple dream of ending all war. Here, now, were the leaders of the two superpowers fighting covert wars: two men unexpectedly united in purpose. Yuri Gorin's was to ensure that never again would Jews be made scapegoats. President Donovan's was to help this Jew in the Kremlin and secure world peace. There must be a way for two such men to outwit Madame O and Uncle Feelie and all that grubby gang with its squalid little ambitions.

The grubby gang just happened to commend unimaginable power. Nobody in the world wanted to trigger the explosion that would wipe out every political viewpoint. Nobody dared take the risk—Talbott stopped himself. He remembered Jacob Slominsky once saying in public that, if necessary, his guards from the Kyrya would bring down the temple of humanity, rather than surrender again to mass slaughter and the death camps.

Jacob, the real Jake, would take the risk

Three thousand miles away, Sol Farkas shared a bird's-eye view of the damage that could be inflicted if anyone took risks. The big time-zone clocks around him in the control room measured the size of the story: the rest came pouring off the news wires.

In the eastern United States, families were starting to watch the drama unfold while they sat at breakfast in front of their television sets. They had been alerted in ways that often baffled foreigners. Some Americans were insomniacs who listened to all-night talk shows, heard the late bulletins, and called friends and relatives. Some had professional reasons for following the news: firefighters, cops and the frequently ridiculed but nonetheless efficient civil defense organizations for dealing with a surprise attack. Americans were not the hysterics often portrayed abroad. Neither were they drugged by too much television drama. They knew the difference between windbags, soap opera, docudrama and reality. They were members of an electronic society, with a mysterious empathy, one to another, each a molecule in the national nervous system. Americans had awoken this morning to a new crisis. They were equipped to evaluate it with a sophistication born of experience and new technologies. But they were today the victims of a technically convincing deception: the perpetrators of the gargantuan crime unfolding before their eyes were made to appear as Jews.

For Talbott's sake, Sol prolonged the torture of remaining in the control room. He had such a strong sense of betraying his own principles that, for a brief moment, he contemplated suicide. He had put the network's facilities at Quex's disposal because the man on the screen who called himself Jake Cooke had come to him; because he wanted Quex to expose any cover-up; because he wanted the truth made public about Hess; because he wanted to avenge a dead producer; and because he was a Jew. None of this would have happened, Sol reflected in his misery, if he had not been a Jew with a Jew's secret fear that nowhere but in Israel was he protected against someone someday saying he was less than human. *Nothing personal had ever in Sol's judgment justified bending the rules of journalistic objectivity.* And that should have included being Jewish.

Someone jogged his elbow. "Call from London!"

He rolled back his chair, eyes still on a wide shot of Talbott sitting alongside Jake Cooke.

"This is very urgent. *I* am Jacob Cooke," said the caller. "I phoned an hour ago."

Sol stared up at the screens. "You bastard. I'm watching the real Jake Cooke right now."

"That man's an imposter."

"Or you could be the imposter—"

"I'll repeat back my phone conversation with you."

"With your resources," said Sol in despair, "you could have bugged it."

Pause. "Okay, you want proof? Naomi."

Sol's big hand tightened around the phone. *Naomi?*

"Naomi was the real reason you pulled out after Deir Yassin."

Sol waited.

"Naomi was captured by Arab guerrillas . . . peaceful farmers by day in the peaceful village of Deir Yassin. You want to know what they did to her?"

Sol was unable to speak.

"Very well. She was still alive when we found her—"

"No," said Sol. "I don't want to hear."

"You were in love, the two of you. You kept that a secret because of her parents. Nobody ever knew. Not even these imposters who have spent years to create a bogus Jake Cooke." There was an inquiring silence.

"Just a minute," said Sol. He reached out a trembling hand to take wire copy from a clerk. He was still gazing at the monitors, but his vision was blurred by shock. If the caller knew about Naomi, he could only be Jacob, who was chief of operational intelligence in Jerusalem at that time. Naomi, fluent in Arabic, had served in the Jewish underground. She had been in that village negotiating with Arab moderates when . . . when she died. Death had been the final, unanswerable argument against violence.

"Yes," said Sol. "What do you want me to do?"

"Write down these numbers. They are public phones in Central London. You are making contact with Sherman."

Sol, scribbling on a pad, paused. Fishhook Sherman?

"Take further instructions from Mr. Sherman," said the caller. "He knows the plan." There was a pause. Then excitement agitated the previously cold voice. "You'll have to do it."

"Do what?"

"Wait . . . Yes, there's no choice. The plan changes with changing circumstances. You must do it."

"Do what?" roared Sol, and glanced guiltily at the others. But everyone was concentrating on the television monitors.

"You have to speak to Talbott."

"It's impossible!"

"It can be done." The voice sounded sure of itself again. "Say you're having technical difficulties your end, you *must* talk with him."

"And then?" asked Sol.

"Hold it." The caller seemed to talk with someone. "Okay . . . There's a time bomb inside the Cenotaph. Set to explode after the Hess Command transmission. You can't say that to Talbott, but here's what you can *do* . . ."

Jacob Slominsky Cooke left the phone booth in a hurry. Everything now was in the lap of the gods. Jacob Cooke had himself resided there long enough to gamble that sometimes the gods were kind.

He moved carefully across the sidewalk, noting the frightened way on-lookers got out of his way. He wore a bright orange-colored skullcap with a stocking mask. He carried a machine pistol. He was flanked by two armed men also wearing orange skullcaps and masks. Except for the difference in the color of their headgear, they resembled the 88's hostage takers. The path opening before them permitted them to break into a rhythmic heel-and-toe stride, covering the ground with speed and economy.

"Four-Ack-Emma to Gross," said Jacob, holding open his paratrooper jacket and speaking into the perforated metal disk above an inside pocket. "Second phase completed. I am moving south toward Mother."

The tiny radio hopped automatically to another channel. "We have you, Four-Ack-Emma." The voice was comfortably familiar. It reached him via an almost invisible fiber-optic line, like a hair between his collar and the plug in his ear.

Yes, the gods were sometimes kind. Thirty hours ago, he would not have said so. He was resigned then to remaining a prisoner of the 88. Held in Ironmongers for weeks, he had inevitably learned the 88's methods. Kraaft had been a regular visitor, perfecting his role as Jake's double. A devout Marxist of the East German school, with a missionary zeal to win converts, Kraaft had told how his mother, a party courier in pre-Hitler Germany, donated her bastard son by a Red Army general to Stalin's special-service institute. There Kraaft graduated as an all-purpose assassin. He could pass as a native-born Basque physician or a Croatian engineer, depending on the revolution's needs. He was fluent in several languages, with a photo-graphic memory. There were many like him. Kraaft just proved to come closest to resembling Jake. There was also a similarity of interests. Didn't Jacob himself suspect betrayal of the Jews by the West in World War II? Couldn't he see the validity of the Hess Command allegations? Near the end of Jacob's incarceration, even Marcus Furneval seemed to think Jacob was sympathetic to the project and conducted several brain-picking sessions with him. The questions told Jacob what was being planned.

Volumes of biographical material had been assembled by Helmuth Henkell's analysts, his squirrels, *Eichhörnchen.* These were built into Kraaft's intellectual disguise and fleshed out the cosmetic alterations. Kraaft had consulted Jacob between sittings with the makeup artists and the posture specialists who had film of Jacob in motion. Technicians measured Jacob's skull while Kraaft memorized bits and pieces from Jacob's life. When they had last met, a month before in Düsseldorf, Jacob had had the disconcerting experience of confronting himself.

Now he was free. The 88 had made a mistake, holding him in London. Perhaps they needed him in reserve, to prop him up like a dummy before the cameras if Kraaft's impersonation should be too shrewdly challenged. His escape, with Sami Esmail neutralized, meant there was a good chance the 88's leadership had only just discovered he was free. He'd gone straight to General Steely Pamir at the Israeli embassy, breaking all rules, pleading an emergency. Pamir had not been too receptive until Jacob told what he knew about Parson Furneval's part in the attempt on Quex's life on Long Island. *That* came as news! What Jacob held back was his knowledge of the Soviet eclipse order. If Radzki, as Yuri Gorin, had issued that order, then the man had sold out. But General Pamir had been in too great a hurry, by then, to linger over Jacob's feelings on Radzki. The embassy's special security force had been mobilized; messages had gone out to Jacob's followers, who by then saw they had been hoodwinked by Kraaft. The orange skull-caps had been Steely Pamir's inspiration, to confuse the 88 and identify Jacob's men if it came to a fight. Poetic justice! The 88 had stolen the idea from Pamir's counterterror groups. Then Nelson had been roped in, producing more logistical support than Jacob could have imagined . . .

Confidence. "That's all you need," Steely Pamir had finally told Jacob. "And that's all you'll have, once you leave here. We know nothing about you, won't take calls . . . Confidence and rapid deployment are your allies now." And the swiftness of the hand that deceives the eye, thought Jacob while the crowd parted like the Red Sea.

A chessboard spread itself before him. There was the Queen. There, the bishop of London. There, the knights of the realm. There, the pawns drawn from the four corners of the globe.

Me against Mother. Jacob swung across the empty space between the crowd and the Cenotaph. The 88's gunmen were taken in by the swift self-assurance of Jacob's party, their use of the 88's same type of gear. But as he moved out alone under the television eyes, Jacob prayed the pictures were not being fed to monitors visible to Kraaft. He glanced quickly at the huge screen confronting the Queen. God be thanked! The Hess Command had started.

Me against Mother. Against Radzki. Now we'll see what species of bastard you really are. Jacob pulled aside his stocking mask and halted in front of the Soviet leader. The shock of graying hair, heavy black brows, long snout, deeply set eyes behind tinted glasses, belonged to the great Russian mother bear of legend. Jacob discerned no trace of the impassioned, skinny refugee. Then he caught some electric radiance. Jacob knew that aura. It overwhelmed his senses.

They were two survivors who have walked the same solitary and dangerous paths; who have changed masks, formed impossible alliances, wormed their way to the core of the enemy. Mother stirred a fraction, senses alert to the same signals.

"I am Jacob Slominsky. You are the same Szmuel Radzki who studied at the feet of Ahad Ha'am, the great teacher at the gymnasia of Herzlia in the land then called Palestine."

Jacob spoke in Hebrew. Yuri Gorin sniffed the air, lowered his gaze, met Jacob's eyes. The old names came flooding back. Lohamei Herut Israel. *Lehi.* Organized by Abraham Stern, killed by the British and replaced by men of iron like this Jacob Slominsky, once also a disciple of Ahad Ha'am, for a while advocating passive resistance until forced to learn that power grows from the gun. So here he was at last. Talbott's man. This skull-capped figure like an avenging angel . . .

Jacob said, "You are either a traitor and I must kill you, or . . . If you remain loyal, I must have a sign."

Mother made a sudden move. Two of Jacob's escorts raised their guns. Mother's hand stopped on its way inside his greatcoat. "I must know your general intent."

"To preserve the land of our fathers."

"Mine," replied Mother, "is precisely so." His Hebrew was flawless and Jacob felt his certainties eroding.

"You flew Hess to England," said Jacob with renewed belligerence. "Wasn't that to sell out the Jews?"

"To *save* the Jews." Mother looked at the escorts. They were too far away to hear the exchange. "I'm not accustomed to discuss matters at gunpoint."

Jacob called curtly over his shoulder. The weapons were lowered.

President Donovan clenched his fists. Was the Soviet leader *negotiating?* He saw how Mother now gestured, then took out a small red book which he handed to Jacob. *Goddammit!* thought the President. He watched Jacob study the book, then talk softly to Mother, who gestured again in the direction of his Soviet officers. One of Jacob's men seemed to be singling out some of the Russians. *Goddammit!*

Mother received back Rebecca's diary and said, "You see, Slominsky, if I were a traitor, I would be guilty of spitting on the graves of two women: the one I revered, and her sister whom I loved."

Inside the makeshift studio, Talbott still watched the continuing Hess Command film. How much would a modern audience believe?

A BBC engineer leaned over the desk, braving the watchful gaze of Kraaft. "An urgent call from New York. I cleared it with the bast— . . . with the guards." He glanced at Kraaft. "Your guards, sir, understand it's a technical problem. Might hurt the broadcast, sir."

Kraaft kept his eyes on the man's face.

The engineer looked back at Talbott with an expression that said: For chrissakes take the call!

"Can I take it here?" asked Talbott.

"Through the squawk box." The engineer pointed tentatively to the transceiver between Talbott and Kraaft. He was fully prepared for the bullet in his head that each move seemed to bring closer.

Talbott called out, "Kill the other mikes."

Kraaft picked up his revolver. "Mind what you say."

The voice of Sol Farkas came through. "Visuals outside keep breaking up . . . You probably can't see it your end . . . Makes the Cenotaph pictures useless."

Talbott listened. The technical taradiddle covered something Sol needed to tell him.

"So get the hostages inside," said Sol. "For their own safety."

Kraaft put his hand over the grid of the built-in mike. Talbott heard him say, "Ask what he means, *safety of hostages.*"

The hand was removed and Talbott relayed the question.

"If the terrorists—if the 88—hear we've stopped transmitting the faulty visuals, they'll think it's deliberate and kill more hostages," said Sol's metallic voice through three thousand miles of space.

Again Kraaft's hand covered the mike. "We have already demanded the hostages move inside. It is the Queen who refuses."

Talbott repeated this, too.

"Convince the Queen it's for the good of all." There was a subtle change in Sol's voice, detectable to Talbott, as if what followed were throwaway lines. "Of course if you can persuade the hostage-takers we really are having technical difficulties this end—"

"Bluff!" This time Kraaft made no effort to kill his own voice. "Your network's looking for excuses to stop its transmission . . ."

Talbott let his breath out. It was Sol, of course, who wanted the President out of harm's way for some desperate reason. The Queen, too, if she'd stop being so stiff-necked.

"Get them inside!" Kraaft ordered the PPS. "Tell your blasted Queen we respect her view but she's putting others in danger. Understand?"

The PPS removed the bloodstained handkerchief he was holding against his face. His eyes flickered quickly to Talbott. They both understood.

Sol Farkas, from his corner of the control room in New York, frantically dialed yet another of the London numbers given him by Jacob.

"Fishhook? Thank God!" Sol steadied himself. Above him, the monitors showed the Hess Command well into the first hour of transmission.

"I now have a location where you will get Nelson," the ex-FBI man said mechanically.

Sol scribbled down the number. "What's this about blowing up—"

"I'm sorry," Fishhook interrupted. "I cannot give you that information. Good-bye."

Sol stared at the softly buzzing receiver, then up at the screens.

The Hess Command had moved into the segment claiming Allied bombers deliberately refused to bomb the death camps.

Sol tried the new number.

"Nelson here," said the voice in Sol's ear. "Back at my old desk. This cockup vindicates me. I wish it could have been done some other way." Nelson had spoken slowly to give Sol time to identify him. Now his voice quickened. "Don't ask questions. Do as I say. Call this number. Ask for Room 101. When a girl answers, say *Matthew, Chapter 5, verse 44*. If she immediately quotes correctly, tell her Phoenix is in operation. Got that?"

Sol repeated back the message and added, "What's the quote?"

"I'm sorry," said Nelson. "I cannot give you that information."

Sol's head spun.

"Next," said Nelson, "call this number. If the Boffin answers, ask for Mrs. Thurson. Never mind who the Boffin is. The message is for Mrs. Thurson . . ."

Sol copied down the message, feeling like a schoolboy. On the monitors appeared aerial photographs. The commentator said, "The Allies could bomb the German factories next door, but not the death camps. Here we see more aerial photographs from Operation Jericho . . ."

Sol stopped writing and stared up at the screens. The phone had gone dead. The commentator went on, "British fighter-bombers in Operation Jericho had no difficulty breaching the walls of this camp to release non-Jewish leaders of an anti-Nazi resistance. Yet the British said they could not bomb the concentration camps without killing the Jewish inmates."

This was something new. This was not in the Hess Command that Sol had received from Talbott. Did it mean the documentary would run longer because of this addition, or had it been edited? How much time were Fishhook, Nelson—*the Hat Men*—and Jacob counting on?

There was a Bible in the newsroom along with standard works of reference. Sol called a copy boy. The eager young face clouded over when he explained what he wanted. "Move it!" shouted Sol.

He got through to the first of Nelson's two numbers. A refined English voice said, "Libyan People's Bureau."

Sol grabbed the Bible from the copy boy. "Hullo," he said, playing for time.

"Libyan People's Bureau."

"Yes, I wonder if you would give me"—he found the New Testament, the Gospel according to St. Matthew—"Room 101?"

"Please hold."

Something from George Orwell's *Nineteen Eighty-four* popped into his head: Room 101 is the worst thing in the world! He flicked the pages and cursed his quirky memory.

A girl's voice came on the line. Sol said, "Matthew, Chapter 5, verse 44."

The girl answered promptly, "But what I tell you is this: love your enemies and pray for your persecutors."

Sol took a deep breath. "Phoenix is in operation," he said.

"I understand. Phoenix is in operation. Thank you, caller."

Again the line went dead.

Sol dialed the second number. "Mrs. Thurson?"

"Speaking."

So the Boffin, whoever *that* was, hadn't answered. Was that bad? Sol hesitated, assailed by sudden doubts. He was far too gone into Jacob's sorcery to turn back. "Mrs. Thurson?" he asked for the second time.

"I am Mrs. Thurson."

What was it Nelson had said? If the girl at the first number responds with the correct quotation, on the next call repeat three times that you wish to speak with Mrs. Thurson.

Sol spoke the name again.

"Yes, what is it?" The woman sounded disinterested, neither surprised nor curious.

"I believe you have a means of reaching Marcus Furneval."

"That is so."

"Please get this message to him at once: Phoenix is in operation."

"Phoenix *is* in operation." The woman's voice quickened a fraction. "I'll see he gets it right away, sir."

Sol put down the phone and mopped his brow. Everyone else in the control room was concentrating on the Hess Command, but one or two quizzical looks had been cast in his direction. A switcher, the man closest to Sol, shook his head, either in astonishment at what he was seeing and hearing on the monitors, or at Sol's odd behavior. To be safe, Sol said to him, "It's a bitch, running things by remote control . . ."

The switcher nodded sympathetically. Probably, thought Sol, he believes I'm masterminding London. I suppose I am, but not in the way he thinks. God, I hope I've pushed the right buttons!

The commentator's voice over the Hess Command was saying, "The military value to the West of giving Hitler the license to kill the Jews may be judged from these statistics . . ."

Two men stood on either side of Nelson's old desk at New Scotland Yard.

"Bob Casey of C-13, this is Mr. Grimweather of SAS."

The new Yard expert on antiterrorism shook Grimweather's hand. "Seems we made rather a pig's breakfast of things."

"Think evil," said Grimweather, wryly quoting the SAS slogan. "We didn't think it enough." He was no longer dressed in the roll-brimmed trilby hat, soft brown shoes and cavalry twill trousers of his earlier appearance outside the No-Man's-Land Tuckshop. Now he wore the kind of dirty brown desert boots known as "brothel creepers" and an unusually long raincoat that failed entirely to conceal somewhat odd black trousers.

Nelson barely noticed this oddity in dress at first. His eye was caught by what appeared on the office television set. It had been presenting a grainy Hess Command until he switched to one of the security cameras watching the Cenotaph, when the palace parson appeared, genuflecting before the Bishop of London.

"The Rev's got the message," said Nelson.

Grimweather asked lazily, "May one inquire, Why did all this go through a *journalist* in New York?"

"Journalists were all I could trust," Nelson replied fiercely.

"I stand corrected." Grimweather reddened. "My men will take orders from you when necessary."

"My men were always willing to take Nelson's orders," said Casey of C-13. "Those chinless wonders around the parson screwed us up . . . How much time left?"

Nelson switched back to the ITN channel. "The 88 are running an updated version of the Hess crap." He checked a report on the interrogation of a mysteriously injured Libyan terrorist delivered to St. Mary's hospital in Paddington. "There's ninety-five minutes of the film still to run."

"We'd better get cracking," said Grimweather and Casey at almost the same time. Casey pulled himself up short and said, "Aren't you running your show from here?"

Grimweather shook his head. "I'll jump with my HALO chaps. It's only fair."

Nelson looked pleased but said nothing. Now he understood Grimweather's odd garb. Under that raincoat, Grimweather would be clad in a one-piece black boilersuit and lightweight, knitted body armor including ceramic "trauma pads." The desert boots were part of the operational gear. Grimweather must want to make up for the earlier fiasco by breaking the traditional exclusion of officers from urban guerrilla warfare. HALO was the acronym for High Altitude, Low Opening. SAS paratroopers jumped from a great height so that the aircraft passed unheard below; the parachute was not deployed until the trooper was so low, the crack of its opening came almost on top of his hitting the ground. If Grimweather's team hoped to prevent slaughter in Whitehall, they would need to drop within a narrow circle around the Cenotaph.

Casey was halfway out the door. Grimweather was taking a last quick look at symbols chalked on a blackboard. Nelson came over and squeezed the SAS man's arm. "Beat the clock," he said, thinking privately Grimweather in his forty-fifth year must *want* his name carved under the SAS barracks-square clock. Some men were like that.

By himself again, Nelson considered the odds. He could not depend on his communications remaining secure from Furneval's treachery. But some at least were made untraceable by working through Sol Farkas.

He chalked new calculations on his blackboard. Among the debits was the Libyan Peoples Bureau, where freshly trained suicide bombers had been identified as followers of the so-called mad mullah, Sayyed Mohammed Hussein Fadhallallah. They would move when they got the message Phoenix was in operation. In a column of unknowns, he chalked "88." Their compulsive partnership with the Libyans must soon fall apart. They might turn vicious. They had lost their true leader, East Germany's General Helmuth Henkell.

Nelson turned to the closed-circuit cameras. The Queen's group came into focus. Already she was leading a move back to the Treasury.

There was President Donovan ambling behind her, one arm half raised from force of habit, turning to the crowds and the cameras with American amiability and just a touch of high noon. Well, it was high noon now; Big Ben tolled the knell.

After Donovan came the Soviet leader. If the 88 and the Libyans went off their collective rocker, he'd be their target too.

Nelson tossed a piece of chalk from hand to hand, and faced the blackboard again. He still preferred the old ways. A computer system lied. It performed its magic but it could be made to lie. The Yard's new stripe of cat was gullible, or lazy, or too dense to recognize that computers would report as true whatever falsehoods were fed into them, and from the unscreened falsehoods breed new lies. He wrote with his bit of chalk "Bullshit Baffles Brains," and as quickly rubbed it out. "B B B," he wrote instead. I'm as fast as any bloody computer, he thought, and I can change my mind a damn sight faster.

His pals had ignored the codswallop on the security computers. They'd rallied to his side because of an old-fashioned gut feeling. Furneval and his MISFIT artists hadn't pulled the wool over the eyes of the woolgatherers.

He regarded another chalked equation. He drew what appeared to be a bubble with smaller bubbles around its periphery. He chalked two tubes leading to the central bubble. One tube was wider than the other. He concentrated on the slender tube, which he marked "Servants' Entrance." He felt compelled to put in some labels lest some virginal secretary should recoil at her master's doodles. They did resemble a gynecological study of the more prurient sort. Come to think of it, the whole bloody place was a kind of manmade womb. He chalked over it, in his old-fashioned way, PHOENIX.

48

Marcus Furneval tipped his parson's hat to a jauntier angle. No need for caution now. He joined the procession winding into the Treasury, falling in behind the chaplain-in-chief and the choirboys of the Chapels Royal. He'd overseen his last nonecclesiastic function.

"It would be advisable to withdraw to the Phoenix chambers," the principle private secretary had whispered to the Queen.

"Phoenix!"

Furneval had watched at a discreet distance while the PPS, under the stern regal gaze, explained. The Cenotaph was crammed with dynamite. "The bomb disposal squads will have a fighting chance," the PPS had said, "if we clear the area of all dignitaries." *Including you* were the unspoken words. To help gallant men, the Queen would take any action. Her presence would impose on them too great a strain. "Very well," she said with a flash of her old humor. "We'll go quietly."

The parson spied General Quex Massey being raised, regal in his wheelchair, by two top-hatted high commissioners of the Commonwealth. Quex stared fixedly at the parson and took a firmer grip on his gold-knobbed cane.

"Can't have you catching your death," said Furneval, whipping off his scarf as Quex was lowered to the floor of the vestibule. Quex recoiled as the scarf was drawn around his neck. "Death of cold," repeated Furneval, glancing round.

The procession was jamming up inside the Treasury. In the makeshift studio, panels rolled back. A few officials vanished into the tunnels. A ragged line of personages formed, amid chatter about nuclear-bomb shelters. Armed terrorists patrolled the lineup. Quex and Furneval were briefly isolated.

"You betrayed me," said Quex, tearing off the scarf.

"By your standards." Furneval laughed. "By mine, I won. It'll all come out. Henkell's dead."

Quex had no idea what Furneval was talking about. The old general's glassy stare conveyed the opposite impression. "I know," he said.

"Then, you also know he made provision for the truth to be publicized if the Kremlin killed him."

"Very awkward, that," Quex said judiciously.

"The truth about Hess, that he negotiated with both the British and Soviets to let Hitler have his Jews?"

"That's what I meant," said Quex, having meant nothing.

"Now the world will know about Soviet complicity."

"I see," said Quex, seeing nothing. "That helps *your* cause."

"You're a shrewd old bugger," said Furneval. "Always said so. You knew all along."

Quex did his best to look omniscient.

"Communism needs new life. We can give it, in the German Democratic Republic." Furneval moved behind the wheelchair and pushed the helpless general into the makeshift studio. A path opened to the concealed stairway. Furneval braked, and moved forward to the head of the stairs. There he turned and descended backwards until his shoulders were level with Quex's feet.

"These bloody fools," said Furneval, encompassing Whitehall with a sweep of his hands, "thought I was *such* a pal of King Edward-the-bloody-Eighth." He banged his chest and then took the weight of Quex and the wheelchair. "I saw him as proof of a rotting past. They tore him down from the throne but tossed him a dukedom, when he should've been shot!"

A tall figure in formal top hat gripped the handles of Quex's chair, relieving the parson of some of the burden. The stairway was very narrow, its walls of brick and plaster changing to packed earth behind timber as they descended. The crowd above had fallen back to make way for Kraaft, the imposter, the terrifying orchestrator of this scene of controlled panic, the man who said he was Jake Cooke.

He waited until the wheelchair reached a bend in the stairway. Quex was illuminated by the emergency blue lighting overhead.

Below the bend, Parson Furneval was knocked aside. His broad-brimmed hat flew backwards from his head. He heard the crash of an exploding gun, and he tumbled down the remaining steps into the tunnel's mouth.

Quex felt the breath of another bullet. Then he glimpsed the man in the tall black hat fire twice. Kraaft's body bumped and slithered towards him, and the man in the black hat blocked its descent with one large foot. Pandemonium broke out above, and Quex thanked God that President Donovan, the Queen and all those other top dogs were already safe inside Phoenix.

"Phoenix!" said Uncle Feelie, coming to Sally from behind. "The bird that rises from the ashes. A clever code name, isn't it? The Phoenix chambers, built to rise from a nuclear holocaust. Monarchs buy their rebirth this way, hey? Smart peoples, hey?"

Sally gritted her teeth. She had been one of the first forced underground.

"Why've we come this way?" she asked. Other hostages had vanished into a second, wider tunnel.

"Phoenix is a state secret, my lovely," croaked Uncle Feelie. "Don't want the peasants to rebel, do we? But we also need servants, even in an underground palace." He gave her a push, then caught her round the waist. "This is the servants' entrance, sweetie. The back door." He was feeling her thighs again. Still she wasn't ready to fight back. She had to learn more. In front, Madame O turned, her breath smelling of garlic and stale beer, and pressed her back against the wall. "Squeeze past," she ordered Sally, cold fingers stroking the girl's face.

Ahead, a brilliant light shone in a cavernous space. In the entrance, a terrorist suddenly twisted round and gestured as if pleading for help. Something had struck him a blow. He staggered back into the tunnel, grasping at Sally. She stumbled and fell, squirmed free, then fell again under the unexpected weight of Madame O. Instinct, not reason, told Sally to bring up one knee with all the force she could muster. Madame O let out an unladylike bellow, and Sally felt her knee sink into a crowded groin. She rolled onto her face and sprang for the terrorist's discarded gun, carrying it with her to the brightly illuminated area. She backed out of the tunnel, ready to deal with the two obscenities who fed on sex like carrion on rotten meat.

"Don't fire, Little Idiot!" Jacob's hand fell lightly on her shoulders.

She fell back reluctantly. Uncle Feelie swayed out of the black shaft. She felt again his sausage fingers, his leering pleasure in Bronfmann's death. She raised the gun.

"No!" Jacob commanded. She saw then that men in orange skullcaps stood on either side, guns raised by their barrels. They must have clubbed other terrorists as they emerged. Her gunfire, she realized, would have given the game away. Madame O joined Uncle Feelie. They stood blinking in the sudden light, slowly aware of the fallen bodies on either side. Uncle Feelie saw Sally and hurled himself at her. The first gun swept down. The metal butt struck the doorman's head with a soft, plopping sound. Madame O flung herself over his crumpled body. She was like a bull. The transformation was immediate. There flashed through Sally's mind the image of bared buttocks and the parody of sex in Düsseldorf. The second guard automatically struck, speeding the transvestite's lunge. Sally side-stepped and claws ripped at her face. Madame O crashed to the ground. A wig rolled from her head. Her arms reached out convulsively and Sally saw razor-sharp shields detach themselves from the creature's scarred fingertips.

It was Talbott's turn to be directed out of the makeshift studio. At the foot of the stairs, a terrorist said, *"This* way, Mr. Talbott."

Something in the man's voice made Talbott pause. He was being stopped from following the main flow into the wider tunnel. "This way," the man repeated, pointing to the space between the galleries. The man wore an orange skullcap, but that was of no significance to Talbott. The man's demeanor was somehow different. As he moved forward, Talbott thought he saw the man wink.

Others in the same orange beanies were separating the few remaining Blitz Kids from the terrorists who had been holding them. Down the stairs behind Talbott came the Libyan walking bombs, thick-waisted in soft plastic explosive, heavy-footed, gait menacing, moving with the swaying vacant-eyed confidence of the mad. Talbott grabbed the boys and pitched them one after another helter-skelter down the central tunnel, suddenly awake to what was happening.

The last man down the steps lifted his feet fastidiously over the dead body of Kraaft. "I'll need that for evidence," he said conversationally. One of the orange-capped men dragged Kraaft by the heels into the open space, then stood aside.

"General Pamir!" exclaimed Talbott.

Pamir raised a steel claw in cheerful acknowledgment. The Israeli was looking rather grand in full diplomatic fig: striped pants, tails, and top hat. He said something in Hebrew. Two men broke out of the shadows and turned into the small opening to their left. "We've bottled up the worst in there," said Steely Pamir. "Walking bombs, hot for self-immolation. We'll help them on their way." He hooked Talbott in tow and moved into the main corridor.

Three military officers stood under the blue lighting. Gold braid glittered on their shoulder boards. Their faces were distinguished by their unusually dark suntans.

"What the hell—?" exploded Talbott.

One of the Red Army officers pushed past him and shouted an order.

"Our orders," said Steely Pamir in a tone of immense satisfaction. "They're giving *our* orders."

A man stumbled out of the small tunnel. He plucked at grenades hanging from his belt. He seemed enormous. Behind him ran a Russian whose grasp he had evaded. Black hair framed the terrorist's face like a lion's mane. His thin khaki uniform bulged between the bindings of plastic. He was screaming unintelligibly. The Russian twisted the Kalashnikov assault rifle out of the Libyan's hand, bending the arm backward and up with such swift force they all heard the cracking of bone. Before the arm had time to fall limp, the Russian had swung the Kalashnikov so that he caught the stock and forced the rifle down across the back of the Libyan's neck. His other hand still grasped the barrel. The Libyan's head jerked back. There was a second loud crack. The Russian broke the fall to the floor, crouched, and ran experienced hands over the weapons and explosives bound to the Libyan's body.

"Hexogen." The Russian rose slowly to his feet. "And PETN." He held up a small container. It looked like the CO_2 bottle in an airliner's flotation gear. "Propane gas. The gas magnifies the explosion. These are very restricted materials in NATO use," he added accusingly. "Difficult to get outside military sources." He stood immobile and immaculate in his Red Army dress uniform, his head cocked slightly to one side as if listening.

"Thanks," said Steely Pamir in grudging admiration.

"We just do what we're told." The Russian held up his hand and added with soft urgency, "Hit the deck, comrades!"

Talbott and General Pamir followed him down to the floor. A rumble gathered inside the small tunnel. The noise grew in volume until it burst upon them with a roar and clouds of earth and dust.

The muffled thunder of the tunnel explosion made itself felt first through earth tremors, causing a gentle snowfall of plaster from the ceilings in the Phoenix chamber. The Queen, Prince Philip and the other royals looked up with studied nonchalance. Some distance away, Nikolai Kerensky watched with pride as his ECLIPSE team went stolidly about its work. Two of his officers spoke English with impeccable upper-class accents. Another sounded as if he had grown up in the Bronx, which was true, since his father had been a near-permanent delegate to the United Nations until caught in some blatant piece of espionage. In their smart uniforms, with their suave manners, they were more than a match for the royal equerries. Diplomacy was not the Russians' immediate concern, however. They had joined up with the Israelis, though why Mother had ordered this unlikely partnership was not for Kerensky to ask.

The Phoenix was arranged like a pinwheel. At the hub was a central chamber reproducing the genteel shabbiness of the less frequented parts of Buckingham Palace, minus the drafts. There were heavy Victorian drapes but no windows; dummy fireplaces; fine Persian and Chinese carpets on beeswaxed wooden floors. Much of the furniture might have been dug up from storage cellars at Balmoral Castle; serviceable and what the Queen called "comfy," although the chamber was the size of a banqueting hall, with a painted ceiling and vaguely familiar pictures on flock-printed walls. Leading off were smaller chambers with an encircling gallery from which extended a series of passages: for palace servants, for Whitehall officials and for the security services. The drawing Nelson had chalked on his Scotland Yard blackboard was a floor plan. He would now have to rub out the most narrow of the access shafts. "We trapped most of the 88 in there," reported Nick Kerensky to Yuri Gorin. "One of the suicide bombers blew himself up."

Mother nodded and lifted a hand in seeming benediction. He was saluting Jacob Slominsky Cooke. The two men were separated by red carpeting that divided the royals from their guests, with the exception of President Donovan, who towered beside the Queen, and the Soviet leader.

Marcus Furneval caught the exchange. He had escaped from the sudden shooting, aware only that Quex was unhurt. He hadn't delayed to learn more, for there were things he had to do. He stared at Jacob, and alarm bells went off. *This was not Kraaft!* He should have been alerted by the way the message "Phoenix is in operation" had come ahead of schedule. He'd assumed the 88 were advancing the timing, for the plan was always to hold hostages here if events took a bad turn. Someone with inside knowledge had outmaneuvered the parson.

But he knew this complex inside out. If London is ever nuked, the Queen or her successor will carry on from here. The role as head of a global commonwealth is taken seriously. There are communication links to the outside world. Three studio cameras sit among potted palms in the library area, dominated by a Balmoral Castle-size fireplace. Phoenix, a cocoon of reinforced steel interwoven with self-contained life-support systems for ninety occupants divided into ten cells which can be sealed independently, will rise from the ashes if anything can. Parson Furneval finished his visual inspection and finally understood the significance of the orange beanies. Technicians now tinkering with the cameras wore them, and they were neither men of the 88 nor palace flunkies.

He looked again. These were Jews. Furneval edged forward. Who the hell was this, directing the new transmission point? Sally Ryan!

So she'd broken out of Ironmongers. And he'd told her the plan of action!

He swung round to study Jacob again, his head spinning. The girl must have helped the real Jake Cooke get away, then. Parson Furneval had been so busy these past hours, making withdrawals from the INTERCOME-CON current file in the Data Center, that smaller events had passed him by. He'd been far too much excited by what he read in decoded traffic from Belgrade to Berlin.

He studied the TV screen built above a massive marble fireplace in imitation of an Adam. The screen was gold-framed. Moments before, it showed only a stag at bay. Now the stag and the heather of the Highlands were replaced by what Furneval recognized as the penultimate segment of the Hess Command.

Fantastic! The plan was still unrolling. On the streets, the 88 and their friends were unaware of the changed situation. Everyone was glued to the screen, sharing that odd compulsion so many humans have to be diverted from unpleasant realities. It had been Talbott's fatal flaw. And could be again? *Above-average pilot but with dangerous tendency to ignore hazards.* So said that Royal Navy flimsy.

It had been so easy to steer Talbott away from the truth. He froze to the wall, and voluntary amnesia wiped out the memory of Rebecca receiving the fatal overdose. All I did, thought Furneval, was chuck lumps of concrete at the poor sod!

It was worth trying again.

The parson stood there, counting his blessings. One: the main entryway is choked with people. Two: Quex is thrusting forward. Three: Mother thinks Quex is dead. Four: Viewers think Israel's the culprit in the hostage-taking. Five: I see how to kill Mother and make it seem like a Jewish atrocity.

Then the parson saw a man in morning coat and tall black hat resting a steel claw on Talbott's shoulder. The claw was removed from the shoulder and a black glove slipped over it.

Furneval, like a pious man of the cloth rising from prayer, gazed up into the Phoenix sky, where it is always light blue, and gave thanks. The game might be finished for him, but the cause would soon be won.

Unconscious of Furneval's presence, Talbott made his way to the Phoenix cameras, his attention half upon the Hess Command commentary. The reels were still turning aboveground. He had not yet won control of the transmission.

"The West seized on Hitler's plan for a final solution to abort the inventions of Jewish scientists in Germany," said a voice over still pictures of weapons. Another TV voice cut in, disregarding the images on screen. "Never disclosed until now is the whole truth about Rudolf Hess . . . an agent of Stalin . . . who sold out the Jews through another agent code-named STIRLITZ . . ."

Talbott looked across the dividing carpet to where Yuri Gorin stood expressionless. Was this how it was to end? Unmasked as Radzki?

"Stalin told Churchill, the Russian Secret Service didn't confide everything. But Stalin also had his secrets . . ." Talbott held his breath, remembering how Henkell had threatened to release documents embarrassing to the Soviets and to Mother in particular. Henkell's dead hand still could strike. The new TV commentary resumed:

". . . The Hess flight to England took place while Communists everywhere opposed war. The flight was Stalin's final desperate attempt to prevent the terrible conflict yet to come. If Hess could win over the British,

he could at least delay and perhaps stop the planned Hitlerite invasion of
Russia. It required an understanding with regard to the Jews, that Hitler
should deal with the problem before it spilled over into British Palestine.
As things turned out, only 260,000 German troops went into combat on
the Russian front out of a total 8.3 million German soldiers. Why? Because
most were busy with the final solution . . ."

Talbott began to relax. East German intelligence and Henkell, after all,
had got it wrong! Henkell must have searched through wartime archives,
stumbled across traces of a Soviet agent high in Hitler's circle, perhaps
even tripped over Radzki's own spoor. If Henkell tracked that spoor to
London, combing through old signals, he could be forgiven for supposing
Stalin's inside stuff was from Hess.

"Are you okay?"

Talbott refocused and saw Sally. She wore a floor director's lightweight
headphones.

"Yes. Of course."

"We're ready to terminate the Hess Command." Sally spoke into a tiny
microphone at the tip of a thin plastic arm curving in front of her mouth.
She said to Talbott, "We're going to outside broadcasts first. The BBC's
dug up some trusted old voice . . ."

To go with my trusted old face? wondered Talbott. He felt suddenly
tired.

"We interrupt this program to bring you a bulletin. For the past three
hours, the world has been held hostage . . ."

The breezy voice took Talbott back to the Battle of Britain and a
broadcaster reporting the clash of warplanes like a cricket match. Alvar
Liddell! But Liddell was dead. For a moment, Talbott thought he heard
again, "Five down for one of ours and there goes another! Oh, well played,
sir!" It had been a clever move, to find a veteran announcer who could
evoke memories of their greatest hour.

"We take you to the scenes in Whitehall . . ."

Remotes fed the street scenes to the transmission. "Several arrests have
been made . . ." Talbott listened while Sally took him to the leather-
topped desk in front of the Phoenix cameras. A tiny screen was recessed to
his right: a feather-light microphone stood discreetly beside a small desk
lamp. He sat where monarchs would sit in a crisis. The unseen BBC man
said, "There is still a time-bomb problem. As you see, the Cenotaph appears to be under siege. Ah, yes—Now! In the middle of your screens . . .
what appear to be puffs of smoke! I'm told these are parachutes! Yes! . . .
bursting open a stone's throw from the ground. Literally, out of a clear
blue sky. Already the first man has dropped into the square so recently
occupied by Her Majesty the Queen. Slap, bang in the middle of the chalk
marks put there for Her Majesty! Someone has just given me a note—
What you're seeing, ladies and gentlemen, are men of the Special Air Service trained in HALO operations to surprise an enemy. And by God the

enemy *is* surprised! Those *were* the last of the terrorists around the Cenotaph. Firing has broken out! There seem to be heavier explosions! Oh, well done, well done!"

The big screen over the Phoenix mantelpiece showed the action. Grimweather and his SAS men were using stun grenades. The noise obliterated other sounds until the voice of the BBC man returned. "There were earlier reports the Cenotaph had been mined. Bomb experts have been digging their way up into the Cenotaph from below."

The picture suddenly broke up. Amplifiers rattled, unable to handle the roar. When the sound and vision returned, viewers in the Phoenix saw that part of the Cenotaph closest to where the Queen had been standing had been ripped open as if it were no more substantial than a big white shopping bag.

Talbott dragged his attention away from the monitor and sought Sally for guidance. She was holding her hands over her ears and talking into her director's intercom. She was half turned away from Talbott. His gaze slid past her and fastened on Marcus Furneval. Black Mac!

Furneval stood behind Quex's wheelchair, his movements unnoticed because everyone was staring at the scenes from outside. Yuri Gorin was in a direct and uninterrupted line with Quex.

Talbott heard the BBC voice battling through the uproar in Whitehall: ". . . may have been several bombs . . . loss of life . . . until further details, returning to underground studio . . ."

The red light gleamed on Camera 1. Talbott straightened up. First thing they'd want to know was, Were leaders here safe?

He found himself uttering the trite reassurances. Sally had one camera pan around the chamber, confirming Talbott's words. The camera paused and held on Yuri Gorin. The Soviet leader filled the tiny monitor at Talbott's elbow, and then he glimpsed a sudden blur of action in a small corner of the screen. He looked up, adjusting his vision to take stock of the reality.

Marcus Furneval was propelling Quex's wheelchair at Yuri Gorin. Quex waved his gold-knobbed cane in a futile gesture to stop the forward motion. Gorin turned. To Soviet eyes, it must appear to be an unprovoked attack. And it was being televised to the whole Soviet bloc.

Worse, Talbott saw at once, Yuri Gorin recognized Quex and could not disguise an initial expression of total astonishment. This was General Quex Massey, supposedly eclipsed, the operational necessity Gorin had ordained to preserve his secret. It must seem to him another massive betrayal, for he had been told Quex was dead. Yet here Quex was, manifestly alive and on the attack.

Millions were watching this attempt on the Soviet leader's life. To switch the scene would be to start a wave of panic speculation. Then Talbott saw something that hurled him out of his chair at Furneval.

The parson carried a weapon. The stubby barrel stuck out from under

Quex's flailing arm. It was the compact Uzi 9-mm submachine gun. Even with metal stock extended, it was just two feet long. Furneval must have had it strapped under his coat. The Uzi was no longer the favorite choice of assassins, *but it was Israel's trademark!*

"Strike a blow for Zion!" bellowed the parson. "Save the Jews!"

On screen, Quex and Parson Furneval seemed partners in a murderous attack. The public knew neither man.

Quex twisted in the wheelchair, the proud head caught in tight close-up. The chin was up. The eyes glittered. But the general could not shift the gun, thrust between his arm and chest, aiming at Mother.

Furneval fired. The bullets from the 25-round magazine would have ripped Mother to shreds. But Quex had thrown himself sideways a split second earlier to cover the gun's blazing muzzle. Talbott, running full tilt, collided with the parson. The only bullet to find a human mark entered General Quex Massey's back and exited from the old general's chest.

Parson Furneval recovered his footing. He yelled to the cameras, "The Jews have avenged themselves on Russia!" In his tight black raincoat, minus his churchman's hat, the gray locks tumbling over the seamed neck and face, he could pass for a Zealot. "Death to the Soviets in the name of Israel! Death to all oppressors of the Jewish people!" He let fly foul curses with each backward leap.

Mother signaled Nick Kerensky to stay put. Some of his eclipse team were converging on the parson. Mother growled and the men froze.

Shock at seeing Quex alive forced Mother to change mental gears. Henkell had spoken the truth when he said Quex was not eclipsed! Quex was staring fixedly at him, hands gripping the wheels of his chair, his chest bloody.

On Mother's right, Talbott's assault on the parson had ended in a stand-off. Furneval began to bob and weave, taunting Talbott with the gun. The two men circled each other. Nobody dared interfere. The parson spoke softly, almost inaudibly, as if . . . as if, many would say later, he was *hypnotizing* the American. Others thought they heard words like ". . . test your nerves, laddie . . ." and ". . . Kim's Game . . . objects in a row . . . one-two-three . . ."

Only Quex and Yuri Gorin ignored the sideshow. Onlookers saw them, as it were, paralyzed; and those same onlookers let attention stray to the mounting drama of Furneval beckoning Talbott like a prizefighter inviting attack, ready to strike at the first opening.

Crimson froth hung from Quex's lips. "Was it all"—he gasped for air— "all lies and deception?"

Mother leaned to catch Quex's words, the last from the man who once walked him through Soho while the sky rained bombs; the man who had almost alone listened to his appeals when he was Radzki the powerless refugee. The two men stared into each other's souls across an abyss.

"Deception brought Hess to England," Mother said in a clear voice. "Lies have covered him ever since. But American perfidy? No! English treachery? No!"

"Then, all the rest is commentary?" whispered Quex.

The effect of these words on Mother was startling. He said, "A king was sacrificed."

Furneval himself heard this. He stood swaying beside the purple damask drapes, and Mother's strange statement reached him as a measured growl. The parson shuddered and lost balance.

Quex, blind to Parson Furneval, also reacted physically to Mother's words, raising his arms as if released from a great burden. Kerensky ran forward at Mother's barked order, and caught the old general as he pitched forward, dead.

A gunshot shifted attention back to Talbott, locked in a fierce embrace with Furneval, whose head hung backward, jaws agape.

Mother swung round, arms dangling, believing he knew what had happened. Four words, uttered in that unmistakable growl, had transfixed Furneval. Talbott's hands had closed around his neck as the parson, in reflex, fired his gun. The bullet had been deflected into Furneval's own face. But even Mother mistook the manner of death. "Son of Rebecca!" The thought flashed through his mind. "You finally strangled your own ghost."

Sally, behind the cameras, held fast. She had no tears for Grandpa Massey. She'd seen his face in close-up when Yuri Gorin delivered him from the past with those few words: *A king was sacrificed.* They'd brought to Quex's eyes a flaming of enlightenment and relief.

President Donovan met the Queen's eyes. Something beyond the violence had affected her. She stood erect, motionless, touched by a radiance that seemed almost divine. Donovan told himself it was the breathtakingly clear English complexion: nothing more. He moved forward.

"Ma'am?" He spoke gently but firmly. "May I make a suggestion."

"Please do, Mr. President."

He waved at the cameras. "The world is watching."

The Queen waited. Surely he wasn't going to push himself center stage now? Her advisers insisted he was a plastic President, a product of the White House spin-control squad, designed for top billing and hot lights, and content with nothing less.

"It might not seem unwise," the President said carefully, "to give the Soviets the floor. Yuri Gorin came within an ace of being assassinated in plain view of millions of Russians. They see him here under your protection, ma'am . . ."

A grandstand gesture? Let Gorin speak? The Queen inclined her head. Why not? Little else would counter the misunderstandings already forming among those who made the nuclear decisions in Moscow when Mother was away.

She turned frosty then and became withdrawn; or so it appeared to those who watched her. "Then, all the rest is commentary." Why had those words transfixed the Soviet leader? What king was sacrificed? She turned her head slightly, as if listening for the answers in the whispered orders being repeated on her behalf.

49

All across the Soviet Union, they saw and heard Big Ben strike three. In Moscow, the time was six on a black winter's evening; at the eastern end of Siberia, already four the next morning. Across this span, Soviet broadcasts had carried the Hess Command. Now they continued coverage, for nobody could stop it without orders. The foiled attack on Yuri Gorin had only tripped a series of escalating military alarms. The announcement that he would speak froze the Soviet defence machine just short of action.

Mother sat where, in the event of a Soviet nuclear strike, the monarch would speak to what was left of the British Commonwealth. The Russian's appearance came as a surprise to many outside the Communist bloc. He was not Big Brother. Nor was he the bloodless chief clerk of popular legend. His opening words were in Russian, and he translated these into English. Then he let Kerensky do the interpreting. "My people," he said, "know what war is."

Inside the Phoenix chamber, nobody stirred. Jacob Slominsky wondered: *My* people?

"This Remembrance Day," said Yuri Gorin, "was invented at the end of the First World War to remind us every year how small incidents grow into major catastrophes. It signaled the intent of all the participants to end war. It led instead to another world war sparked by 'an incident.'" His words evoked the phantoms behind recent news reports that began with a

missing submarine and grew into explosive front pages: SUNK BY SOVI-
ETS . . . SUB WAS NUCLEAR, MISSILE-LADEN, AMERICAN.

"You have a saying, 'to nip in the bud,'" said Gorin. "A small incident I
shall now tell you. Nothing, though, was nipped in the bud. An evil man
was arrested in Germany—on exactly a Remembrance Day such as this.
His name was Schicklgruber. It was November 11, 1923. If men had
prayed less that day, and acted more, Schicklgruber would not have escaped justice in order to cast a shadow across this century as . . .
Hitler . . .

"The last kick from the dark ages of Hitler is this Hess Command. The
Soviet Union repudiates it . . .

"We must not give Hitler a posthumous victory."

Jacob held his breath.

"We were all Hitler's victims," said Gorin. "We all know a specific hatred was directed at the Jews . . ."

This, thought President Donovan, would be a hard act to follow.
Mother had stolen his lines about hatred lurking in all men. He caught
himself, and concentrated again on Mother's words.

"A Jew repeated to me, before he died in Warsaw, the message of another Jew of the same name who, two thousand years ago, wove it into the
Talmud: 'What is hateful to thee, never do to thy fellowman. That is the
whole of the Law. The rest is commentary . . .'"

There was a moment of stunned disbelief after Mother finished. He
began to applaud himself in the Kremlin fashion. Donovan joined him.
Soon the chamber echoed to the applause.

Sally directed the cameras to show the Soviet world the manifestation of
goodwill as Mother padded out of the studio area. He knew his protocol
and went first to the Queen. Then, because he also knew his *Realpolitik*, he
took the U.S. President by the arm and drew him to the cameras. Donovan
had to think fast. Whatever he said would be studied like chicken bones
before soothsayers. He had his enemies back home. But, thank God, he did
not have a politburo.

So he spoke frankly. He welcomed the Soviet initiative, and was careful
not to make it sound like Mother's sudden inspiration. He agreed that
Hitler was a symbol of how monsters grow from small beginnings. Prayer
was not enough. And therefore he proposed a Pax Americana-Sovietica to
guarantee the territorial integrity of all who feared persecution.

He looked around. He'd catch hell in Washington. "Let's confess," he
said, "the two most powerful allies against Hitler have lost our way . . ."

He could feel the stir around him. He must take care not to upstage
Mother. "In all humility," he said, "I call on all citizens of Earth to join us
again in two minutes of silence while we seek guidance for future action
. . . together."

The Queen beckoned the PPS to her side as the applause broke out
again. Donovan had spoken of another silence *at the foot of the Cenotaph.* It

would be an act of gratitude for a safe deliverance. Could it be arranged? The PPS nodded and hurried away. How right he had been, thought the Queen, about the President's love of the grandstand gesture. And how very lucky that was for everyone.

The urgent message from New York was patched through in record time. Everyone in that long chain was on Talbott's side; from secretaries to sound engineers, they were vital links between Sol Farkas and the man they perceived as, in every sense, the anchorman. Talbott was moving out to the Cenotaph when he got Sol's message and found a mobile phone.

"There's a woman in Rome," said Sol, "claims to be one of ours. Needs help migrating to America."

"Hey!" protested Talbott. "This is urgent?"

"Well, yes. She threatens to tell her story to some other network. She worked on the TITFER project."

"Vesna!" Talbott relaxed. "Sol, promise her anything in reason." He thought for a moment. "Just ask what the hell TITFER means."

Sol began to laugh. "You need a Serb to explain cockney rhyming slang?"

"Sol, there isn't time for games."

"It's where the whole thing began. Tito! His favorite wartime distraction was that BBC radio comedy "It's That Man Again"—ITMA. And Tito's cockney wireless operator. Remember?"

It came back to Talbott. The ITMA hat. The slang for hat, rhymes with tit-for-tat, tit-fer-tat, *titfer.*

"We won," he heard Sol shouting.

"Who won?"

"All who wore the big black hat, old buddy."

"The hat was death," said Talbott. "It came down, made us invisible, stopped us from living. Hat Men! Nobody knew who or where we were . . . I'm not sure," he added before putting the phone down. "I'm not at all certain we've won, not yet."

The day was dying.

Every step of the way back to the Cenotaph was guarded by men indoctrinated by tradition or ideology to love or scorn the monarchy, distrust the Russians, or view with alarm the Americans. They set aside differences to serve a common aim: to protect their leaders. The bodies of men killed in the fighting between the 88 and the SAS still lay beneath the slab-sided sepulcher of the illuminated Cenotaph. Here, for the first time in all the decades of remembering the dead, there were dead visible to remember.

Jacob walked between Sally and Talbott, followed by some of the Kyryan guards.

"Can Mother get away with this?" asked Sally. "He'd no politburo sanction."

"He spoke over their heads," said Jacob. "He spoke directly to the Soviet people. He said what they want desperately to hear."

"If a few in the Kremlin had a glimmering of the truth," Sally speculated, "they'd still think twice before touching him, I suppose. Our cameras will have turned him into a popular hero."

Talbott said, "There's still a piece missing."

"Hess," said Jacob. "Hess is the missing piece. How *did* Radzki the penniless refugee make that first vital jump into Stalin's confidence? Stalin only saw, in the beginning, a devoted Soviet agent in the Nazi camp. With all other wartime agents, Stalin grew distrustful. He was afraid his experts in conspiracy could turn into conspirators against himself. *Something* made Radzki an exception, and gave him eight vital postwar years to build his own power."

"This is only guesswork," objected Sally.

"No." Jacob stopped at the edge of the floodlit square. "Yuri Gorin, today, to win the collaboration of my Kyryan guards, *was obliged to persuade me of the truth.*"

The military bands were striking up. Army searchlights quivered into life.

Jacob said, "I'll give you the proof. Not here, though. It's in the Düsseldorf synagogue. You know where—"

"There's only one synagogue left," said Talbott.

He was caught up in the rush of broadcast technicians. "They need you," someone shouted. "It's still your show."

"Well, back to *my* little idiot box," Talbott murmured.

Sally frowned, and then laughed. "Little Idiot" had been Jacob's line.

Talbott saw Nelson and Fishhook standing by the Cenotaph. Its stark profile was broken where the bomb had torn loose great chunks of stone. He walked to the mobile unit and saw Mother in the dazzling light . . . If only he could be sure Jacob was right, but Jacob was holding back the missing piece. And so Talbott could not yet be certain if there survived in Mother that same old Radzki of the cardboard case and refugee rags who swore the next time he had to face powerful men, he would have the power to make them listen.

Do we exercise power over the Soviets through him? Talbott wondered. Maybe this man who moved heaven and earth to pile up power has achieved something nobody on earth expected: an ultimate balance of power, his heart in the West and his head in the Kremlin.

This time, the two minutes of silence really did fall like an enchantment. The networks were now responding to hope instead of fear. They showed a universal readiness to meet the American President's appeal. The pictures came in from all quarters. Humanity was spellbound. And Mother bent his head and thanked God for Bomber Harris, who taught him never to put his faith again in prayers and petitions.

In the aftermath, Talbott returned to Düsseldorf to look for the missing link in Radzki's story. The only synagogue is guarded by German soldiers. It has been granted this special protection by the West German Government as one more gesture of atonement. The cost of the gesture far exceeds the total income of the few Jews who still remain in Düsseldorf.

It would be good to do something here for Bronfmann's memory, thought Talbott. But you cannot re-create a congregation. He was drawn towards the carved doors guarding the Torah inside. A wintry light set fire to stained glass. A hand touched his. "I'm not sure about the rules for women," said Sally. "Jacob wants me to take you to him. I guess it's okay."

Talbott put an arm around her. She seemed vulnerable in a simple plaid dress. The borrowed and mannish clothes of recent days had concealed her fragility. "A synagogue's for worship, not discrimination," he said, and together they walked through the temple to the tabernacle.

Jacob was waiting on the balcony. "The Greek word was *synagoge*, meaning congregation." He had heard them talking. His tone was rabbinical, as if he had slipped back into his true vocation. "The Jews in Babylonia, far from the ruined Temple in Jerusalem, kept up their religious life in exile and adversity by such assembly. There, in Babylon, Hillel the Elder gave us the Golden Rule. Everything else that comes out of theological disputation *is commentary*."

"So that's what Grandpa meant!" exclaimed Sally. "And why Mother answered the way he did?"

"Yes," said Jacob. "The words bridged the gap between now and your grandfather's first meeting with Radzki, when he explained something terribly important. He'd rediscovered his Jewishness through another Hillel: Zeitlin Hillel, who died in Nazi hands."

"Why did Mother say, *'a king was sacrificed'*?"

Jacob lifted a hand as if to beg her patience. He leaned over the rail. "To congregate here and commune with God," he said, "was always a joyful occasion. They're dead now. But you can feel the vibrations from all that worship. Feel the complex energy still. It's their souls, clasped within the temple."

He straightened up. "Come," he said brusquely. He seemed suddenly fearful of sentiments that once made the devout unwary enough to be devoured. "This is what I want you to see, exactly as it was." He stopped before a wooden panel. It opened under his gentle pressure. He reached in and withdrew some tightly folded oilskin.

"This was airtight," said Jacob. "It contained a roll of film. I had the frames printed."

He handed the oilskin to Talbott, who spread it open. It was an escape map issued to airmen, so flimsy it could be compressed in the bowl of a pipe.

Jacob took four printed sheets from the inside of his topcoat. "Letters," he said, "between Mrs. Simpson, her Duke and Hess. Photographed at the time."

Sally held one to the thin light coming through the stained glass.

"Government House," she read from the letterhead. "Bahamas." She looked at the date, scanned the text, and gave it to Talbott.

"So the ex-king was in touch with Hitler *after* the Battle of Britain?" said Talbott.

"Not exactly," Jacob answered.

"But it looks like absolutely treasonous communication with enemies of the time!"

"A king was sacrificed . . ." quoted Jacob. "The signature is forged."

Talbott leaned back, baffled. *"Forged?"*

"At the time."

"Why?"

"For reasons that seemed good at the time."

"How can you be sure?"

"Radzki," said Jacob. "Radzki first saw the letters—and there were many—when he was still Hess's pilot. They seemed genuine. He photographed them. He sent the microfilm to Moscow. He kept a duplicate roll. He put the originals back in the files for Hess to show Hitler. Hitler thought they meant Britain was ready to give up and all it needed was to put the Duke of Windsor back on the throne."

"If you knew this, why—?" began Talbott.

"I didn't until Mother told me."

"At the Cenotaph?"

"Yes. Conspirators with things in common talk in shorthand. Mother had to convince me. Rebecca's diary wasn't enough."

"Who forged the letters?"

"The British Secret Intelligence Service. Someone knew the Duke had been indiscreet. The Windsors *did* write foolish letters. The forged ones went further. This one's dated mid-1940, the Germans have blitzed Western Europe, Britain's alone and the Duke's hanging around in Lisbon. The next letters show the Duke apparently letting Hitler know he wants peace and fancies being returned to the throne, both with the help of England's 'thinking plutocracy.' That sort of thing keeps up until May 1941. Meanwhile, Hitler's issued the July 16, 1940, directive saying Britain's isolated, let the invasion begin. Operation Sea Lion will conquer Britain starting September 15, final plans to be ready a month earlier. Hitler kept putting it off. Generals on both sides couldn't understand why he gave up the initiative. Now we know! These letters kept Hitler dangling. British intelligence knew about his fear of crossing open water, and played on it. He *wanted* to believe those letters. Finally, in May, he sent Hess over. Within weeks, he turned against Russia. All those intervening months were critical for Britain. She'd made Hitler hesitate too long by using the only aggressive weapon available: deception."

"And created a monster for the future!" said Sally.

"Who worries about the future when the present is at stake?" Jacob shrugged. "Only Radzki. He made himself indispensable as Hess's controller after the war. He had Stalin believing if the Soviets wanted to pressure Britain, they'd only got to threaten to trot out Hess. Hess would testify the Windsor letters were genuine if Radzki told him to."

"But the British recovered the real Windsor letters," said Talbott. "Didn't they steal many of them from a German castle?"

"Right. But Hess, and Stalin, thought *all* were genuine. The irony is, Parson Furneval was dispatched to help get such letters. For his services, he enjoyed the palace privileges you know about. And all the time, he'd made copies of those originals for the East Germans."

"The Hess story isn't finished," said Sally.

"Never will be. Hess was, is and forever—Hess, symbol of evil in all of us," said Jacob. "Bad luck for him. That's why four great powers who disagreed on everything else agreed to lock him up in that monstrous jail at enormous cost on the flashpoint of new conflicts. It satisfied a primitive urge to confine evil, stop the past coming back, knife in hand . . ."

Sally shivered and glanced at Talbott. He held up the roll of film. "Radzki's past came back . . . *here?* You took his word for it?"

"He couldn't have been lying," said Jacob. "Not under the Cenotaph. I believed him. I found everything here just as he described. He wanted to keep himself square with God; that's why he took the risk in the Nazi time." Jacob was leading them through the synagogue to the street. The light from outside made him look old and gray. "He even left a self-compromising note. Oddly enough, it only became dangerous to him when your Bronfmann came here with something between his teeth, learned from a British intelligence genius—"

"The Boffin!" said Talbott. "*He* forged the letters."

But there were still things Jacob thought better left unsaid. He went on, as if there had been no interruption, "Bronfmann put things together and set off alarms." He fished in his pocket. "Here's what Radzki wrote, and left with the oilskin package here: 'Truth is God's seal. Talmud: Shabbath 54.' "

Sally stood still. "Nobody would ever know the truth without breaking the seal? Poor Grandpa. I teased him so much about knowing everything. Yet he did know enough to quote from the Talmud . . . You know? 'All the rest is commentary.' "

"That did shake Mother," said Jacob. "Those words reduce all religious sophistry to the simple 'do unto others.' "

"Which is what the world heard a Soviet leader work into a speech?" suggested Sally. "His way to beg forgiveness for the things done to get where he is. Well, good for Grandpa!"

"Your grandfather," Jacob conceded, "reminded the Radzki lurking inside Mother of the nature of the burden. Your grandfather knew the Talmud to be a never-ending dialogue between scholars, a monumental record of the Law as interpreted through the ages. Radzki explained this at their first meeting. It convinced your grandfather of his integrity, but he never reported it, because it seemed not to be relevant to the conduct of a war. When he did refer to it, finally, he said enough. At the end of his life, he reminded Mother of what he had said that time in Soho, that the Talmud is full of mental acrobatics but boils down to a basic question of conscience. And true to type, Quex Massey conveyed all this in a coded sentence!"

Outside the synagogue, in that dreary landscape, Talbott felt again the loneliness of such an exotic temple in such mean streets. He thought of Bronfmann, who had spoken to the few surviving Jews, too poor to leave, certain they had been forgotten, and unable to shake off the memories. "I've one more question for your Talmudic scholars," he said to Jacob. "I'd like to be married here."

"In synagogue?" Jacob managed to look startled, pleased, and apprehensive, all at the same time.

"For Bronfmann," Talbott explained. "To let him know, not all the world's against Israel."

"Steely Pamir's view?" Jacob smiled. He quoted: " 'And we needn't behave as if it is.' "

Sally broke in. "Married to who?"

"You, of course," said Talbott.

"You never asked if I'd work with you." Sally backed away. "And you don't even ask if I'll agree to marry!"

"But you did. And you will."

"You're *worse* than Grandpa!" Sally began to laugh in spite of it all. "So absolutely sure you're right. He even said I'd end up marrying you!"

Jacob left them to it. They'd be after him soon enough with more of their questions . . . He saw the armed Germans circling the synagogue. Instinctively, he crossed to the other side of the street. Then he scolded himself. They were there to protect Jewish property, and too young to remember anything else, weren't they?